Night of Destiny Book 1

Copy Right@2024 Sect Elder Breeze
All rights reserved.

Chapter 1

Unexpected One Night Stand

Jessica Miller, female, 18 years old, with a well-proportioned figure, a beautiful girl, and a freshman in college.

She was wearing a light pink shirt, washed blue jeans, and plain canvas shoes, with a pure and pretty appearance, and big eyes, filled with innocence.

Today is her boyfriend Raymond Davis's birthday, and she wanted to give him a surprise.

The bag contained the carefully selected luxury brand watch, which was expensive, and she saved for half a year to afford it.

Raymond was one year ahead of her and was a prominent figure in the school, the dream boy of all the girls in the school.

As soon as she entered the house, she felt that something was not right. There was a pair of red crystal high heels in front of the shoe cabinet, and red shawls, tops, skirts, and long stockings were scattered all over the floor.

Men's shirts, trousers...

The red underwear lay quietly on the man's pants, looking quite erotic, and there were sounds of a woman's groan and a man's low growl coming from the bedroom...

An erotic reality show?

If this weren't her boyfriend's house, Jessica might have been interested in watching the performance from outside the door.

Sect Elder Breeze

The messy floor and the musky smell in the air made her realize what was happening, no matter how naive she was.

"Do you love me, Raymond?" A seductive voice asked.

Florence Black? Her good friend? Um... She's been playing games too much lately, hallucinating, hallucinating...

"Of course, I love you, Florence, you're amazing..." Raymond's voice was filled with comfort and pleasure...

Jessica approached the bedroom step by step.

The ambiguous voice became clearer, the door wasn't closed tightly, and she stood there, clearly seeing the intertwined silhouettes of two people, Florence arched her neck, her curly hair wild, her face flushed, and her red lips kept moaning.

"Tell me, who's better in bed, me or Jessica?" The lust-rendered voice was particularly charming.

"Of course it's you, Jessica is too conservative, we've been dating for a year, and the most intimate thing is holding hands. She doesn't agree to have sex with me. She's just a boring beauty, with no taste, how can she compare to you? Oh, darling... faster..."

Cut, your mouth smells bad, only an idiot would be kissed by you.

Really fierce!

Their postures are too difficult, right?

Damn, how did they manage to make that pose?

Jessica was a little impressed with herself, she had the mind to study their posture at this moment.

"Oh... Jessica..." Raymond noticed Jessica, frowned and quickly pulled the quilt to cover their bodies.

"Jessica..."

Florence stood up calmly, disregarding her naked body, which still bore the marks of lovemaking.

"Her figure is really hot like she's got the potential to be a playgirl," Jessica thought to herself.

Florence casually tossed a set of clothes to Raymond, and she put on his shirt.

Night of Destiny

Jessica remained calm, though her face was pale, her eyes contained a hint of laughter, innocence, and sweetness. Her mother had said that no matter what, one must always smile, as it's the best disguise.

"Jessica, you've seen it now, we're together, so you should break up with him!!" Florence provocatively hooked Raymond's arm, and with an air of superiority and a condescending tone, she showed off to Jessica.

How could someone like Jessica, from such a humble background, be worthy of the handsome and dashing Raymond? Only someone like herself, Florence Black can be with him.

"Why are you doing this, Raymond?" Jessica asked.

Even if you were cheating, don't involve my friends, especially since this girl's reputation is so bad. She is a well-known playgirl.

Raymond coldly smiled, shook his head, and with a look of disdain on his young and handsome face, proudly said, "Jessica, let me tell you the truth. I pursued you in the beginning because I made a bet with a few of my buddies. All the boys in the school knew it was difficult to pursue you, so I made a bet with a few of my friends on whether I could successfully pursue you. Honestly, look at you, bare-faced, dressed in rubbish, are you worthy of me?"

Even if she's beautiful, it's still humiliating to take her out.

"So that's how it is," Jessica nodded with understanding, and sweetly smiled, "How much was the bet?"

"1 million dollars!"

"You wouldn't have won the bet without me, so give me half of the winnings!" Jessica smiled even more sweetly, and her eyes emitted the glow of money.

Damn, since you lied to me, it's not unreasonable for me to get half of the money, right?

Raymond's face turned pale.

See, this woman is so tacky. As soon as the money is mentioned, her eyes light up, like she's got a scamming look on her face, damn it!

He had sex with another woman in her presence, yet she still smiled so sweetly, and even wanted to know about the bet and demanded money?

Damn! What kind of monster is she?

Florence couldn't contain her anger, "Jessica, have you no shame?"

"Of course I have shame. At least my face is worth something, I can sell it for a higher price than you," Jessica said with a sweet smile. "You're so stingy. If you don't want to give, then don't. Taking all the money for yourself, be careful, may you be struck by lightning."

"As you wish, we're breaking up. I wish you all the best in love."

Both of them turned pale.

Jessica smiled and walked away gracefully.

******

Night fell, and the city of W was bustling.

The bar, located in the prime area of W, was bustling with activity. On the stage, seductive dancers twisted their waists like water snakes, their heavily made-up faces exquisitely beautiful and alluring, their seductive eyes captivating the men in the audience who cheered non-stop.

The music was thunderous, and the air was filled with the intoxicating aroma of alcohol.

This was a place of revelry and debauchery.

At the bar, Jessica kept drinking, her face flushed with alcohol.

Raymond had cheated, and they had broken up. She acted carefree, but deep down, there was still a twinge of pain, just a tiny bit.

Night of Destiny

"Jessica, come on, be a good girl. Forget all the unhappy things and drink some more," her stepsister Karen Brown encouraged her to drink more and discreetly slipped a pill into her drink.

"Could you stop chattering in my ear? Let me have a moment of peace," Jessica calmly said and downed her drink.

Damn it, if I didn't need you to pay the bill, who would tolerate your noise?

After Jessica's mother passed away, her stepmother married her father and brought Karen into the family. Despite being together for four or five years, their relationship had always been strained. Karen's social circle was a mix of unsavory characters, and she changed boyfriends as easily as flipping through a book. Jessica had never liked her stepsister.

But she was broke and had no money to pay for her drinks, so she had to rely on Karen.

Karen suppressed her anger. She saw Jessica drink the glass of wine, smiled smugly, and had the bartender pour a few more drinks for her before slipping away to the dark corner by the side door.

"How is she? That's my sister. Isn't she beautiful? 5 million dollars, the price is non-negotiable!" Karen cunningly said to a shady-looking man. She owed loan sharks and couldn't afford to repay, so she had to trick Jessica into the bar and sell her to the underground market to clear her debts.

Anyway, Jessica just happened to have a heartbreak and wanted to get drunk. Karen didn't feel the least bit guilty.

"Deal!" The man rubbed his chubby chin, his eyes filled with lust.

This was a prime catch. A woman like her could fetch up to 10 million dollars at the underground market.

Sect Elder Breeze

Jessica drank to the point of feeling tipsy but not completely drunk. Damn it, Raymond said she was old-fashioned and boring. She wanted to show him what fun meant, but buying drinks for such a bad man was downright foolish.

Jessica got up, placed down her glass, and stumbled forward, then suddenly lurched and fell into the arms of a young man.

A very young man, looking like he was in his early twenties.

His features were carved to perfection, exquisitely beautiful with an almost otherworldly allure. He exuded a natural elegance and nobility, yet his eyes were excessively cold, almost bordering on indifference.

An elegantly indifferent man.

Marcus Smith looked with disgust at the woman who was actively throwing herself at him, he detested this kind of actively pursuing woman.

As he looked into her eyes, suddenly...

He was stunned!

As if the whole world was filled with bright colors.

She had a pair of beautiful eyes, bright, clear, and spiritual as if filled with the brightness of the whole world.

"Wow, are all the money boys so good-looking now?" Jessica murmured to herself.

This man is too good-looking. Jessica thought to herself, according to Karen, the money boys in this bar are all outstanding, with extraordinary looks and elegant demeanor. And this man fits the bill perfectly, so Jessica took him as a money boy.

Marcus's face darkened, and his slender eyes narrowed dangerously.

Money boy? He, Marcus Smith, is a money boy? Damn it, that girl is dead!

Before he could say anything, Jessica grabbed his collar and asked fiercely, "Hey, how much for a night?"

Veins popped on Marcus's forehead, his cold eyes emitted a daunting cold light, and he tightened the hand around her waist, her soft body hitting his hard chest, "Are you looking for a man?"

"Nonsense, if I wasn't looking for a man, why would I ask you?"

Not only is this man good-looking, but even his voice is so magnetic, being a money boy must be very profitable, Jessica thought.

"Very well!" Marcus's voice was chilling. For some reason, hearing her say that, a surge of anger rose in his heart, so he dragged her into his private elevator. Since she came looking for a man, he didn't need to waste time, right?

Tonight he had rejected countless women who had tried to chat him up, feeling quite uninterested, but she had aroused a fire in him.

When Karen and the sleazy man returned to the bar with the check, Jessica was gone, which made Karen stomp her foot in anger, and the sleazy man's eyes glinted ominously.

Sweat broke out on Jessica's body, a raging heat rising within her. In the elevator, the innocent girl turned into a seductive goddess, her young body constantly rubbing against Marcus's body, exhaling fragrance.

The ambiguous moans floated teasingly in the man's ear, bewitching his soul.

Hmm, this man smells so good, with a faint tobacco scent, no artificial perfume, clean and warm. She didn't know what was happening to her, her body was unbearably hot, and she could only keep rubbing against his body to relieve the heat.

So comfortable...

Moans escaped her lips, her small hands greedily reaching into his chest...

Damn! Has she turned into a seductress?

Sect Elder Breeze

Marcus was teased by her warmth, his breath becoming erratic. His proud self-control was on the brink of collapse. This woman was simply a demon in disguise, she twisted restlessly in his embrace, her beguiling eyes and intoxicating fragrance overwhelming.

He forgot his anger and wickedly lifted her chin, dangerously gazing into the girl. Unable to resist, he leaned down and kissed her red lips.

So sweet.

The sweet taste was intoxicating, Marcus never lacked women, as the heir of the Noblefull Group, there were plenty of women waiting for him to ravish them. Marcus had countless women, changing them as often as changing clothes. However, he never kissed a woman on the lips, in this regard, he was somewhat fastidious.

But this time he made an exception!

His skillful lips pried open her teeth, invading every corner, enticing Jessica's delicate tongue, suckling and nibbling lightly, caressing every inch of her tender skin. Jessica's spine was electrified, her whole body trembling, her legs weak, if Marcus hadn't held onto her, she might have embarrassingly collapsed on the ground.

This man really knew how to captivate!

The dominant kiss, rough and tumultuous, made it impossible not to sink into it!

Jessica, inexperienced and passionate, completely aroused Marcus, almost making him lose control, nearly making love with her in the elevator.

This woman was like opium, dangerous and deadly.

The two young bodies rubbed desperately together. Jessica's face flushed, Marcus breathing heavily, their low moans and panting intertwined in the confined elevator, the whole space filled with an ambiguous air.

Ding...

Night of Destiny

The crisp sound brought Marcus back to his senses, gritting his teeth, suppressing the overwhelming desire. He dragged the almost collapsing Jessica to his exclusive room, his eyes suffused with a dark mist.

Damn it, can't you be a bit gentle?!

Jessica, her wrist aching from being dragged, exploded in anger!

Marcus slammed the door shut. He was unable to bear it any longer, and pushed Jessica against the door, one hand against her forehead, the other gripping her waist, his hard chest rubbing against her soft breast, he lowered his head and fiercely kissed her on the lips.

His handsome face was flushed with a terrifying redness, the ambiguous sounds of mingled saliva making the whole air boil with intense heat.

Never had a woman aroused such a strong desire in him.

Like a wild beast, he frightened Jessica.

"Wait... wait... let go... you jerk..."

"What, now playing hard-to-get? " Marcus's eyes were deeply red, filled with danger and malice as he pinched Jessica's chin. "You ignited this fire, and you must bear the consequences!"

Damn it, can't you use some fresh words? Jessica rolled her eyes. Fire, fire, what the hell, I'll burn you alive!

Jessica swallowed hard. She was starting to feel scared. But, what was this surge of heat inside her? Her body was getting hotter, her face redder, and she felt a faint glow of green in her eyes as she looked at Marcus.

She really wanted to kiss him... touch him...

Damn it!

What the hell did Karen give her to drink?

Chapter 2

100 Dollars For One Night

The strange sensation made Jessica's gaze start to blur. Having already drunk alcohol and then drugged, she had managed to hold on for so long, which was quite a feat.

"You've been drugged, haven't you?" Marcus finally noticed something was off about her, no wonder her body had been so hot since earlier. He had thought it was... The girl's flushed cheeks, seductive eyes, her clothes half-exposed, her sexy shoulders, alluring collarbones, and soft breasts that were half-revealed...

This was a vividly seductive scene, and no man could resist such temptation.

"Damn it, you come here alone and get drugged, and you didn't even notice?"

Anger, the usually icy Marcus could not contain it. The thought of what might have happened to this girl if she had run into someone else... And did it even matter to her?

The thought of other men seeing her in this seductive state made Marcus want to kill.

No, to kill her!

Jessica groaned uncomfortably, her mouth dry, and unable to resist, she licked the corner of her lips. This action, in Marcus's eyes, undoubtedly became a seduction. An absolute seduction!

Night of Destiny

Marcus gave a wicked smile, provocatively lifting her chin, his fingers ambiguously caressing her soft and rosy lips, hot breath teasing Jessica's ears, sending shivers through her body.

Damn, this man was such a devil, why did he have to look so good for no reason? She was falling into his trap.

"If this is your way of playing hard-to-get, congratulations, you've succeeded!"

Lowering his head, he wanted to kiss her.

Damn it, still playing hard-to-get, aren't you a bit too self-absorbed?

Jessica had a starry-eyed expression on her face and sweetly smiled, "First, let's clarify, how much for a night with you?"

If it was too expensive, and she couldn't afford it. Originally, she had planned to wait for Marcus to name a price, then she would say she couldn't afford it and make a quick escape. Who would have thought that plans always fail to keep up with changes?

Marcus's face turned ashen.

Damn it!

He, Mr. Marcus, had never thought he would fall to the point of being bought by a woman.

Furious, he chuckled and provocatively lifted Jessica's chin, his deep eyes possessing a mesmerizing charm that made Jessica unable to help but indulge in it.

"1 million US dollars, I'll buy you for a night!" Marcus said.

Boom!

Jessica's mind exploded!

Oh no, what she currently hated the most was someone who relied on money and acted high and mighty.

Her burning anger erupted like a roaring fire, and with a sweet smile, Jessica arrogantly lifted her head, exuded a queenly aura, proud and defiant, "10 million US dollars, I'll buy you for a night, how about that?"

Damn it, who has more money? I can use the money to crush you to death!

Tell me how many hell bank notes you want, and I'll burn as much as you want!

It had been a chaotic night, filled with ambiguity to the extreme.

Jessica woke up in the morning, feeling sore all over her body, cursing Marcus in her heart countless times.

This man was nothing but an inhuman person, too ruthless!

Her body was covered with numerous bruises and marks left by him – some from gripping, some from kissing. Jessica purposely ignored the marks she left on Marcus's back, cursing him in her heart over and over again.

Her petite body had been tightly held in his embrace, and it took Jessica a great deal of effort to break free. With the dawn approaching, she hastily put on her clothes, enduring the pain in her lower body. She couldn't help but curse Marcus a few more times. Finally dressed, she reached into her pocket, finding only a hundred dollars.

A hundred dollars for 10 million hell bank notes, is that enough?

She didn't care. He was the one who benefited from it, while she was the one who suffered losses. If it was not enough, he would have to make up for it.

Spending a hundred dollars, she felt extremely distressed. She scolded herself for exchanging money for pain. Was she out of her mind?

In Jessica's calculations, Mr. Marcus wasn't worth a hundred dollars. It was truly a bargain. She reckoned Mr. Marcus would be close to spitting blood when he found out.

With this in mind, Jessica felt completely justified leaving the money on the table and kindly tearing a piece of paper to write a few words: inhuman person, this is your selling-your-body money. Goodbye!!

Jessica surreptitiously slipped out of the room, fleeing like a fugitive.

Night of Destiny

She would go home and settle accounts with Karen. How dare she drug her? Did she want to die?

******

Mr. Marcus woke up, and the sky was already beginning to brighten. Its comfortable embrace and a pause later, he felt something amiss. Suddenly opening his eyes, the room was empty, leaving only him. His eyes narrowed slightly, his bewitching features taking on a dangerous hue in the morning light – looking both lazy and deadly.

Damn that little brat.

She actually managed to escape?

Well, nobody escapes from the hands of Marcus. This naughty girl...oh... tastes pretty good.

He was a bit intrigued. Mr. Marcus was now a classic example of acquiring the taste after the first bite.

His gaze fell on the hundred dollars on the table, its vivid color catching his attention. An unpleasant premonition arose within him, and Marcus's eyes twitched at the corners. It better not be what he was thinking.

He had underestimated Jessica's evil nature.

When he saw the graceful words on the paper, Marcus's eyes darkened, and a murderous aura emanated from his body.

Inhuman person?

A hundred dollars?

Selling-your-body money?

Alright, very well!!!

Mr. Marcus grabbed the paper, crumpled it into a ball, and smiled twistedly.

******

The old and dilapidated slums of City W.

Sect Elder Breeze

The old and dilapidated houses, the dirty and smelly streets, and the crowded crowds, everywhere exude the hardships of the lowest level of urban life. Surrounded by skyscrapers, only this section is dilapidated.

Jessica carried a small suitcase and walked out of the crowded street.

"Jessica, have a good time with your aunt in France, don't worry about Dad. Study hard, Dad is sorry for you." Mr. Miller's eyes were swollen and he cried all night. Since marrying Karen's mother, he has felt guilty towards Jessica. "Dad is incompetent. And I have been mediocre all my life, unable to do anything for you. Fortunately, your aunt is taking you abroad, so you don't have to suffer with me. I can also give an account to your mother."

"Dad, don't say that." Jessica hugged her father. "I'm going to France, not disappearing. Dad, you can rest assured. I'll come back in the future and I'll make sure you live a comfortable life."

"Brother-in-law, don't worry, I will take good care of Jessica." Agnes Lopez said lovingly.

"Dad, Karen is very shady outside and owes a lot of money. You must not get involved, just live your own life well. She's already an adult, she will take care of herself. Besides, you have no obligation to do anything for her, remember?" This was what Jessica was most worried about.

Mr. Miller nodded.

After returning that day, Jessica directly beat up Karen. Despite her innocent appearance, she had a strong temperament and forced Karen to confess everything. However, Karen was still not giving up, trying to sell Jessica to an underground auction. Luckily her aunt had taken her to France to study, otherwise, she would have been in big trouble. She was worried about her father.

The taxi started and Jessica watched her slightly stooped father, tears streaming down her face.

Night of Destiny

Dad, wait for me to come back, I will make sure you live a comfortable life.

******

At the traffic lights, a silver luxury sports car was parked.

Mr. Marcus's recent temper was very bad. He was about to return to Australia and he couldn't find the whereabouts of that girl.

That bad girl, he was determined to find her and make her pay for what she had done. Even if she ran to the ends of the earth, he would find her and make her pay the price.

Those pair of bright eyes were very charming!

Her taste, so addictive, is captivating.

Damned girl!

Mr. Marcus was unwilling to accept that their relationship would end like this. There was always a voice in his heart shouting that she was the one he was looking for. This special feeling made his heart race, and he didn't reject it.

His slender eyeliner slightly lifted, suddenly stopped. Was that the bad girl?

In the taxi, Jessica was absentmindedly looking at the necklace Mr. Miller had given her, not noticing Mr. Marcus's gaze.

The traffic lights changed, and the car started moving. It was rush hour, with heavy traffic. Marcus had to closely follow, afraid of losing her.

Driving like this was very dangerous.

On the high curve, as a result of the taxi in front of him turning, Marcus became anxious and recklessly cut in, and as a result, tragedy struck. A truck coming from behind violently collided with his sports car, causing Marcus and his car to flip several times...

Bad girl, don't go...

Before falling into a coma, Marcus's only thought was intense and persistent!

Inside the car, Jessica's heart skipped a beat, and she felt a sharp pang before she turned her head blankly. Who was calling her?

"There's been a car accident at high speed," the driver said.

Jessica felt somewhat uneasy, and it took a long time for her to calm down.

As the ambulance rushed Marcus to the hospital, Jessica also boarded a flight to France.

The girl waved with a bright smile and shouted, "Goodbye, America, I will be back soon!"

******

Eight years later
W City, airport.

A finely dressed little boy stood in the airport lobby with snow-white skin, delicate features, and a tender and lovable appearance. Despite his adorable face, he wore an elegant smile, resembling a child version of a gentleman.

Every detail was unbelievably perfect, causing a sensation among many travelers, from elder people to little children.

"Henry..."

"Mommy, I'm here!" Henry Miller waved his little hand, smiling to greet his beloved mother.

Jessica had golden curly hair, wore sunglasses, a red shirt, a wide black belt with scattered diamonds around the waist, cropped denim trousers, and a pair of red high heels, stylish yet pure.

Finally, they were back!

After missing their hometown for seven years, even the air felt fresher than in Paris.

"My darling, how does it feel to be back home?" Jessica steadied the suitcase, leaned down, and planted a big kiss on Henry's face. She loved him so much.

"The weather is better than in Paris."

Jessica took off her sunglasses, revealing an extremely pure face with a sweet smile, concealing her devious thoughts, "Let's go, let's go see our Aunt Grace. Remember, when you see her, you have to give her a big kiss so that we can have a feast for the two of us."

"Understood, Mommy!" Henry nodded solemnly.

The mother and son conspired as they headed toward the exit.

Her son was truly clever.

******

"Sir, what are you looking at?" The Smith family's steward at the airport lobby asked curiously.

Old Mr. Alston's sharp gaze was fixed on the mother and son's silhouettes, lost in thought.

"Did you see that little boy just now?" Old Mr. Alston's voice was slightly cold.

The steward followed his gaze, only catching a glimpse of Henry's tender back.

"What's wrong?" the steward inquired.

That child and Marcus... bore a striking resemblance. Though it was just a passing glance...

But that little boy's face, though tender, resembled the one he had seen when he first met that child years ago.

Old Mr. Alston's face darkened as he shook his head, "It's nothing, perhaps I saw it wrong. Let's go."

"Yes."

Grace Wright was Jessica's close friend during her studies abroad, and their relationship was very deep. She returned to the country three days before Jessica and her son.

As soon as Henry arrived, Grace hugged and kissed him without stopping, immediately welcoming them and preparing to entertain them.

This was a very famous local restaurant known for its unique regional flavors, attracting customers from far and wide.

After getting out of the car, Jessica went to the restroom. Grace let Henry get out the car and wait as she went to park. When Henry got off, Grace came over from the other side and waved to Henry, "Sweetheart, come over here."

Henry ran over with a smile, but he didn't notice and bumped into a man, almost falling, and his little foot stepped on the man.

"Sorry!" Henry quickly apologized and bowed. He grew up in France and was an elegant young gentleman.

After apologizing and seeing that the man wasn't angry with him, he walked over slowly. Grace saw that he was unharmed and felt relieved, and then took him into the restaurant.

"Marcus, what's wrong?" A pretty woman intimately hooked her arm with his and asked with a sweet smile.

Why was he staring at that kid all the time?

Marcus shook his head, his cold eyes narrowing slightly. For some reason, when the child bumped into him, it seemed to touch the softest part of his heart, causing a slight flutter. Marcus regretted a bit that he hadn't seen the boy's face more clearly.

"It's nothing, let's go!" The two of them walked arm in arm into the neighboring restaurant.

Chapter 3

The Brilliant Son

Jessica returned to America for two weeks and everything went smoothly. Grace rented a house for her and her son near the school, just a ten-minute walk away. The area had convenient transportation, complete facilities, and a quiet neighborhood, which was very suitable for them.

Jessica took Henry to see Mr. Miller.

Mr. Miller and his second wife, Irma Baker, still lived in the slums. Seven years ago, Karen was caught by the underground market for owing high-interest loans and since then, she had disappeared without a trace. The person behind it was sinister and vicious, not Mr. Miller, and Karen's mother, as commoners, could provoke.

Due to their difficult life, Irma's temper worsened, but Mr. Miller was a very gentle person and often endured her. They lived a very hard life.

In recent years, Jessica had been busy with her studies, taking care of Henry, and working part-time. She had been too busy to return to her home country, only calling Mr. Miller every week to catch up.

Eight years had passed and seeing Mr. Miller with white temples, Jessica felt an indescribable sense of discomfort.

"Jessica? Is that Jessica?" Irma's eyes lit up when she saw Jessica's fashionable appearance. "Jessica, hurry up and take us away from here. I've had enough of it here. Your father is useless, working hard all his life and not saving a penny. Fortunately, there's you, a good daughter, to take care of us. Hurry up and take us away. I'm legally your mother, and you must support me!"

"I only have one mother, and you are just my stepmother," Jessica smiled sweetly.

Damn it, a leopard can't change its spots. She's talking about support obligation. If it weren't for my father's sake, I'd dismantle you. If it weren't for you and your daughter's greed, my father wouldn't have suffered so much over the years.

"What are you saying? You are being unfilial! Oh, why is my life so miserable? Jessica, I don't care, you must take me away!" Irma wailed and cried on the ground while Mr. Miller appeared helpless.

Henry tugged at Jessica's sleeve with his tender voice full of innocence, "Mommy, you taught me what 'brain-dead' means last time, and I understand now."

Irma's voice was stunned and stopped as Jessica laughed, "My darling is so clever!"

"How dare you curse me, you wild child... Ouch!"

Snap!

The sharp scream suddenly stopped, and Jessica slapped without hesitation, "You dare, say it again!"

Jessica had a very innocent appearance, always wearing a harmless smile that was clear and attractive. Only those familiar with her knew that this woman was a first-class schemer. Even if she wanted to cut you into pieces in her heart, she would still be smiling on the outside.

At this moment, she finally tore apart this sweet and innocent mask, her eyes flashing with anger. If it weren't for the lack of resources, she would have wanted to break a stick and hit her with it.

Anyone who dared to touch her baby, she would strike back for one, and for two, she would strike for a pair.

Irma was frightened by her and cried out, "Daughter hit her mother, daughter hit her mother... Come and reason with her...Oh...no..."

Damn!

Why don't you become an actress? You could easily win some kind of best-acting award just like that.

"Have you had enough of your tantrum?" Mr. Miller, unable to bear it any longer, took Jessica and Henry away. How could he have been so blind to marry her back then? She had ruined his entire life!

"Dad, come and live with me, let me take care of you. I've been working in France for a year, working part-time during my studies and I've saved up some money. I can take care of you and Henry, no problem."

Mr. Miller sighed, and patted his grandson's head, "Jessica, don't worry about it. You know Irma's temperament. If I go to live with you, she will too, and she has a gambling habit. If there's no money at home, she can restrain herself a bit, but if she knows you have money, she will be extravagant. I can't burden you. It's not easy for my daughter to have success. I can't ruin it for my sake. Besides, you have to think of Henry too."

"Dad... Do you want me to just watch you suffer?"

"Dad is used to it. As long as you all are doing well, Dad is satisfied."

"Well, Dad, I'll bring Henry to see you when I have time. If you have time, come and stay with us for a few days. Henry will be very happy too."

"Yes, Grandpa, Henry wants to hear your stories."

"Good boy. Grandpa understands."

******

Sect Elder Breeze

After school, Little Henry went to the nearby market to buy vegetables, meat, and groceries. As he passed by the park, he saw an old man sitting on a bench.

He was wearing a fitted suit and exuded a very dignified aura.

Not far away, a long Rolls-Royce luxury car was parked at the side of the road, and a man was anxiously making a phone call, urging someone to tow the car.

It looks like the car broke down!

The two were almost face to face, Old Mr. Alston suddenly stood up in excitement, his face changed dramatically, startling Henry.

"You..."

Henry was puzzled, and then he smiled gracefully, "Hello, sir!"

Old Mr. Alston was shocked, the little boy he met at the airport that day, that glimpse, looked a lot like Marcus, and now, even more so!

Those facial features, that disguised elegance, were almost identical.

"Who is your father?" Old Mr. Alston suddenly asked, too shocked, the dominant figure in the business world for many years, he couldn't control his trembling voice.

"Sir, do you always ask a stranger who their father is?" Henry smiled.

Old Mr. Alston paused for a moment, and suddenly the phone rang, he picked it up. Henry was about to leave, but he stopped in his tracks when he heard the first thing he said.

"Marcus's secretary needs to be replaced?" Old Mr. Alston asked sternly, his face darkening.

Henry raised an eyebrow, with a pensive look on his face.

"Well, in that case, let Crystal be his secretary. With Crystal watching over him, I can feel a bit relieved at least!" Old Mr. Alston's voice was extremely cold.

Henry's lips gracefully curved but with a hint of coldness.

Night of Destiny

His blue pupils flashed a hint of mockery, then disappeared, returning to the graceful young gentleman.

"Yes, that's it!" Old Mr. Alston hung up the phone, locked his eyes on Henry's face, and repeated, "Who is your father?"

Henry smiled, exceptionally elegant, "He is a teacher, you don't need to know!"

He stepped forward and left.

"A teacher?" Old Mr. Alston pursed his lips, then sighed.

Perhaps it's just a coincidence, how could Marcus have any relation with such common people?

As Henry approached the apartment door, he took out his phone and dialed a number, "Aunt Grace, please do me a favor..."

******

Noblefull Group, President's Office

Marcus sat on the genuine leather sofa, wearing a well-fitted suit, with a devilishly handsome face and a cold, piercing gaze. This young president exuded an air of elegance mingled with indifference.

The slanting sunlight poured in, casting scattered, mesmerizing shadows on him, adding a layer of captivating charm.

Marcus Smith, 28 years old, the third young master of the Smith family, graduated from Harvard University and took over Noblefull Group four years ago. With his talent and abilities, he made a name for himself in the business world within a few short years, elevating Noblefull Group to new heights.

His iron-fisted style and decisive decision-making consistently made him unbeatable in the business world, wielding immense influence.

Sect Elder Breeze

At the same time, he was known as a playboy president. With his immense wealth and handsome appearance, Marcus was the object of affection for elite ladies and sought after by celebrities, regardless of their background, they all couldn't escape his charm.

Rumors had it that Crystal Walker, the heiress of the Walker Family Group, was his official girlfriend, and they were already at the stage of discussing marriage. Major newspapers had also reported intimate photos of the two of them together.

Even so, Marcus' frequency of changing partners still astonished people. Whether they were actresses, elite ladies, or innocent girls, as long as Marcus set his sights on them, they couldn't escape his pursuit.

Except for Crystal, no woman had ever stayed by his side for more than ten days. Mr. Marcus' rules of engagement were simple: easy come, easy go. His wealth and handsomeness were alluring, while his coldness and iron-fisted approach kept these women from daring to get too entangled with him.

Hence, he was known as the playboy president.

At this moment, he furrowed his brows, looking quite displeased, as his icy gaze fell upon his secretary, Nancy Scott.

Nancy broke out in a cold sweat. Although she was the wife of his friend, she couldn't help but feel afraid when faced with Marcus' icy gaze. Who knew she would suddenly become pregnant and have to take a leave?

"Mr. Marcus, I will choose a suitable secretary to take over my position."

"No need!" Marcus said coldly, his slender eyes narrowing. "Go and inform the HR department to recruit a new one."

Nancy hesitated for a moment, taking the risk of being scolded to say, "Mr. Marcus, I have a suitable candidate to recommend. Can you consider?"

Night of Destiny

Oh, no! Marcus' expression was truly terrifying. Would she fail even before she started?

"Speak!"

"Yes, I have a friend who worked as a secretary under the president of Husdow Group for a year. She is currently looking for a job in the country, and I am certain of her outstanding abilities. She is more than capable of taking over my position as a secretary."

Husdow Group? Being able to serve as a secretary for a year under that control freak, there was no doubt about her capabilities. Lionel, that pervert, changed his secretary every month, with many quirks and strict demands. He rejected secretaries who fawned over him and those who were just decorative. Any secretary who could last under him for three months was considered one of the most top-notch in the world.

"Submit her resume directly to the HR department. No need for an interview!" Marcus decisively stated, "Let her start formally on Monday!"

"Yes!"

******

An Apartment.

Jessica, holding the phone, was stunned and speechless for a while after hearing Grace's words.

"Darn it, Grace, are you out of your mind? You gave my resume to Noblefull Group! Ugh, I'm going to kill you!"

"Hey, sis, I had to ask Nancy to put in a good word for you. What's your problem? The salary is 70,000 dollars a month! If I had the ability, I'd have taken the job myself. Is it your turn now? Also, your sweetheart, Little Henry said you agreed. I only gave Nancy your resume because of that. Oh well, I don't care. It's done, anyway. Report to Noblefull Group's CEO's office on the 36th floor on Monday. Got it? I'm busy, gotta go. Talk tonight."

Jessica, "…"

"Mommy, I'm sorry. I thought you were in a hurry to find a job, so I agreed to Aunt Grace," Henry sat at the table, looking distressed, his fair face on the edge of tears.

"Sweetheart, it's okay. Mommy initially promised Mr. Quincy to work at his company... It's nothing, we can just push it back. It's nothing. I will talk to Mr. Quincy."

"Mommy, are you not mad at me?" Henry raised his head and asked softly, with tears still shimmering in his eyes.

"If Henry sells mommy, mommy will help Henry count the money," Jessica kissed her son's tender cheek, not noticing the cunning smile that flashed across Henry's lips.

Oh, Mommy, I did sell you!

Chapter 4

Eerie Encounter

Jessica and Quincy Lee agreed to have dinner at a French restaurant.

Quincy, Jessica's senior, was two years older than her. He came from a prominent family, with handsome looks and a gentle demeanor, always wearing a light smile. He was a distinguished gentleman well-known in high society.

Night of Destiny

When they were studying in France, Quincy and Jessica had a good relationship. He was gentle, generous, and courteous, a dream lover for most girls, like a prince charming, always gentle and noble.

Two years ago, Old Mr. Lee summoned Quincy back from France and officially handed over Gootal Group to him.

This gracious man had a keen sense of the business world, and under his leadership, Gootal Group had been advancing steadily. Knowing that Jessica was about to return to America, Quincy intended to recruit her into Gootal Group.

Jessica had been considering for a long time and only agreed yesterday, but unexpectedly, Henry and Grace made a mistake, leaving her with no choice but to Jessica could only refuse his offer.

Stuck in traffic, she arrived at the restaurant twenty-five minutes later than the scheduled time. Regretting deeply, Jessica rushed towards the restaurant while muttering curses at W City's terrible traffic.

Lost in thought, she missed a step in her high heels and screamed as she stumbled forward, "Oh…"

Colliding with the man's solid chest, a faint tobacco scent hit her face, clean and comforting. In her panic, Jessica instinctively grabbed the man's hand.

It felt warm!

"Sorry, sorry…" Jessica lifted her most sincere smile and was about to apologize when suddenly… her heart skipped a beat, and her mind went blank in an instant.

Marcus was waiting for Crystal for lunch. Just as he got out of the car steadily, he saw a woman stumbling towards him. He instinctively reached out and caught her, feeling a fragrant warmth enveloping him. Jessica's soft strands of hair scattered, revealing her fair skin and delicate features, everything about her appearance and touch felt strangely familiar to Marcus.

Her deep, watery eyes, bright as sunshine, made it hard to look away, while her fair skin, dainty features, and flushed cheeks from running made her look like a tender peach.

Jessica's smile froze!

How could it be him?

It was not that her memory was too good, she still remembered the Marcus she had sex with eight years ago, but the mini version of Marcus, Henry, that she saw every day, she couldn't forget even if she wanted to.

Even his elegant demeanor was a perfect match.

Jessica's first instinct was to run away.

Marcus pressed his lips with a half-smile, "Miss, am I that scary-looking?"

Without thinking, Jessica shook her head.

Marcus asked, "Why do you run when you see me?"

He had forgotten her?

Forgetting was normal, it had been eight years, and their relationship was only a passing acquaintance.

But why did a wave of sadness well up in her heart?

The man wore a high-quality suit, showcasing his tall and muscular figure with impeccable tailoring and strikingly handsome facial features. His elegant yet aloof demeanor, piercing gaze, and every move exuded a kingly demeanor.

Jessica muttered to herself, "Are all money boys like this? Are they all so otherworldly? It's truly sinful!"

"Sorry, I'm in a rush," Jessica smiled, politely nodded, swept away her surprise, and calmly walked past him into the restaurant.

When she left W City for France, she found herself pregnant just a month later. Her first feeling was surprise, followed by joy.

At the time, she was studying the language and facing a lot of difficulties in preparing for school. Her aunt suggested that she should terminate the pregnancy.

Night of Destiny

However, Jessica stubbornly decided to keep the baby, delaying her studies for a year for the sake of Henry. She had no regrets.

This child was her everything!

Regardless of how the child came to be, Jessica was very grateful to Marcus for giving her a child. In a foreign country, because of him, she could endure boundless loneliness, endure the ridicule of others, and endure the hardships of life.

Jessica floated into the restaurant like a ghost, feeling like the ground was swaying beneath her. She never expected to see him again.

Marcus gazed deeply at Jessica's back, lost in thought. Her figure was so familiar, with the sunlight gently falling on his shoulders, casting a faint halo. Why?

"Marcus, sorry for being late!" Crystal arrived in a light blue dress, her delicate features filled with apology.

Suddenly, Marcus realized why he found her so familiar. That girl's eyes, figure, and the atmosphere were similar to Crystal's.

"Let's go eat!" Marcus smiled gently, put his arm around Crystal, and walked towards the restaurant.

The ambiguous lighting and elegant atmosphere made this restaurant perfect for couples dining.

Jessica secretly prayed she wouldn't run into him again. Her fragile heart couldn't handle this constant emotional rollercoaster.

"Jessica, why aren't you eating?" Quincy asked gently, his face full of concern.

Jessica quickly came to her senses, apologetically smiled and sheepishly touched her nose, which Quincy found adorable, increasing his fondness for her.

"Senior, I'm sorry for standing you up again. You must scold me for it!" Jessica said.

"Jessica, what nonsense. I am happy that you finding a satisfying job. I can't scold you. Even though it's a pity we can't work together, as long as you're happy, nothing else matters," Quincy said tenderly.

Feeling guiltier, Jessica couldn't understand why she didn't have feelings for this kind and patient man. He was flawless like white jade. Why couldn't she feel attracted to such a wonderful man?

If she did, it would be perfect. Quincy would be the perfect lover, the perfect husband.

Damn it, this stupid heart. It wouldn't leap when she wanted it to but jumped uncontrollably at the wrong times.

"I'm sorry," Jessica said softly.

"Jessica," Quincy reached out and lifted her chin, wearing an indulgent smile on his face. "As long as you're happy!"

In his eyes, Jessica was the most precious. Caring for her silently for so many years, he couldn't bear to push her even a little. He wished to give Jessica the best in the world.

He wouldn't let her be unhappy.

Jessica smirked and grimaced, feeling her appetite return.

Not far away, Marcus narrowed his eyes slightly. His profound gaze showed no sign of emotion. He had noticed them as soon as they entered. Quincy Lee, the president of Gootal Group. What was their relationship?

He had engaged in business confrontations with Quincy before. Quincy was always courteous and friendly, but his smile always had a sense of distance and coldness.

But now, a face full of gentle indulgence; the girl seemed like his pearl in his palm. As a man, Marcus knew exactly what that passionate look in Quincy's eyes meant. That girl didn't seem to reject his intimacy.

Could it be that they were lovers?

Night of Destiny

This realization made Marcus extremely upset. Fury surged in his eyes as if someone had coveted his most precious possession. That damn, tricky girl had just been cold and indifferent to him, and now she was smiling so sweetly in the blink of an eye.

Feeling the burning gaze, Quincy raised his eyes slightly and quickly met Marcus's displeased gaze. He was startled as the tender look in his eyes was overlaid with a layer of indifference. They nodded to each other from a distance and each politely had a drink.

Jessica bowed her head and ate, not noticing the silent showdown between the two men.

"Eat slower, don't be so hasty, your lips are dirty," Quincy gently wiped her with a napkin, still with a doting and cherished smile, indulging in his beloved's mischief.

Jessica was taken aback, feeling extremely embarrassed. Was this gesture too intimate? However, she didn't pay much attention to it, just smiled at him apologetically.

Marcus's eyes narrowed dangerously, an air of danger emanating from his handsome face.

In the battle between men, men understood it the best. Quincy was declaring his possessiveness, clearly telling him, "This woman is mine!"

The war between men was always full of flames and dominance. Especially for two men who were rivals in the business world. Whether they were gentle or cold men, they would have a unique way of showing each other, "This is mine!"

Marcus's eyes were cold, as expected, they were lovers, and that man had torn apart his gentle facade. There was nothing but dominance in his gaze.

"Marcus, what are you looking at?" Following his gaze, Crystal widened her eyes in surprise. "Mr. Quincy? Is she his girlfriend?"

Marcus remained silent, bowing his head to eat.

Sect Elder Breeze

Crystal said softly, "Marcus, you should learn from Mr. Quincy. No scandals at all, just look at yourself..."

"Crystal, are you complaining that I've been neglecting you? Tonight, I'll be as passionate as fire," Marcus said with a devilish smile.

Crystal blushed, feeling coquettish.

He loved Crystal, and over the years, only Crystal had managed to capture his gaze, but he always felt unsatisfied, always searching. One woman after another, but there was an empty place in his heart that no one could fill. Crystal was beautiful, and her family background was good. He loved her, and she loved him, clearly a deeply bonded couple. He didn't know what he was still unsatisfied with.

When Quincy and Jessica left, Quincy held Jessica's waist and whispered in her ear, "Jessica, I see an acquaintance, please play along." Saying this, he affectionately held her and walked out, looking every bit like a couple.

Jessica just smiled understandingly and didn't refuse. She just wanted to be helpful!

Marcus's eyes instantly turned fierce. Why, as soon as he saw them being intimate, he couldn't help but be furious?

Outside the restaurant, Quincy suddenly asked, "Jessica, do you know Marcus Smith?"

"Marcus Smith?" Jessica looked puzzled. The CEO of Noblefull Group, her future boss, currently she doesn't know him.

Quincy smiled gently, "No, it's good that you don't know him!"

Jessica, you really don't know Marcus Smith? Henry's face looks seventy percent like Marcus's. Anyone who sees them would not doubt that they are not father and son.

******

Monday morning.

Night of Destiny

Henry got up very early, raised an elegant smile, and lightly knocked on Jessica's door, "Mommy, it's time to get up, you have to go to work today!"

"I know, I know..." Jessica responded drowsily.

Henry smiled, washed up, dressed up, went into the kitchen, washed the pot, lit the fire, fried eggs, and skillfully made two nutritious breakfasts, the fragrant sandwiches came out of the oven, he heated milk again, and this time opened the door directly, jumped onto the bed with his small body, and kicked Jessica off with one foot.

Thud...

"Ouch, it hurts..."

Henry jumped down gracefully, ignoring his mommy's resentful eyes, got water, squeezed toothpaste and put it, smiled, and gestured to come in.

"Mommy, Noblefull Group is very strict, if you're late, you'll lose your job, and we'll have to suffer."

Jessica wanted to cry but had no tears...

"Henry, I hate you!" Jessica roared and resentfully went to the bathroom to wash up.

Henry helped her fold the blanket, picked out the outfit she should wear to work today, and neatly placed it on the bed.

When Jessica came out dressed and did her hair, Henry had already packed his bag and was in the middle of having breakfast, "Good morning, Mommy, hurry up and have breakfast, we'll leave together."

Jessica resentfully bit into the sandwich, of a five-star standard, and felt slightly twisted in her heart.

Usually, isn't it the mommy who serves the son in the morning? Why did it turn into her son serving the mommy here?

Her son was a genius, and he did the chores so well, her life had hope.

"Henry, I'm sorry for not being a good mommy to you!"

Henry solemnly nodded, indicating he understood, and elegantly urged Jessica to have breakfast. Everything about his dear mommy was good, but she was lazy and couldn't do housework. Poor him, at such a young age, he was good at housework and could cook a table full of dishes.

"Henry, you shouldn't marry a wife in the future, you should take care of Mommy for your whole life, you know?"

"Okay!"

So obedient! Future daughter-in-law, go aside, this son is so outstandingly good, how could anyone snatch him away for nothing? This time Jessica understood why the mother-in-law and daughter-in-law relationship had always been very delicate.

******

Noblefull Group building, situated in the most prosperous central area, towering into the sky, was magnificent and extraordinary.

Jessica took a long breath.

Come on, Jessica!

For the money, rise!

Chapter 5

New Secretary

Night of Destiny

Jessica went up to the 36th floor.

This floor was spacious and luxuriously decorated.

There were several secretaries for the CEO of Noblefull Group, working together. At first glance, they were all beautiful and shrewd.

Jessica took a long breath, relieving the tension in her heart.

Nancy saw her at first sight and walked over with a smile, "Hello, are you Miss Jessica? I'm Nancy Scott."

Jessica politely shook her hand, "Hello, I'm Jessica Miller, nice to meet you!"

"Don't be so polite, I'm Grace's friend, we'll have plenty of opportunities to meet in the future." Nancy was very surprised. She looked young in the photos, but in person, she looked even younger.

Pure and fresh, the professional suit didn't match her, is she really the top secretary trained by Lionel?

The other four women also whispered to each other. They had known for a long time that someone was going to replace Nancy's position as the executive secretary. It was said that she was the only secretary of Lionel of the Husdow Group who had completed a full year and had even automatically resigned. In their impression, she should be a very competent woman.

Why does she look like a college student?

Everyone looked at Jessica with questioning eyes.

"Mr. Marcus, Miss Jessica is here!"

"Come in!"

A low, magnetic voice came. Jessica's heart skipped a beat. This voice sounded familiar as if she were hallucinating...

Pushing the door open, Jessica... froze!

This world... became surreal!

Darn it! How small was this world?

"Is it you?" Marcus dangerously squinted his eyes, his thin lips uttering a dangerous question. He never dreamed that the new secretary was her, and even more surprising, she was Jessica Miller.

Time froze!

Marcus's handsome face was deeply inscrutable, showing no emotion. No matter how he looked at her, she seemed very young, maybe in her early twenties, fair-skinned, with a pure appearance and eyes filled with bright colors.

To confirm her capabilities, he deliberately called Lionel. Upon learning that Jessica had joined Noblefull Group, Lionel was livid, shouting for Marcus to bear his losses. The talent he had trained under his perverted methods had been given to Marcus for nothing, which really grated on Lionel's nerves.

This also confirmed Jessica's exceptional abilities.

This young girl was the leading figure in the Parisian secretary world. It was truly unbelievable.

Jessica felt heartache and resentment in her heart for her youthful ignorance eight years ago!

Even eight years ago, if Mr. Marcus hadn't been so oppressive and cold, she shouldn't have been so ignorant to treat him as just a "money boy" and even throw a hundred dollars at him as payment for sex.

Jessica, you fool!

If Mr. Marcus remembered this misunderstanding and found out that she had secretly given birth to Henry without telling him, she would be in big trouble with no way out.

Can she have the chance to say that she came to the wrong door?

What does his expression mean? A beast is always a beast, with eyes that seem to glow green. Hey, can you not make such a sinister expression?

"Are you sure you're of legal age?" Marcus leaned back, lazily lifting a curve. This girl, why is she so expressionless? Couldn't she show some emotion?

Shame, it's an absolute shame!

Damn it, eight years ago, when you took my virginity, why didn't you think to ask if I was underage?

Jessica seemed to forget that it was her who seduced him first.

"Mr. Marcus, I am twenty-seven years old and of legal age," Jessica replied seriously.

Marcus raised an eyebrow, his hands crossed, resting on his chin, staring at Jessica with a sly expression that made her think of a snake.

A cold, moist snake.

Jessica felt uneasy.

Does he not remember her at all?

Jessica's heart pounded, and a cold sweat broke out on her back. Her nerves suddenly tightened. Normally, Mr. Marcus was played by her, and then being dumped for a hundred dollars, this kind of humiliation was a first for him. It should have left a deep impression, he couldn't possibly forget.

Could it be that Mr. Marcus is used to this kind of thing and has become indifferent because of it?

Jessica's thoughts were in disarray.

"Miss Nancy will tell you the specific workflow. Since you are the leading figure in the Paris secretary world, let everyone see your abilities. Go out now!" Marcus's tone was as indifferent as ever.

His profound gaze revealed no emotions.

"Yes, Mr. Marcus!" Jessica breathed a sigh of relief.

Nancy told her about the work process, and familiarized her with the environment, and Jessica quickly adapted, but she was tired and almost exhausted by the end of the day.

After work, Henry was busy in the kitchen wearing an apron. The busy figure of little Henry made Jessica, as a mother, feel a little guilty. Yes, a little guilty...

"Baby, I love you!" Jessica put down a pile of documents and grabbed his little face, kissing him. His skin was so tender, kissing him felt so comfortable, unlike that man, so cold as an ice machine!

"Mommy, I love you too!" Henry elegantly kissed her back.

And Jessica, exhausted from the day, was moved to tears.

"Mommy, how was work today?"

"Don't ask me yet, let me eat a few bites first," Jessica swiftly devoured the delicious meal her son had made. She was starving.

"Hey, baby, what's with that expectant look in your eyes?"

"What expectant look? That's me despising your table manners!"

"Ugh!"

"Mommy, do you like the working environment at Noblefull Group?"

"No, I don't!"

"Why?"

Jessica clenched her fist, her inner fire blazing, "Because there's a wild beast emitting green light!"

Henry, "..."

"Did you see anyone you know?"

"Know anyone?" Jessica tilted her head, trying to remember the department managers she met today, filtering through the people she had seen, "Lots of strangers, but no one I knew."

"I give up on you!"

"Henry, what's with that expression on your face? Are you despising me?"

"Mommy, you're a pseudo-lady! Well, let's eat, let's eat. I really shouldn't have expected too much from you."

Jessica: "..."

Feeling despised by her son felt darn awful.

******

Night of Destiny

A week passed in the blink of an eye, and Jessica had already established her presence in Noblefull Group. As Mr. Marcus's chief secretary, her abilities had earned the respect of everyone, even prompting Nancy to happily take a vacation, seeing that Jessica could handle things on her own.

Even the four women in the secretary's office, who started with mocking, had started to show respect. With her abilities, Jessica had proved her worth.

Noblefull Group was a fiercely competitive environment where only merit mattered, particularly among Marcus's secretaries who were all carefully selected, each with their unique qualities. They were proud and self-assured, and it took a lot of effort for Jessica to earn their recognition.

The only thing that bothered her was facing Mr. Marcus's handsome face every day. For Jessica, it was torture to say goodbye affectionately to her son every morning and then bump into the big boss in the company. She had to constantly remind herself not to give Marcus a kiss.

Speaking of the extent of perversion, Lionel was no less than Mr. Marcus. During her time in France, she had to meticulously record all of Lionel's interactions with his mistresses. Whenever he felt like it, he usually just mentioned a mistress's name, and Jessica had to recall the details of that woman from her memory and pass it on to him.

What annoyed her the most was that Lionel's perversions were not inclined towards socialites or stars, but rather towards affluent women. Regardless of whether the woman was married or not, if he set his sights on her, he would flirt and seduce her.

It is imaginable how fiercely Jessica's inner fire must have burned, as she specially handled these matters for him, wishing she could throw him to Mars.

Sect Elder Breeze

Marcus wasn't much better. He had a deeply devoted girlfriend, a socialite. He had so many mistresses that they could line up several streets. In just one week of taking office, he had already received calls from over 30 women, all wanting to have a rendezvous with Marcus, and he pushed all of this onto Jessica, asking her to shield him from them.

She accepted the lamenting, the pleading, and the insults in full.

Initially, he just wanted to see her in distress. After all, even the experienced Nancy felt extremely flustered and often became furious while handling these romantic affairs.

But Jessica exceeded his expectations.

When his mistresses called, she welcomed them all with a smile, listened to them attentively, and came up with a perfect excuse every time to fend them off. She could tell every mistress that the CEO was in a meeting, without ever using the same excuse twice.

Her countless creative excuses left him speechless.

Once, he pushed the door open and happened to hear the young girl smiling and saying, "Mr. Marcus is making love with Miss Crystal in the rest lounge and may not be available for a while."

This statement twisted Marcus's handsome face.

However, it couldn't be denied that she was the most competent secretary and handled such matters with ease.

"Mr. Marcus, sorry for the lie, but this is more in line with your style," Jessica said innocently, with a sweet smile.

Damn it!

She scolded people without using dirty words!

The person that perverted Lionel raised, is perverted too!

******

Eight years later, seeing Raymond Davis and Florence Black again, Jessica was also surprised.

"Jessica, what are you doing here?" Raymond exclaimed in surprise when he saw Jessica.

Night of Destiny

Beside him, Florence looked astonished and then jealous, with a fierce glint in her eyes.

"Raymond, I am Mr. Marcus's secretary," Jessica smiled.

"Jessica, I didn't expect to see you here," Raymond exclaimed excitedly, rushing over and grabbing Jessica's hand. There was a calculating glint in his eyes. This was his chance to save the Davis Family Group, and he had to seize it.

It had long been rumored that Marcus had a very capable secretary, but Raymond didn't expect it to be Jessica.

Jessica looked so young, seeming like a college student. What could she have done to become Marcus's secretary? It must be because Jessica was pretty, and there must have been some unclear relationship between the two for Jessica to get this job.

Raymond felt jealous in his heart. He had been dating Jessica for a year but hadn't even received a kiss, and now that man had jumped ahead. He felt an indescribable jealousy.

But for now, the most important thing was to save the Davis Family Group. As for Jessica, he hadn't expected her to have changed so much in eight years, still looking uniquely pure, but the past greenness and simplicity were gone, making her even more beautiful.

She made his heart flutter! She could sleep with Marcus, what couldn't she sleep with him?

For now, asking her for help was the real deal. They could take their time later...

"Do you miss me? I missed you so much in these seven years. I've been asking about your news all the time. Where have you been?" Raymond said with excitement, holding Jessica's hand.

Jessica was speechless, her eyes slightly lowered, looking at Raymond excitedly holding her hand. Were they that close?

Also, dude, you're embarrassing yourself. It's been eight years, not seven, okay?

Could you please rehearse before acting? It's so easy to see through.

Besides, your new girlfriend is right there beside you. Is this how you disregarded your girlfriend's feelings?

Damn it!

Who do you think you are? She knew that Raymond was coming today, to be honest, she had even forgotten Raymond's face; she only remembered when she saw him, his presence in her memory was too weak.

"Raymond, Mr. Marcus is waiting for you inside," Jessica said with a faint smile.

"A secretary? I'm afraid she's more like a bedfellow," Florence sharply mocked.

After all, everyone knew that Marcus was quite fickle, and it was common for him to flirt with his secretary. Back in their student days, Florence didn't like Jessica at all.

She only pretended to be close to Jessica to get closer to Raymond. She didn't feel the slightest guilt about taking Raymond away from her. This woman always deceives people with her innocent and pure face.

"As long as they're not married, an unclear relationship between a man and a woman can be called a bedfellow. Miss Florence, how many beds do you change in a day?" Jessica sarcastically asked Florence with a smile.

Anyone can be sarcastic; I can poison you just by opening my mouth!

"Jessica, you ..." Florence was livid.

"What are you doing?" A cold voice floated over, carrying a hint of anger, making the entire floor feel like mid-winter.

Chapter 6

Difficulties Created By Mr. Marcus

Marcus glanced at Raymond and Jessica holding hands, and his eyes narrowed slightly, his cold gaze carrying a hint of anger. Jessica quickly let go of Raymond's hand and stood still without a word.

Other secretaries were trembling with fear; Mr. Marcus's expression was truly terrifying.

Florence, upon seeing Marcus, revealed a faint green glow in her eyes, like a hungry wolf seeing sweet food, displaying her best side with seductive eyes.

What a showoff!

What kind of coquetry is that!

"Raymond, if you're here to flirt with my secretary, please leave. And you, Jessica, please be professional during work, stop flirting around!" Marcus sternly said as he entered his office.

Jessica shook. You were the one flirting around, okay?

Florence sneered at the scolded Jessica and arrogantly strode away in her high heels.

Boring woman!

If Marcus could be interested in this kind of woman, Jessica would seriously doubt his taste.

After making three cups of coffee, Jessica delivered them and was about to leave when Marcus's eyes darkened, and he coldly said, "Miss Jessica, stay and listen!"

A perfect secretary is not allowed to question their superior's orders.

Sect Elder Breeze

"Yes!" Even though Jessica didn't understand his intentions, she quietly stood by.

This man is cold and ruthless, unfathomable. She should be more restrained to avoid getting in trouble.

Why did Marcus ask Jessica to stay? Raymond couldn't figure out their relationship for a moment. A man as inscrutable as Marcus is not someone everyone can understand. Jessica always wears a mild, sweet smile, it's hard to read her.

Florence had been throwing seductive glances at Marcus, hoping he would notice her. Seeing Jessica being asked to stay, she looked resentful.

Damn woman, always ruining her good opportunities.

Marcus was worth billions, incredibly handsome, influential, and powerful.

Marcus had a net worth of billions, he was incredibly handsome, powerful, and influential. That was the kind of man Florence had her sights set on. If Marcus noticed her, she was confident she could win his heart. When that happened, she intended to sweep away Jessica, who was a hindrance.

Jessica could tell what Florence was thinking by the jealous look on her face. She quietly smirked and thought to herself, "This lady should go buy a bed from the market and get some rest. Maybe she can achieve her dreams faster in her dreams."

The Davis Family Group was an established household goods enterprise in City W, of considerable size. That year, the group had been impacted by the financial crisis, causing Raymond to lose a considerable amount of money in the stock market. The company's cash flow was tight, leading them to seek funding from the Noblefull Group, hoping to turn the tide.

Night of Destiny

"Mr. Smith, we have a large number of stable manufacturers and loyal customers. Our company has a significant potential for growth. Our cash flow issue is only temporary. Mr. Smith, as long as you provide the funding, I am confident that we can restore normal operations. For you, it's just a drop in the ocean, with no real loss, isn't it?" Raymond flattered Marcus.

Marcus's deep, inscrutable eyes revealed no emotion as he reviewed the Davis Family Group's performance for the year and the plan for the following year. His slender fingers tapped lightly on the table, creating a rhythmic sound that made Raymond's heart race, causing him to gulp nervously as he watched Marcus.

With just a few words, Marcus could determine the Davis Family Group's fate.

"Mr. Smith, please consider it. We truly have many advantages over our peers. We can all earn money together," Florence cooed in a seductive voice.

The seductive voice made Jessica shiver. Damn, can't you tone down the flirtiness a bit?

She turned to look at her own arm, where a swarm of goosebumps had appeared.

"Miss Jessica, do you have any objections?" Marcus unexpectedly asked Jessica, lifting his head.

Raymond's eager gaze fell on Jessica, with a look that said "You have to help me". At least they had a relationship before, Jessica won't just stand by and do nothing.

Florence sneered disdainfully, silently cursing Raymond for his audacity to seek help from Jessica in front of her. Wasn't he disrespecting her by doing so?

Marcus looked on coldly at the ugly scene, his lips curling up coldly.

How many men is his secretary involved with?

Quincy, Raymond...

Looks can be deceiving; that's for her, he wanted to see what she would say.

Sect Elder Breeze

Jessica lowered her eyes and humbly said, "Mr. Marcus, I'm just a secretary. In this kind of decision-making issue, you're asking the wrong person. If the Noblefull Group's stock price fluctuates, I would become the scapegoat."

Mr. Marcus dangerously narrowed his eyes, coldly sweeping over Jessica. This young girl had quite the talent for insulting people, daring to call him incompetent.

"As you say, it's so simple. As my chief secretary, you can't even provide any opinions, Miss Jessica, are you sure you're capable of this job?" Mr. Marcus's tone was even colder than his indifference.

Florence could tell he was displeased and secretly delighted, wishing that Mr. Marcus would just kick Jessica out of Noblefull Group on the spot.

"Mr. Marcus, since you're my boss and insist on asking, I have to say something. You can take it as a reference," Jessica said, "Davis Family Group is an established daily goods company with many loyal customers and a good corporate image, leaning towards tradition, which is its advantage in competition. However, in recent years, Raymond has frequently misappropriated company funds in the stock market, repeatedly incurring losses and showing no improvement, and the product quality is also not as good as before. Doing business, especially in traditional enterprises, is better to be down-to-earth. Such speculation carries too much risk. I believe that even if Noblefull Group injects capital, it may not effectively improve Davis Family Group's current situation, but rather be a futile effort."

Jessica dared to bet on her precious son's high IQ, Mr. Marcus, the cunning man, had already made up his mind, deliberately pushing her out as a scapegoat.

Sly, dark-hearted.

Perverted!

With such a boss, no wonder the subordinates' minds are twisted.

Night of Destiny

"Jessica, you're talking nonsense, you're slandering me!" Raymond became angry and stood up from the sand with a swish, cursing Jessica.

Marcus's lips curved into a smirk. His secretary, with such a poker face, it's so cute to see her criticize Raymond seriously. He wonders how she curses him in her heart.

"Mr. Marcus, don't listen to Jessica's nonsense, she's resentful that Raymond left her and chose me. She is deliberately retaliating against Raymond. Mr. Marcus, don't listen to her nonsense, she's jealous of us and can't stand to see us doing well." Florence stared at Jessica with resentment, then turned to Marcus with a pitiful look, hoping to turn the tide.

Jessica, "..." Oh gosh.

Oh, no! If it weren't for you needing Marcus, when they met in the office, she would have forgotten what Raymond and Florence even looked like.

Jealous?

Are you kidding?!

What exactly is there to be jealous of on both of you, inside and out?

Marcus raised an eyebrow. She was abandoned? They were lovers? Mr. Marcus narrowed his eyes and smirked, "Miss Jessica, your love life is truly rich."

Jessica humbly bowed, pulling off a bright smile, "Oh, come on now, Mr. Marcus, your love life is so colorful, and as a subordinate, it wouldn't be right to fall behind, it would make people laugh."

Which means, if the boss is so strong, how could the subordinate dare to fall behind?

A twitch at the corner of Marcus's eye, staring at Jessica with a murderous glint. Why can she say such biting words with such a bright smile?

Hit the nail on the head!

Sect Elder Breeze

Poker-faced, just smiling and smiling, but the words she spit out make him furious, yet she's smiling so sweetly, speaking the truth. He doesn't even know where to direct his anger.

"Raymond, look, even my secretary said that the investment is a one-way street, we can only hope for our next cooperation. Miss Jessica, please see our guests out!"

Raymond and Florence were unwilling and still wanted to persuade, but Marcus swept a chilling glance, instantly filling the entire space with a terrifying sense of intimidation, making everyone's nerves tense in an instant.

This is a kind of coldness that belongs to the dark side!

He just sat there quietly, with an elegant and indifferent face, a cold gaze, not saying a word. This kingly dominance made everyone feel oppressed.

Even the calm and wicked Jessica felt that this man was truly terrifying!

This man was powerful to the point of being frightening.

With such an enchanting face, if he were to smile more, it would be so alluring. Maybe she would go to him with her son and start fawning over him.

"Raymond, Miss Florence, please!" Jessica courteously showed them out.

"Jessica, I am so disappointed in you!" Raymond glared at her, as if not defending him just now was a heinous crime.

Jessica remained silent!

What did she see in him back then? Indeed, people are very ignorant when they are young!

******

At noon, take a one-hour break.

"Jessica, let's go to lunch!"

"I'm not going, you guys go, I brought a packed lunch." Jessica raised the bento box in her hand, looking happy. Her son made this loving bento, which was even better than the food at a five-star hotel.

Night of Destiny

"Oh, your boyfriend makes you a bento every day, you're too lucky, deliberately making us jealous."

"Alright, I'm so hungry, let's eat!"

"..."

Jessica waved goodbye to them and then took out the bento that Henry made.

"Your boyfriend made you a bento?"

A cold voice appeared, causing Jessica's spine to chill, and her heart to skip a beat.

Hey, Mr. Marcus, can you stop being so mysterious? The way you scare people is enough to give them a heart attack.

Jessica forced a smile, "Mr. Marcus, this is my matter, no need to answer."

Mr. Marcus crossed his arms, his deep gaze swept over her face and slowly shifted down to the bento.

Today, Henry made chicken wings, which were beautifully arranged to form a heart shape. Paired with sautéed asparagus, the color was vibrant green with a sprinkle of chili, and in the middle of the heart-shaped chicken wings was a small red tomato as decoration.

It was a true heart-shaped bento!

Mr. Marcus smirked, his gaze mischievous and teasing as he looked at Jessica. Jessica followed his gaze, her face flushed, feeling as nervous as a deer caught in headlights.

Ridiculous! The melodrama her son concocted, damn it, this man must have misunderstood!

"The food at the company cafeteria isn't good?"

"I'm used to eating what he makes."

"Him?" Mr. Marcus furrowed his brow, his gaze inscrutable and slightly mocking, "A man?"

Jessica coughed twice and nodded.

Why doesn't this man go eat?

She looked at the dishes, smelled the aroma of the food, and her mouth watered.

You're not hungry, but I am!

Sect Elder Breeze

Mr. Marcus laughed even more coldly. Humph, Quincy cooked for this woman? What a miracle! Why flaunt the affection, afraid that people don't know how intimate you two are?

"It looks very delicious," Mr. Marcus said lightly.

Jessica's lip twitched fiercely. What did he mean? Jessica was still pondering why he said that.

Mr. Marcus had already shown with his actions that he meant it, elegantly taking the bento box, the fork lightly picking up a chicken wing, and then into his mouth.

The first bite tasted the asparagus, it was delicious, and this bento was of high quality. It may be home-cooked, but the taste was very delicious.

Jessica was stunned, and she felt completely disoriented for a while. Damn it, he dared to steal my bento.

"Mr. Marcus, what are you doing?"

"Eating!"

"That's my bento."

Calm down, calm down, impulsiveness is the devil.

"I'm hungry!"

Really delicious! Quincy, you are talented. Damn it, even cooking, that man is so perfect, beware of lightning strikes.

Henry, who was teaching at the elementary school, elegantly sneezed.

As Mr. Marcus continued to eat, Jessica glared at him with her eyes burning, an expression as if she wanted to devour him. He paused, raised an eyebrow, then took another bite of the chicken wing.

He got up elegantly, carried the bento, and walked into the CEO's office, leaving Jessica outside.

Jessica, "???"

With eyes fixed on the CEO's office, Jessica took a deep breath, clenched her fists, and felt her anger building.

Damn it! Marcus, you despicable, heartless, beastly pervert! Do you think I'm just a decoration?

Night of Destiny

Stealing her bento wasn't enough, and he also dared to lock her outside the door. Did he feel like he couldn't eat because she was glaring at him?

She'd seen shameless people before, but never this shameless one.

Don't be so despicable. Watch out for karma!

She was about to storm in when Mr. Marcus floated out of the CEO's office with her bento and casually tossed her a red object.

Instinctively, Jessica caught it.

Instant noodles?

Chapter 7

His Sadness

Oh, no... Marcus, you're filthy rich, so why are you eating such a common brand of instant noodles?

"Miss Jessica, eat your instant noodles!" Mr. Marcus said calmly, as if nothing had happened.

To Jessica's ears, it was like nails on a chalkboard, and she had to restrain herself from attacking him.

His expression seemed to say, "Enjoy your instant noodles!"

"Mr. Marcus, you stole my bento."

"As a qualified secretary, you have to consider your boss's stomach." Mr. Marcus confidently took a second chicken wing.

Jessica was salivating with envy.

"A normal boss wouldn't steal their subordinate's bento." Jessica smiled graciously, but internally, she wanted to knock him down and trample on him.

Implicitly, "You're not normal, are you?"

"You didn't know I'm not normal?" Mr. Marcus calmly retorted, raising an eyebrow and a mischievous gleam in his eyes. "I have a history of mental illness. Do you want to see it and confirm?"

Jessica choked on her breath after hearing this shameless lie.

One day, I will crush you!

In the face of the situation, Jessica had to lower her head and leave. Instant noodles were just that; she had eaten them before.

"Miss Jessica, check the expiration date. It should still be good."

Jessica's footsteps stumbled. Damn, this deceitful man must have done it on purpose, intentionally!

If she ever ended up killing him accidentally, he probably deserved it, and the judge should not find her guilty.

Jessica took hold of the instant noodles, her composure nowhere to be seen.

Marcus felt no guilt as he enjoyed the bento, feeling satisfied and full. It had been so long since he had eaten such delicious home-cooked food.

How long had it been?

It had been so long that he couldn't even remember.

Throughout the afternoon, Marcus was unpredictable. His handsome features were as icy as can be. If the usual Marcus was elegant and cold, today's Marcus was dark and chilling.

Night of Destiny

For no reason at all, Jessica had been scolded by him several times, making the atmosphere in the secretary's office as chilly as midwinter, with everyone on edge. Anyone summoned by him would emerge after being reprimanded.

Jessica could sense that Marcus was very agitated.

As the end of the workday approached, Marcus asked Jessica to make him a cup of coffee. When she brought it in, Marcus stood by the floor-to-ceiling window, his tall and imposing figure exuding an overwhelming pressure.

With the setting sun casting its warm light, the entire office was filled with a comforting warmth.

Gently placing the coffee on his desk, Jessica gave him a reminder.

"Miss Jessica, rearrange my evening schedule," Mr. Marcus did not turn around, his voice slightly hoarse.

In the president's office bathed in the twilight glow, his tone exuded a deep sense of melancholy.

"Yes!"

As she slowly exited the president's office and closed the door, Jessica couldn't help glancing back at him.

This man possessed a powerful charisma that naturally drew people's gazes. He was elegant, cold, and ruthless... possessing all the qualifications of a ladies' man.

In her eyes, Mr. Marcus was always formidable, to the point of seeming nearly invincible.

But today, Mr. Marcus was filled with a sense of sadness, mixed with the sorrow of longing. It was as if he was reminiscing about someone. The warmth of the twilight, which seemed unrelated to him, unable to blend with his thoughts and sadness.

Jessica felt a slight pain in her heart. The more powerful a person was, the more they concealed their own weaknesses. They couldn't cry, couldn't show weakness—yet they were often the most fragile and tender inside.

Sect Elder Breeze

Damn, under this specific light, with that specific person, and that specific silhouette, it felt like something straight out of a melodramatic soap opera with its tragic male lead.

Mr. Marcus, are you going for the tragic route?

That's just... too kitschy!

******

This area was a wealthy district, with fashionable villas in various styles such as American, British, and Gothic nestled on the mountainside. The scene was luxurious and spectacular.

A silver Rolls-Royce stopped in front of an American-style villa, and Marcus opened the car door, gracefully walking into the villa. He seemed even more distant than usual.

"Mr. Marcus, you're back. The master is waiting for you." The elderly butler respectfully ushered Marcus inside.

The villa was decorated extravagantly, with the touch of a renowned designer, almost bordering on opulence. The glittering gold nearly dazzled Marcus's eyes.

A hint of hidden mockery flashed through Marcus' eyes.

The villa gave him the feeling of nothing but coldness, piercing to the bone.

Alston Smith sat in a dignified manner at the head of the table, with white temples and a cane. This man, who had once dominated the business world, exuded an air of dignity. Although his eyes were cloudy, they still had a sharpness to them.

His third wife, Monica Collins, who was not yet thirty, sat on the side with a cold smile. Her seven-year-old son, Leonard Smith, sat quietly, with a timid expression that was quite endearing.

His second brother, Dennis Smith, was also present, and his upright face could not conceal the greed in his eyes.

Night of Destiny

"Dad, I'm back!" Marcus called out in a flat tone. It was the Old Mr. Alston's rule to come back for a meal once a week.

"Our busy man has finally returned, with such a grandiose manner that keeps us all waiting," Monica said coldly.

"He's the president of Noblefull Group, of course, he's grand. Hmph!" Dennis said snidely.

Marcus remained expressionless, "Dad, the company has been busy lately. I apologize."

Although he said that, there was no hint of apology in his tone, and his expression remained indifferent.

"Dinner is served!" Old Mr. Alston's sharp gaze swept across everyone, and he uttered these words, silencing everyone.

Marcus sneered inwardly.

Leonard timidly called him "Brother Marcus", and Marcus glanced at him and nodded. Leonard then smiled, but Monica pulled her son's clothes, making him lower his head timidly.

"Marcus, Dennis is going to open a jewelry store. Allocate some funds to him and help him network," Old Mr. Alston commanded sternly.

"Yes, Dad."

Every time he stepped in here, it felt like stepping into an ice cellar, suffocatingly cold. In the eyes of Old Mr. Alston, he was nothing but a tool. This old man who once dominated the world was accustomed to controlling everything.

The true master of the Smith family was Old Mr. Alston, and the true heir was Dennis Smith. Old Mr. Alston's most beloved son was Leonard.

As for him...

He was nothing more than the illegitimate offspring produced in a moment of passion.

A clandestine son.

The inadvertent murderer of Old Mr. Alston's most beloved son.

Marcus sneered inwardly, knowing that one day, he would make Old Mr. Alston see how a man could fight back against emotional abuse!

******

In an apartment, Jessica collapsed on the sofa as soon as she got home. Her little son had not returned today, and she furrowed her brows.

Hmm, at this time, should Henry be cooking?

She had already become accustomed to the smell of food upon returning home.

Worry was just a passing thought. Jessica sprawled out on the sofa, feigning death. Her son was a pure genius, absolutely incapable of such a ridiculous farce.

She lay there, feeling at ease, waiting for her son to come back and cook for her.

Not having eaten Henry's cooking for a day made her feel unwell. In the afternoon, being scolded harshly by Mr. Marcus and then suddenly having to rearrange his schedule, she was too tired to even move a finger.

Unconsciously, she thought of Mr. Marcus standing in front of the window, impeccably dressed, full of loneliness as if the whole world had abandoned him.

The Mr. Marcus she knew was cold, elegant, cunning, and psychologically dark... but could that person have anything to do with sorrow?

What happened to him?

"Oh, snap out of it," Jessica thought, shaking herself, "Jessica, have you been abused by him and developed a masochistic tendency?"

Maybe it's better to think about the face of her precious son than Mr. Marcus's?

Turning her thoughts about the two faces of Henry and Mr. Marcus, which were the same except for their sizes, Jessica calmed down.

Night of Destiny

"Mommy, it's not you who has a masochistic tendency, it's your son who does." A child's tender voice floated in.

Henry closed the door and came in with two bags of vegetables and meat, giving her a disdainful look.

"Henry, you're finally back, mommy's starving to death!" Jessica shamelessly complained to her son that he hadn't fed her in time.

Henry took off his backpack, threw it at her, and smiled, "Mommy, you should eat something to fill your stomach first, I'll cook right away."

Henry was a genius, hardly paying attention in class. His schoolbag was always lightweight, but today it was unexpectedly heavy. Curiously, Jessica pulled it open, and there was a pile of snacks pouring out.

Chocolate, cream puffs, candy... apples, bananas... and bread?

So many things filled a large backpack. Jessica's immediate reaction was, "Henry, when you find money, you should use it to honor mommy. Buying things haphazardly is wasteful."

Henry arranged the vegetables and meat, then washed the pot and turned on the rice cooker before coming out. He had an extremely elegant smile on his face as he blinked and said solemnly, "Who said I found money? These are gifts from the girls at our school."

"What did you do to receive so many gifts from them?"

What's wrong with my son? Why does he inherit this playboy personality from his father? Is it possible that being a playboy is also hereditary?

"I'm also puzzled!" Henry said innocently. "They all say that I have a charming smile, and they give gifts to express their interest in me."

These kids nowadays, falling in love at such a young age?

"Didn't I tell you not to smile for no reason? I will make you go out and sell your smile when we can't survive one day."

Henry, "…"

"Moreover, is your smile only worth this much? It's too cheap," Jessica tilted her head and thought about it. "Let's make a blank check one day, then it will be worth it. Understand?"

"What if the check bounces?"

"Don't you investigate the details first?"

Henry nodded seriously after thinking for a moment, "Makes sense. I'll try it next time."

"You're such a good boy!" Jessica calmly patted his head, not feeling like she was destroying a little boy's future.

"Henry, mommy has a question for you, um…" Jessica's face turned a little red, she approached her son, hugged his little body, and asked, "Aren't you curious about your father at all?"

Chapter 8

Why He Didn't Have A Father

Henry's beautiful face was full of smiles, "Mommy, didn't you say that my dad died? You even said that the grass on his grave is taller than me."

Mr. Marcus, who was coldly dining at his villa on the mountaintop, suddenly sneezed.

Jessica, "…"

Night of Destiny

Since Henry was old enough to understand, he had asked once why he didn't have a father.

At that time, Henry was three years old and attending kindergarten in France. There was a boy in his class who lived next door to them, and he often insulted Henry at school, calling him a wild child without a father.

One time, Henry got into a fight with him and lost. He returned home in tears with a large bruise on his arm. He asked Jessica why he didn't have a father.

At that time, Jessica felt as if her heart was being torn apart.

Henry was the best gift she had ever received in her life. He was her precious baby, and Jessica wouldn't allow anyone to harm even a single hair on him. But what hurt him the most was her, his mother.

She clearly remembered the resentment in Henry's eyes when he asked her this question.

He was a child prodigy, with an intelligence higher than other children from a young age. But at the age of three, he was still too young, just a little more sensitive than other children. Misled by other children, he thought it was his mother's fault that he didn't have a father, so he couldn't help but blame her.

That's when Jessica told him that his father had died. She even melodramatically made up a story about how the his parents fell in love, and his father was hit by a car and died, leaving his mother alone to raise him out of love.

From then on, Henry never asked about his father again.

It was really tough for Jessica to raise the child alone all these years, studying, working, earning her own tuition fees, and earning money for Henry's formula.

She was in Paris, where the cost of living was ridiculously high. During her hardest times, she had slept for less than 4 hours a day on average for a whole year.

As Henry grew older, he also understood the hardship Jessica had endured. With age, his intelligence grew in proportion, and his personality became so impressive that it left people astonished.

The topic of being a single parent could no longer hurt him. And naturally, he ignored the absence of the man who should have been a part of their lives.

Now that the topic of his father, which they had ignored for years, was suddenly brought up, Jessica felt awkward. The lie had gone too far. If she had known earlier, she would have told Henry that his dad had gone to Mars. At least he could have come back.

She didn't know if there was still time for her to say that his dad had come back to life.

Actually, Jessica didn't want Mr. Marcus to know about Henry's existence, but she also didn't want to lie to Henry.

Damn it, she was torn.

"Henry, have you ever seen someone come back to life?"

"Yes," Henry replied calmly.

Jessica fell silent, and Henry added, "On TV."

Well, Marcus Smith, let's talk about this question when you meet my son someday. I don't want to dwell on this question anymore.

"Never mind, let's not talk about it. Sweetie, next time tell that girl who likes you that you like chocolate." Jessica tore open the beautifully wrapped package and threw the chocolate into her mouth.

It was delicious!

"Got it, Mommy. What else do you like to eat? Something challenging, and I'll give it a try." Henry shook his head and smiled.

He liked his mommy just like this, a money-loving, cunning, and occasionally a bit silly.

"Durian."

Henry's eye twitched a bit, "Mommy, have you ever seen anyone confess to a boy with a durian?"

"That's why I want you to try it. You should know that practice is the sole criterion for testing truth."

"Understood!" Henry calmly accepted the challenge and then kissed her on the face with a smile. "Mommy, sometimes you are really not just ordinary silly."

After saying that, he looked at Jessica with a sideways glance, as if to assure her that she didn't need to worry because she was his mommy.

******

In a luxury apartment located in the city center, clothes were scattered all over the floor, with torn dresses and sexy lingerie, and a man's tie...

The dim lights created a mysterious atmosphere, with a temperature of desire swirling in the air, a scorching passion that seemed to melt everything, intertwined with the low moans of the man and woman.

On the white bed, the bodies of the man and woman entwined like vines, fierce kisses landing hard, like a storm passing through, leaving marks of scratches and kisses on the pure female body that were shocking to the eye.

The man's ferocity and the woman's meekness made this affair sexy and sizzling.

"Marcus..." Crystal gasped.

Tonight, Marcus was wild, ravaging her from the moment he entered, his face dark, as if releasing something.

His emotions hovered on the brink of collapse. Rarely rough, he pinched her delicate skin, leaving marks bit by bit.

Her seductive eyes, filled with mist, Crystal was beautiful, a combination of delicacy and innocence. Marcus suddenly stopped and looked at Crystal intently.

"Marcus, what's wrong with you?" Her desires stirred, uncomfortably rubbed against him, her voice, tainted by passion, was seductive.

Marcus's gaze was deep and his exquisitely handsome face showed no emotion.

Sect Elder Breeze

The woman beneath him inadvertently transformed into Jessica's poker-faced smile, a face that was also very innocent.

Compared to Crystal, it appeared even more innocent. And it also possessed a purity that Crystal lacked.

Marcus couldn't help but wonder, if it were Jessica lying beneath him at this moment, what expression would she have? He was truly fed up with her trademark poker-faced smile.

"Marcus..." the seductive voice awakened his overflowing thoughts like a splash of cold water extinguishing all his enthusiasm.

Marcus got up from Crystal's body, his clothes slightly disheveled, and walked to the window expressionlessly, looking at the dim lights outside.

What was wrong with him? Why was he thinking of Jessica?

Crystal didn't know why he stopped, she hugged him naked from behind, wanting to kiss his lips, attempting to reignite his desire.

Marcus calmly turned his head away, and Crystal's lips landed on his chin.

Crystal gave a bitter smile, this kind of outcome seemed inevitable.

Marcus's lips were his forbidden zone.

No matter how intimate they were, he never kissed her. Nor did he let others kiss him.

Marcus's eyes fell on the bustling cityscape outside the window, his exquisitely elegant face half-illuminated by the night, adding a touch of desolation and melancholy.

"Marcus... what's wrong with you?" Crystal was a woman who understood the bigger picture, bitterness and jealousy fleeting moments. In front of Marcus, she was always gentle and considerate.

"I saw my father today." Marcus's deep voice revealed a cold resentment.

Night of Destiny

Gently, Crystal hugged him from behind. She could guess that after all these years, his emotions would always spiral out of control after seeing his father.

"It's okay, everything will be fine!" Her gentle voice brushed past Marcus's heart, allowing his tense muscles to slowly relax.

Crystal only knew that Marcus was a bastard child, his mother was a dancer who raised him alone for ten years, and he returned to the Smith family when he was ten years old.

Old Mr. Alston had originally planned to Marcus's mother as his third wife, but on the third day after their return to the Smith family, the young master of the Smith family, Charles Smith, was found murdered in Old Mr. Alston's bed, with clothes disheveled, and the prime suspect was Marcus's mother.

As she was being taken away by the police, Marcus's mother suddenly broke free from the detective's grasp and ran towards a truck, and was instantly killed in the collision.

The truth behind Charles's murder also became a mystery along with the death of Marcus's mother, and in the end, the case was left unresolved.

Naturally, Marcus would never tell her about these things.

At that time, this scandal of the aristocratic family was widely known, involving affairs and taboos such as a woman serving both father and son... Rumors filled the air.

Old Mr. Alston used his connections to forcefully suppress this scandal and married his current wife just ten days later.

The storm gradually subsided, but it was tough for Marcus. He had been present at the crime scene, witnessing his mother being taken away and running towards the truck to her death.

Because of this incident, Marcus had not spoken for three years.

He suffered from serious psychological problems.

Crystal had been with him for a few years and had never heard him mention anyone from the Smith family or his mother. In Marcus's world, it seemed like he was always alone, forever alone.

"Marcus, have you ever truly loved anyone?" Crystal asked softly, her hand resting over his heart.

"I love you!" Marcus's gaze swept over the small hand on his chest, his voice calm.

Love, what is it? For him, it was an extravagant luxury.

All the people who loved him would ultimately leave him, so Marcus learned at a young age that he should not love anyone.

After all, what use was love if it all ended in separation?

By not loving, he wouldn't feel sadness when parting ways, he wouldn't cry, he wouldn't close himself off like a fool, and he wouldn't lose the courage to keep living.

He had had enough of the pain of loss.

His mother, his sister...and who else? He couldn't remember; he just had a vague sense that there was another, but he couldn't recall her face. But Marcus knew they had all left him.

He had tried to hold on, but only emptiness remained at his fingertips.

Nothing was left.

If he could forget the cold loneliness and the empty void of the night, Marcus thought that living life like this wouldn't be so bad. He didn't want to endure another loss.

But some things are too important for certain individuals to lose, so they lack the courage.

Crystal smiled gently, her beautiful face filled with happiness and contentment, "No matter what, I'm happy to have been by your side all these years."

She knew that Marcus didn't love anyone else.

Although there were rumors that she was his beloved woman and that their relationship was deeply passionate.

Night of Destiny

But which man who truly loved his girlfriend would constantly change women? It was too much for her to bear.

Crystal knew that Marcus was just lonely... and lacking a sense of security.

It may sound ludicrous. Mr. Marcus, who ruled the business world with an iron fist, lacked a sense of security?

It seemed like a fairy tale, but Crystal knew that Mr. Marcus truly lacked it because he had closed himself off for three years and had suffered from severe psychological problems. He was indifferent to the whole world.

But sometimes, she also felt that he was waiting for someone.

He would often get lost in her eyes, he wouldn't kiss her mouth, but he would often kiss her eyes, tenderly, full of compassion.

Only in those moments did Crystal feel cherished.

A woman's intuition is often accurate. She knew that everyone was just a substitute for someone else, but she had searched for all these years and still didn't know who that girl was.

Who exactly was this mysterious girl who had remained in his thoughts all this time?

Chapter 9

It Was Just A Flutter

"Crystal, if I ever get married one day, I would choose you to be my wife!" Marcus stated, his refined features emanating a cold and calm determination, without hesitation.

Sect Elder Breeze

Crystal nodded with a gentle smile. Was this enough? Wasn't it?

Marcus's lips were off-limits, just like they were specially reserved for someone. Just like his heart. But at least, Marcus was willing to marry her, and that was enough.

Wasn't it?

"Thank you!" Crystal smiled gently.

Marcus suddenly became a bit restless. His emotions had been tense and out of control all day, making him feel a bit exhausted when faced with Crystal's tenderness.

Glancing at his tie nearby, he said while fastening it, "I have to go now, goodnight!"

Without waiting for Crystal to respond, he opened the door and left.

The silver Rolls-Royce raced through the streets, the lights of the underground tunnel flickering between brightness and darkness, reflecting a dangerous edge on Marcus's refined face.

Suddenly stepping on the brakes, the sound of the wheels screeching on the street. Marcus slapped the steering wheel and leaned forward, the dim streetlights giving his handsome silhouette a faint glow.

In an instant, he raised his eyes, his finely crafted face gaining a touch of wickedness. In the darkness of the night, he exuded a bewitching aura as he took out his phone.

Momentarily hesitating, he dialed a number.

******

In Jessica's apartment, the phone rang while she was taking a shower, and she casually called out to Henry to answer it.

Henry was busy making her bed when he saw the caller ID: Bastard Marcus?

Henry, "???"

"Miss Jessica, come out to Times Square!" a magnetic and deep voice commanded in its usual manner.

A bright smile curled up at the corner of Henry's lips. Could it be Marcus?

"Are you mute?" Marcus mocked impatiently when she didn't respond after a long silence.

This father seemed to have a bad temper. No wonder Mommy always came back with a face of exhausted despair.

"Who are you?" This was the first time Henry listened to his voice, the first time they conversed. His mood felt complex.

Slightly excited, somewhat thrilled, like a child trying hard to earn praise, his voice became even more elegant than usual.

Marcus was briefly taken aback by the unique sound of a child's voice. He glanced at the phone and furrowed his brow, "Who are you?"

"My name is Henry Miller!" Henry said, unable to hide the laughter in his voice.

His childish voice was like a gentle breeze, like rain falling on a desert. Mr. Marcus's irritable mood instantly improved significantly.

"Let your sister answer the phone." Knowing the other person was a child, Mr. Marcus's tone became gentle as well. His surname was Miller, and since Jessica was young, Mr. Marcus naturally assumed that Henry was her little brother.

Internally, he couldn't help but criticize. Look at this polite child. His voice is so pleasant to listen to. How can there be such a difference between children born from the same mother?

"My sister?" Henry elongated his voice and chuckled softly. This is what he said, not what he said. He just didn't argue back.

The law doesn't require him to refute someone's preconceived misconceptions.

Right?

Sect Elder Breeze

Henry is a cunning child, mentally mature and strong-willed. His favorite person is Jessica. If Jessica doesn't want him to do something, he won't do it. Even though he has so many, many curiosities about his biological father.

The bathroom door opened, and Henry smiled, "Wait a moment!"

"Darling, whose call is it?" Jessica asked while drying her hair, her voice trembling.

"Someone surnamed Smith."

Jessica froze, the towel falling to the ground. She stood still like a wooden chicken, her mind conjuring up a scene of Mr. Marcus about to strangle her.

She was taken aback and rushed over to grab the phone, covering the receiver, and looking at Henry in panic.

With a smile, Henry shrugged and picked up the towel, helping her dry her hair.

Jessica was restless. Because of nervousness, her voice trembled, "Mr... Mr. Marcus, is there something wrong?"

"Come out to Times Square!"

"Just a moment... It's already 10 o'clock."

"A competent secretary should be available at any time."

After Marcus finished speaking, he decisively hung up the phone.

A fire ignited in Jessica's heart. Damn it, will I quit or not?

"Mummy, calm down!"

"Henry, what did you say to him?" Jessica was restless and uneasy. She could face anything calmly, but Henry always made her feel flustered.

"Mummy, he just said for your sister to answer the phone, and I was about to say that you are my mummy, but you came out." Henry's gentle voice carried reassurance.

That's good. Jessica's tense heart finally relaxed, feeling like she had taken a step off the edge of a cliff but was pulled back just in time.

******

Night of Destiny

When Jessica arrived at Times Square, she immediately saw Mr. Marcus' silver Rolls-Royce. It was almost 11 o'clock and the department stores and counters were all closed, with hardly anyone in the square.

Mr. Marcus sat arrogantly on the front of the car, exuding a mixture of arrogance and laziness. He smoked a cigar, surrounded by a faint haze of smoke that enveloped him.

Why was he still awake at this hour?

"Mr. Marcus, it's late. What can I do for you?" Jessica asked with a smile.

Mr. Marcus turned his head, his delicate facial features combining wickedness and elegance, creating a captivating and enticing aura.

His deep gaze, devoid of the daytime coldness, now held a shimmering allure in the night, like the seduction Adam used to tempt Eve into sin, with just one glance, one could be captivated.

On this hot night, the wind carried a hint of summer heat. Jessica's heart was pounding, and her cheeks turned slightly warmer. In this particular atmosphere, emotions that were usually suppressed by pride and reason seemed to stir restlessly.

This man can be quite alluring sometimes, Jessica thought to herself.

Mr. Marcus stood up, flicked away his cigarette butt, crushed it harshly with his foot, opened the car door, and turning his head, gave an order, "Get in the car!"

Jessica wanted to defiantly ask him where they were going, but when she saw Marcus's expression, she hesitated for a second and obediently got into the car.

It was better to not provoke this man whose mood was always changing.

As Marcus got into the car, he gave her a sideways glance. Jessica sat up straight, forcefully maintaining her signature smile. Suddenly, Marcus leaned over.

"What are you doing?" Jessica nervously tightened her nerves.

Marcus didn't say anything. He reached out and fastened her seatbelt.

A purely masculine scent overwhelmed her, mixed with the fragrance of Henry Rose's "Menace." As Marcus' chief secretary, Jessica had all the information about the women he was currently involved with stored in her mind.

She knew what they liked, and what they used, everything was crystal clear to her.

"Menace" by Henry Rose was Crystal's favorite brand: fresh, elegant, and with a unique taste.

A slight twitch of Jessica's eyebrows, pursed lips, and a slight turn of her face away. Her signature smile seemed a bit stiff.

Did he just leave Crystal?

This thought grabbed Jessica's mind like a demon. A faint, not very deep but very apparent bitterness surged from the bottom of her heart. She knew very well that this man was promiscuous.

Women came and went like clothes for him, and he also had a serious girlfriend with whom he had a strong bond. They were a perfect match, both in terms of social status and looks.

However...stripped away were Jessica's pride and hidden self-esteem.

It seemed like such raw emotions easily surfaced.

It was said that the darkness of night provides the best protection, but she believed that it also exposes one's truest side.

In the day, the bright sunlight was so dazzling, making one's arrogance and elegance impossible to go unnoticed.

But at night, when the brilliance of the day faded away, people's darkest sides unconsciously revealed themselves. Because the night was dark enough to conceal ugliness, and there was no worry of being exposed.

Night of Destiny

Eight years ago, they had a one-night stand, not knowing each other. Jessica's knowledge of Marcus was solely based on his prowess in bed.

In these eight years, she hadn't thought of him much. But whenever she looked at Henry's face, there would occasionally be a fleeting thought of that man.

Love at first sight?

That was just a fairy tale.

It didn't exist in the harsh realities of life, and Jessica's character wasn't inclined towards such melodrama.

The true realization of Marcus came eight years later, when she worked as his secretary.

It seemed...

There was a small flutter in her heart.

But it was just a flutter. She had always been rational. From childhood to adulthood, except for that one hot-blooded incident at the bar, Jessica had never done anything too impulsive.

Marcus' promiscuity snuffed out the flutter in her heart.

If it wasn't the only emotion, Jessica wasn't interested!

Maybe every woman wants to be the one to change a playboy, hoping to be their destined one.

But to Jessica, this was a foolish dream. Because a playboy will always be a playboy.

Raising Henry all by herself for eight years, she had long transcended the age of innocence. Even eight years ago, Jessica had never entertained such foolish thoughts.

So...

The flutter was simply a flutter, nothing more.

Silence exploded in the carriage.

This was Jessica's first close encounter with Mr. Marcus, a man with delicate facial features. From a distance, he looked beautiful. But up close, he was not impressive.

Mr. Marcus belonged to the kind of enchanting beauty that was even more exquisite up close as if every feature had been carved perfectly.

Sect Elder Breeze

    Well, she had to admit that she was superficial and had no resistance to beauty.

    Having such a delicate appearance and a gloomy personality was truly a waste. Her son, Henry, on the other hand, was much better, always polite and charming.

    When she was alone, she loved to let her thoughts wander. Sitting next to Marcus, she felt a bit pressured, her nerves taut.

    After all, she had a passionate one-night stand with this man.

    And they created a genius named Henry.

    She still vividly remembered the terrifying expression on Mr. Marcus's face when she said, "10 million, I'll buy you for one night." It was truly horrifying.

    Well, he had so many women, with better figures and sweeter personalities than hers. For the first time, she felt a bit jealous.

    It was normal for him not to remember.

    But, after giving him $100 and leaving him with the words "selling-your-body money," it was a shame for someone as proud as Marcus.

    It should be unforgettable for him.

    He didn't have bad eyesight, and he held her all night. She hadn't had any plastic surgery in 8 years, no changes. Is it reasonable for him to completely forget her?

    It's not that she's self-obsessed...

    Jessica was indeed a bit conflicted. Why was he behaving so calmly? Could it be a plot?

    Her whole body trembled as she couldn't help but think of the plot of a melodramatic revenge drama, where he would seek revenge on her...

    Conspiracy theories emerged. She had some darkness in her heart as well.

    "Mr. Marcus, can I ask you a small question?"

    "Go ahead!"

Jessica carefully considered her tone, tightened her fingers slightly, nervously gripping her clothes, and after several mental preparations, she finally asked, "Have you ever been dumped by a woman?"

Mr. Marcus slammed on the brakes, causing Jessica's body to lurch forward, only to be rebounded by the seatbelt, making her dizzy and disoriented...

Damn! Even if he was dumped by a woman before, he shouldn't have to be so harsh!

Her gaze caught a few shiny English letters, and Jessica was struck like lightning, fearfully turning her head to look at Mr. Marcus...

The bar from eight years ago?

Chapter 10

Met Quincy

Marcus's face was gloomy.
Damn it, how many men does she have?
One Quincy, one Raymond, and now another pretty boy?
But she looks so innocent, is it an illusion?

Sect Elder Breeze

Compared to Marcus's jealousy, Jessica's mind was captivated by the bar in front of her. She could never forget, eight years ago, it was here that she and him had the most absurd night of their lives.

"Mr. Marcus, why did you bring me to the bar so late?" Jessica couldn't help but ask, feeling tense. Memories of eight years ago played in her mind like a slow-motion film.

To her surprise, Jessica remembered all the details between them eight years ago.

Her recklessness, his coldness, her impudence, his arrogance...

People from two different worlds, but they sparked a flame for one night. Jessica's heart was pounding, nervously sweating in her palms, and her face growing hotter with each passing moment.

She couldn't figure out Mr. Marcus's thoughts at all.

What does he mean? Does he recognize her?

Seeing her flushed face, Mr. Marcus snorted coldly in his heart. When she was Lionel's secretary, she had been to places like bars. She was just pretending to be innocent?

"Drink!" Mr. Marcus coldly dropped the word and entered the bar.

Jessica was stunned, her suspended heart finally relaxed, and her nerves weren't as tense anymore.

Putting aside the tension of Marcus recognizing her, reason returned to Jessica's mind once again. Marcus seemed restless today, why?

He was gloomy the whole way, on the verge of losing control.

Despite his usual cold silence, Jessica could tell that he was in a very bad mood.

Jessica pursed her lips and walked into the bar she had hurriedly fled from eight years ago.

Night of Destiny

The ambiguous and intoxicating lighting filled the air with a seductive charm. On the stage, the hot and sexy dance made the men in the audience scream and cheer. The flexible waist movements of the dancers exuded a seductive allure. Screams filled the place!

This was a bar with extremely high-class decoration, noble-like furnishings, and a luxurious visual experience. Jessica noticed that almost everyone who came here to spend money was an influential figure.

This was a top-notch private bar. She couldn't help but fall silent. How did she manage to get in here eight years ago?

"Jessica? What brings you here?"

Jessica was just thinking of finding Marcus when a gentle and splendid voice floated over.

Quincy?

Jessica froze. Quincy was wearing a very formal suit, standing straight and tall, his refined features had a jade-like texture under the colorful lights.

Clean, pure, it seemed sacrilegious to even take an extra glance.

Most of the people who come here to enjoy themselves are elite individuals who have had too much pressure during the day. Once it's nighttime, they tear off their masks of social elitism and let go of their pent-up stress.

"Hi, Quincy. I came with someone to have fun, and you?" Jessica secretly prayed that Quincy wouldn't run into Marcus.

Suddenly, she realized why Quincy asked her if she knew Marcus that day. He probably noticed something.

"I have some business discussions to attend to."

A drunken man stumbled and ran towards them, almost colliding with Jessica. Quincy's perceptive reflexes kicked in, he grabbed her slender waist, swiftly turned, and avoided the collision.

"Be careful!"

Sect Elder Breeze

Their bodies bumped into each other, tightly pressed together, softness and strength merging into a picturesque scene. Jessica's heart was still pounding, a faint scent of cologne filled the air, adding a touch of elegance to the smell of alcohol.

This was the familiar scent that Quincy always had.

This scene caught Marcus's eye. Naturally, it felt ambiguous and passionate. He raised his glass and downed a shot of wine.

His cold eyes emitted a cold gleam, and a flame ignited silently, spreading like wildfire. He was even astonished by it himself!

Damn Jessica!

If he had known this would happen, he wouldn't have asked her to come out.

Marcus called Jessica to accompany him for a drink purely on a whim.

"Mr. Quincy, nice to meet you!" Marcus's cold voice interjected between them.

Jessica felt a surge of electricity, a shiver ran through her whole body. She immediately broke free from Quincy's embrace, her heart pounding. This was bad, as expected, things don't always go as planned.

"Mr. Marcus, I've heard a lot about you!" Quincy reached out his hand, a glimmer of surprise flickered in his gentle eyes, but he skillfully hid it. He gracefully greeted Marcus.

Two pairs of eyes engaged in a battle, the noisy background music faded away, and the air was filled with tension that belonged to the fiery clash between men.

The sharp edges were revealed!

It was the most primitive wildness between male animals.

Jessica's heart pounded, vaguely uneasy.

The Smith, Lee, Moore, and Brown families divided the city of W into four powerful forces, each dominating a different direction. The four families had always kept their distance from one another, even though they were renowned across the city and had made a significant impact.

Just like Marcus Smith and Quincy Lee, the two of them had been engaged in intense rivalry for the past years. Although they had met before, this was the first time they shook hands so formally and truly got to know each other.

Quincy, the CEO of Gootal Group, was a humble and gentle gentleman, a dream lover for the social elites. He and Marcus, though belonging to different types, were equally capable, ambitious, and charismatic. They were evenly matched.

There was a saying in high society:

"Ladies all want to marry their daughters to Quincy while dealing with Mr. Marcus themselves."

"The internal rumors have long circulated. Mr. Quincy has a 90% chance of winning the bid for the infrastructure project in the northern ore mill. Noblefull Group had no choice but to admit defeat," Marcus said with a faint smile.

"Mr. Marcus, you exaggerate. You abandoned the northern ore mill just because you set your sights on that real estate in Stanley Bay. It happened to be a bargain for me. We owe our success to your generosity," Quincy replied.

"Mr. Quincy, you're too humble."

"Mutual compliments!"

...

The two men smiled at each other, brushing off the intense competition in W City that had caused stock market crashes and bankruptcies of many companies in the past three months.

Successful men always had a certain charm, the ability to conceal their deepest thoughts and reveal the most elegant smile.

Like Quincy.

Like Marcus.

From the beginning, these two major projects were battled over by Noblefull Group and Gootal Group. Both sides spared no expense, sabotaged each other, manipulated stock market transactions, and disrupted the equilibrium prices of the entire market, creating chaos. In the end, they both profited from it.

Even Jessica could feel the intensity and strong rivalry behind it all.

In the end, it all dispersed calmly in the smiles of the two men.

That was what they called being a true powerhouse!

"Mr. Marcus, I heard you have a versatile female secretary by your side. Who is she? It turns out to be Jessica. Congratulations, I have been trying to recruit her for so long without success," Quincy said, his gaze lightly sweeping over Jessica with his unique doting expression.

Jessica's throat tightened, feeling somewhat guilty. To be honest, it was indeed a misunderstanding, something she didn't expect.

Marcus smirked, "Oh, Mr. Quincy, you didn't know?"

Quincy smiled warmly, a jade-like purity shining in his eyebrows as if he had the most selfless tolerance between lovers.

"Yes, Jessica had been avoiding suspicion and refused to come to my Gootal Group. So, I lost a great talent."

This statement was ambiguous, but it sounded particularly grating to Marcus's ears. It was obvious that Quincy was telling him that Jessica didn't want to mix work and love, which was why she chose to go to Noblefull Group instead. It was he, Marcus who benefitted from it.

"Miss Jessica is indeed a great secretary. She provides top-quality service for both personal and business matters, right? Miss Jessica?" Marcus's elegant smile turned slightly twisted. Under the enchanting light, his deep gaze was filled with a wicked charm.

He emphasized the words "personal" and "service."

Night of Destiny

You know how to provoke me, but I might just know how to disgust you!

Quincy's warm gaze remained unchanged as before as if Marcus had casually mentioned the weather today. Only the slightly tightened grip of his hand revealed his hidden endurance at the moment.

Marcus sneered inwardly, noticing that Jessica's expression remained the same with her poker-faced smile, yet her flickering eyes betrayed the fire in her heart.

Damn it! Marcus, can you be any more twisted?

Marcus seemed to imply that she had a fling with him. Oh well, no matter how desperate she was for love, she would never choose him.

Jessica clearly forgot that she willingly chose Marcus eight years ago.

The competition between successful men was always invisible to the naked eye, every move hidden behind an elegant smile.

Marcus successfully counterattacked, feeling surprisingly good. His lip curled slightly, "Mr. Quincy, care for a drink?"

"Sure!"

Both their hands reached for Jessica's shoulders simultaneously, possessing the same tall and upright figure, along with the same determined and profound gaze, exerting an equal amount of pressure.

Cold and intimidating!

Even the gentle Quincy, at this moment, was declaring his possessiveness with his actions. When Marcus looked at him, he changed the direction of his hand, wrapping his arm around Jessica's waist and leading her toward the bar.

Marcus's gaze darkened as he watched their intimate backs.

Jessica felt a shiver down her spine, wondering what exactly Quincy was up to.

This was the most nerve-wracking gathering for Jessica in the past few months.

Sect Elder Breeze

As the chief secretary for both Lionel and Marcus, Jessica was already comfortable and adept in social events. But this time, she felt that the air beneath her nose was too thin.

Quincy and Marcus seemed to be competing with each other, and it wasn't her imagination. Jessica carefully filtered through the information in her mind, but she couldn't find any grudge between them.

In the business world, even if they fought tooth and nail, it was all consensual, a willing gamble with winners and losers.

The atmosphere between these two men was so eerie that she wanted to scream. If it weren't for maintaining a perfect smile, Jessica would have liked to turn and walk away.

She had no idea why Marcus called her out.

To accompany him?

Only these two could treat expensive brandy that cost over ten thousand as plain water.

"Mr. Quincy, Miss Jessica, you seem to have a good relationship," Marcus said playfully, his delicate features showing no expression, but his deep and smirking gaze passed over Jessica.

Jessica pursed her lips, wondering when the hell Marcus started to care about her relationship with anyone.

Quincy responded with his trademark indulgent smile for Jessica, "Yes, it's been eight years!"

Another vague response.

Marcus silently took a sip of his drink, maintaining an elegant gentlemanly demeanor. His noble and handsome looks made girls scream.

Eight years, enough of showing off!

The bar was exclusive, and the expensive prices made it out of reach for ordinary people. The attendees here were mostly high-profile individuals, naturally including Marcus and Quincy.

The drinking competition between these two friends-who-maybe-enemies added a layer of mystery to the business battle they had built up in the past few months.

"They're so treacherous..." Wealthy individual A said. "Are they conspiring against us?"

"No doubt, look at their demeanor, probably!" Wealthy individual B said. "They're cunning and sly. I knew Mr. Marcus, but I didn't expect Quincy to be this cunning, a wolf in sheep's clothing."

Jessica, silent!

Come on! Men! Even if Quincy doesn't look pure, it's your bad judgment.

It was amazing that she could make a sarcastic remark in such a tense atmosphere.

Jessica took a trip to the restroom and this time, the two men who had been wearing polite masks all night finally tore off their disguises.

Quincy's usually gentle gaze turned sharp and cold like a knife, his indifference chilling, "Marcus, if you dare touch Jessica, I will make you regret it!"

Those words, as ruthless as the god of the underworld, sounded even more astonishing coming from this gentleman.

The surrounding air suddenly dropped.

Cold and sharp, it pressed against them.

Marcus's seductive eyes flashed with a hint of cruelty, as he coldly laughed, "You still want to challenge me? Quincy, I could crush you with a single finger. If you've got what it takes, then bring it on."

"Such big talk!" Quincy's coldness glanced at him. "I doubt you can afford to play this game!"

"I doubt you can handle losing!"

Two powerful gazes clashed, instantly producing sparks of intense battle, with the smell of combat boiling in the air. Without Jessica present, the plunder and ferocity between men were unabated.

When Jessica came out, the two men were already toasting again, smiling as they lifted their glasses and downed their drinks!

Chapter 11

Affectionate Quincy

When three of them left the bar, Jessica found herself in a dilemma again.
"I'll take you back!" Marcus and Quincy said simultaneously, their eyes meeting and both focused on Jessica.
Marcus's coldness and Quincy's warmth both expressed unwavering determination.
Compared to Quincy's smoothness inside the bar, he appeared much more relaxed now, calmly saying, "Mr. Marcus, there's no need for you to trouble yourself with such a trivial matter. What do you say, Jessica?"
Quincy whispered something in her ear, his warm breath brushing against her earlobe. To outsiders, it seemed like Quincy was kissing her earlobe, indicating an intimate relationship.
Jessica was shocked, her body stiffening, her face flushing and paling interchangeably. She felt like a child who had done something wrong, completely at a loss...
What did Quincy say?
Henry?
What did he mean?

Marcus narrowed his eyes, displaying a trace of cunningness. He couldn't insert himself into the familiarity and intimacy between the two of them.

"Mr. Marcus, it's late. You don't have to bother. It's enough for Quincy to take me home," Jessica tried to remain calm, avoiding eye contact with Marcus, and got into Quincy's car.

The Lamborghini disappeared in an instant, leaving Marcus in the dark, his eyes filled with malice. He clenched his fists tightly and angrily kicked the car to vent his frustration.

The elegant and perfect exterior was finally torn apart in the dark!

The expensive Rolls-Royce silently endured its owner's anger, trembling several times.

The journey was silent. Jessica, who knew that Quincy had already figured out the truth, felt extremely nervous. Her heart raced, wondering if she could still deny it.

At this moment, she couldn't help but resent Marcus for having such bizarre genes. Henry resembled him to a staggering extent, his youthful appearance resembling a younger version of Marcus.

Indeed, his genes were bizarre, causing her to lack the confidence even to deny it.

Did Quincy already know about it a few years ago? Why didn't he mention it all this time?

The car stopped outside Jessica's apartment, and Jessica wanted to escape from this awkward atmosphere. However, Quincy wouldn't let her go that easily.

"Henry, he's Marcus's son," he said, not asking but affirming.

Jessica looked calm, even indifferent, as she stared directly at Quincy and nodded, "Yes!"

Struggling in desperation would only reveal her more vulnerable state. Henry's presence was the final proof. How could someone as clever as Quincy not have guessed it?

Sect Elder Breeze

The dim and weak streetlights cast a half-light on Quincy's face. His eyelashes drooped slightly, concealing the pain in his eyes. Quincy was such a proud person, how could he be willing to show his vulnerability in front of his beloved?

"I suspected it a long time ago. Two years ago, when I returned to the country and first met Marcus, I felt a sense of familiarity. As Henry grew up, I realized they were like a mold, stamped out the same. When Noblefull Group and Marcus were mentioned, you didn't react, so I thought it was just a coincidence."

Jessica listened quietly. Over the years, Quincy had helped Jessica and her son a lot, and she was very grateful to him.

Besides not being able to reciprocate his feelings, Jessica was willing to give everything to him.

Eight years of silent giving, expecting nothing in return. Jessica had wanted to speak up several times, but in the end, she said nothing.

In truth, they were all intelligent people, and they were both well aware of each other's feelings.

"Marcus doesn't know about Henry's existence," Jessica said, not hiding anything. "Eight years ago, it was just a misunderstanding."

It was a beautiful misunderstanding that gave her the most precious gift in the world.

"So, besides being tied together by Henry, you two have no other relationship?" Quincy asked.

"Quincy, we've known each other for eight years, and you should know that if I can't be his only girlfriend, I don't care about having any relationship with him," Jessica thought of the countless mistresses Marcus had, feeling a tinge of bitterness.

"In that case, be my girlfriend. I've loved you for eight years," Quincy said decisively, his warm eyes filled with determination and a faint hope that was hard to discern.

"Quincy, don't joke around, I..." Jessica was shocked, her pupils suddenly widened. She didn't expect Quincy to confess. For eight years, they had both kept to a boundary, not crossing it, as if it were an unspoken agreement.

"You know my entire past, and you also know I have Henry. You deserve a better girl than me, Quincy. I'm telling you the truth, I've never seen a better man than you in my life. I'm not worthy of you..."

"I don't care!" Quincy suddenly pulled Jessica into his arms, his tone firm. "I don't care about any of that. I only know that I love you, Jessica!"

"Quincy..." Jessica wanted to push him away, but he held her tighter. She secretly smiled bitterly, thinking that tonight's Quincy was too unexpected.

Could it be Marcus's appearance that disturbed Quincy's tranquility?

"Don't say anything. Just listen to me," Quincy held her tightly as if he wanted to merge the fragrance of her body, the one he had loved for eight years, into his very soul, never to be separated again.

"Jessica, I love you, I swear to God, I love you. I don't care that you already had a child. When I fell in love with you, I already knew that you had Henry, but what does it matter? I once thought about giving up. I played a very difficult game, and no matter what, I couldn't pass the final level. I thought that as long as I passed it, I would give up on you."

"It's been eight years, and this game is no longer as challenging as it used to be. Countless times, I challenged the final level, countless times, all I had to do was press the enter key, and I would have made it through. But in the end, I couldn't bring myself to do it. I don't want to give up."

"Jessica, believe in my true feelings. In this lifetime, I have only ever had feelings for you."

Sect Elder Breeze

His voice, warm and with a touch of hoarseness, resonated with a faint sorrow and pain in the night as if the entire night sky wept for this man's deep affection.

Moved to tears, Jessica's heart ached like a twisted pain, spreading thread by thread through her veins. She felt a strong desire to cry.

With a mouthful of bitterness, this love was too heavy. She would never be able to repay it in her lifetime.

"Quincy... I..." Jessica didn't know how to refuse this heavy love. If it were any other man, she would have slapped him long ago, rejecting him mercilessly, leaving no trace of tenderness.

But he was her senior in college, who had been by her side for eight years, silently giving without ever asking for anything in return.

"Jessica, if love is an investment, why not invest all your energy and time in me? I, Quincy, guarantee your lifelong happiness."

Jessica opened her mouth, biting her lower lip, remaining silent.

Eight years of emotions surged out like a volcanic eruption, hot and intense. If Jessica claimed she wasn't moved, it would be a lie.

Quincy was a good man, and it was precisely because of that, Jessica didn't dare to hurt him so recklessly. If she agreed, it would be a lifetime commitment.

"Please think carefully about what I said, alright?" Quincy didn't want to push her too hard. He withdrew the slight disappointment in his eyes and filled it with indulgence. Suddenly changing the topic, he said, "Jessica, even though I don't want you to immediately agree with me, can you do me a favor?"

"Quincy, just say it. As long as I can do it, I will help." In this situation, no one wouldn't refuse his request.

Night of Destiny

"Can you pretend to be in a relationship with me for a while, be my fake girlfriend? My grandfather is pressuring me to get married, I'm truly tired of coming home every day and finding a woman I don't know waiting for me." Quincy spoke earnestly, full of anguish.

Jessica simply smiled, hiding the bitterness as she nodded, "Okay!"

Jessica went upstairs, opened the door, and turned on the lights. She leaned heavily against the door and took a long breath. She was really tired!

Marcus, Quincy, everyone made her tired, so tired...

"Mummy, you have a face that looks so beaten up, so pitiful..." The cute boy, Henry, wearing cute cartoon pajamas, held a cup of hot milk, and leaned against the wall.

Looking at this mini-version of Marcus, Jessica had a sense of time and space confusion.

Her eyes narrowed suddenly, she kicked off her shoes, walked over, and grabbed his collar, "What time is it? You're still not sleeping. Do you want to die?"

"Be gentle, be gentle, Mummy. Act like a lady..." Henry affectionately rubbed against her chest, smiling mischievously as he passed by, "AD has a new defense system, I challenged it."

Jessica felt speechless. Her son was good in every aspect except for this. He was so mischievous at such a young age and he could still smile so elegantly.

This twisted personality, she didn't pass it on to him.

"A challenge? More like teasing, right?" Jessica slapped his forehead, "You little brat, behave yourself."

When Henry was five years old, he demonstrated an astonishing computer talent. He often provoked other people's defense systems. When they were in France, there was a time when Jessica accompanied Lionel to a business banquet and ended up being splashed with alcohol by his mistress.

Sect Elder Breeze

Under Henry's calm demeanor, he shattered the internal defense systems of Lionel's company three times within a week. Every time Lionel replaced it, Henry stepped on it and boldly left a small pink pig on Lionel's office computer, twisting its butt and speaking in a childish voice.

"Sir, you're so bad at this!"

The screen turned black, and the pink pig spat out these shiny gold words, twisting Lionel's handsome face in anger.

Jessica knew that her son was considered the top hacker in the world. He had a group named "Freaks Assembly", filled with world geniuses.

"I know, I know... Mummy, did someone bully you? Tell me, I'll make them regret it."

"Save it. Bullying others with your talent, huh?"

"So what if I do? If he's so capable, let him bully back!" His childlike tone carried an extraordinary elegance and arrogance.

Jessica remained silent.

"Mummy, your boss called you out, but Uncle Quincy brought you back."

"It's just a coincidence."

"Oh, really... so cliché."

"What did you say?"

"Nothing. I'm so sleepy, going to bed now. Goodnight, Mummy!" Henry finished drinking the milk, handed the cup to Jessica, floated into the room, and closed the door.

Gossiping over. It was just a melodramatic play, so boring. Time to sleep.

Jessica, "..."

******

The next day at work, Marcus remained as cold and intimidating as ever, with an extra touch of frost in his gaze. Because of him, the entire Noblefull Group seemed to freeze over.

Night of Destiny

The secretary's office was as busy as ever, with Jessica spinning around like a top, arranging suitable schedules, dealing with Marcus's mistresses, answering endless phone calls, and handling a never-ending pile of documents. Her hands barely stopped moving.

Marcus called her into his office for the fifth time.

"Clear your schedule for tonight," Marcus ordered in a cold tone without even looking up. "Accompany me to a banquet."

Jessica was taken aback. She was his secretary, so it was natural for her to accompany him, but shouldn't Crystal be the one to go with him?

She didn't dare to say much and quietly left the office.

At noon.

The elevator on the 36th floor rang, and Crystal arrived!

She wore a light blue designer dress, blue crystal high heels, and light makeup. She appeared soft, elegant, and trendy, causing Jessica to secretly admire her.

"Hello everyone, I'm here to see Marcus," Crystal smiled and greeted all the secretaries, heading straight towards the CEO's office.

Jessica stood up, maintained her smile, and politely said, "Miss Crystal, Mr. Marcus instructed me not to disturb him. Would you like me to inform him of your arrival?"

Crystal was taken aback. This was the first time someone had dared to stop her. She couldn't help but look at Jessica a few more times. Rumor had it that Marcus had a capable female secretary, and Jessica was considered the top secretary in the Paris office.

However, she seemed too young and too beautiful.

There was a somewhat decorative feeling about her.

Crystal felt a bit displeased, but Jessica followed the rules and informed Marcus. Lately, his temper had been unpredictable, so she decided to play by the book.

"Come in!"

"Miss Crystal, I apologize for keeping you waiting. Mr. Marcus requests your presence."

Crystal nodded and gave Jessica a deep look. Without saying a single word, Crystal elegantly entered the CEO's office.

Jessica carried on with her work without a care, swiftly typing and archiving files.

After a while, Marcus and Crystal emerged together, looking like a perfect couple as they left hand in hand. Marcus glanced at Jessica but didn't say anything.

Crystal looked at Jessica with a subtle, almost imperceptible hint of hostility.

Jessica was confused. Why?

Chapter 12

Felt Jealous

When Quincy called her, Jessica was getting ready to have lunch with her colleagues. Henry had slept late last night and woke up late, so he didn't have time to make her lunch.

She declined her colleagues' invitations and headed downstairs.

Night of Destiny

A black Lamborghini was parked in front of the Noblefull Group Building, with Quincy holding a large bouquet of roses and leaning on the car with a gentle smile, looking warm and charming.

Jessica hurriedly walked over, feeling embarrassed, "Quincy, why are you here?" Still holding the bouquet of roses?!

She felt awkward. It was lunchtime, and many employees entering and leaving the Noblefull Group Building. Their gazes were filled with astonishment and ambiguity.

She could bet that rumors would be flying around.

The rivalry between Gootal Group and Noblefull Group had been going on for many years, and it was no secret. Usually, the competition was behind the scenes, but recently, Mr. Quincy and Mr. Marcus had brought the rivalry to the forefront, causing a lot of commotion.

Both companies were fighting against each other but also maintaining an unusual relationship. No one could really understand the relationship between the two families. It was the first time Mr. Quincy had appeared so openly at the Noblefull Group Building.

Quincy's girlfriend was Marcus's secretary. This news would cause a sensation.

"I've come to take my girlfriend to dinner!" Quincy smiled gently, his eyes filled with tenderness. He lovingly placed the roses in Jessica's hands.

Holding a bouquet of red roses, Jessica didn't know whether to laugh or cry.

Quincy smiled and continued, "I have something to discuss with you. Today is my grandfather's birthday, and I would like to invite you as my dance partner. Come, let's eat and talk at the same time."

Sect Elder Breeze

"Hello, Mr. Quincy," Marcus's car parked next to them, and he rolled down the window and glanced at Jessica. "Miss Jessica, the company is a working place. If you want to talk about love, find a different place. Don't affect the corporate image of Noblefull Group. There's already enough news about the families of Mr. Quincy and mine."

Jessica forced a polite smile. Damn it, with your promiscuous and philandering behavior, Noblefull Group has already lost its image. She was even worried that joining Noblefull Group would affect her pure image.

Quincy asked with a smile, "Mr. Marcus, does Noblefull Group have a rule against having a romantic lunch? I'm just here to invite my girlfriend for a meal. Mixing business and personal matters, is that not your style, Mr. Marcus?"

Marcus elegantly tapped his slender fingers on the steering wheel in a rhythmic manner. Jessica's heart skipped a beat as she tugged at Quincy's sleeve, signaling that they could leave.

"Mr. Marcus, we'll go ahead. We won't interrupt your time with Miss Crystal."

"Miss Jessica, prepare for Old Mr. Lee's birthday banquet tonight. I hope you can truly separate your personal and professional life."

With that, Marcus stepped on the gas pedal and disappeared before their eyes.

"Quincy, I'm sorry! I had no idea beforehand." Jessica apologized; she had no clue that Old Mr. Lee had invited Marcus and her to attend his birthday banquet.

After all, accompanying her boss to a banquet was quite common. At first, Jessica thought it was a business event, but she didn't expect it to be...

She was certain that Marcus had done it on purpose.

"Since you had already agreed to him beforehand, let's just forget about it this time. There's plenty of time in the future, no need to rush." Quincy still smiled, graceful and charming. He knew all too well what Marcus was thinking.

Night of Destiny

His tender gaze turned towards the window, reflecting a pair of deep and serene eyes. The usual warmth in his eyes was replaced by a hint of sharpness. Marcus, do you have to provoke me?

After lunch, Jessica returned to her office. Her colleagues had also returned and upon seeing her holding a large bouquet of red roses, they all came over with smiles, gossiping.

Jessica managed to navigate through their questions, but the women were persistent, causing a commotion in the secretary's office. They all assumed that Jessica and Quincy had a deep relationship and started teasing her about their romantic history.

These beautiful women were carefully selected secretaries of Noblefull Group, highly capable and with unique personalities. They were all shrewd. If Jessica didn't satisfy their curiosity, they would hound her for answers for days on end.

Feeling helpless, Jessica casually made up a melodramatic story to shut them up, which made them gasp in admiration and ask when they would get married.

Jessica sighed inwardly. It turned out that no matter how sharp and intelligent women were, when they gathered together, they would gossip.

As they were getting louder, Marcus and Crystal returned.

"Have you all finished your work? How can you have time to chat and drink coffee? If you don't want to work, pack up and leave!" Mr. Marcus's cold voice froze the entire floor.

The gossiping women immediately fell silent and returned to their seats as quickly as possible.

Marcus's icy gaze swept over Jessica, catching sight of the big bouquet of red roses. He found them glaringly annoying and walked straight into his office, slamming the door shut.

Crystal looked at the door in astonishment, then glanced at Jessica. A tinge of jealousy flashed across her delicate face as she clenched her fist.

"Miss Jessica, hello, I'm Crystal Walker!" Crystal greeted Jessica with a gentle smile and extended her hand, making Jessica feel a sense of crisis.

Though he had many women, Marcus never cared about any woman. And Crystal knew that those women were just tools for him to alleviate loneliness.

She had been by Marcus' side for years and had never seen him care so much about any other woman, only Jessica...

And this girl gave her such a familiar feeling, familiar to the point that it made Crystal fearful, fearful of losing Marcus.

Jessica politely greeted, "Hello, Miss Crystal!"

"Miss Jessica, so young and capable, I envy you..." Crystal leaned closer to Jessica, lowering her voice, a hint of maliciousness flashing across her beautiful face. "Miss Jessica, don't covet what doesn't belong to you, understand?"

The last question she asked was barely audible, but it carried a chilling tone.

In the blink of an eye, she returned to her submissive and sweet demeanor, as if the previous exchange was just an illusion.

Jessica curved her lips into a perfect arc and smiled, "Miss Crystal, what are you talking about?"

"Miss Jessica, being so intelligent, how could you not know? You and Mr. Quincy are a good match. I won't disturb you any longer. Goodbye!"

"Miss Crystal, take care!" Jessica smiled and saw Crystal off.

Crystal glanced at Jessica, a cold smirk flickering across her eyes before she turned and left. The threat from this woman was too heavy!

Jessica sat down, a layer of coldness tinting her eyebrows.

Night of Destiny

Crystal's words were a warning and a threat. That sinister smile tore through her outward appearance of gentleness and humility.

Do women truly disregard everything for love?

One face in public, another in secret. How can they live without exhaustion? She and Marcus were truly a perfect match, no wonder Marcus chose her as his girlfriend, but...

What does this have to do with her?

A cold smirk formed in Jessica's heart.

Crystal actually thought she coveted Mr. Marcus? Damn it, maybe she needed to see an ophthalmologist.

Near the end of the workday, the door of the CEO's office opened, and Mr. Marcus, who hadn't made a sound all afternoon, walked out with a silent expression. His eyes were cold, his demeanor elegant, and his exquisitely seductive features showed neither joy nor anger.

Jessica sensibly stood up and left with him. Why did this man have such a limited range of facial expressions? Was he missing a nerve somewhere?

She couldn't help but analyze Mr. Marcus' genetic makeup. Walking with him this summer was truly... refreshing!

******

In the busiest street of W City, there was a boutique for luxury brands that was known for its understated elegance and combining romantic elements, highly favored by socialites and ladies.

"Lucy, this woman is your responsibility!" Marcus threw Jessica to the store manager, his gaze swept over Jessica with a hidden meaning. "She is my companion."

"Understood, Mr. Marcus!" Lucy, the mature and elegant beauty of a store manager, snapped her fingers crisply.

Two fashionable and beautiful young women came over to assist Jessica in choosing clothes and styling her hair.

"Hey, Mr. Marcus, is this on the company's tab?" Jessica smiled and asked.

Even the usually aloof and elegant Mr. Marcus' face darkened slightly. His cold gaze swept over Jessica as he squeezed out a few words through his teeth, "What do you think?"

Jessica felt relieved, and the other beauties quickly understood the situation. They gave her a thumbs up, and Lucy smiled at Mr. Marcus and then at Jessica, understanding it all.

Her unfriendly attitude towards Jessica had suddenly become amiable.

Marcus intentionally wanted to put her in a difficult position, but he didn't expect Jessica's words to turn the tables. She made it clear to the other beauties that she wasn't Mr. Marcus' mistress, just an employee.

This woman was too clever!

However, he liked that!

Mr. Marcus thought to himself as his deep gaze fell on the figure in front of the dressing mirror, remaining silent for a while.

Makeup, hairstyling, accessories, shoes... Women took a long time to dress up, but Mr. Marcus had already finished preparing, patiently waiting for her for over two hours.

"Mr. Marcus, it's done. Take a look, are you satisfied?" Lucy pushed Jessica forward, smiling teasingly. "As expected, you have a good eye. Miss Jessica looks her best in this dress. She is the most beautiful lady that our store has received in the past six months."

Marcus put down the magazine, raised an eyebrow slightly, and a flash of astonishment passed through his cold, deep gaze. His pupils narrowed slightly, reflecting a hint of depth.

Beautiful, so beautiful!

Night of Destiny

The swaying sea-blue gown highlighted her slender and exquisite figure. The soft silk clung to her body, revealing her curves. The slightly fluffy design on the right side of the hem flowed down from the waist, accentuating her long lower body. The dress accentuated her waist, and full chest, and on the left side of her chest, there was a large sea-blue rose, extremely unique. It showcased her bare shoulders and delicate clavicle, and the low-cut design further accentuated her ample chest, with suggestive lines that aroused imagination.

This sea-blue dress seemed to be specially designed for Jessica, complementing her charm that was somewhere between innocence and maturity, captivating everyone's hearts and souls.

Pure yet glamorous, coupled with her signature smile, it was simply a breathtaking beauty that dominated the room.

Marcus' gaze made Jessica slightly uncomfortable. Her heart raced, and a blush crept onto her cheeks. A pair of bright and beautiful eyes showed a hint of shyness, which was rare.

"It's beautiful!"

Marcus stood up and approached Jessica, his cold eyes filled with astonishment. She was slim and petite, but her chest was quite impressive. He had thought that such a dress wouldn't suit her, but the stunning beauty was beyond his expectations.

The thought of someone else appreciating her allure filled Mr. Marcus with a strange sense of displeasure as if he wanted to keep her hidden in his pocket.

"Miss Jessica, you look beautiful," he unabashedly glanced at her ample bosom, his eyes carrying a hint of wickedness. The snow-white skin and the tantalizing cleavage made him want to tear apart her dress.

Jessica suppressed her anger and put on a perfect smile, saying, "Thank you for the compliment, Mr. Marcus!"

Sect Elder Breeze

This woman's smile was clearly fake, so why was it so bewitching?

Marcus lightly traced his fingers over Jessica's exposed skin, relishing the silk-like touch. A surge of electricity shot up Jessica's spine, rushed to her head, and then spread throughout her body. She trembled uncontrollably, her skin turning a faint shade of pink.

When it came to seduction techniques, who dared to compete with Mr. Marcus?

His wicked and deep gaze, like a captivating vortex, made people succumb to its irresistible charm. Jessica's perfect smile was starting to falter, and her heart was pounding like thunder.

Everyone said that if Mr. Marcus wanted to seduce someone, no one could resist.

With exquisite features and a perfect figure, exuding an elegant and mysteriously wicked aura, every action of his easily captivated the hearts of numerous women.

Just as Jessica couldn't bear this ambiguous atmosphere any longer, her heart pounding in her throat, Mr. Marcus grabbed her waist and said wickedly, "Don't move!"

He put a blue gemstone necklace around Jessica's neck, with the tear-shaped pendant hanging on her chest, complementing her clothes and demeanor.

It added a touch of mystery to Jessica.

Chapter 13

The Limited-edition Necklace

"You're my woman, dress you up a bit nicer so that I won't be embarrassed!" Mr. Marcus whispered in her ear with a wicked tone, and then pushed her away, saying, "Miss Jessica, let's go!"

Jessica lowered her head to look at the necklace on her chest. Her heart skipped a beat once again. It wasn't her imagination - this necklace was a limited-edition treasure from Noblefull Group called Angel's Tears.

The jewelry company under Noblefull Group was one of its main industries, together with real estate and media, making them the three pillars of Noblefull Group. This Angel's Tears necklace was launched five years ago at the Milan Jewelry Exhibition and caused a sensation in the entire jewelry industry, sweeping the globe. It attracted countless celebrities and big names.

Jessica had learned about this when she studied the exhibition history of Noblefull Group, paying particular attention to a certain person - and that person was the designer of this necklace, Marcus Smith!

Jessica silently looked up at the countless stars in the sky, her heart pounding incessantly. She struggled to maintain her usual composure.

What did Marcus mean by all this?

Could it be...

A counterfeit?

Only with this thought could she control her wildly beating heart.

Silent all the way, the silver Rolls-Royce drove into the mansion of the Lee Family. It was a manor filled with British style, with a spacious courtyard, tall trees, and a quiet and majestic atmosphere. An ancient and solemn dominance permeated the air, along with elegance and luxury.

"Mr. Marcus..." The waiter parked the car and Jessica called out to Marcus. She really wanted to ask him a question: Was this necklace a counterfeit?

Marcus coldly glanced at her, as if he guessed what she wanted to ask. A wave of anger flickered in his deep eyes, and Jessica wisely remained silent.

"Miss Jessica, put on your signature smile," Marcus smirked, exuding a wicked aura.

He was dressed in a formal suit, and the devilish wine-red tie added a touch of wickedness to his whole being. With his elbow slightly bent, he gestured for her to follow.

Jessica put on her signature smile, linking her arm with his. It was the first time they had been so intimate since that night eight years ago. A slight feeling of unease lingered in Jessica's heart, making her nervous and awkward. Her usual indifferent and calm demeanor seemed to have disappeared into thin air.

It felt like something would tighten in her heart whenever he approached. It wrapped around her like coils, making it difficult to breathe, and her nerves were stretched tight. This feeling was terrifying.

"Miss Jessica, are you nervous?" Marcus's deep and magnetic voice was mesmerizing, making her heart flutter.

Was she nervous?

His lips quirked up, his mood becoming even better. He liked her nervousness!

Jessica didn't reply. Nervous? Can nervousness be more important than saving face? No!

"No one is forcing you, don't act like a dead fish."

What is he talking about?!

Night of Destiny

Anger surged, and she had the urge to stomp her sharp high heels fiercely on his feet. However, the anger dispersed the nervousness, and Jessica's signature smile became even more prominent!

Without a doubt, they were the most outstanding and eye-catching pair at the entire banquet. Since they entered the banquet hall, all eyes were focused on them. Envious, jealous, disdainful...all kinds of gazes were directed at them from all directions.

Jessica noticed that most of the gazes were not focused on Marcus and her exceptional appearance but on her chest...

Those gazes unmistakably carried blatant greed and jealousy.

Crystal's face turned pale as paper in an instant, her fists clenched tightly. Those gazes carried sinister hatred as if they wanted to tear Jessica apart.

Quincy's usually gentle eyes also darkened, with a hint of hostility passing through!

The vintage palace-style banquet hall was resplendent with exquisite and luxurious chandeliers, masterful oil paintings by both domestic and international artists, and seemingly inconspicuous vases that were priceless antiques. Every element in the banquet hall contributed to the atmosphere of utmost opulence.

"Isn't that Jessica?" Raymond and Florence, not far from the banquet, were shocked as they saw Marcus leading Jessica towards Old Mr. Lee.

Old Mr. Lee was a titan in the industry with an extensive network. His birthday banquet was a gathering of the upper echelons of society, an event that Raymond was not originally invited to. However, he managed to secure an invitation by leveraging his connections in order to seek investment.

Sect Elder Breeze

At this moment, Jessica appeared stunningly elegant and refined, evoking envy and causing saliva to flow from Raymond's mouth. She was truly beautiful, a far cry from the poverty-stricken girl she was eight years ago.

On the other hand, Florence's face twisted with jealousy. The girl she once envied and ridiculed for her lowly status now wore a limited-edition evening gown. It was not an outfit that money alone could obtain, let alone the Angel's Tears necklace she wore, which made all the ladies in the room green with envy.

Crystal's pale complexion was also due to Angel's Tears. This necklace was the crown jewel of the Noblefull Group, prized by Marcus as his masterpiece, and the only necklace he personally designed in his lifetime.

After the worldwide popularity of Angel's Tears, the Noblefull Group released many necklaces with a similar design. At first glance, they looked similar, but the lines and cutting techniques were far inferior to the smoothness and uniqueness of Angel's Tears. Marcus made subtle adjustments in the details before launching it on the market.

Although this series of necklaces became a bestseller worldwide, a darling of socialites, cementing Noblefull Group's position in the international jewelry industry, it was common knowledge that there was only one true Angel's Tears in the world.

At the Noblefull Group's 50th anniversary celebration, Crystal, taking advantage of her relationship as Marcus's girlfriend, asked him to let her wear it for one night. However, Marcus refused and even became angry on the spot.

Since then, Crystal dared not mention wearing Angel's Tears anymore.

This man had many taboos, from the grudges of the Smith family to a bloodbath more than a decade ago, and his mother as well as this necklace... No matter how intimate one may be with him, he would not allow anyone to touch his taboos.

Why did Jessica have special treatment?

Night of Destiny

Crystal's jealousy burned her eyes, to the point that she was consumed by the mad desire to slash Jessica's smiling face.

Marcus looked at Crystal, but saw her face full of sorrow, her eyes filled with tears. She turned around abruptly and walked away.

Marcus's eyes flickered, he released his hand from Jessica's waist without even looking at her, and chased after Crystal.

This scene was witnessed by everyone present, and Jessica instantly became a laughingstock.

They made such a high-profile entrance, but when Mr. Marcus saw his girlfriend, he immediately let go of Jessica. In the eyes of others, Jessica was just a substitute for Mr. Marcus' girlfriend. As for why she wore Angel's Tears, it was probably just a reward for being Marcus' mistress.

Jessica hadn't been Marcus's secretary for long, and this was her first time accompanying Marcus to a party. Not many people knew her.

Furthermore, her appearance was indeed too innocent, resembling a freshly-sprung college student, which was a far cry from the image of the number one Parisian secretary as rumored.

Naturally, one would think that she was Marcus's mistress.

Being the first one to draw attention can be risky. And the necklace itself attracted envious glances from all the ladies in the room. To be then discarded by Mr. Marcus in such a manner turned Jessica into a laughingstock in the eyes of others.

Jealousy and disdain came at Jessica from all sides like needles.

With a smile on her face, she had grown accustomed to being used as a scapegoat by Lionel. Being resented and envied by other women had become a daily occurrence for her. Jessica had long cultivated a thick skin and a strong will.

However...

Why did it taste so bitter this time?

Marcus, you damn bastard!

If you wanted her, why did you bother bringing me along in the first place?

"Hey, Jessica, I actually thought you had transformed from a sparrow into a phoenix and soared to greater heights. Turns out, you're just a sparrow dressed in phoenix clothing. Mr. Marcus is busy comforting Miss Crystal. Why are you still here? How embarrassing!" Florence taunted sharply. Dressed in a black evening gown with a low V-neck, her ample cleavage was tantalizingly revealed, oozing sex appeal.

"This Angel's Tears necklace is fake, isn't it?" she mocked, covering her mouth. "How can you afford such a necklace? Mr. Marcus might have only given you this fake necklace just to trick you into bed. How pitiful."

Florence's sarcastic remarks seemed addicting, while Raymond beside her lusted after Jessica's beauty, his eyes filled with lasciviousness, looking extremely sleazy.

Jessica smiled calmly, "Excuse me, do we know each other? Why are you talking to yourself?"

Florence's face turned red instantly. What he said was nothing compared to Jessica's humiliation.

"Why are you pretending not to understand when you clearly know what I'm talking about," Florence clenched her fist and sneered coldly. "Hmph, even your ex-boyfriend abandoned you for me."

Raymond pulled Florence's hand, looking slightly embarrassed. He was still contemplating how to win Jessica back, and he never expected her to be so beautiful. If only he had made his move earlier back then, avoiding the situation where he could only look but not touch.

"I must say, Florence, is it honorable to be a mistress, picking up someone else's discarded man? After all these years, you still boast about it. Do you not have any other glorious history to speak of?" Jessica smiled.

Her words struck Florence's face with a slap.

Night of Destiny

Florence's expression changed dramatically, and she reached out to hit Jessica, but her hand was firmly grabbed by someone else.

Quincy, whose face was usually calm, had a sinister look as if he were a devil. His blue eyes flickered with a fiery light, and he tried hard to control the impulse to twist her wrist and break it. "This is my grandfather's birthday banquet. If you want to cause trouble, please leave!"

"Mr. Quincy, it's a misunderstanding, just a misunderstanding..." Raymond immediately put on a flattering smile upon seeing Quincy.

His ugly behavior made Jessica coldly laugh.

Raymond, who used to be arrogant and capricious as a young man, had completely changed within a few years.

Quincy's icy gaze swept over Raymond and Florence, his eyes narrowing slightly, revealing a dangerous gleam.

With a gentle tone mixed with sarcasm, he said, "Who are you, I don't remember we sending an invitation to you."

"I'm Raymond from Davis Family Department Store. Nice to meet you, Mr. Quincy."

Quincy coldly glanced at the hand he extended, showing no intention of shaking it, only furrowing his brow.

He warned Florence with a glance, "I don't care how you managed to get in here, but if you dare to cause trouble again, don't blame me for being impolite."

"Yes, yes, it's just a misunderstanding," Raymond quickly apologized and pulled Florence away.

Florence also put on a gentle smile, trying to show her best side. She always had this confidence that no man could escape from the palm of her hand, and this confidence had made her forget her self-respect.

"Yes, Mr. Quincy, it was just a misunderstanding," Florence said softly and coquettishly.

Raymond could no longer provide her with a life of luxury, so she naturally had to find another way out. Marcus and Quincy were undoubtedly the best options.

Sect Elder Breeze

"Miss Jessica and I were old classmates. She is vain and easily deceived. I just kindly advised her not to be deluded, so as not to become a laughingstock. Old Mr. Lee's birthday banquet was such a grand occasion, and she came with fake Angel's Tears. Wasn't that embarrassing? It also embarrassed Old Mr. Lee."

Jessica looked at her contemptuous face and sneered, shaking her head. She really couldn't understand why this woman could be shameless to this extent.

People should have self-awareness. Last time, Florence desperately flirted with Marcus when she saw him, and this time, when she saw Quincy, she also tried hard to show her charm. She really was...

Florence was just belittling her to raise her own value, reaching such a shameless extent, which was rare.

"Only ignorant people would think that this Angel's Tears is fake, just like you. No matter how branded your clothes are, you still look like a fake!"

Quincy was about to get angry, but a cold and chilling voice interrupted, instantly freezing the atmosphere.

Marcus's delicate features were as cold as a devil from hell, his gaze sweeping Florence with indifference and mockery, "Have you ever seen the real Angel's Tears?"

Compared to Quincy's gentle demeanor, Marcus was obviously more ruthless, with a devilish aura that sent chills down one's spine.

Some people, if they provoke him, he would repay them tenfold, regardless of gender. In Marcus's world, gender often didn't matter, only the line between friend and foe.

This was Marcus, the cold-hearted Marcus.

"I..." Florence was speechless.

Yes, how could she have ever seen Angel's Tears? She had only seen it a few times in magazines. It was a symbol of honor and wealth. Who wouldn't love it? But very few truly understood it.

"Just overestimating yourself!" Marcus said coldly. "Pathetic woman, instead of envying others, you'd better find a place to die and be reborn, to reshape your cultivation."

Whispered conversations filled the surroundings, accompanied by the faint mocking laughter of women.

Chapter 14

Strange Conversation

Florence's face turned red, completely devastated by Marcus's remarks. The disdainful gazes of others fell upon her, making her feel so embarrassed that she wished she could find a hole to hide in.

She had originally wanted to witness Jessica's humiliation, but unexpectedly, it was Marcus who mercilessly mocked her, making others laugh at her instead. Florence regretted it deeply.

Marcus's powerful presence silenced her completely.

"Jessica, are you an idiot?" Marcus suddenly turned his head, his deep gaze brushing with a hint of anger. "Do you have no brains to stand here and let someone like her insult you? Where's that sharp tongue of yours?"

Jessica remained silent.

Truly ruthless!

With just a few words, he insulted both of them.

Sect Elder Breeze

It wasn't that she didn't fight back, but Quincy spoke up for her and his sharp tongue left her no room to perform!

"Mr. Marcus, if it weren't for you abandoning her, she wouldn't have to endure this embarrassment!" Quincy calmly remarked, sarcastically blaming Marcus as the cause of Jessica's embarrassment.

"Mr. Quincy, are you feeling sorry for her? As my secretary, can't you handle such matters well? Miss Jessica, should I question your abilities?" Marcus's devilish gaze flashed with a cold light, directing his criticism towards Jessica.

Jessica gave a faint smile, "Mr. Marcus, you speak the truth. It's all my fault."

Quincy frowned disapprovingly, while Marcus's lips curled coldly, "The next time you're bullied by someone like her, you better fight back properly. Don't embarrass me."

Only he could bully his woman; no one else could touch a single hair of her!

Quincy's eyebrows raised, and a sense of danger instantly engulfed him. Marcus's concern for Jessica was truly... odd!

This worry was played out by him in an unconventional way, not something that everyone could accept - this alternative, twisted yet genuine care.

Jessica maintained her calm composure, still wearing her signature smile, "Understood." Pausing for a moment, she arched an eyebrow at him. "Mr. Marcus, do I have to retaliate against anyone who bullies me? What if things go wrong?"

"Hmph, is there anything I can't handle?" Marcus dangerously narrowed his eyes, his deep gaze exuding a demonic aura, along with his own arrogance.

In the entire business circle, apart from the other three big names, there were really few who could compete with him.

Crystal happened to come in and heard his words, her expression suddenly changed, and she looked at Jessica with a hint of resentment in her eyes.

Night of Destiny

Quincy's warm gaze narrowed slightly, passing a hint of danger, "Mr. Marcus, my girlfriend doesn't need your concern!"

"As long as she is my secretary, I have a say," Marcus replied coldly with a smirk, hooking his arm around Jessica's waist and brushing past Quincy, heading towards Old Mr. Lee, who was chatting with someone else.

This little drama came to an end like this. There had long been rumors that the girlfriend of the CEO of the Gootal Group was Marcus's secretary. It turns out she wasn't Marcus's mistress, but Quincy's girlfriend!?

Oh my god...

The ladies and noblewomen whispered to each other, discussing the disputes between them. Jessica undoubtedly became the most mysterious woman at this banquet.

"Marcus, why?" Jessica lowered her voice, her gaze scanning Crystal, and happened to meet her resentful eyes. Her heart pounded, what had he just said to Crystal?

And what was the matter with this necklace?

"Why did you make me attend this banquet? Why did you make me wear Angel's Tears? What exactly are you trying to do?"

Jessica wasn't a fool. The eerie atmosphere between him and Quincy, the occasional expressions of hatred, what was it all for?

She noticed that Marcus had too many secrets, and unknowingly she had been pulled into it.

She hated this feeling of being manipulated.

Marcus lowered his head, and his clean scent filled Jessica's nostrils. His warm breath brushed against her ear as he whispered, his voice like a bewitching melody, "Miss Jessica, what do you think?"

He held her waist with one hand, his head next to her ear, gently murmuring. From any angle, this scene was ambiguous.

Sect Elder Breeze

Marcus teasing her made her heart skip a beat, rippling like a stone dropped in water, spreading layer by layer...

As she turned her head, she happened to meet his devilish eyes, deep and devoid of warmth, mixed with a bit of restrained hatred that Jessica couldn't understand.

All the ambiguous ripples within Jessica vanished, as if falling into an icy abyss.

This Marcus... was like a devil!

Jessica absentmindedly was led by him to Old Mr. Lee. This was her first time meeting Old Mr. Lee, the business tycoon who once dominated the market.

He was over seventy years old, still in good shape, with cloudy but sharp eyes. After years of accumulation, that dominant aura was completely hidden, but not disappeared, instead, it appeared even stronger, revealing the coldness and decisiveness that once ruled the business arena. His features still retained traces of youthful beauty.

Jessica had a strange feeling as if she saw... a resemblance to Marcus fifty years later.

An astonishing... similarity between their eyebrows.

"Old Mr. Lee, it's been a while. Your vitality seems to have increased. I wish you good fortune and a long life," Marcus smiled, his tone more elegant than ever, conveying a sincere respect from a junior to an elder.

However, Jessica, who was holding his arm, clearly felt that Marcus's muscles were tense and rigid as if he were a fighter jet activating its full defense system, preparing for an attack.

This kind of Marcus, Jessica had never seen before. He smiled so sincerely, the smile reaching his eyes, but not his heart.

She hadn't been Marcus's secretary for long, and she couldn't claim to completely understand him, but she knew very well what every action of Marcus meant.

Night of Destiny

"Thank you. Amid your busy schedule, you came, I have truly inconvenienced you." Old Mr. Lee said with a smile, his sharp gaze scanning Marcus, revealing a complex meaning that was soon hidden beneath his cloudy eyes.

"You are a legendary figure in the business world. It is only natural for me to personally congratulate you on your birthday celebration."

"I am old. Can't keep up anymore. It's your young people's world now."

"Old Mr. Lee, you're too modest. There are many things that I still need to learn from you, whether it's business or other matters."

"Aha, Mr. Marcus, you're too polite. Your methods are many times more ruthless than me when I was young. There is nothing I can teach you."

"..."

Jessica, beside Marcus, felt his body becoming increasingly tense, greatly puzzled. This conversation between the two of them was too strange.

Gootal Group and Noblefull Group had been in fierce competition for many years, with deep-seated grievances. Old Mr. Lee and Old Mr. Alston had not interacted for decades, yet every time it was Old Mr. Lee's birthday, Marcus would personally come to congratulate him.

But...

This conversation was too bizarre, Jessica couldn't find the words to explain it. She faintly felt that at this moment, there was a surge of animosity brewing in Mr. Marcus's heart.

"Old Mr. Lee, let me introduce my companion, Miss Jessica."

Old Mr. Lee looked at Jessica and his face suddenly changed...

"Diana..." Old Mr. Lee trembled all over as if he had been struck hard, his face turned pale, and his hand shook so violently that his cane fell to the floor.

Clang...

A deep shock and... excitement surged in Old Mr. Lee's cloudy eyes, trembling as if he was about to grab Jessica's hand.

Marcus's lips curved into a sinister smirk, his eyes shimmering with a devilish light, smiling as he looked at the discomposed Old Mr. Lee.

Suffer!

Suffer intensely!

You can't compare to even one percent of what I suffered back then.

What you did to me, from now on, slowly, bit by bit, I'll repay you a thousand times over!

Jessica's heart pounded, she turned her head to look at Marcus, only to see a trace of ruthless hatred flickering at the corner of his lips, instantly sending chills down her spine.

"Old Mr. Lee, you've mistaken me for someone else, I..."

"Grandfather, what happened to you?" Quincy was drawn to the sound of Old Mr. Lee's cane hitting the ground.

Old Mr. Lee trembled all over. All of his emotions quickly converged.

His emotions stabilized remarkably fast, as if the earlier excitement and shock were just a momentary illusion to Jessica.

Marcus narrowed his eyes, squatted down in a leisurely manner, picked up Old Mr. Lee's cane, and when he looked up, his smile was gentle and humble, embodying his usual elegance.

"Old Mr. Lee, here is your cane."

Old Mr. Lee took it as if nothing had happened, but his gaze towards Marcus held an indiscernible glimmer. He patted Quincy, who was concerned, and said, "It's nothing, Quincy, just slipped for a moment."

Jessica was filled with astonishment but dared not speak out.

Night of Destiny

Intentionally, Marcus glanced at the Angel's Tears necklace around her chest and smiled, asking, "Old Mr. Lee, are you surprised, to see the Angel's Tears again?"

Quincy frowned, seeing the Angel's Tears again? What does that mean? When this necklace became popular worldwide, Old Mr. Lee once said that the designer of this necklace must be a gentle and passionate girl.

Later, it was discovered that the designer of this necklace was Marcus. Old Mr. Lee just smiled and didn't say much.

This necklace, apart from appearing at the Noblefull Group's 50th anniversary gala, rarely appeared in public. What does Marcus mean by this?

And his grandfather seemed to be too indulgent towards Marcus.

"I am indeed surprised. Everyone knows that Angel's Tears is your masterpiece, and it's the only one. Such a precious necklace appears at my banquet, it truly surprises me," Old Mr. Lee looked deeply at Marcus, "Mr. Marcus, you really give me face."

He almost bit the words out, but his complexion no longer showed any disturbance.

"Well," Marcus embraced Jessica's waist, almost pulling her close to him, intimate and inseparable. His exquisite features were elegant and charming, "Gem matches the beauty. Miss Jessica is the most important woman to me. With her wearing this necklace, it is worthy!"

As soon as these words were spoken, Quincy's gaze suddenly darkened, shooting out a sharp light, while Jessica remained silent, standing quietly by Marcus's side.

"Mr. Marcus, what do you mean by important woman? She is my girlfriend. When did she become the most important woman to you?" Quincy smiled gracefully, like a gentle breeze brushing against the face, but with a hint of chilling determination.

Sect Elder Breeze

Quincy's words shocked Old Mr. Lee, his sharp gaze swept over Jessica, and he asked in a deep voice, "Quincy, what is going on? Your girlfriend?"

Mr. Marcus smiled innocently, gently, and tightened his grip on Jessica's hand slightly, "Mr. Quincy, Miss Jessica is my chief secretary, an indispensable person to me. She handles all my affairs efficiently. Isn't she an important woman to me?"

"Mr. Marcus, your fiancée is standing right there watching. Aren't you feeling guilty saying this?" Quincy smiled elegantly, with a touch of mockery. "Or perhaps, you're just used to it?"

"So what?" Marcus sneered arrogantly.

There was nothing anyone could do about what he wanted to do!

His provocative gaze carried arrogance and disdain as if he were the ruler of the entire world. This confidence was cultivated through years of endurance and experience.

Quincy's flawless temper seemed to be on the verge of collapse. His complexion grew colder and colder.

Old Mr. Lee glanced at Jessica, and she couldn't quite decipher his gaze. She had the feeling that it was complicated, tinged with something she couldn't understand.

Marcus smirked, and looked at her askance, his demonic gaze flashing with a chilly light.

Jessica slightly freed herself from Marcus's embrace and greeted Old Mr. Lee, "Hello, Old Mr. Lee, my name is Jessica."

Old Mr. Lee took a deep look at her, made an acknowledging sound, and withdrew his gaze, "You said you wanted to introduce your girlfriend to me tonight, is this Miss Jessica?"

"Yes, Grandfather!"

Old Mr. Lee nodded, and glanced at Jessica once again, and weariness appeared in his brows, "I'm feeling a bit tired. Can you help me greet the guests?"

"Yes!" Quincy looked at Old Mr. Lee curiously, then had the butler assist him to leave.

The old man's once straight back seemed somewhat hunched, stained with the desolate burden of time.

What just happened?

Jessica glanced at Marcus, confused. Why did he provoke Old Mr. Lee?

No, it wasn't just a provocation, it was a form of revenge.

When he smirked at Old Mr. Lee, his gaze was filled with the satisfaction of revenge.

Diana?

Who is this person?

Why did her name come out of Old Mr. Lee's mouth? Does she resemble her? What secrets does this Angel's Tears hold?

Chapter 15

Jessica Was Considerate

Old Mr. Lee stumbled upstairs, dismissing the butler and looking as if he had aged ten years. He knelt on the ground in pain, clutching his head, and sobbed softly.

"Diana..."

The curtains in the study were pulled back, allowing moonlight to pour in and cast a layer of melancholic light upon the old man's figure, filled with despair and desolation.

The low sobbing sound was heart-wrenching to anyone who heard it.

After a while, Old Mr. Lee regained his composure and opened the safe in the study, carefully retrieving an exquisitely carved box from inside.

Trembling, he opened the box, revealing an Angel's Tears necklace.

The age of the necklace was quite distant, the chain had turned yellow, and the color of the gemstones was also uneven. It was made of synthetic gemstones and was not valuable. It was apparent that the materials used were rough. Its design was the same as the Angel's Tears necklace designed by Marcus, even down to the rose on the gemstone.

"Diana..." Old Mr. Lee tenderly caressed the necklace, murmuring as tears streamed down his face.

Downstairs, the banquet continued.

Quincy stopped Marcus, his warm gaze tinged with questioning, "What did you just say to my grandfather?"

Marcus smiled, devilishly elegant, "Mr. Quincy, today is Old Mr. Lee's birthday celebration. Besides congratulating him, what else can I say?"

Jessica's heart ached. Marcus was smiling so carefreely, but why did she feel this heartache? It seemed like he was hiding something. There was an overwhelming sense of grief and despair emanating from him, yet he laughed so freely.

"Mr. Marcus, congratulations have already been given. Can we leave now?" Jessica smiled, maintaining her perfect facade. She knew Marcus had used her.

But strangely, she felt no resentment, only pain for him. No matter what he said or did, physical reactions couldn't be hidden. He clearly didn't want to stay here.

Night of Destiny

Marcus turned his head, the smile on his face slightly fading as he looked deeply into Jessica's eyes before quickly shifting his gaze away.

Wasn't she angry?

Jessica had always smiled in front of him, but it was a mask, and he had always known. Yet, was her smile now one of anger or falsehood? He could tell.

At this moment, she seemed neither angry nor false, just genuinely smiling, inquiring.

In normal circumstances, she would have been pointing fingers and criticizing by now, right?

This girl was truly unpredictable.

This was the first time Marcus felt that a woman's heart was as elusive as finding a needle in the sea.

"Jessica, how about I take you home later? Let my grandfather rest for a while, and I'll introduce you properly," Quincy suggested.

Jessica smiled and said, "Quincy, there will always be opportunities in the future."

"I'm afraid Old Mr. Lee won't recover just by taking a rest," Marcus sneered coldly.

"What do you mean, Marcus?" Quincy's voice filled with anger, causing Jessica to be greatly surprised.

Quincy always had a gentle temperament and rarely got angry. But now, she could sense a fierce aura emanating from him.

Just as she was about to intervene, Quincy took a step forward, and the two men faced each other, creating a tense atmosphere filled with icy chill.

Sect Elder Breeze

Quincy spoke in a cold voice, "Your family and my family have been bitter enemies. And whether in secret battles or open fights, I'm not afraid of you. But Marcus, if you show any disrespect towards my grandfather, don't blame me for being impolite. My grandfather may have tolerated your mocking and provocation multiple times, but it doesn't mean I will. Listen carefully, if you don't want to come to my Lee Family, the Lee Family may not welcome you either!"

Marcus's eyes turned sinister like a demon, filled with a dangerous and contemptuous smirk. He spoke with arrogance, "He tolerated me? Hmph, Quincy, do you know why our two families have been at each other's throats all these years? Do you know why he tolerated me? Quincy, go ask him. As long as I, Marcus, am alive, I will play the Lee Family to your deaths, at any cost, using any means necessary!"

Jessica's heart raced at these words. An ominous aura enveloped Marcus' refined features, revealing a sense of ruthlessness. He was willing to perish along with the Lee Family just to annihilate them.

Quincy, too, was panicked and intimidated by the dark aura emanating from Marcus. He had always believed that the grudges and conflicts between their two families over the years were simply due to their struggles in the business world.

But...

It seemed that he was wrong!

Marcus was a proud and arrogant man. If he lost, he would naturally find ways to turn the tide. He respected his opponents rather than harbored hostility towards them.

Could there have been something Quincy didn't know about the grudges between the two families?

Their voices were not particularly loud, and the sound of the banquet music filled the air. There were no people nearby, apart from Jessica, who could hear what they were saying clearly. However, this scene could easily be misunderstood.

Night of Destiny

With the leaders of the two families, along with tonight's topic Queen Jessica, and the recent scandals involving the two young masters and Jessica, this scenario naturally appeared as a rivalry between two men for a woman in others' eyes.

"Quincy, let's stop talking," Jessica shook her head, gesturing for him not to engage with Marcus for the moment. Mr. Marcus's emotions were clearly not right.

She had already noticed that Marcus was an unfathomable man who had many untouchable taboos. On regular days, his emotions seldom fluctuated. He was elegant, cold, and profound. But once you touched his taboos, his emotions were likely to spin out of control.

Seeing Mr. Marcus, who had just restrained himself in front of Old Mr. Lee, made her feel sorry for him; and now, witnessing Mr. Marcus almost losing control of his emotions, made her worry.

"Mr. Marcus, can we leave now?" Jessica asked with a smile.

Florence felt a mix of envy and resentment. She had been momentarily stunned by Marcus, embarrassed in public. She blamed Jessica and, disregarding Raymond's attempts to stop her, mocked harshly, "Jessica, your son is already so big, yet you still can make Mr. Marcus and Mr. Quincy jealous and compete with each other. You're truly impressive!"

Jessica felt as if she had been struck by lightning, her face turning ashen-white as paper.

All the people at the banquet fell silent.

Florence intended to embarrass Jessica, and her words were spoken loudly enough for everyone to hear.

There was a deafening silence as everyone's gaze focused on Jessica, Marcus, and Quincy.

This scene felt like a farce, and everyone seemed to be waiting to see how it would end, waiting for the jokes about Marcus, and Quincy.

Sect Elder Breeze

Marcus, cold and ruthless, and Quincy, gentle and polished, were both figures in the business world who no one dared to provoke.

Some genuinely admired them, but most were envious.

The secret that Marcus and Quincy were both pursuing the same woman had long spread among the upper class. Everyone was eagerly waiting to see how the romantic rivalry would unfold, and who would win the woman's heart. But no one expected the bombshell revelation that the leading lady had a child.

It could be imagined how gleefully they were, waiting to see Marcus, and Quincy become a laughingstock.

"Butler, kick her out!" Quincy was the first to regain his composure and gave the cold order.

Florence thought they would become furious and redirect their anger at Jessica. She never expected to get caught up in trouble herself and shouted, "Mr. Quincy, believe me, what I am saying is true. Don't let her deceive you. Jessica's son is already in elementary school."

Florence had once happened to see Jessica picking up Henry from school. She had observed them, laughing and leaving together from afar. Florence initially thought they were distant relatives. But her niece told her that Jessica was Henry's mother, and Henry was a single-parent child.

This explosive revelation left her stunned. Florence calculated the timeline and realized it coincided with the period when Raymond and Jessica broke up. Raymond had even mentioned that he had never even kissed Jessica. Florence had intended to investigate further, but just now, she was humiliated by Marcus because of Jessica, which made her lose control and try to expose Jessica's true nature to Marcus and Quincy.

"Believe me, what I am saying is true!" Florence was being dragged away, yelling frantically.

Raymond wanted to plead, but Quincy gave him a cold glance.

Night of Destiny

"Everyone here, listen carefully. Anyone who dares to support Davis Family Department Store will have a problem with me, Quincy!"

With that statement, Davis Family Department Store was destined to become history!

Raymond Davis, pale-faced, was kicked out by security.

Marcus's gaze locked onto Jessica's face, while Jessica's mind was in chaos, her thoughts blank. She couldn't even dare to meet his eyes.

Marcus's deep and icy gaze swept over Jessica, who had been bowing her head. Then he glanced at Quincy. His narrowed eyes flickered with hidden hostility.

Not far away, Crystal's beautiful face flashed a satisfied smile. She had a child? What great news!

"Mr. Quincy, I'll take my leave!" Marcus said in a deep voice, not waiting for Quincy's response. He took Jessica and left the banquet.

Quincy watched them leave with concern.

Crystal wanted to chase after them but hesitated, revealing a triumphant smile. Since Jessica had a child, she couldn't possibly be a threat to Crystal.

How could a woman with a child be deserving of Marcus?

******

Inside the car, it was silent.

Jessica's heart was pounding, almost pounding out of her chest. Her cool mind could no longer stay calm.

If Marcus investigates her, he will find the existence of Henry. Will Marcus make any connections when he sees Henry?

Those forgotten memories, now only she alone remembers them. Marcus had long forgotten, but there was no telling if he would remember when he sees Henry. What should she do then?

Henry was everything to her, and no one could take him away, not even Marcus!

What should she do?

Panic, and fear, overwhelmed her mind, making her face turn pale.

Suddenly, the brakes screeched, and Jessica's heart skipped a beat. She looked up and saw Marcus's devilish eyes fixated on her.

"How old are you this year?" he asked calmly.

This question sounded calm.

"26!" Jessica truthfully stated, feeling anxious and uneasy.

"26?" Marcus bit onto this number with a hint of amusement. "How old is your son?"

"Mr. Marcus, that is my personal matter," Jessica replied calmly. "Haven't you always emphasized the separation of public and private affairs?"

In what tone are you speaking? You are only a few years older than me. Look down upon me for being so young and having a son. You might as well look down upon yourself.

Marcus seemed to not have heard what she said. He remembered something and his eyes turned dangerous, "Was it your son who called last time?"

Jessica didn't respond, which tacitly confirmed it.

A dangerous atmosphere filled the cramped car compartment, and Jessica's usual trademark smile couldn't hold up.

Yes, so what?

Her palms were sweaty from nervousness, her heart pounding. She didn't dare to look at Marcus's gaze at this moment.

Marcus's hand slowly tapped on the steering wheel, one after another, in a rhythmically and heavily. Each tap struck Jessica's heart heavily, suffocating her.

Marcus was angry!

No, he was furious!

What would happen if he knew about Henry's existence?

Night of Destiny

"Miss Jessica, you really know how to play pretend!" Mr. Marcus turned his head, the corners of his mouth curling with a smile. His gaze was filled with anger, but also a sense of mischief.

Jessica's face turned pale, and Mr. Marcus lifted her chin, his long fingers rubbing against her delicate skin. A pure masculine aura filled the air, sending shivers down her spine. A blush appeared on her cheeks.

Marcus's gaze swept over her graceful figure, his face filled with mischief, "Miss Jessica, I can't believe you have a son in elementary school, with that face and figure of yours."

Jessica's eyes deepened, and her lost smile reappeared as she reached out and brushed away his hand, "Mr. Marcus, my personal life is none of your business."

Mr. Marcus sneered, a teasing smile playing on his lips, "I can fire you!"

"Feel free to do so. With my qualifications, I have plenty of job opportunities. Losing me, Jessica, would be your loss," Jessica said with a slight smile, a hint of confidence and provocation in her expression.

"Such confidence!" Marcus smirked, his gaze suddenly turning heavy.

His gaze made Jessica feel uneasy.

She couldn't discern the emotions in Mr. Marcus's eyes - whether it was danger or boiling anger.

She had a child! Mr. Marcus was seething with anger, a fury bubbling up from within, almost consuming his rationality.

The thought of her alluring beauty and her intimacy with another man ignited a destructive rage in Mr. Marcus's piercing gaze. He wished he could tear apart her beauty and the man who had once possessed her.

A sudden shock ran through his heart, and Marcus's gaze grew even deeper. Was he going crazy?

This woman was the girlfriend of his sworn enemy, and her face... It resembled the woman who had caused him a lifetime of misery to a great extent.

If they were involved, how could he bear it?

He looked into the night with intensity, his thin lips pressing tightly together, his perfect profile appearing exceptionally cold and heartless in the darkness.

Chapter 16

Hatred

Jessica let out a long breath, successfully diverting his attention. If Marcus were to find out about her child, he would only be shocked. But the affair of the Lee Family was his taboo.

She forced herself not to think about the conflicts between the two families, as an outsider like her could never comprehend them. It was best not to touch them.

"Miss Jessica, you're unmarried but have a child. Who is the father? Quincy?" Marcus suddenly spoke.

Jessica's heart skipped a beat, a shadow enveloping her, almost taking away her every breath. She thought Marcus's attention had shifted.

"He had an accident... and passed away," Jessica said calmly, a tinge of sorrow appearing between her brows.

Marcus glanced at her, silent for a while. He couldn't help but sympathize with the child, because he also had grown up in a single-parent household and only returned to the Smith family at age ten, his heart aching.

A car accident, just like his mother...

He couldn't help but feel sorry for that child. He remembered that day's phone call, a very elegant child's voice.

When he was young, he was polite in order to receive praise from his mother. Timidly, expectantly, waiting for his mother's compliment.

That day, it seemed like he could sense that feeling of that child on the phone. Because he had experienced pain, he could empathize.

Jessica tightened her fist, the moisture in the palm of her hand revealing her nervousness. She couldn't let Marcus ask again. If he started to suspect and investigate her, everything could fall apart.

No one would believe that Henry's face was a mere coincidence.

"Mr. Marcus, please find someone else to accompany you to future Lee Family banquets!"

"What? Not happy?" Marcus sneered.

"You Smith Family and Lee Family have your own grievances, don't involve me in it. Mr. Marcus, I am just your employee, not a tool for your revenge," Jessica said with a faint smile. "Your father and Quincy's father have been competing in the shadows for decades, and now it's your turn to fight with each other. That's your world, it has nothing to do with me. Please don't disrupt my peaceful life."

A hint of fierceness flashed in Mr. Marcus's narrowed eyes, "Do you think you can just withdraw like that? Miss Jessica, you are too naive!"

Jessica's smile turned icy, her face darkened, and her sharp gaze swept over Marcus, "Has anyone ever told you that you are despicable?"

Mr. Marcus smirked mysteriously, seeming indifferent and distant as if he had a protective shell around him, "So many people have called me despicable, what difference does one more make?"

Despicable?

Jessica, your world is too pure. It seems, you still don't know what despicable means.

I... have long been sinking and struggling in hell!

A lifetime in darkness!

Jessica's breath hitched, she was furious. How could this man speak with such indifference and act as if nothing mattered when he cared deeply?

She despised this kind of Marcus.

This man always hid everything deeply, no matter how displeased he was, he forcefully kept it hidden, suppressing it with all his might. Even when his emotions were on the verge of collapse and there was life-saving driftwood by his side, he arrogantly refused to reach out, choosing to destroy himself. And to destroy others!

Clearly, he cared. But he pretended as if nothing mattered. This kind of Marcus infuriated Jessica.

After the anger, there was a hint of bitterness in her heart.

Has he lived this kind of life for over a decade?

"Miss Jessica, you resemble someone," Marcus suddenly said, his gaze fixed on Jessica's face, a flicker of emotion passing through. "If not for the age difference, I would almost think... Do you know? These past few days, looking at your face, I wanted to tear you apart."

Jessica's eyes flickered with surprise. But Marcus looked nonchalantly at the night sky, "Don't worry, I was just talking."

Jessica's heart raced.

Does he mean Diana? Who is this person? And why did Diana make Old Mr. Lee's face change so dramatically? Is she his ex-lover?

Night of Destiny

According to Jessica's knowledge, Old Mr. Lee had three mistresses throughout his life and had a son. After the birth of his son, he dismissed the mistresses and raised the son alone. However, in the second year of his son's marriage, after giving birth to Quincy, both the husband and wife died in a plane crash while on a business trip to Paris.

The Old Mr. Lee and his grandson, Quincy depended on each other, with Old Mr. Lee living a lonely life. The column for his spouse remained empty.

Could this be related to Diana?

But this is a grudge from the previous generation. What does it have to do with Marcus? Why does Marcus hate the Lee Family so deeply?

Marcus took out a photo from his pocket and handed it to Jessica. Her heart tightened as she took it, her face changing slightly.

The photo was a bit dated and slightly yellowed. The girl in the photo had a pure and lovely appearance, wearing a similar dress to the one she was wearing, and she was even wearing the Angel's Tears necklace.

Jessica looked at the photo in shock. The girl's facial features were remarkably similar to hers, especially her eyes...

"You two look alike, don't you? If she hadn't passed away several decades ago, I might have thought you two were sisters."

The man's refined features carried an eerie smile, looking somewhat sinister, "I always thought you looked familiar, but I forgot where I had seen you. It turns out it was through this photo. If it weren't for the day I glimpsed this photo in the study at the Smith Mansion, I would have completely forgotten about the existence of this woman."

"So, is that the reason you brought me to attend this banquet?"

"You're quite clever!"

Sect Elder Breeze

"Thank you for the compliment, Mr. Marcus. But in this world, are many people look alike." Jessica calmly concealed her shock.

It seemed like there was a grudge between Old Mr. Lee and Old Mr. Alston. Because of the hatred from the previous generation, Marcus had suffered. Is that why he hated her?

No wonder, in the past few days, his gaze towards her had been particularly cold!

But...

She just happened to resemble the person in the photo. Mr. Marcus, you're being too ruthless, aren't you?

So, isn't Marcus the original creator of this necklace?

Does that mean Mr. Marcus is plagiarizing someone else's design?

Old Mr. Lee and Old Mr. Alston must have known. Why didn't they say anything?

Jessica couldn't help but admire Mr. Marcus. It's rare to see a thief being so open and unapologetic.

Truly astounding!

"Diana Brown, do you know her? What's your mother's name?" Marcus asked sternly.

Jessica furrowed her brows slightly, a hint of annoyance flickering across her face. Seeing his distraught expression, she wondered why he was asking this. Could it be that he suspected her of having a connection with someone he hated?

"Miss Jessica, if you won't say, I can still find out. Do you want me to dig into your background?" Marcus warned coldly.

Jessica thought of her beloved Henry, her heart pounding. After a moment's hesitation, she said, "I don't know the Diana Brown you mentioned. My mother's name is Judy Black. She passed away when I was very young. Mr. Marcus, I am not so forgetful that I wouldn't recognize my mother. I have never even heard of this Diana Brown you speak of."

No connection?

Night of Destiny

Marcus had already suspected that Jessica was Diana Brown's daughter, so he deliberately showed her a photo to test her reaction. But her face showed nothing but confusion.

He felt shocked. Just a coincidence? Could there be someone who looks so much like Diana in this world?

When Marcus saw the striking resemblance between Jessica and Diana, he could have investigated her background. He even used his connections for that purpose but stopped midway.

He glanced at the girl beside him. She had a pair of bright and enchanting eyes, radiating a pure and innocent charm, always wearing a smile that seemed as warm as a spring breeze.

Her smile was fake, and Marcus knew it, but he still found it comforting. As her eyes swept over him, he felt a sense of familiarity, as if they had met before.

Marcus now realized that he was afraid of uncovering the truth through the investigation. Hence, he stopped midway.

It was ironic that Marcus, who feared nothing, would actually be afraid...

There were too many memories that had been left behind, carried away by the wind. Marcus forced himself not to dwell on those past events.

However, in the depths of the night, the haunting memories still lingered vividly, as if it were just yesterday. He wanted to forget, but he couldn't.

The Smith and Lee families, since the empire you both constructed are now crumbling.

Then, let's all...

Descend into hell together!

Why should I be the only one, wandering alone in this hell?

Even if it involves innocent people, he would spare no one!

Marcus tightened his grip on the steering wheel and abruptly turned the car. Jessica's heart raced, and due to her nervousness, a faint blush spread across her face.

What has Marcus gone through in the past? Why does he carry so many secrets, and so much pain in his heart?

Jessica still remembered him at the banquet, his tense body and deep, enigmatic eyes. Even when a hint of ruthlessness occasionally flickered in his gaze, it made her feel that he had endured too much. It was heart-wrenching.

How could the esteemed third son of the Smith family, who was upright and resolute, possess such despairing and sorrowful eyes?

She must be going crazy! If not, why is he constantly on her mind?

Jessica looked up at Marcus. Mr. Marcus stared straight ahead with his cold and indifferent eyes, deep and enigmatic, showing no emotions.

"Wait, how do you know where I live?" Jessica suddenly realized that Marcus's car was not far from her residential area, instantly raising her alertness to the highest level.

Marcus cast her a cold glance as if he was looking at an idiot, "It's on your resume."

"Um, it's fine to stop here, it's not easy to reverse over there." Jessica quickly came up with an excuse, calmly requesting to get out of the car.

But Marcus remained unfazed, "You're talking nonsense!"

It was a straight road, not easy to reverse? Was Jessica afraid of something while speaking nonsense with her eyes wide open?

The car stopped in front of her building. Jessica nervously tightened her dress and tried to open the car door in a hurry without even unfastening her seatbelt, but she was bounced back.

Suddenly, Marcus extended his long arm and firmly pressed Jessica's hand, raising an eyebrow to prevent her from getting out.

Marcus's palm felt warm, pressing against the back of her hand. Jessica felt the fiery heat of their skin on contact.

He leaned in, his presence exuding pure masculinity.

Night of Destiny

In this confined space, his scent filled every breath. It made her blush.

Jessica realized that her heart was becoming more and more unruly, almost bursting out of her throat.

Up close, Mr. Marcus's exquisite face was impeccable, as if it were God's most proud creation. His blue eyes shimmered with ripples, carrying a hint of devilishness and an elegant indifference, as well as a touch of mischief.

"Miss Jessica, what are you afraid of?" Mr. Marcus was in a very pleasant mood.

Seeing her nervousness while still smiling only gave him a sense of accomplishment.

Suddenly, Marcus had a strong desire to bully her, to make her cry profusely.

What would it be like to bully a woman like her? Just the thought of it made his blood boil and burn. Some women could ignite a man's protective instincts, while others sparked their desire for conquest.

It was apparent that Jessica fell into the latter category.

"I was afraid that you would meet your son," she thought to herself.

"Mr. Marcus, I don't understand what you're saying," Jessica tried to remain calm, shrinking her body as much as possible.

"Don't understand?" Mr. Marcus smiled, even more devilishly, leaning closer to her. His rigid body almost touched her breasts, his voice like a bewitching chant, "It seems like you really don't want me to find out anything about you."

Jessica's smile became even more perfect, but her heart raced. How could she forget that this man was intelligent and perceptive? He could decipher someone's thoughts by just looking at them.

Mr. Marcus, you are really terrifying.

While Jessica's mind was in turmoil, Marcus's attention was no longer focused on prying her secrets. His whole mind was captivated by the beauty in front of him.

Jessica's gown was designed with a deep neckline. Marcus's body almost pressed against hers, and his height advantage allowed him to admire the cleavage. The snow-white skin was as smooth as cream and exuded a subtle fragrance.

Nothing could be more captivating to a man's gaze than this.

Chapter 17

Second Kiss

Marcus's eyes darkened, sparks flickered, and he fixed his gaze on her two rosy lips. His throat tightened as the desire burned even stronger. His Adam's apple bobbed, unable to resist any longer.

He kissed her tempting lips, the ones that had enticed him throughout the night.

Her eyes widened suddenly, filled with astonishment. Her heart pounded faster, losing control to the point of feeling weak and powerless.

Had he gone mad?

Mr. Marcus held her lips, sucking lightly and biting, intertwining passionately.

In the end, he couldn't be satisfied with just a taste. He lightly tapped his teeth, his agile tongue conquering her like a wild beast, brutally plundering her sweetness in her moment of daze.

Night of Destiny

It was a brutally naked ravishment, almost taking away Jessica's breath and sucking out her soul.

The usually calm and cunning woman had her rationality shattered, stood there dumbfounded as Mr. Marcus unexpectedly kissed her.

This was her second time kissing Marcus, and in her whole life, she had only been kissed by this one man.

The feeling was exactly the same as eight years ago.

Panic, dizziness.

Her mind went blank, not thinking about anything else, as if the whole world was filled with only his face, his breath, and his scent.

The tingling sensation ran down her spine, rushed to her head, spun around, and spread through her limbs.

Mr. Marcus didn't know what had come over him.

Why did he impulsively kiss her like that?

Why?

In Mr. Marcus's memory, he had never kissed a woman before.

He believed that To love and to be loved was a sacred thing.

How many married couples could stand by each other for a lifetime?

When this thought entered Mr. Marcus's mind, their lips already parted.

Both of them were breathing heavily, their gazes locked firmly on each other.

His gaze was like a whirlpool, seemingly trying to suck out her entire soul. Her face blushed, and her heart raced like thunder.

Suddenly pushing him away, she hurriedly unbuckled her seatbelt and got out of the car.

A cool breeze blew, but couldn't dispel the heat and blush on her face.

She felt that if she didn't leave Marcus and breathe fresh air, she would die.

This feeling...
It was terrifying.
It made her both anticipate and fear.

She should have slapped him hard. Jessica thought to herself, a bitter feeling rising in her heart. Damn Marcus, what game is he playing again?

Daring to treat her as a woman he plays around with outside, she would have his son kill him.

"Miss Jessica, your kiss technique is quite inexperienced. Have you really been dating Quincy for eight years?" Marcus followed suit and got out of the car, with a smug expression, teasing her in a way that only a shameless flirt would.

His face was not ordinary. His deep and seductive gaze was like poppies, beautiful yet deadly.

It was said that men with deep gazes are the most passionate.

But Marcus, where is your passion?

Jessica smiled, keeping herself separated by the distance of the car, avoiding overly intimate contact. Her lost rationality began to return. She calmly said, "Mr. Marcus, actually, your technique is also quite inexperienced."

Honestly, Marcus's kissing skills were terrible, as if he hadn't improved at all in the past eight years. Several times, he even hit her teeth.

Though she didn't have any previous experience to compare it to, she knew that this guy's skills were really bad.

Marcus's eyes flickered, and his handsome face instantly darkened! His blue eyes brewed a storm.

That damned woman dared to despise him?

Why is she always able to smile and stab people with a single blow, hitting them right where it hurts?

Well, he admitted it. He was terrible at kissing. As the saying goes, practice makes perfect, but he had no one to practice with, so naturally, his technique was not good.

Night of Destiny

Being criticized for having bad kissing technique was as taboo as questioning his abilities in sex. It hurt his self-esteem!

Mr. Marcus glared at her fiercely, as if he wanted to tear off her dress, push her into the car, and prove his abilities in sex.

Jessica felt a looming crisis and cleared her throat, saying, "Mr. Marcus, I'm home!"

Mr. Marcus looked at her with narrowed eyes, unmoved, standing coldly.

Jessica froze.

You can't even understand such an obvious signal to leave, Mr. Marcus, when did you become mentally challenged? What does it mean to stand still?

Marcus looked up at the lights upstairs, his lips curling upward, "Miss Jessica, don't you invite me upstairs for a drink of coffee?"

Jessica was petrified, staring stiffly at the silhouette swaying upstairs...

Soon, she regained her composure, calmly took out several coins from her bag, and flashed a dazzling smile, gently placing them in Marcus's hand.

"Mr. Marcus, walk thirty meters to the left, turn right, there's a small shop. It's on me. Goodnight, goodbye!" Jessica maintained a high posture, as if offering Marcus a cup of coffee was a great favor to him.

As soon as she said it, she didn't have the courage to face Marcus's furious face. She knew the right time to leave and quickly disappeared into the residential area.

Jessica entered the elevator, panting like a cow, her face red like fire.

Did he just want to visit her home? Or was he interested in her son?

Mixed emotions flooded Jessica's mind, but whichever it was, it was not a good thing for her.

"80,000..." Jessica pondered, contemplating whether or not to resign, considering her monthly salary.

If this continued, she would have a heart attack.

"Money must be more important, right?" Jessica touched her chest and suddenly realized that Angel's Tears were still on her.

She furrowed her brow, fine, she could repay it tomorrow. This thing gave her an ominous feeling.

Like a cursed gem.

"Mommy, you're so beautiful that you're dazzling my eyes," Henry elegantly whistled and made a heart gesture with his hands. "I'll use mommy as the standard when looking for a wife."

Jessica giggled, her emotions stirred by Marcus and then alleviated by his son.

"Looking for a wife?" Jessica turned Henry around regardless of her image, embracing him tightly and playfully tugging on his ear. "Why look for a wife? Shouldn't you take care of mommy for your whole life?"

Henry furrowed his brow, pondering with a thoughtful expression, and reluctantly said, "Mommy, with your standards, I won't be able to find anyone. My mommy is one of a kind. Rest assured, trust me!"

In the eyes of little Henry, his mommy was the most beautiful person in the world.

Jessica smiled brightly, "Darling, your way of complimenting people is becoming more and more impressive. Come here, kiss me."

She planted a loud kiss on Henry's fair face, and all of her worries vanished.

"Mommy, your lips are so red," Henry's beautiful eyes narrowed into a seductive slit. He had seen everything clearly from upstairs.

His dad was quick!

Night of Destiny

Over the years, countless men pursued his mommy, but no one had ever gotten a kiss from her. Even with Quincy, whom she had the deepest relationship with, they only held hands at most.

Indeed, his dad had charm. Just for being able to kiss his mommy, little Henry gave him extra points. After all, it took courage to do that.

Jessica calmly cleared her throat, "It's lipstick."

"Really?" Henry cutely furrowed his brow, using an innocent expression to prove his purity. "Why does it look a bit swollen?"

Jessica couldn't bear it anymore and playfully tapped his head, blushing for the first time in ages, "It's not suitable for kids to see such a scene."

"What scene isn't suitable for kids? You can see people kissing in the park easily. Mommy, you're so out of touch."

"Henry..." Jessica gritted her teeth...

"Hush, mommy, be good. Let's see your signature smile. Being angry is not good for your skin." Henry elegantly touched Jessica's head.

Jessica suddenly remembered that Marcus had also said at the banquet, "Miss Jessica, show your signature smile."

The expressions of this father and son were indeed eerily similar. Blood relation was truly a complicated thing.

Jessica slumped her shoulders, on the verge of tears.

"Mommy, who is that man?" Henry knowingly asked, after all, he still wanted to know what the probability was for his mommy and dad to become a couple.

Jessica turned her head and squinted her eyes as she looked at her son.

"This high up, even if Henry were to see them kissing, he probably wouldn't be able to clearly see Marcus's face," she thought.

She felt slightly relieved and touched her belly, pretending to be pitiful, "Baby, Mommy's hungry..."

Henry, speechless, watched her play dead on the sofa.

Sect Elder Breeze

Little Henry scathingly gave her a disdainful look, "Mommy, you're such a glutton!"

Although he said that, he obediently went to the kitchen to heat up food that had already been prepared, and brought it out for Jessica.

"Baby, you are so considerate. As a mommy, I felt such a sense of accomplishment," Jessica said with a smile.

Henry smiled but did not respond. Because she was his beloved mommy, that's why he took such good care of her. As for others, he didn't even spare them a shred of mercy.

In terms of personality, Marcus and Henry were very much alike. The only difference was that Henry's disguise made him appear kinder than Marcus.

"Mommy, this necklace looks familiar."

Jessica choked on the food and coughed desperately. She loved spicy food, and Henry had put quite a few chili peppers in the food. The choke made her tear up.

"Why are you panicking, Mommy?"

Henry quickly poured her a glass of water, and it took Jessica a while to catch her breath.

"Do you recognize it?"

Since when did her son have knowledge of jewelry?

Henry shook his head, "It just looks familiar."

"Oh!" Luckily, she worried for nothing. Usually, Angel's Tears would appear when Marcus was around.

"Mommy must be tired. I'll go prepare a bath for yourself, and Mommy will take a bath and go to sleep after eating."

Jessica nodded, and the little boy casually walked into the bathroom.

Jessica suddenly realized that she had discovered her son's potential as a nanny perfectly.

******

In the study, Henry logged into WhatsApp.

Third Young Master had a glowing profile picture, and Henry's lips curved into a smile.

Night of Destiny

Henry was a computer genius, maneuvering global online transactions behind the scenes effortlessly. Obtaining Mr. Marcus's contact information was like a piece of cake for him.

A week ago, he had become interested and hacked into Mr. Marcus's account.

Mr. Marcus had been using WhatsApp for many years, and he had deep emotional attachments to it. Apart from anger, being hacked also presented a challenge to him.

After all, Marcus was also a computer genius and a rare one at that. Someone being able to hack his account naturally ignited Mr. Marcus's fighting spirit.

Father and son battled it out on the internet for two days. Henry emerged as the victor, and they developed a special bond during their exchange. Late at night, Mr. Marcus occasionally chatted with Henry.

Love My Mommy The Most: Hey, still not asleep at this hour?

Third Young Master: Annoyed.

Love My Mommy The Most: ??

Third Young Master: I kissed a woman tonight, annoyed.

Love My Mommy The Most: (⊙o⊙)...... Annoyed because you didn't get to sleep with her after kissing her, is that it?

Third Young Master: o(╯□╰)o, go away!

Love My Mommy The Most: Mr. Marcus, don't be angry.

Third Young Master: This woman has a face that I hate.

Henry pondered with his head supported. When did his mommy become so detestable? She was a great beauty. Could it be that his father had a unique taste?

Love My Mommy The Most: If you hate her face, why did you kiss her?

Chapter 18

Conversation Between Father And Son

Third Young Master: Who knows? If I knew, would I bother?

Love My Mommy The Most: You're strong! Beasts are truly impulsive.

Third Young Master: You brat, watch your mouth, I might turn against you.

Love My Mommy The Most: Aha, you're probably searching for my ID now. There are 1001 million IDs. You're going after them one by one, who knows, you might find out me among them.

Third Young Master: ...

Night of Destiny

Love My Mommy The Most: Mr. Marcus, how was the woman who accompanied you tonight? She must be amazing, with a beautiful face, good figure, and a good temper. She can do laundry and cook too, a perfect wife and mother. Are you tempted?

Henry promoted his mommy to his dad. After all, he was only stating the facts. At most, he could do the laundry and cooking, it's the same thing. Besides, it's a buy one get one free deal.

There was silence for a long time. Henry blinked his eyes. Is his dad petrified?

Third Young Master: Who are you exactly?

Love My Mommy The Most: Your son!

Third Young Master: ... Why don't you say you're my grandson?

Love My Mommy The Most: You're 28 years old, how can you have a grandson? Third Young Master: ...

Love My Mommy The Most: Mr. Marcus, should I help you find a date?

Third Young Master: I have many women, I didn't need anymore.

Love My Mommy The Most: ...Be careful not to make other women pregnant, I don't to have a younger brother or sister, otherwise I'll deduct points from you.

Third Young Master: Are you done blabbering? What date are you talking about? You can keep it for yourself.

Love My Mommy The Most: Oh, from now on, I'll use her as the standard when looking for a wife. My mommy, I feel sorry for her even suggesting her to you. Don't regret it if you don't want her.

Love My Mommy The Most: Plus, it's a buy one get one free deal, giving you a talented son for free. Such a good deal.

Third Young Master: Cheap things are not good quality.

Love My Mommy The Most: ...

Henry stayed silent, indeed, he underestimated his dad's sharp tongue.

Third Young Master: Let's chat another day. I will arrange a conference call with Saxon.

Love My Mommy The Most: As a filial son, it is necessary for me to remind you that there have been power disputes within the mafia recently. William and Saxon are double-crossing each other, and the diamond smuggling route is very dangerous. Saxon is a fickle and selfish person, so be careful. After all, it is an illegal business. If you get caught, who will take care of me, dear father?

Third Young Master: My good son, you can take down all the banks in the world by yourself and open an offshore account. How much do you want? Your dear father cannot afford to raise you, you know.

Love My Mommy The Most: Dear father, you have a wicked tongue. Be careful, my mommy might despise you.

Third Young Master: My good son, go wash up and go to sleep!

Love My Mommy The Most: Alright then, let me put it this way. Dear father, feel free to engage in smuggling and illegal activities. If anything happens, your good son will cover for you!

Third Young Master: My good son, feel free to manipulate behind-the-scenes online transactions. If anything happens, dear father will cover for you.

Love My Mommy The Most: !!!

My dear father, you will surely regret your words.

If you get into trouble, I will definitely protect you. After all, you are playing in my territory, you are a sideline, and I am the main event. If I get into trouble, I'm afraid no one will be able to protect me, unless Victor and Truman wipe out the FBI.

The little boy in front of the computer showed an elegant smile and opened the chat group of the aberrant assembly.

Marcus crossed his hands and supported his chin, his deep gaze falling on the pink piglet wagging its tail on the computer, feeling speechless.

Night of Destiny

Indeed, he was checking Love My Mommy The Most's ID, and there were actually 10.01 million IDs. Immediately after, the screen turned black and a pink piglet with a wiggling butt popped up. Love bubbles constantly emerged.

"Dear father, am I cute?"

Luckily, he did not have any water in his mouth, otherwise he would have spewed it all over the screen.

Who is he exactly? The profile shows that he is 7 years old and based in Paris. Could he be an idiot? How can a 7-year-old child manipulate such powerful behind-the-scenes transactions?

He almost controls 70% of the global arms trade, with involvement in money laundering and diamond smuggling, but even he cannot determine the exact extent of his control.

Truman was the world's largest arms dealer and the number one terrorist worldwide, but he just laughed and spoke in a familiar tone.

He even managed to dig up the highly confidential information about the diamond smuggling between him and Saxon.

Who exactly is this person?

Looking at the international arrest warrants, the top three are Truman, Victor, and Robin, one by one ruled out, and none of them fit the description.

It was evident that he meant no harm, and Marcus could even feel the goodwill and fondness conveyed by the other person through the screen.

A strange emotion.

The chaotic feelings caused by the banquet and Jessica unexpectedly subsided, and Marcus relaxed his whole being.

Is Saxon really fickle and selfish?

Marcus sneered. The present Marcus is no longer the Marcus who could be easily manipulated. Who could take advantage of him now?

******

Noblefull Group.

The next day at work, Jessica returned Angel's Tears to Marcus. The necklace was too valuable, and the feeling it gave her was too ominous. Holding it in her hand made her feel uneasy.

A smile crept across his lips, and his gaze fell on her white cheek, then lowered, his devilish gaze revealing a hint of wickedness.

The image of their kiss from the previous night flashed in her mind, and a chaotic feeling overwhelmed her. She felt completely disoriented.

Her smile was slightly forced.

Luckily, Marcus looked away after a brief moment, "You may leave now!"

"Yes!" Jessica breathed a sigh of relief.

Marcus only lifted his head after she left his office, and stared deeply at the closed door.

This woman sparked his desire for conquest.

What should he do about it?

Marcus crossed his hands and supported his chin, his blue eyes radiating a determined perseverance.

Jessica made a phone call to inform the department managers to gather in the first conference room. As soon as it hit 9 o'clock, Marcus went to the meeting with three secretaries, leaving Jessica and Susan in the office.

Recently, Noblefull Group had been planning a hot springs resort project. From the development department to the design department, people were busy and there seemed to be a routine meeting almost every day to report on the progress of their work.

After Marcus left, both women breathed a sigh of relief. They had done all the work they needed to do, and aside from occasionally taking a few phone calls, they had nothing else to do.

Night of Destiny

Susan came over holding a gossip magazine and teasingly winked at Jessica, "Jessica, how does it feel wearing Angel's Tears?"

Among all the secretaries, Jessica and Susan got along the best. Jessica liked her.

She didn't know which entertainment magazine it was, but they took a photo of her and Marcus. The sea blue Angel's Tears necklace was incredibly charming, with a hint of mystery that captivated the soul.

"How does it feel?" Jessica thought for a moment, smiled, and said, "Like eating a fly!"

Susan laughed and scolded her, pointing to the two people in the magazine, "Seriously, Jessica, you really have a queenly aura when you dress up. You're a perfect match with Mr. Marcus, a handsome man and a beautiful woman, truly a natural couple!"

Jessica took a glance at the magazine, then casually returned it with a slight smile, "I didn't feel that way!"

"How is that possible?" Susan teasingly winked, "Being with Mr. Marcus, didn't you feel a spark?"

It's more than just a spark, it's almost suffocating. If Mr. Marcus' handsome aura dares to be recognized as the second, then no one would dare to claim the first.

"Feel a spark? I don't know what you're talking about." Jessica denied it flatly, slapping away her teasing smile, "He's engaged, so give up!"

"Hmph... Mr. Marcus is like a poppy flower, charming yet deadly. We can only admire from afar, but not get too close. It's a pity!" Susan sighed.

"Poppy flower? I think he's more like a rotten egg with a crack in it, attracting only flies."

Susan laughed, "That's a good metaphor and quite apt. But speaking of which, this kind of man isn't suitable for us in our lives. Miss Crystal is Old Mr. Alston's chosen daughter-in-law. How can we compare to her? So as Mr. Marcus' secretaries, we must be able to withstand the spark."

Sect Elder Breeze

Jessica lowered her gaze, nodded, and covered the fleeting moment of trance.

Susan was right. She couldn't enter Marcus' world, and he couldn't enter hers either. So, Henry was destined to never have a father!

There was no possibility for her and him.

The elevator door chimed, and Jessica and Susan stood up. Susan's brow showed a hint of annoyance, but she respectfully bowed, "Hello, Mr. Dennis, Mr. Marcus is in a meeting. Please wait in the reception room."

Jessica understood in her heart. It was Dennis Smith, the second young master of the Smith family.

"Marcus intentionally, isn't he? He knew that I was coming today. Go and call him back now!" Mr. Dennis looked impatient and incredibly rude.

Susan sneered, while Jessica smiled, "Mr. Dennis, please wait in the reception room. Mr. Marcus will be back soon."

"You're the new secretary?" Old Mr. Alston didn't let him enter Noblefull Group, but he was still the second young master of the Smith family, Marcus' older brother. Marcus' subordinates didn't show any respect towards him at all.

Because of this, Dennis held deep grudges.

"Yes!" Jessica smiled.

Dennis felt pleased. His anger subsided a little, and seeing Jessica's innocent and beautiful face, he felt a desire to tease her.

Well, he had to wait for Marcus anyway, might as well pass the time. This new secretary was quite attractive.

He reached out and lifted Jessica's delicate chin.

Jessica's eyes turned cold, and she took a step back with a smile, "Mr. Dennis, please behave yourself!"

Dennis was taken aback. He had assumed that this young secretary was probably just an assistant who hadn't seen much of the world. He didn't expect this naive girl to ignore him too. Anger surged within him.

Night of Destiny

"Mr. Dennis, please wait in the reception room!" Susan said coldly.

Dennis pointed directly at Jessica and ordered, "You, go and make me a cup of coffee!"

"Yes!"

Jessica went to the pantry and made a cup of latte.

Susan pouted and whispered, "How annoying. How can he and Mr. Marcus be brothers? They are like night and day!"

"Jessica, let me take the coffee in. He seems to have taken a liking to you. Every time he comes to visit Mr. Marcus, he tries to harass someone. Last time it was Dora, and now it's you. He truly lives up to his reputation as a rotten egg."

"I'll take it in. He specifically asked for me. If it were you, he might unleash his anger on you. Don't worry, it's broad daylight. What harm can he do?"

Jessica pushed open the door to the reception room. Dennis was seated on the couch, with an air of unparalleled arrogance.

"Mr. Dennis, here's your coffee."

As soon as her hand left the tray, he grabbed her wrist and pulled hard, causing the tray to fall onto the carpet. Jessica was caught off guard and found herself being embraced tightly by him.

Dennis grinned, "A mere assistant secretary dares to defy me, huh? You've got guts. I'll show you how capable I am."

After saying that, grabbing Jessica's head, he moved towards her cheek to kiss her.

Jessica was filled with both anger and embarrassment. She never expected Mr. Dennis to be so barbaric and violent. There was a difference in strength naturally between men and women, and she was no match for him.

"Let go, you bastard!"

"Marcus has had a taste of you, right? Hmph, I want to taste it too!" Dennis smirked, pressing down the struggling woman, wanting to take advantage of her forcefully.

To be honest, with his status and position, even if he did something to Jessica, he could resolve it. Even if he couldn't handle it, Old Mr. Alston could handle it. With this assurance, Dennis dared to act so recklessly.

Jessica was furious and slapped him across the face. Did he think she was made of clay?

The slap made Dennis see stars, Jessica may appear innocent and lovely, but she had quite some strength.

"Susan!" she shouted.

Jessica took advantage of his momentary panic and poked his eyes while kneeing him hard in the crotch. Dennis screamed in pain, clutching his lower body, rolling on the carpet, and crying out in agony.

The three strikes for dealing with sexual predators have been tried and tested repeatedly, and never fail.

The door was forcefully kicked open.

Marcus silently walked in, his eyes deep and serious, even more calm than usual. But the intangible pressure he emitted made people fear from the depths of their hearts as if Yama was present.

"Second Brother, how interesting!" Marcus grinned, his cold gaze fixed on the struggling Dennis on the ground. A sneer filled his thin lips, full of mockery, a coldness that made people shudder.

Jessica quickly stood up from the ground, her clothes a bit disheveled. Her face was flushed, a mix of shame, anger, and more anger.

"Damn it, Marcus, she seduced me and pretended to be coy. You should fire her!" Dennis endured the pain and stood up in front of Marcus. Even if he was in excruciating pain, he couldn't show weakness and be humiliated.

This annoying girl, her kick was really heavy. He had to wonder if his cock was hit so hard that it couldn't get erect. The pain was unbearable.

She seemed so weak and small, but her power was unexpectedly great.

Night of Destiny

"Oh..." Marcus elongated his voice with a meaningful tone, his gaze sweeping over Jessica. Seeing her disheveled hair, and flushed complexion, slight anger appeared in his blue eyes.

"Mr. Marcus, Mr. Dennis is talking nonsense. It was he..." Susan wanted to defend Jessica, but Marcus gestured for her to be quiet.

If they had to explain such matters, then Marcus wouldn't be Marcus.

Anyone who dared to bully him was seeking death!

Jessica had no intention of defending herself, and Marcus was unlikely to ask her about what had just happened. Although they had only been together for a short time, their understanding of each other was complete.

How Marcus teased and played with Jessica daily was his source of amusement, and anyone who wished to get involved could dream of it!

Dennis couldn't figure out Marcus's attitude. Marcus exuded hostility and remained as cold as ever, but Dennis was certain that he wouldn't openly oppose him for an insignificant woman. Even though Marcus didn't consider him important, he couldn't get past their father's authority.

"Marcus, fire her!" Dennis commanded, glaring at Jessica.

Chapter 19

She Was Spoiled By Me

"Second Brother, are you the boss of Noblefull Group, or am I?" Marcus coldly retorted, a hint of cruelty crossing his blue eyes. "If you have the ability, take my position, and I won't stop you then!"

"Marcus, if you don't fire her, don't think you can get through our father!" Dennis threatened.

Marcus's gaze darkened, becoming even colder. The entire reception room seemed to freeze over. "Second Brother, what kind of words are these? You came to Noblefull Group to harass my secretary, and she simply defended herself. You were in the wrong from the start. Do you still have the audacity to make accusations?"

Jessica smirked inwardly. Honestly, if she hadn't known in advance that Marcus had a second brother named Dennis, she wouldn't have been able to connect the two. As biological brothers, they were so different from each other, weren't they?

Although Marcus had a dark side and ruthless methods, he was resolute and sharp-witted, an exceptional talent. Even his appearance was a rarity of good looks.

On the other hand, Dennis had a dignified appearance, a sarcastic manner, and no talent or virtue. Making him associate with Marcus felt like an insult to Marcus.

"Marcus, are you protecting her?" Dennis glared, suddenly bursting into laughter. "An insignificant woman who dares to hit the young master of Noblefull Group. Who spoiled her temper? Marcus, is this your subordinate?"

Night of Destiny

Marcus's eyes darkened, his aura domineering, arrogant, and arrogant. "She was spoiled by me. Do you have a problem with that?"

Dennis was taken aback, retreating in embarrassment!

Jessica's heart skipped a beat, her ears burning. This arrogant Marcus was the real Marcus, as if in the world, he was the only one who mattered and no one dared to say otherwise.

Regardless of the reason, this domineering and possessive tone made Jessica's heart feel complicated. It was like a mixture of happiness and worry, sweetness and bitterness.

These secretaries behind him looked at each other, sensing that the CEO's words were like those between lovers, a possessive love.

These women didn't think too much about it. After all, they had been working in this company for a long time. They also had some knowledge of the conflicts between the two young masters of the Smith family and simply saw it as their struggle.

Dennis held his breath and didn't want to get entangled with Marcus any longer. He was determined to retaliate for the humiliation. "Approve the money!"

His purpose for coming today was to get the money!

Marcus's eyes turned cold. A hint of coldness flashed across his lips. Money? He had already planned to give him that money. Dennis was a typical rich second-generation, indulging in all sorts of vices without any business acumen.

It seemed like all the business acumen of the Smith family was concentrated in Marcus.

That's also why, after weighing the pros and cons, Old Mr. Alston pushed Marcus into the position of the CEO of Noblefull Group, even though he disliked his son and even hated him.

"You want to open a jewelry chain store, and I agree with it. Dad said he would approve your funds, and I have no objection. However..." Marcus's voice elongated, "Recently, Noblefull Group has needed of funds as we are preparing to launch Angel's Tears no.4. So, unfortunately, your matter might have to be postponed."

Dennis flew into a rage, pointing at Marcus and yelling, "You did this on purpose?"

Saying that Noblefull Group was short of funds was simply spreading falsehoods!

"So what if I did?" Marcus coldly retorted, his brows icy. Even if he burned all the money, he would still be hundreds of times stronger than giving it to Dennis.

Jessica and the other women could sense the high tension between the two young masters of the Smith family. While one exuded dominance, the other was quick-tempered and easily enraged. In terms of dominance, Dennis was no match for Marcus.

Jessica secretly contemplated that it was an insult to Marcus to compare him to Dennis.

"You dare oppose me for a woman? Hmph, who do you think you are? Just a bastard born to a whore. What right do you have to be arrogant? Noblefull Group will still be mine in the future, and you won't claim a single cent. Let's see how you can convince Dad!" Dennis shouted.

Everyone's expression changed, including Jessica!

A bastard born to a whore?

Damn!

Could he really say such words? Jessica felt a surge of anger burning inside her, the first time she had felt such intense anger in so many years. This insult felt as if it were directed at her.

Marcus tightened his fist, making a crackling sound. Veins bulged on his forehead. Everyone could feel a strong, suppressed killing intent emanating from him. His eyes turned cold as if he were ancient ice.

Night of Destiny

Such heavy killing intent!

Yet, he remained standing straight. Despite Dennis's anger and desire to leave, Marcus was confident that he wouldn't dare to truly engage in a fight with him.

"Wait, Mr. Dennis!" Jessica suddenly spoke up, picking up a cup of coffee with an elegant smile. "You haven't finished your coffee."

"You, woman, are you crazy..."

Before he could finish speaking, Jessica flicked her wrist, and the entire cup of coffee poured down on him. The scalding heat made Dennis cry out in pain...

The women clapped their hands and cheered, delighted by the turn of events.

Marcus, with a murderous aura, slowly faded it away, his gaze towards Jessica now filled with surprise and complexity.

Dennis, in a disheveled state, brushed off his clothes and the coffee spilled on his head, raging with humiliation. He raised his fist to strike Jessica but was stopped by Marcus. With a stern glance, Marcus forcefully pushed him away and angrily scolded Jessica. Under the fierce gazes of the women, Dennis hurriedly fled in embarrassment.

"Jessica, well done! You taught him a lesson!"

"Jessica, you're amazing!"

"Jessica, I admire you..."

"..."

The women laughed heartily, bringing comfort to Jessica's heart. She didn't expect that Marcus, who seemed so twisted and dark in his mind, would gain the favor of others.

As everyone noticed Marcus's strange expression, they fell silent and left the reception room together.

Jessica's face burned brightly, her heart pounding. She couldn't understand why she had acted so impulsively when she could have restrained herself, just as Marcus had done.

Why couldn't she?

When Dennis had been about to bully her, she didn't become so enraged as to lose her rationality. It was only when she heard him insult Marcus that she became so furious, solely wanting to defend Marcus's honor.

But she knew she had caused trouble!

Dennis was the second Young Master of Noblefull Group, the beloved son of Old Mr. Alston. Although Marcus was the president of Noblefull Group, the Board of Directors was still under the control of Old Mr. Alston.

"Mr. Marcus... I, oh..." Jessica tried to explain her earlier outburst but suddenly felt her arm tighten, and her body collided with Marcus's broad and comforting embrace. Her face instantly flushed red.

"You..." Her question, which had been on the tip of her tongue, came to a sudden halt. She had completely lost the ability to speak.

"Don't say anything. Let me hold you for a while!" Marcus's voice was hoarse, and he held her tightly in his arms. His voice sounded as if it had been rubbed with sand, tinged with a touch of pleading. "Just for a little while!"

Throughout his life, Marcus had experienced countless hardships, but there was only one person who had protected him in such a way, his mother.

When he returned to the Smith family, Charles and Dennis had often bullied him. Beatings and scolding were commonplace, and young Marcus could only endure it without fighting back, because he didn't have enough strength.

After his mother's death, Marcus was sent to Australia. During those years, he didn't utter a single word. He escaped from the sanatorium and was sold to the black market for boxing matches. Those two years were the most humiliating and yet the most resilient years of Marcus's life.

Marcus had been on the edge of death, struggling and coming back time and time again, transforming from a child into a resilient teenager, going through a sharp change.

From then on, he repaid tenfold whatever he received, suppressed whatever he should hide, and endured as much as possible.

In the eyes of others, Marcus, with his strength, seemed almost invincible. But who had ever thought about him, fought for him, and protected him?

Only Jessica!

This woman he had known for a short time, in such a powerful and fearless manner, stood up for him and protected him, breaking the hard ice in his heart.

Jessica trembled as if her heart was wrapped in a thick cocoon, feeling as if her heart was being twisted by a knife. Biting her lip, she almost teared up.

This side of Marcus, she had never seen before. It was as if he was a child who had been wronged and was seeking comfort. Even someone as strong as him had this vulnerable side.

Her small hands clenched into fists then relaxed, clenched again, and finally, emotions triumphed over reason.

She embraced Marcus!

Just this once, Jessica, only this time!

She yielded to her own compassionate heart for him.

Marcus shook, his body slightly stiffening, his arms involuntarily tightening as if he wanted to pull her into his bone and blood.

Sunlight filled the entire room, casting a faint silhouette tinged with sadness.

After a moment, Marcus let go of her, and his deep gaze carried a complex layer of joy and worry. Jessica couldn't understand it clearly, or perhaps, she didn't dare to delve deeper.

Mr. Marcus's eyes were captivating, as if with one more glance, she would uncontrollably fall into them. This feeling was frightening, indescribable, and though she didn't reject it, she was somewhat afraid.

"I'll leave first!" Jessica heard her voice, calm and ordinary, without any fluctuations.

This warm embrace seemed to be just an illusion after Marcus's exhaustion.

As she turned around, her arm was pulled, forcing Jessica to turn back.

A faint smile brushed across the corner of Marcus's lips, his eyes were deep and calm. "Do you love me?"

With a bang, Jessica heard something in her mind suddenly shatter. A blush exploded on her cheeks, embarrassed and resistant. If there was a hole in the ground, she would probably not hesitate to crawl into it.

She loved Marcus?

How is that possible...

She had always been trying to avoid him, right?

She instinctively wanted to retort, but Marcus's index finger pressed against her lips, his eyes filled with a playful smile.

"Miss Jessica, do you think it's too late for an explanation now?"

His smile was clean. Unlike his usual coldness or indifference, it momentarily puzzled Jessica, unsure of his intentions.

"Mr. Marcus, your level of narcissism has reached a new high!" Jessica smiled.

Does she love Marcus?

Perhaps, he was a little special to her because he had a face that resembled her son's.

Henry was Jessica's everything, and she wouldn't let anyone bully him. Loving someone also meant defending them, and when she saw Marcus being bullied, she naturally thought of her son. It was this impulse that made her protect Marcus.

But looking at the towering Marcus, she couldn't express this tender feeling.

Everyone has their pride. In her heart, there was always a line that others were forbidden to cross.

He got too close, his heartbeat just an inch away from hers, yet their worlds felt so distant.

Close, yet a world apart.

Just as she was about to step back, she was held by the waist, and Marcus's eyes slid over her with a hint of amusement.

"Thinking of running away?"

The man's arm exerted a strong force, and she was tightly trapped in his embrace, unable to move. Marcus's aura surrounded her like a storm, suffusing her with a crimson flush. Her heart raced, and her thoughts became dull.

Mr. Marcus's domineering approach had an alluring charm.

Jessica felt annoyed, and when she looked up, she saw Marcus's half-smiling face, as if he was certain that she had fallen for him. He felt a mix of satisfaction, pride, and a hidden excitement.

She calmed down and gradually regained her rationality.

Peeling away her usual facade, Jessica's brows furrowed with determination, her gaze unwavering. She raised a confident smile that surpassed Marcus's.

"Mr. Marcus, do you love me?"

Marcus froze, his long eyes narrowing slightly.

Love her? Was she joking?

Only women have ever loved him, how could he possibly love anyone else, let alone someone with a face he despises?!

Chapter 20

The Hatred From His Father

"I do not love you!" Mr. Marcus's voice tightened as he denied decisively, hesitating for a second.

He admitted that this woman was intelligent, wise, beautiful, and capable, and was a mature and independent urban woman with all the qualities that make men attractive.

But he wouldn't love her.

Marcus would never love anyone again.

The people he loved would always leave him in the end, so what's the point of investing emotions from the beginning?

With her, he only desired conquest and plunder.

No woman could ever make him feel such a strong desire to conquer, and no woman had ever made him want to take away everything from her.

He wanted to ruthlessly tear apart her innocence. It was precisely because of her innocence that his darkness was highlighted.

Jessica smiled, the answer was within her expectations. With a bit of provocation in her smile, she said, "Mr. Marcus, since you don't love me, why would you lose control like this? Or is it that every woman who interacts with you, you care about whether she loves you? I don't think so, right?"

Provocative, who wouldn't be?!

Marcus had just pushed her into a corner, so why wouldn't she do the same to him?

Jessica never backed down.

Night of Destiny

Marcus's face darkened, and with narrowed dangerous eyes, he warned, "Miss Jessica, you're audacious!" His tone already carried a warning.

Jessica's lips curved up in a defiant smile as she took a step forward, locking her gaze onto Marcus's eyes. Her delicate hand pressed against his chest, and with slightly parted lips, she said each word forcefully, "Marcus, don't ask me whether I love you or not, you will never find an answer. If you want me to love you, it's simple, exchange it with this!"

With that, Jessica lightly tapped his chest and left gracefully while Marcus was still stunned.

She made Marcus truly understand what it meant to be audacious.

When the other women saw her coming out, they asked about the situation one after another. After all, Jessica had offended Dennis, the second young master of the Noblefull Group, a man who, although immature, was under Old Mr. Alston's protection. Marcus might not be able to protect her.

"I don't know, let's just go with the flow!" Jessica smiled faintly. From beginning to end, she hadn't mentioned this matter with Marcus.

She knew that she had caused trouble! Dennis would not let it go, and most likely would use Old Mr. Alston to pressure Marcus. If Marcus couldn't protect her, she could just leave.

She waited patiently for the outcome, being his secretary until Marcus found the right words to say. That was her top priority at the moment.

It was almost time to get off work. Jessica still had one document left to finish when she received a call from the supermodel Nydia. Nydia wanted to invite Marcus to dinner.

Among all of Marcus's women, Jessica disliked Nydia the most. Nydia always carried an air of arrogance, looking down on everyone with her spoiled and bossy attitude. She spoke in a commanding tone that irritated people.

Sect Elder Breeze

Especially towards Marcus's secretary, she seemed to have an inexplicable hostility. Every time she called, her tone was unpleasant.

Jessica wondered why Mr. Marcus was so indiscriminate. Could he tolerate a woman with such a personality?

Marcus didn't have any social engagements that evening, and Jessica couldn't understand his attitude. She asked for a moment and then transferred the call.

Susan finished her work for the day and saw Jessica's disdainful expression. She giggled and said, "When Nancy was still here, she detested Nydia the most. Her temper would always become so irritable after talking to her on the phone."

"Wow, Mr. Marcus's taste..." Jessica murmured sarcastically, "Not flattering at all."

Susan propped up her chin and opened a magazine. It listed more than ten of Marcus's women, including his official girlfriend Crystal, "See, find anything here?"

Jessica glanced over and flipped a few pages. Marcus's taste in women was a bit strange. They generally had a pure and innocent look, whether they were refined ladies or charming girls next door. Including Nydia, regardless of her personality, she was indeed beautiful.

She thought he would prefer hot and sexy beauties.

Well, judging by the list, he seemed to like women who appeared innocent!! Jessica thought mischievously.

"Look, they all have a pure look, and they all have a pair of similar eyes," Susan gossiped, playfully pushing Jessica's shoulder. "We've privately speculated that Mr. Marcus is looking for a high-end replacement."

Jessica was astonished and then snorted, "Susan, it's just a coincidence. Which beautiful woman doesn't have beautiful eyes?"

It was true that each woman had a similar charm upon closer inspection.

"It's not a coincidence, it's true. A few of us have studied it. Nancy thinks so too. Her husband has known Mr. Marcus for a long time, and she heard that Mr. Marcus used to like hot and sexy beauties. He must have someone in his heart but can't have her, so he's been looking for a replacement." Susan said mysteriously.

"Your imagination is too rich."

Is Marcus falling in love with a woman? Unimaginable, Jessica couldn't believe it, but looking at all these beautiful women, a strange thought crossed her mind. Susan's words made some sense.

As a ruthless and dark Marcus, what kind of woman would he fall in love with?

"Jessica, you better believe it..." Susan pouted her lips, suddenly stopped, and looked at Jessica, then at Crystal in the magazine, with a strange expression. "Jessica, haven't you noticed that you look somewhat similar to Miss Crystal?"

"Nonsense, where do we look similar?" Jessica glanced at her and pouted her lips. She always thought she looked more beautiful.

Jessica was quite self-centered.

Susan stared at Jessica, looking shocked, "Oh no, all of us have been secretly studying Mr. Marcus's women every day, and we never noticed that we have someone in our office who fits the criteria so well."

"Susan, you're nosy!" Jessica couldn't stand her. "Stop shouting as if I have a thing with him. I come from a poor family, and I'm genuinely innocent."

"I got it, I got it. Why are you so scared!" Susan looked at Jessica, then at Crystal's photo, clicking her tongue in admiration. But she would only blabber about this, as she knew better than to spread rumors, to avoid misunderstandings and gossip.

Although they initially doubted Jessica's abilities, just after a week, she proved herself to be a truly top-notch secretary with her outstanding skills. They were a few years older than Jessica and admired her.

"Jessica, Mr. Marcus had been quite calm lately. No scandals in the past couple of weeks," Susan said, wide-eyed with surprise, raising her voice unintentionally.

"Lower your voice!"

After Susan mentioned it, Jessica also realized that Mr. Marcus has been relatively well-behaved recently.

Did Mr. Marcus no longer live a promiscuous lifestyle?

The two shrugged, and Jessica smiled. As secretaries, it seemed they were all accustomed to gossiping about their bosses. In France before, she and some close friends almost gossiped about Lionel every day.

******

The door to the CEO's office opened, Marcus walked out with a cold expression, and the two gossiping women immediately separated. Susan skillfully hid the magazine under the computer desk, and looking guilt-free, displaying loyalty.

Marcus glanced at them, snorted coldly, sarcastically curling his lips, "Miss Jessica, you are really dedicated!"

"Oh, worrying about Mr. Marcus is my responsibility."

Marcus scanned her coldly, then looked at Susan, "Miss Jessica, Miss Susan, keep your voices down when gossiping about your boss!"

The two women froze.

Mr. Marcus, you're quite sharp-eared!

Marcus left with a flourish, and Jessica and Susan breathed a sigh of relief only after the elevator doors closed.

"Jessica, what did he overhear us gossiping about him?"

"You said he has been behaving well lately!"

But it didn't take long for him to misbehave again.

Susan sighed helplessly, on the verge of tears.

The two quickly packed their belongings and headed downstairs.

******

As soon as Marcus got downstairs, he received a call from Old Mr. Alston.

"Come home!" A brief command that couldn't be refused.

Marcus's thin lips curled coldly, brushing off the sarcasm. So soon?

In the dimly lit carriage, Marcus's gaze took on a shade of darkness.

Upon entering the Smith family mansion, both Old Mr. Alston and Dennis Smith were present.

Old Mr. Alston's expression was extremely sour, while Dennis tried to look pitiable. Seeing Marcus returning, Dennis wore a gloating expression, eagerly anticipating how Old Mr. Alston would scold Marcus.

It would be best if Marcus's power were to be stripped away, allowing him to take over Noblefull Group. Then he could do as he pleased.

"Marcus, why did you withdraw your second brother's funding? Give me a reason!" Old Mr. Alston slammed his cane against the floor, his anger surging, shaking the chandeliers in the hall.

After all, he had dominated the business world for decades. Even in his old age, that domineering presence remained. He had never felt much affection for Marcus. More than a decade ago, after the mysterious and perplexing case involving the Smith family, Old Mr. Alston grew to detest Marcus even more. If it weren't for Marcus's intelligence and exceptional business acumen, Old Mr. Alston wouldn't spare him a single glance.

Sect Elder Breeze

Old Mr. Alston, the titan of the business world, along with Old Mr. Lee, was once known as the overlords of the industry. However, due to Marcus and his mother, he became a laughingstock in business circles. Although this incident had happened over a decade ago, Old Mr. Alston still carried deep grudges, blaming Marcus for all the mistakes.

On a regular day, his gaze toward Marcus was filled with disgust and contempt, as if looking at something filthy.

This child was a stain on his life, a disgrace. Old Mr. Alston wished he had never had Marcus and his mother in his life.

"Noblefull Group is planning to launch Angel's Tears No. 4 soon. Best Wish International Group requested additional funding, and I have already approved it. The second half of the year's plans for Noblefull Group, aside from the spa resort and Angel's Tears No. 4, involve partnering with Best Wish International Group. Foreign businesses are more important compared to domestic ones, as Dad should be aware. Most of the funds for the second half of the year are allocated to these major projects. It's quite tight. As for my second brother wanting to open a jewelry store, let's postpone it for now!" Marcus said confidently.

Dennis disagreed and sneered, "Dad, he's just making excuses!"

"Dennis's jewelry store won't need much money. Marcus, are you deliberately making things difficult for him?" Old Mr. Alston sneered, giving Marcus a sharp look. "This is my command!"

In Old Mr. Alston's mind, although this son was detestable, if something were to happen, he would not hesitate to push him away and let him die. But his abilities were indeed commendable. As long as he obediently followed orders, the position of Noblefull Group's president would still be his. Otherwise...

Night of Destiny

Hmph, a sinister glint passed through Old Mr. Alston's eyes. He wouldn't give any consideration to father-son sentiment. Neither of them had any real feelings for each other.

"Dad, Noblefull Group has seized 60% of the jewelry sales market in W city, ranking fourth in the second half of the year. They are also going to launch new models, showing strong momentum. Second brother wants to open a jewelry store, is there a market? Even if I give him a Noblefull Group counter, he might not be able to afford it. It's a known loss-making business, why agree to it?"

"Marcus, don't look down on me!" Dennis became angry and countered in a stern voice.

Damn it! Marcus was just a son of a bitch, what right did he have to look down on him? If anyone should be looked down upon, it would be him, Marcus.

Old Mr. Alston gave Dennis a harsh look, implying him to shut up.

"I don't care if he can afford it or not, you must approve the funds for him, that is an order!" Old Mr. Alston said coldly, without any emotion, his tone carrying a warning.

Marcus may be the president of Noblefull Group, but Old Mr. Alston is the one truly in control.

Marcus may be ruthless and clever, but he wouldn't be able to overturn his ownership of Noblefull Group in just a few years.

Old Mr. Alston's current concern was not whether Marcus would approve the money or not, but whether Marcus would listen to him. The feeling of having someone firmly under his control was fulfilling. He didn't regard Marcus as his son, just as a tool, a money-making tool to help him manage Noblefull Group.

Family ties, oh, what a laughable thing!

Sect Elder Breeze

Marcus made up his mind this time and refused to give in, "Dad, I've mentioned before that we are short on funds. You can't just ignore Noblefull Group's expansion plan for the second half of the year, right?"

Old Mr. Alston became angry and stared coldly at Marcus. What had happened to his third son who was always like a puppet to him, allowing him to control everything? He was always challenging his authority.

Old Mr. Alston had always thought that he had him under control, Marcus wouldn't dare to contradict him and would obey his every command. Even if he despised the Smith family mansion, Marcus still had to obediently come home for dinner once a week.

When he favored Crystal as the daughter-in-law, Marcus didn't hesitate and immediately pursued her, succeeding in winning her over within three days, showing his loyalty to his father.

He had always believed that Marcus would always be in the palm of his hand, allowing him to mold and manipulate him as he pleased.

But recently, he had been constantly defying him.

He changed his chief secretary, favoring Crystal, who could keep an eye on Marcus closely. Just to ensure he wouldn't make a move.

But he ignored his command and hired a young lady as his chief secretary the next day, openly claiming that she was the top secretary in the Parisian secretarial world. When it came to hiring, Marcus only looked at one's ability.

This had already displeased Old Mr. Alston, but he could tolerate it considering it was Marcus's first act of defiance.

Who knew that there would be a second? He dared to challenge his authority again. It was unforgivable.

Chapter 21

A Tool For His Revenge

"Do you dare to disobey me?" Old Mr. Alston's voice was as cold as ice, each word was like a sharp rock.

Marcus remained expressionless and refused to back down, "Dad, please consider the overall situation!"

"I'm just burning money for your second brother to play with, do you have any objections? Do you really think Noblefull Group belongs to you?"

Marcus's coldness and calmness made Old Mr. Alston feel greatly embarrassed, and he couldn't help but reprimand him. There was inevitably a hint of mockery in his tone.

A pawn being played by him, daring to defy his orders, what an audacious person!

Marcus's lips curled into a cold smile, "If you want to open a store for second brother, use your personal funds. Noblefull Group is indeed short on funds!"

He repeated this excuse for the third time, which was considered unreliable by both of them.

Just because Dennis dared to tease Jessica on his territory, Marcus would never approve of this funding for him!

"Marcus!" Dennis trembled in anger, unable to believe that Marcus would defy their father.

Old Mr. Alston narrowed his murky yet sharp eyes, pursed his lips, and spoke sarcastically, "Marcus, the Noblefull Group is short on funds, and yet you have money to indulge in diamond smuggling. Do you think I'm a fool?"

Don't think he doesn't know about any shady business he's involved in. Does he really think that once he retires, he won't care about anything anymore?

"Smuggling?" Dennis screamed, wide-eyed and incredulous. "Dad, are you serious? Diamond smuggling is illegal, and the authorities have been cracking down on it in recent years. Marcus, you have some nerve to engage in such illegal activities!"

Marcus sneered coldly, responding to Dennis' outcry with a mocking smile. Did he think everyone was as foolish as him?

However, how did his father find out about this?

Marcus recalled the night when he opened WhatsApp because he was feeling annoyed. Love My Mommy The Most had mentioned that there have been power struggles in the mafia lately, and things were getting messy. There might be some treacherous moves.

He had a conference call with Saxon and probed subtly, but there were no loopholes.

Generally, once such treacherous acts were exposed, Saxon would become a target in this business. Who would dare to trade with him in the future? Marcus didn't quite believe that Saxon would willingly take losses to play this game. If there was a hidden hand on his side, that would be a different story.

"Dad, your information is indeed well-informed!" Marcus sneered. He had always known that there were his informants within Noblefull Group. His diamond smuggling operations were also carried out discreetly, without any evidence for others to catch.

He had confidence in this aspect.

Could it be that someone had set him up from the beginning?

Night of Destiny

"There's nothing in the underworld that I can't find out," Old Mr. Alston thought he had caught him by the neck and said arrogantly, "When I was involved in smuggling, you hadn't even been born yet. In terms of connections and routes, I am broader than you, young man. You still have a lot to learn."

"Is that so?" Marcus merely gave a cold smile and asked in a mocking tone, his icy eyebrows raising slightly. "So what?"

"What did you say?" Old Mr. Alston became angry and embarrassed.

"Dad, do you see his attitude?" Dennis complained dissatisfiedly. "Noblefull Group is your life's work, and he is using Noblefull Group's name to engage in such illegal activities. If he is exposed, all your hard work will go down the drain. Dad, are you going to let him continue tarnishing the reputation of Noblefull Group? Our Smith family will be ruined."

Right now, Dennis couldn't wait for Old Mr. Alston to immediately remove Marcus from power so that he could take over as the President of Noblefull Group.

Who is Marcus? Just a son born out of wedlock. Why should Dad let him take charge?

Dennis never thought of himself as inadequate. He only knew that Marcus had taken away his rightful power.

And Marcus, with a cold smile, said, "Dad, if you think there are problems with my management of Noblefull Group, or if you can't overlook my illegal smuggling activities, then it's okay. I am willing to step down from Noblefull Group. Second brother has always wanted to sit in this position, and I have no objections."

The elegant and cold man now showcased his elegance to the extreme, and no one could mistake the sincerity on his face.

Dennis's eyes lit up, but Old Mr. Alston's expression became somber.

Sect Elder Breeze

A storm was brewing in his eyes—how dare Marcus threaten him?

Although Dennis was his beloved son, Old Mr. Alston indulged him, yet he was not capable. Besides eating, drinking, and having fun, he didn't understand anything. If the vast Noblefull Group were entrusted to him, it would surely be ruined.

Although Old Mr. Alston was old, his mind was still sharp. Noblefull Group was his lifelong work, his pride. No matter how much he loved Dennis, there was no way he would hand it over to him. That would be equivalent to destroying Noblefull Group. Even if Old Mr. Alston despised Marcus, he still wanted him to keep the Noblefull Group going, until he nurtured Leonard.

He didn't believe that Dennis couldn't do it, and neither could Leonard!

At this moment, Marcus could by no means leave. If he left and Noblefull Group fell into Dennis's hands, within three years, before Leonard grew up, Noblefull Group would be destroyed.

He simply viewed Marcus as a tool. Until his goal was achieved, this tool could not be discarded.

Their gazes clashed directly in mid-air, sparking a fiery clash. Old Mr. Alston seethed with anger, Marcus remained calm, but their auras were equally strong, and neither was willing to back down.

Marcus made it clear—worst case, I leave Noblefull Group. Even if the Smith family blacklists him, he's not afraid. Marcus's main business is already overseas, and without Noblefull Group, he isn't concerned about survival. Noblefull Group was only a tool for his revenge.

Smuggling was merely a means to restrain Old Mr. Alston, preventing him from ousting Marcus until he had a firm grip on power and buying him time. Otherwise, he would drag Noblefull Group down with him!

Night of Destiny

"Dad..." Seeing that Old Mr. Alston didn't respond, Dennis impatiently urged, wondering how he could miss out on such an easily obtainable position and wealth.

"Shut up!" Old Mr. Alston scolded sharply. You idiot!

Dennis was afraid of Old Mr. Alston, and instantly fell silent.

"Marcus, won't you approve the funds for your younger brother, will you?"

"No money!" From Old Mr. Alston's tone, Marcus knew that he had taken a step back. His arrogance increased, and he spat out the two words, infuriating Dennis.

Old Mr. Alston was choked up and almost fainted. Marcus, you are truly arrogant!

"If there's nothing else, I'll go back first!" Marcus said calmly.

Old Mr. Alston stared at him with cold eyes. Marcus's lips curled into a cold smile as he turned and left.

Very well, Alston Smith, this is just the beginning!

"Dad, Marcus is too arrogant. Why do you indulge him like this?" Dennis was displeased, his eyes red with anger.

"You shut up!" Old Mr. Alston shouted angrily, Dennis was taken aback. After calming down for a moment, Old Mr. Alston continued, "Marcus had originally planned to approve the funds for you. Why did he change his mind? What did you do in his office?"

Old Mr. Alston, being a cunning and shrewd person, quickly sensed that something must have happened.

Dennis's face turned pale. He didn't expect Old Mr. Alston to ask him this question. He had teased Jessica first, and he knew it was his fault. He had always teased Marcus's secretary and was a lustful man by nature. Marcus was well aware of his character.

Sect Elder Breeze

In the previous instances, Marcus would at most mock him or watch from the sidelines with a cold gaze. Dennis had also insulted him many times, but he had silently endured it. He truly didn't expect Marcus to turn against him over a secretary.

"Tell me!" Old Mr. Alston thundered, striking the ground with his cane.

Dennis exaggeratedly recounted the whole incident, absolving himself of all blame. "Dad, Marcus must have been enchanted by that woman to behave this way."

Old Mr. Alston snorted coldly and cursed inwardly. Such a useless waste. If he had even a tenth of Marcus's capabilities, he wouldn't have had to endure this. He would have long ago kicked that irritating son out the door.

"Go out, Dennis. Can you at least do something worthwhile? Don't just laze around all the time, doing nothing!" Old Mr. Alston was frustrated with Dennis's lack of ambition.

He had dominated his entire life, so how could he have raised such a useless son?

"Dad, I understand..." Dennis awkwardly laughed, his expression filled with greed. "Dad, what about opening my own shop?"

Old Mr. Alston's gaze swept over, sharp and intimidating, causing Dennis's heart to race. It was terrifying! He almost tried to come up with an excuse to escape, but he couldn't let go of that money. He was unwilling.

Old Mr. Alston was extremely disappointed in Dennis. But no matter how much of a failure he was, Dennis was still his son.

"Go back to your room for now, and I'll have Vincent send you the money tomorrow!"

Upon hearing this, Dennis smiled with satisfaction and contentment as he went back to his room.

Night of Destiny

Old Mr. Alston sneered. It seemed that Marcus had developed ideas of his own. He couldn't tolerate it. This time, he must firmly keep him under control.

"Sir, please have some coffee!" The butler, Vincent, brought a steaming cup of coffee with a delightful aroma.

Old Mr. Alston had a special preference for coffee.

Rubbing his temples, Old Mr. Alston looked exhausted and asked his long-time loyal butler, "Vincent, do you think Marcus has rebellious thoughts?"

Vincent, a man with a loyal and honest face, had been with Old Mr. Alston for decades. He was incredibly loyal, witnessing Old Mr. Alston's glorious life and all his regrets.

"Sir, it may just be a misunderstanding!" Vincent wasn't speaking up for Marcus, but stating the truth. "Mr. Marcus personally chose the secretary for Noblefull Group and trusts her. Young Master Dennis's actions at Noblefull Group have caused some scandalous incidents before, and this time it might have gone too far. Perhaps it was a way for Mr. Marcus to teach him a lesson, not necessarily a deliberate act of rebellion against you, sir!"

"Hmph!" Old Mr. Alston felt anger. "Dennis is just useless, always causing trouble. I give him money to open a shop, and he'll most likely squander it away. They're brothers, but how can they be so different?"

This was Old Mr. Alston's concern, a very serious one. This was also why he disliked Marcus so much, even though he was his son.

Vincent knew the ins and outs of everything but didn't say much.

The grievances between the father and son of the Smith family were truly complicated.

"Sir, how about calling Young Master Charles son back?" Vincent suggested.

Sect Elder Breeze

"That's not possible!" Old Mr. Alston immediately vetoed. "Who doesn't know that Charles has been gone for over a decade? If he suddenly comes back, all the scandals from over a decade ago will resurface. Isn't the mockery of the Smith family enough?"

Vincent understood and remained silent. He knew that Old Mr. Alston would never agree to his proposal. The incident from years ago had far-reaching consequences. If Marcus were to find out that Charles hadn't died but was sent abroad by Old Mr. Alston after a severe injury, which resulted in the death of his mother, the Smith family would likely be thrown into chaos.

"Sir, it has been over a decade, and Young Master Charles's appearance has changed. Others may not recognize him. If he were to come back as your adopted son or some other identity, wouldn't that work?" Vincent suggested, opting for a middle ground.

Old Mr. Alston narrowed his eyes, closed them, and slowly said, "It's not that it's impossible, but it's too risky. If Marcus were to find out, he would risk his own life to bring Charles down with him. Otherwise, I would have brought Charles back already."

Vincent became even more silent. He was loyal to Old Mr. Alston and had watched the Smith family's children grow up. He knew how much Old Mr. Alston favored Charles, and he understood that he was being unfair to Marcus. But he couldn't say anything. The persistence can be deadly in one's life. Although Marcus was his son, he was treated as an enemy. Why bother?

Mr. Marcus was undoubtedly the best choice to take over the Noblefull Group, no matter how he looked at it. His abilities and skills surpassed the other three young masters by far.

But Vincent knew that Old Mr. Alston didn't like to hear such things, so he never said them.

"Call Old Mr. Walker and invite him to dinner!"

"Yes!" Vincent received the order.

Old Mr. Walker? Crystal's father. Could it be that the master wanted Miss Crystal to marry into the Smith family?

Considering Marcus's recent rebellious attitude, this matter was probably hanging by a thread. Vincent didn't know whether Marcus liked Crystal or not. There were rumors about their deep affection for each other. But...

Chapter 22

Henry's Secret

Jessica rented a spacious apartment with four bedrooms and two living rooms. It was Friday, and Jessica returned home only to find that she couldn't smell the aroma of food. She pouted. Hadn't her precious son returned yet?

As she set down her briefcase, she noticed that the door to Henry's study was slightly ajar. Jessica smiled. What was this kid so busy with? He even forgot to prepare a meal for her?!

Curiously, she pushed the door open.

Jessica had always given Henry plenty of space. She knew that her baby often spent time on the computer and had some secrets he kept from her. However, she never interfered. As long as her son was happy, she wouldn't interfere in his personal matters.

Her love for Henry was unconditional. He hadn't developed a spoiled and arrogant personality, but rather remained elegant and considerate, which had surprised Jessica.

"Sweetie, what are you doing?" Jessica entered the room.

Normally, when she entered, Henry would always close some things and switch to playing games. At first, Jessica thought he was genuinely playing games. It seemed that whatever her son was doing had little to do with her. She only knew that her son was caring and filial, and she didn't concern herself with anything else.

The little boy was sitting properly in front of the computer, fingers flying across the keyboard, seemingly unaware of Jessica's words. His pale face was tense, his eyes fixed firmly on the screen, showing a serious and even chilling expression.

This was the first time Jessica had seen her son not smiling. Her heart skipped a beat as he resembled a small Marcus, looking quite scary.

She almost thought that Marcus had possessed her precious baby.

A few drops of cold sweat formed on Henry's perfectly white forehead. He was tense all over, with an extremely terrifying and cold aura surrounding him.

"Sweetie?" Jessica called out with some concern. What was he doing?

Her gaze was fixed on the computer screen, which looked like a map with intersecting lines, forming a network. It also seemed like a three-dimensional space, with four red dots and one black dot moving rapidly.

It was a mess of addresses, forming a bizarre map.

It was a model of a city. Jessica wondered what he was doing.

The little boy kept entering commands. Accompanied by some strange sounds that made her heart tremble.

Night of Destiny

Jessica couldn't understand. She had never understood such profound things. She had always wondered how her baby understood them.

Henry's hands were constantly typing on the keyboard without pause.

The room was quiet, with only the sound of the keyboard clicking, unusually quiet, so quiet that Jessica felt a terrifying dread.

As a mother who knows her child, she had a gut feeling that her son was in trouble. Her hand slowly rested on his shoulder.

The little boy stiffened, and Jessica silently conveyed her comfort and support. No matter what her baby did, she would support him because she believed in him! Afraid of affecting him, Jessica didn't speak anymore and slowly left the room.

That brat, if he doesn't confess soon, he's done for!

Returning to her room, and changing her clothes, she started cooking. Jessica's cooking skills couldn't be compared to Henry's at all. That's why after Henry learned how to cook, she stayed away from the kitchen. It had been a long time since she cooked, and it was estimated that she had become even worse at it. Jessica sighed.

Should she wait for Henry to come out and cook?

She now realized that she was really spoiled. Without her son, she couldn't even have a meal.

In the study, Henry narrowed his eyes, a hint of a smirk passing over his lips. He quickly tapped a few keys on the keyboard, and soon, the black dots disappeared in the three-dimensional space, and the labeled place names swiftly switched.

Boom... Several sparks burst out suddenly as if there was an explosion.

One after another, Henry laughed, claiming victory!

Challenge me, hm, overestimating your abilities!

The little boy opened a chat group, and it was in chaos. Everyone was speculating on the results.

Sect Elder Breeze

Henry smiled slightly, watching them stir, and casually pulled up the file from earlier, infiltrating the counter-terrorism organization's database with a sinister smile.

Truman: That bastard Cornell used foul means. Damn it! Tonight I will issue an arrest warrant. I can't let go of my hatred without killing him.

Monster: Killing him is simple, wiping out his entire family is the true deal.

Robin: No news for such a long time. He didn't really get caught, did he?

Truman, Monster: Shut up!

Robin: ...

Counter-Strike: You bastards, didn't I warn you not to mess with Cornell? Dammit, you already have control over the Mexican arms market, do you still want to swallow the entire Middle East? Oh, my God...

Never Give Up: Captain, this time it's unexpected. Cornell joined forces with the FBI. Why didn't you inform us earlier?

Everyone: Exactly!

Counter-Strike: Dammit! You guys are terrorists. I'm the Chief Inspector of the International Counter-Terrorism Special Action Group!

Robin: That's true, different factions, but... Captain, honestly, you're not being generous enough this time.

Monster: It's alright. Those weapons were equipped with the latest explosive systems. As long as Henry destroys the evidence, it's fine.

Truman: Henry, say something, hey...

Counter-Strike: You deserve it, aha... Once you all were arrested, I invited you to have coffee at the FBI headquarters! It's so glorious, five of us in the top ten of the international most-wanted list, oh ahahaha...

Everyone: Get lost!

Never Give Up: My Henry, you have to hang in there...

Night of Destiny

Rainbow: Actually, it's Victor and Truman's fault. You guys don't understand who Cornell is. You dare to fall into their trap. So stupid. It's tough on my Henry... I don't know if my talented Henry can handle the four of them together.

Miracle Doctor: Stay calm, everyone!

Love My Mommy The Most: It's settled!

Counter-Strike: Dammit! Henry, did you hack the counter-terrorism organization's database???

Love My Mommy The Most: Yes!

Counter-Strike: ...Dammit!

Everyone: Henry truly is Henry, the most formidable!

Never Give Up: Henry, now that this matter is resolved, you should deal with the other ones as well. Truman, talk to Henry as soon as possible.

Never Give Up: Recently, the FBI has been acting too frequently.

Truman: Henry, the Mexican arms...

Counter-Strike: Truman, you terrorist, do you think I don't exist?

Truman: ...Captain, I was wrong! ...Henry, the money laundering lines were blocked by the federal authorities. Can you help me fix it and transfer the funds to a dummy account?

Robin: In addition to the lines being blocked, the underground bases in the Middle East are also under surveillance by the federal authorities. They captured an undercover agent just yesterday. Most likely there's a mole. Henry, set a trap and catch the mole!

Counter-Strike: Dammit, you guys are committing crimes!

Never Give Up: Captain...

Monster: Henry, Truman's issue is the most urgent. The Australian cabinet has already formed a Special Action Group to intercept. You need to destroy the evidence immediately. Robin's case can be put on hold for now.

Counter-Strike: No! Henry, if you dare to do this, I will arrest you!

Robin: Captain, did you find evidence? If you find the evidence, I will surrender myself to the FBI.

Counter-Strike: ...

Miracle Doctor: Captain, you're all alone here, everyone here is a terrorist. Shouldn't you go home and get some rest?

Rainbow: Captain, look here, smile...

Others suddenly fell into silence!

Counter-Strike: Henry, give me the evidence of Robin's money laundering!

Robin: Hey hey, Counter-Strike, I'm still in this chatting group, are you provoking me?

Counter-Strike: So what if I'm provoking? If you guys don't commit crimes, won't you die?

Robin: No!

Monster: No!

Truman: No!

Counter-Strike: Dammit!

Counter-Strike: Truman, Robin, Victor, I warn you, the FBI has arrested you on charges of drug smuggling. Be careful, if I catch you, I'll have you shot.

Truman: Captain, my main business is arms smuggling. Captain, you have to believe in my innocence, I'm just a scapegoat.

Robin: Captain, my main business is money laundering and online transactions. Please believe me, I'm innocent.

Monster: What you said is what I wanted to say.

Never Give Up: Hahaha, Captain, you're leaking information...

Miracle Doctor: We have to understand the Captain's difficulties.

Never Give Up: Captain is truly a saint.

Rainbow: I told you, Captain is very fond of us...

...

Love My Mommy The Most: Truman, give me three days. You'll get every penny to be deposited without a single deduction.

Night of Destiny

Love My Mommy The Most: Robin, I want you to personally go to Arabia and find Edward. He is an expert in this field. Let me greet him later and avoid the FBI's surveillance. He has the most experience.

Love My Mommy The Most: Victor, your internal security has been breached. I'll get you a new one in a couple of days.

Love My Mommy The Most: Captain, you want their criminal information? No problem, I'll give you a file. As long as you crack the password, it's all yours.

Counter-Strike: Damn, are you talking nonsense?

Love My Mommy The Most: Captain, I have a suggestion - the Middle Eastern arms dealers and the largest Chinese gang in Australia are allying. This case is going to give you a headache. I suggest you withdraw the undercover agents from Robin, Victor, and Truman's side and engage in insider trading. It will be much easier to catch them that way.

Truman: Henry, you're so cunning! Are you sure this isn't for our benefit to monopolize the arms trade in the Middle East?

Love My Mommy The Most: What do you think?

Counter-Strike: Damn, you terrorists.

Robin: Henry, I love you. Captain, I'm willing to cooperate.

Monster: Thanks, Henry. Captain, as a law-abiding citizen, I'm willing to support all your actions. By the way, they have already established contact with me.

Robin: I would also like to add that we just had a conference call an hour ago.

Truman: Well, I won't say anything then. We all understand.

Counter-Strike: Damn it!

Never Give Up: Wow... As they say, the authorities and criminals are in cahoots. You guys are really shameless.

Rainbow: Henry, I adore your cunningness. I want to marry you!

Sect Elder Breeze

Love My Mommy The Most: Hmm, if you were 20 years younger, I might consider.
Everyone: ...
Miracle Doctor: Antarctica is a good place.
Counter-Strike: You guys just wait, don't end up in my hands. Henry, when will the alliance take place?
Love My Mommy The Most: Next month!
Counter-Strike: I'm going to a meeting!
Everyone: Get lost!
Never Give Up: Henry, did you really give him our criminal records?
Love My Mommy The Most: I already sent them to him!
Everyone: ...
Love My Mommy The Most: One should be fair!
Everyone: ...
Love My Mommy The Most: Truman, last week, didn't Noblefull Group have a batch of light weapons trade with you?
Truman: Yeah, Marcus is quite ruthless. I've never encountered such a badass businessman before. He almost made me lose money by bargaining hard on the price.
Love My Mommy The Most: Destroy your trade records, or give me the original documents.
Truman: ???
Love My Mommy The Most: No reason.
Truman: I won't give it. It's our internal information.
Love My Mommy The Most: Don't force me to challenge you.
Truman: Hey, hey, hey, Henry, is he your father? Why are you protecting him so much? Fine, I'll give it.
Never Give Up: (^o^)/ Don't you know? He destroyed all of Marcus' criminal records. Oh, oh, oh, there's an affair involved.

Night of Destiny

Robin: Exactly, Mr. Marcus had a money laundering deal with me a few years ago. When Henry asked for the records last month and I refused, he wiped out my database that same night.

Monster: Who is Marcus to you, Henry? Come clean.

Rainbow: On a side note, I've always admired Mr. Marcus' performance in the boxing ring in Australia a few years ago. He was amazing.

Never Give Up: That was over a decade ago, right?

Love My Mommy The Most: Boxing ring? What's going on?

Robin: Don't you know? Mr. Marcus spent two years in the underground boxing scene. Lennon is a freak. When Mr. Marcus was only 12 years old, he had him fight against Michael Lee and he actually won. It caused a sensation in the whole underground boxing world.

Never Give Up: Wasn't he autistic for three years? At that time, he was the hottest person in the underworld. People thought he was mute. As long as there was a boxing match, Lennon made him participate. They saw him as a money-making machine. But he seemed to be reckless as well. Even when he was beaten half to death, he still went back into the ring.

Miracle Doctor: Apart from his time in the boxing ring, Mr. Marcus had some even more sensational accomplishments in Australia over the years. I was young at the time and only had a brief encounter with him. I thought he was from a poor family somewhere, but who knew he was the young master of the Noblefull Group?

Sect Elder Breeze

Monster: All of these things have been erased. That underground boxing ring he was in in Australia a few years ago, mysteriously disappeared. And, about a decade ago, there were rumors that Marcus was taken away by Tony from the Myron Church for training. Then, eight years ago, the entire Myron Church was annihilated overnight. All of these things have something to do with him, but almost all of the evidence has been eliminated.

Robin: There were two main figures in the Ghost Gang, one light and one dark. It was rumored that Mr. Marcus was the mastermind behind it all.

Rainbow: Henry, why aren't you saying anything? Are you still here?

The little boy in front of the computer had a gloomy expression. On the small pink face, there was a murderous aura.

Love My Mommy The Most: Robin, Truman, use your connections to cover up his past completely.

Robin: Marcus himself is a computer genius. He erased his own past a long time ago. I'm afraid, apart from us, there are very few people in the world who know about his past.

Monster: Henry, who is Marcus to you?

Robin: Whoever he is, if you don't want Mr. Marcus to get into trouble, we have all the criminal information about Marcus. We will destroy it all, don't worry.

Truman: From now on, I owe you a favor. I'll give him a 70% discount, fair trade. I'll personally connect him to the arms smuggling route, guaranteeing that everything will go smoothly.

Never Give Up: Speaking of which, Noblefull Group has a batch of diamond smuggling activities. However, the contact person is Saxon from Italy. There must be something fishy going on during the power transition recently. The current route is not secure. They probably want to play a trick. You should tell Mr. Marcus to be careful.

Love My Mommy The Most: I've already reminded him!

Night of Destiny

Monster: How about this, Henry? Let him come to me. I will take care of the diamond smuggling for Noblefull Group in the future, guaranteeing that I won't take advantage of him and nothing will go wrong.

Miracle Doctor: What can I do? Oh, I got it. If Mr. Marcus ever gets a terminal illness, as long as he is still breathing, come to me. I guarantee everything will be fine.

Everyone: ...

Love My Mommy The Most: Thanks. Victor, when you go to Italy, please investigate Saxon for me. I feel like something is not right about this.

Monster: Understood!

Almost in unison: Henry, who is Mr. Marcus to you?

Love My Mommy The Most: He's My Dad!

Everyone: Shocked!

Everyone: You're playing us!

Henry propped up his head and muttered to himself, "I'm telling the truth, why doesn't anyone believe me?"

Chapter 23

Ex-boyfriend's Visit

Love My Mommy The Most: We've been having quite a few issues lately. Have you all been on vacation for too long and gotten lazy?

Everyone: ...

Love My Mommy The Most: Those four FBI guys are pretty good. Victor and Robin, find a time to play with them. I suspect they have a special tracking system. With that, it'll be much easier to infiltrate their systems and maybe even find a list of undercover agents.

Miracle Doctor: Is this the legendary 'catch them all'?

Robin: Hey, babe. You're really smart. Got it, Victor and I will join them to play right away. If we can't handle it, then we'll let you go in.

Love My Mommy The Most: Okay, I'm logging off now!

After saying goodbye, Henry logged off.

He closed the computer and propped up his head, pouting. His mommy caught him. He smiled and left the study.

Sure enough, Jessica was leisurely sitting on the sofa, looking at her reports, waiting for her baby to come out and cook for her.

"Mummy, I promise I won't get into trouble, don't worry!" Henry walked over, kissed her on the cheek, and gracefully smiled. "Aren't you happy?"

Jessica rubbed his head and patted it hard. Henry frowned and looked at her with a pitiful expression, his eyes portraying an innocent.

"What were you doing just now?" Jessica asked.

Henry sighed and didn't hide it.

"I have a few friends who are involved in an arms deal. The buyer is colluding with the FBI, trying to catch them all. Luckily, my friends had a contingency plan in place, rigged with a bomb system. When something went wrong, I went to cover up the evidence. The FBI happened to have four people tracking them, so I played along for a while."

He also blew up the counter-terrorism organization's database, since they had been annoyingly entangling him and mom found out.

Jessica's heart skipped a beat. A few friends? Arms deals? FBI?

Was she in a fantasy?

Damn it!

"Who are your friends?" she asked.

Henry smiled mysteriously and gently placed his little hand on Jessica's heart. "Mummy, you have to stay calm..."

Jessica instantly had a bad feeling.

"Truman, Atwood, Victor, Robin, Gordon..."

"Stop!" Jessica's voice trembled as she shouted to stop. Even though she was usually calm, she found it too unbelievable. The three names her son casually mentioned were actually the top three global terrorists.

Because Lionel was also involved in shady dealings and arms trading, he had even had a conference call with Truman. As his chief secretary, Jessica knew everything.

Not to mention, there were often terrorist events happening abroad, and these three names were well-known to anyone who paid even a little attention to international affairs!

Her well-behaved son, how did he get involved with these people?

"Baby, how long have you known them?"

"For a year!"

"So, does that mean this year, you've been involved in illegal activities?" Jessica's voice trembled, where had her innocent baby gone?

Henry elegantly smiled and rubbed Jessica's hand with his small hand.

"Mommy, there are too many loopholes in arms control, even if they don't smuggle, others will. Although Truman and his group are terrorists, walking on the edge of the law, they can't be considered good people in the traditional sense... but they are worth befriending!"

They may be cold and ruthless, but they always have consistent principles - I don't bother people if they don't bother me, and they value loyalty and emotions. While the world sees them as terrifying, Henry thinks they can be adorable at times.

Their ruthlessness always has reasons behind it.

Who would willingly become a globally wanted person for no reason?

"I thought you would be content with being a top-level gangster, why did you directly upgrade to being a terrorist?" Jessica sighed helplessly.

Henry elegantly laughed, "Mommy, let's consider the situation in city W. There are also quite a few people playing arms smuggling. Mr. Quincy, who you consider a good person, also commits crimes. That's how the business world is - money reigns supreme!"

"Besides arms, what else do you dabble in?" Jessica felt it necessary to thoroughly understand her precious child.

Henry cleared his throat and pouted, "Diamond, smuggling, money laundering... those are my specialties."

"What about drugs?"

"I swear on my integrity, absolutely not!" Henry said earnestly, "I would never touch that, Mommy, trust me!"

"Trust my foot!" Jessica lightly hit his little head. She couldn't help but wonder why this little child had so much knowledge. Why was he so twisted?

Mr. Marcus, did your genes go wild?

Or has Henry mutated?

Night of Destiny

"Sweetie, a counterterrorism inspector from the FBI once said that there are people behind the three major terrorists, manipulating them. Is it possible that person is you?" Jessica could no longer stay calm.

She admired herself for still being able to sit there calmly.

Henry cleared his throat again, his voice getting quieter, "Seems like, perhaps, it might be!"

Jessica was completely struck, looking at Henry with an expression of "I don't know you."

"Sweetie, Mommy wouldn't mind breaking the mother-son relationship, you know? Maybe they switched babies at the hospital, just look at you, you don't look anything like me." Jessica was flustered!

"Mommy..." Henry stared at her with a pair of innocent eyes, accusing Jessica of being heartless.

With a serious expression, Jessica nodded calmly as if afraid that Henry wouldn't believe her, "Mommy is being serious!"

Henry pouted, and Jessica immediately surrendered, thinking that if her son was a bit twisted, she had a part in it too.

"Whatever you choose to do in the future, just be careful and don't tell Mommy about such thrilling things. Your old mother has a weak heart!"

Henry,"..."

Henry smiled and continued, "Mommy, I know that senior inspector from the FBI... "

Jessica's first reaction was, "Collusion between officials and bandits?"

"You could say that!" Henry said slowly, "Mommy, so-called terrorists are not as terrifying as they are made out to be. Captain and Truman have been old friends for many years. They even came from the same training camp. Anyway, no matter how they try to control arms smuggling, they can't. Instead of letting strangers smuggle, which would increase the instability of international terrorist organizations, it's better to let someone familiar with it do it. Captain can discreetly divert the flow of arms, avoiding the chaos of fluctuating prices in the arms market. Moreover, by having people he trusts to control the arms market, he can engage in insider trading, and exchange information with international gangs and drug trafficking organizations. Every major international crime that has been solved was helped by Truman and Victor. These smugglers have become so adept at their crimes that it's not easy to catch them. So, if you want to talk about collusion between officials and bandits, it's not entirely incorrect."

Jessica looked at her son in astonishment. She had always known that this kid was abnormal, with an extremely high IQ, but he shouldn't be this frightening, right?

"So, you mean someone is protecting you, so nothing will happen?" Jessica just wanted to confirm this.

Henry sneered, "Even if no one is protecting me, nothing will happen!"

"Can't you be a little more arrogant?" Jessica gave him another tap on the head, and Henry covered his head, pouting in protest.

"Mommy, aren't you angry?" Henry asked with some concern. If Mommy got angry, he could immediately withdraw and obediently be her intimate little darling, as he loved her mother the most, just as his online nickname suggests.

"I'm not angry. My son is so successful, and mommy is very proud..." Jessica praised first, then said, "As long as you don't go astray, mommy doesn't mind."

Henry secretly thought, Mommy, this isn't considered going astray, then what would be?

Jessica's idea was that whatever path her son chose, it would be the right one!

What is called spoiling, this is it!

This mother-and-son duo got along the best in history!

"Alright, I won't meddle in your affairs, baby. It's time to cook, Mommy is starving!" Jessica complained. Whatever he did, he had to take care of her stomach beforehand; that was the important matter!

"Yes, my dear Mommy!" Henry smiled and obeyed her order, going to the kitchen to cook.

"Baby, Mommy is free tomorrow, do you want to go out and play?" Jessica picked up the report and said while reading it. She decided to let her son enjoy his childhood to the fullest.

Being too mature too early, he missed out on so much fun! It was a pity.

She could only try to compensate and make him happy.

Jessica put one hundred and one percent of her effort into Henry, always thinking about giving him the best of everything in the world.

"Great!"

"Where do you want to go?"

"How about a picnic?"

"Okay, let's go to the amusement park for a picnic while we are at it."

"Okay, no problem, Mommy, you have to keep up, don't give up after one roller coaster ride."

"Don't underestimate me!"

Henry smiled and thought while cutting vegetables, it would be even better if Daddy could come too. He loved having both of his favorite people by his side; it would be such a wonderful feeling.

When could they be together?

Henry turned his head, in the living room, Jessica was focused on her report, circling and marking. She was very serious.

The soft light coated her feminine figure with a thin warm glow, calm and peaceful.

Time was good, warm as it could be.

A smile curled up on Henry's lips, that day would come! Until then, he would patiently wait!

When Jessica received a call from Raymond, her first reaction was, what audacity this person has, he had the nerve to contact her?

"What did you say?" Jessica frowned, stood up, walked to the window, and pulled up the curtain. Sure enough, she saw Raymond standing downstairs.

Jessica sneered, over these years, he became less and less of a man, acting subserviently towards Marcus and Quincy, so ingratiating that it was repulsive. She remembered feeling uncomfortable when she met him at Old Mr. Lee's birthday banquet that day.

"I'm busy!" Jessica coldly refused.

Raymond asked her out for dinner, it was ridiculous. Were they that close?

They hadn't seen each other in eight years, she couldn't even remember his face. To Jessica, Raymond and Florence were strangers, or even less than strangers. Unless it was necessary, she didn't want to see him.

Even her little toe knew why he was looking for her. It was nothing more than asking her and Quincy to plead for mercy, to let him spare the Davis Family Group.

After the banquet, Quincy did indeed suppress the Davis Family Group, and no one dared to lend a helping hand in the business world. Mr. Quincy was furious, pushing the Davis Family Group to the brink of bankruptcy.

Jessica had heard about it. But she didn't care, because the affairs of the Davis Family Group had nothing to do with her.

Night of Destiny

After years of life experiences, her personality was slightly cool and extremely protective. The people she cared about, she protected to the extreme. Those who had nothing to do with her, she never cared about.

"Jessica, if you don't come down to see me, I'll come up to find you!" Raymond said shamelessly, confident that Jessica couldn't refuse.

A hint of anger flashed in Jessica's eyebrows.

Raymond, you jerk! Shameless!

"Mommy, who is it?" Henry brought a dish from the kitchen and curiously asked when he noticed his mommy's expression wasn't right.

Generally, his mommy had a great temper, rarely getting angry. Even when she was angry, she would still have her trademark smile. Such an obvious display of anger was rare to see.

"Wait here, I'll go down!" Jessica hung up the phone in anger. "An annoying fly!"

With Raymond's shamelessness, he wouldn't give up until he saw her. If she let him come up, it would disturb the peace and if she opened the door, he would see Henry. Considering everything, Jessica could only agree to go downstairs to meet him.

"Baby, don't ever become a man like this. Otherwise, Mommy would rather let you undergo gender reassignment surgery to save you from embarrassment!" Jessica used a harsh example for education.

Henry smiled, "Yes!"

After changing her outfit, Jessica instructed Henry, "If you're hungry, eat first, don't wait for mommy. Who knows when he'll leave!"

Henry nodded, and only then did Jessica go downstairs.

"Jessica, you look so beautiful!" As soon as Raymond saw Jessica, his eyes lit up. He approached her with admiration in his tone.

She was wearing a beige casual outfit, with her hair tied up in a ponytail and running shoes on her feet. She looked refreshing. She had always possessed unparalleled purity, and with such attire, she was like a student who had just entered college.

She was youthful and stunning. Raymond was completely captivated and full of praise.

"What do you want from me?" Jessica asked calmly, wearing her usual smile, but her voice was slightly cold.

Raymond reached out to hold Jessica's hand, but she cleverly dodged with a slight curve of her thin lips.

"Raymond, if you have something to say, don't touch me!"

His expression darkened, but quickly resumed a smile, "Jessica, I've wanted to come see you for a long time, but I've been busy with the Davis Family Group, unable to free myself. I miss you so much!"

Actually, you don't need to miss me so much!

Jessica shook slightly. The once handsome and flamboyant man now looked sleazy no matter how she looked at him. It was an insult for him to utter such sacred words as miss him. The changes in eight years were truly significant.

She had almost forgotten about the past, but she still couldn't forget the sarcastic and cruel words Raymond had said when he and Florence betrayed her, trampling on her dignity, pride, and womanly honor.

In that instant, she smiled sweetly, but deep down, she hated him fiercely.

A man and a woman in a relationship, no matter the reason or sincerity, should at least maintain a basic level of respect for each other. Raymond, however, clearly lacks even the most basic qualities of being a man.

No wonder he has become so sleazy after eight years.

It was precisely because of that hatred back then, unable to swallow her anger, that she ended up going to a bar to get drunk, and as a result, she met Marcus and had Henry.

To her, Henry was the most precious gift given by this incident.

Jessica eventually let go of her grievances and no longer held any grudges.

That's just how her personality is. For people who are unrelated to her, she simply throws them out of her mind, not leaving even a trace. As a result, she completely forgot about him.

There are so many passing acquaintances in life, who has the energy to remember an unimportant person?

Raymond saw that Jessica remained unmoved, silently cursing in his heart. He was extremely annoyed, but he didn't show it on his face, after all, he needed something from her.

Chapter 24

Raymond's Plea

Raymond attempted to use their past connection to move her.

"Raymond, I've almost forgotten about what happened eight years ago! Why bring it up now?" Jessica sneered.

When she was with him back then, she didn't love him. They were just one of the many couples on campus, following the trend, simply dating for fun.

Young Jessica was passionate and impulsive, occasionally a little confused and naive. If it weren't for the difficulties of raising Henry alone for these eight years, the ups and downs she experienced, and the warmth and coldness of human relationships, she wouldn't have become the independent, calm, and steady Jessica she was today.

To her, the so-called "past connection" was just a joke.

What had Raymond done to her?

Nothing at all, right?

Even though they were boyfriend and girlfriend, the most they did was hold hands and go on a few dates. They had dinner alone a few times and attended one of his friend's gatherings, but they had never even watched a movie together.

The most Raymond did was mock her taste in clothing, ridicule her lack of sophistication, and betray and humiliate her.

She admitted that she had indeed done a lot of foolish things when she was young, and the relationship with Raymond was a prime example of her foolishness.

"But I can't forget you!" Raymond said affectionately, his eyes filled with tenderness and passion.

Jessica trembled, a hint of a sneer flashing in her bright eyes.

Oh my God, you're not an actor, so stop acting. It's disgusting.

She secretly guessed, how long has he been rehearsing this scene?

"Raymond, just say what you want to say. I'm not the Jessica from eight years ago. Talking about these things, I feel embarrassed listening to it," said Jessica rudely. One-sided wishful thinking should have its limits.

Raymond's face turned purple with anger and shame, almost bursting into a rage.

He clenched his fists tightly and exerted a great effort to suppress his grievances. He was a pampered young man from an affluent family, used to getting whatever he wanted, but in recent years, he had fallen on hard times, relying on others' approval at every turn. Raymond kept his composure, not daring to say a word.

He didn't expect that now he had to consider the look on Jessica's face. There was some unease in his heart. Eight years ago, he was the one who abandoned Jessica voluntarily, the one who didn't want her.

He had looked down on her and mocked her.

Now that the tables had turned, how could Raymond feel comfortable in his heart?

"Jessica, you're really heartless. Don't you cherish our past relationship at all?" he pleaded.

"What relationship do we have to cherish?"

"I know it was my fault in the past. I don't mind if you hit me or scold me. Can you please save the Davis Family Group, considering the old times we had?" Raymond lowered his voice and begged Jessica.

As long as the Davis Family Group got through this crisis, he would definitely "repay" her generously.

Humph!

Who does she think she is? Quincy is from a prestigious family. How could Jessica be worthy of him? What's worse, she also had a seven-year-old son. He's probably just playing with her. Raymond thought maliciously.

Ever since he found out about Jessica's seven-year-old son, Raymond's hatred grew immensely. During their time together, he didn't even get a single kiss from her. The child was definitely not his.

He concluded that Jessica had cheated on him eight years ago!

"Mr. Raymond, are you mistaken? I'm just a mediocre secretary. Whether the Davis Family Group experiences any difficulties has nothing to do with me. I can't save your company. I'm sorry!" Jessica said coldly. How shameless can you be?

"No, it's not like that. I'm asking you to plead with Quincy. It was he who ordered a complete blockage. No one in the business world dares to invest in the Davis Family Group anymore. If this continues, my company won't last long. Jessica, please, help me out. I'll give you whatever you want. It was Florence who seduced me back then. I can abandon her, as long as you help me!" Raymond begged with a low voice, his face filled with entreaty and slight anxiety, afraid that Jessica wouldn't believe him.

Jessica's eyebrows furrowed. Honestly, over the past few years, she had been studying and raising Henry at the same time. At first, because she was young, she could only do odd jobs like washing dishes, delivering newspapers, and delivering milk. As she grew older, she started working part-time in various companies, trying almost every job she could find and encountering all sorts of people.

Among them was no shortage of lecherous men who thought their money could buy her for a night or take advantage of her. When she worked as Lionel's secretary, she dealt with the upper echelons of Paris, including a few scumbags who were sleazy to the extreme.

But never had she encountered a man as shameless as Raymond. He was practically breaking all records for Jessica's experiences with shameless men.

No decency, no responsibility...vile, shameless, and uncouth. A man reaching this level, it's truly a disgrace to his ancestors!

Night of Destiny

"Raymond, can you please understand the situation? I can't help you. Whatever Quincy wants to do, it has nothing to do with me. Your company's situation is also not my concern. I have no responsibility or obligation to help you," Jessica said coldly. It was all his fault, not to blame others. "To me, you're just a stranger, even more unfamiliar than a stranger. Please, don't try to establish any connection with me. I can't bear it."

Raymond's face turned pale, and anger filled his eyes. Feeling humiliated by Jessica's insults, he felt extremely embarrassed.

"Jessica, how can you be so heartless? To you, it's just a small favor, but do you know how many people will lose their jobs, how many people will cry if the Davis Family Group goes bankrupt?" Raymond shouted sharply, his face flushed with anger.

"Why do you have to be so indignant? Raymond, as a man, don't you feel ashamed to beg a woman for the sake of your career?" Jessica taunted mercilessly, narrowing her eyes and a cold smile playing on her lips. "Don't think that just because I've returned to America, I don't know anything about your dirty deeds. These past years, to win over investors, you didn't hesitate to send Florence to accompany those old men. Can you still call yourself a man?"

"How... how do you know?" Raymond gasped, realizing that Jessica was right. For the sake of winning over investors, Florence did indeed sell her body, and he felt repulsed by her actions, yet he couldn't break free from her help. Raymond believed that no one knew about this.

"If you don't want anyone to know, don't do it in the first place. In the business world, everything is known by everyone. How can any secret be hidden?" Jessica sneered, a trace of mockery crossing her eyebrows. She accidentally overheard it one time when she was accompanying Marcus to meet some clients next door.

Those people were shamelessly discussing how skilled Florence was in bed in such a public setting.

It must be said that it was a tragedy. The tragedy of both of them.

"I... " Raymond tried to defend himself. "It was Florence's idea..."

"Your affairs are none of my business, Raymond. Let me emphasize once again, that your matters have nothing to do with me. We have no connection or relationship worth mentioning. If you want to determine the fate of the Davis Family Group, do it yourself. Maybe you can go beg Quincy." Jessica said coldly. "I'm going back. I hope you won't bother me in the future!"

"Jessica... wait!" Raymond saw her turning to leave and panicked, quickly reaching out to grab Jessica's arm. "I'm begging you, help me just this once!"

"Will you ever stop?" Jessica waved her hand back, her face showing impatience.

She squeezed her fist, calculating the angle, trying to figure out which angle would maximize the impact of her punch!

Despite her innocent and lovely appearance, she had a violent side to her.

"Jessica... "

"Do you want to get beaten up?" Jessica's voice turned cold, and her innocent and beautiful face emitted an extremely domineering aura. No one dared to underestimate her at this moment.

A woman who could raise Henry to be so strong would never let anyone bully her without fighting back.

Raymond was truly intimidated, watching her walk away helplessly, his eyes filled with hidden resentment. Damn woman, refusing to help him, she will have to taste the punishment!

"Florence, it failed. She refused to help!" Raymond angrily dialed Florence's phone. "That bitch!"

"Didn't you mention your past?" Florence was surprised.

"Forget about it! I've tried everything, but she just won't agree. Looks like I'll have to take the final step. That damn woman. I don't believe she won't help me like this!" Raymond was furious, got in the car, and closed the door. "She better wait for me. She brought this upon herself!"

The current Jessica was stubborn. Well, he would use the ultimate trick. Let's see how she would beg him on her knees then!

******

Jessica went upstairs. Henry was studying a defense system program. Three dishes and a soup were already cooked on the dining table, emitting steam. The little boy was waiting there considerately for her to eat.

"Mommy, are you starving?" Henry smiled, and put down his books. "Mommy, when did your skills regress? It took you so long to drive away a fly!"

"Blame it on the shamelessness of this fly!" Jessica coldly snorted, a disgusted expression on her face. In front of her son, there was no need for pretense.

Henry laughed and lovingly picked up food for her. "Who is he? The person chasing after you?"

"Your Mommy's ex-boyfriend from eight years ago!"

Henry was sipping soup and choked on it, continuously coughing. His rosy cheeks turned red.

Jessica quickly took a tissue and handed it to him, pouting. "Darling, don't get too excited. This person has absolutely no relation to you. Please don't make any baseless assumptions. That would lower your Mommy's standards."

Henry couldn't help but laugh, tears in his eyes. "Mommy, I won't indulge in self-deception. You can rest assured. By the way, didn't you break up eight years ago? What happened now? Did he realize your good qualities and want to get back together?"

Sect Elder Breeze

"He's just bringing disgrace upon himself. Let's not bother with him. In any case, it has nothing to do with us." Jessica said calmly. "By the way, let's visit Grandpa tomorrow. Shall we bring him along for some fun?"

Henry nodded. Almost every week, Jessica would go visit Mr. Miller, and she would take Henry with her to accompany her father.

"Mommy, whoever you can't handle, leave it to me. I'll take care of them for you!" Henry suddenly spoke up, driving away the flies for his Mommy and defending his father's rights. As a son, it was his duty.

"Deal, if I can't handle it, I'll let you handle it!" Jessica slyly smiled.

Early the next day, Jessica and Henry dressed in matching mother-son outfits and went out. They first picked up Mr. Miller, then headed to the largest amusement park in W City.

Jessica had wanted to bring Mr. Miller over. She wanted to take care of her father, but unfortunately, Mr. Miller adamantly refused. Karen had been sold for a few years and hadn't been seen since. Mr. Miller was worried that her return would bring trouble to Jessica, so he refused to live with her under any circumstances.

Every month, Jessica would give Mr. Miller an allowance. Life was no longer as difficult as before, and it didn't matter where they lived. Jessica couldn't persuade him, so every week, she could only bring Henry to have a meal with him and chat. This way, Mr. Miller could enjoy the pleasure of doting on his grandson.

Her biggest wish now was for her father and son to be safe and sound. Everything else could wait.

The three generations of the family had a great time at the amusement park.

Night of Destiny

Jessica had a difficult childhood, where every penny was stretched to its limits. She never had extra money to go to an amusement park. She was very mature from a young age, helping Mr. Miller with household chores. Sometimes when Mr. Miller set up a stall on the street, Jessica would go and help him.

The joys of childhood were a distant dream for Jessica.

Back then, when she passed by the amusement park and heard others' joyful screams, Jessica couldn't help but feel envy.

Later, she went to France, and her aunt's life was still manageable. She became pregnant with Henry and didn't want to burden her aunt's family too much. She worked, studied, and took care of Henry all at the same time, juggling her busy life. She didn't have time to play.

It was only in the past year or two that their lives became more comfortable.

When she gave birth to Henry, she vowed to give him the most comfortable life. She would not let her son experience the same regrets she had in childhood.

She was grateful that she had achieved that goal!

In reality, she was just a big kid. She appeared more innocent than those college girls who came to the amusement park. With the stress of working on weekdays, she cherished her weekends and wanted to relax.

They specifically chose the most thrilling games to play. Gentle games were not suitable for them.

They teased each other along the way, constantly stimulating each other, and the laughter never stopped. Mr. Miller was beside them, unable to stop smiling, looking at the smiling faces of his daughter and grandson, he felt that his life was complete!

After the picnic, Jessica was not satisfied and wanted to play another round.

Mr. Miller laughed and said, "You little girl, you're the one having all the fun. You're not just here to entertain the child!"

Jessica smiled slightly, pouted cutely, and tugged at Mr. Miller like a little girl. "Dad, I'm a child too!"

Henry elegantly inserted a straw and handed drinks to Mr. Miller and Jessica, smiling. "Grandpa, Mommy's still young at heart. We're men, we don't need to worry about the same things as her."

"You brat!" Jessica lightly tapped his head and laughed.

Mr. Miller laughed heartily, hugging his precious grandson. Love filled his gentle face. He had worked hard his whole life, and only now did he feel the kindness of heaven.

He had a beautiful, caring, and capable daughter, and a smart, adorable, and considerate grandson.

They had gone from bitterness to sweetness.

It was enough!

Jessica truly dragged Henry to play another round of thrilling rides. Her elegant and beautiful face was filled with pure laughter. Henry accompanied her without hesitation. These games weren't very exciting for him.

His precious Mommy wasn't braver than him. Sitting beside him, her screams almost pierced his eardrums.

Chapter 25

Car Accident

When they came down, Jessica was covered in sweat, but Henry remained calm and composed, creating a stark contrast.

"Baby, you're too boring. Even in a place like this, you can't put on a suitable expression." Jessica was unwilling to accept that her son was more composed than her. She pinched his rosy cheeks in retaliation.

"Mummy, it's not exciting enough to begin with!" Henry smiled, behaving like a little gentleman, charming everyone at the amusement park.

During an arms deal, Victor had a conflict with an Arab arms manufacturer. The negotiation process decided who would be in command by playing Russian roulette. This scene was recorded, and Robin showed it to Henry, who chuckled and praised Victor for his boldness.

That's how games should be, to be stimulating enough!

When they returned to their original spot, Mr. Miller smiled at Jessica, and Henry nodded repeatedly, causing Jessica to protest in dissatisfaction. The three of them sat down to rest, planning to go home after a little while.

However, Jessica did not expect that danger was lurking dangerously close to her.

******

Recently, Dennis was pursuing a lively and adorable college student. To win her over, Dennis disguised himself as a sophisticated gentleman, charming and polite, which made the girl fall for him and develop a strong liking towards him.

Sect Elder Breeze

Coincidentally, it was the weekend, and the girl wanted to come to the amusement park. Dennis felt displeased deep down. How could he, the second young master of the Smith family, come to a place like this, full of crowds?

But to please her and win her heart, he pretended to be considerate and accompanied her to the park.

He never expected that he would encounter Jessica at the amusement park. A few days ago, he had harassed her, but she had fiercely fought back and poured coffee all over him. He hated that arrogant woman.

Dennis was narrow-minded and vengeful. He held a grudge against the humiliation he had suffered at Noblefull Group that day.

Whenever he thought of Marcus's superior demeanor that day, Dennis would seethe with anger. If you asked him who he hated the most, it would definitely be Marcus.

In his eyes, Marcus was just the son of a whore, but he had taken everything away from him. Every time he went to Noblefull Group, Marcus's attitude was like begging for mercy. Dennis had suffered a great deal.

He had been pondering how to seek revenge for this incident, and the anger had been stuck in his heart for days.

But what shocked him was that Jessica was accompanied by a boy who looked exactly like Marcus, with the same features, the same charm, it was clearly little Marcus.

After the shock passed, Dennis felt furious, his gaze becoming sinister. Jessica and the little boy were wearing matching outfits, although she looked unusually young, many people initially thought they were siblings.

But Henry unabashedly called her "Mummy." Dennis naturally assumed that he was the son of Jessica and Marcus.

Anyone who had seen Henry and Marcus would undoubtedly think they were father and son.

Night of Destiny

Dennis couldn't contain his anger. No wonder Marcus had tried to make things difficult for him for the sake of that woman. He had almost been scolded by his father, and that money almost went down the drain.

So that woman was his lover. They even had such a big son.

Besides anger, Dennis felt a sense of crisis.

The Smith family had four brothers, and the eldest had already passed away. Although their father didn't like Marcus, he had handed over Noblefull Group to him. Now, Marcus was in control of Noblefull Group, and his father could only control Marcus through the board of directors.

This made him somewhat concerned.

His father, Old Mr. Alston, had hinted to him before, telling him not to be impatient, to gain experience outside first. If he made some achievements, then it wouldn't be too late to hand over Noblefull Group to him.

Dennis was dissatisfied and protested but to no avail.

He knew that his father was now grooming Leonard, hoping that he would take over Noblefull Group when he grew up.

Now there was another member of the Smith family. Dennis was jealous and hated him. After all, the little boy was the eldest grandson of the Smith family.

Marcus was currently in charge of Noblefull Group, but their father was getting old. Who knew what would happen in the future? He would never allow anyone else to compete with him.

So he found an excuse to leave the amusement park, sat in the car, and stared fiercely at the exit with a menacing look in his eyes.

People came and went, and cars passed by. Dennis became increasingly irritated.

When Jessica and the others came out, Dennis narrowed his eyes and a trace of ferocity crossed his face. Marcus, you are heartless, don't blame me for being unrighteous!

This woman and child are your treasures, right?

I will make you taste what it means to be in unbearable pain.

The car followed closely, moving slowly. Dennis stayed put, following Jessica and Henry until they reached a quiet street, where a bus could take them directly to their apartment.

Little Henry was telling jokes to Mr. Miller, and Jessica was chiming in with stories of their time in Paris. The three of them were happily chatting and not sensing any danger.

After Mr. Miller and Jessica had moved a distance apart, Dennis suddenly pressed the accelerator, ruthlessly crashing toward Jessica and Henry.

Under the scorching sun, the entire quiet street was deserted, except for the three of them and a few young men and women. When the car came rushing at them, someone screamed...

The sound pierced through the air, and Jessica's heart tightened. She turned her head sharply and saw Dennis's car coming towards her.

Jessica's pupils suddenly shrank. The car was too fast, and she couldn't evade it in time. Out of her motherly instinct, Jessica pushed Henry forcefully!

In the face of danger, she chose to protect her precious child.

Boom...

The car violently collided with Jessica, and her delicate body was thrown several meters away, rolling several times on the ground, leaving behind an eerie trail...

"Mummy!"

"Jessica!"

Henry and Mr. Miller shouted and rushed over, while pedestrians screamed in horror...

Seeing that Jessica was injured but Henry was unscathed, Dennis clenched his fist and fiercely pounded the steering wheel, "Damn it! You brat, you're lucky!"

Night of Destiny

To avoid causing trouble, he quickly drove away.

Henry suddenly lifted his gaze, a fierce intensity in his innocent eyes, oozing with a ferocity beyond his years, a murderous vibe.

Squinting, numbers flashed through his mind!

Jessica had already lost consciousness, her long hair scattered, blood oozing from her head, staining her once pristine face. Underneath her, blood continued to seep, staining the hot ground.

She lay in a pool of blood, her breath weak, shattered as if she would vanish from the world in the next second.

Mr. Miller trembled in fear, reaching out to pick up Jessica, "Jessica, Jessica..."

"Grandpa, don't move Mommy! Call an ambulance!" Henry's voice was calm, sounding as innocent as usual, without a hint of panic.

If it weren't for the cold sweat on his forehead and his trembling hands, Mr. Miller would almost think that it wasn't Jessica who had been hit.

This collision was severe, he didn't know where his Mommy had been injured. If he moved her and worsened her condition, the consequences would be even more serious.

Stay calm, Henry, you must stay calm!

Henry kept reminding himself, but his little hand kept trembling. An ominous feeling gripped his heart.

An inexplicable fear almost drove Henry to the brink of collapse. His instincts had always been accurate.

He had never been wrong!

Mommy, you can't die, absolutely not!

"Jessica..." Mr. Miller trembled with fear, tears streaming down his face. "Jessica, you can't die. What will I and Henry do if something happens to you?"

A few passersby gathered around, whispering among themselves.

Henry raised his small face, reached out his hand, and held onto Mr. Miller. His young voice was slightly hoarse, "Grandpa, Mommy will be fine. Don't cry..."

Upon hearing this, Mr. Miller's tears flowed even faster.

Why wasn't it him who got hit? He was old, so it wouldn't matter if something happened to him. But Jessica was only 26 years old, her life had just begun. She still had a long, long way to go, and she had Henry...

Henry remained very calm, a terrifying calmness. His eyes were tightly locked on Jessica's face, his little fists clenching tightly. In those eyes, so similar to Marcus, a frightening coldness lurked. He seemed completely different from the elegant and smiling little gentleman of usual days.

An ambulance arrived quickly, and Jessica was taken to the hospital!

Outside the operating room, Mr. Miller and Henry sat silently, their hands tightly held together. Mr. Miller trembled incessantly, his eyes filled with fear...

Jessica, you mustn't be dead!

God, please bless my daughter!

Henry whispered softly comforting Mr. Miller. The old man was always nervous and easily flustered in such situations.

He knew he couldn't lose his composure.

Mommy's life was hanging in the balance, and his grandfather couldn't bear any more stress at his age. If he panicked, who would shoulder everything?

Though he was young, he was capable enough to take on everything at home. He mustn't panic, Mommy would be fine, she would be fine.

Time was passing little by little as if life itself was also slipping away. The wind blew in quietly, bringing a hint of heat.

The door to the operating room opened.

Night of Destiny

Mr. Miller quickly stood up and rushed over, trembling as he grabbed the doctor's hand and asked, "Doctor, how is my daughter doing?"

Henry waited quietly for the results, barely even breathing.

"The patient needs surgery!" The doctor in all-white attire glanced at Mr. Miller and Henry, his eyes showing a hint of pity, sympathizing with their plight.

"Okay, as long as my daughter can be saved, that's great!"

"This is not an ordinary surgery. We need the consent form signed by a family member."

"Doctor, just tell me, what kind of surgery is needed?" Henry calmly spoke.

The doctor looked at the little boy who had been silent all along, secretly admiring how delicate and beautiful he was. It was rare for such a young child to have such a strong and determined demeanor.

"Amputation!" The doctor uttered the words.

Henry and Mr. Miller were stunned, as if thunderstruck!

The face of the little boy turned colorless in that instant, almost transparent, with his big eyes opening wide to their limit.

Amputation?

His mommy was going to be amputated?

Absolutely not!

"The patient's right leg is fractured, with a bacterial infection. It needs to be removed immediately to prevent further illness," the doctor truthfully explained. In the hospital, life and death were ordinary occurrences. Though the doctor sympathized, as a doctor, he could only choose the most beneficial approach for the patient.

Save her life! That was his responsibility. Even though it was cruel, at least she could survive!

Mr. Miller panicked, "There will be a risk to her life... What about Henry? My Jessica..."

Sect Elder Breeze

In an instant, Mr. Miller seemed to age by ten years. His once straight back was now slouched, tears streaming uncontrollably. It was a pain as if a piece of flesh was forcibly ripped from his heart - his precious daughter...

He couldn't imagine what Jessica would look like after the amputation.

This girl had always been proud and intelligent. Having to spend her whole life in a wheelchair, how could she bear it? His grandson was still so young and in need of care. How would they face the days ahead?

The more the old man thought, the sadder he became, and the faster his tears fell!

"You need to make a decision quickly. The longer you delay, the more dangerous the patient's condition will become!" The doctor, though reluctant, could only urge them. As a doctor, the patient's life was of utmost importance.

"No, it's not possible!" Henry decisively spoke out, resolute!

The doctor and nurses all looked at him in disbelief.

The child had a pair of beautiful eyes, deep as the sea. At this moment, he was so calm that it was terrifying. It seemed as if the critically ill person was not his mommy.

"My mommy must not undergo the amputation surgery!" he looked into the doctor's eyes, articulating each word with great clarity.

"Boy, do you know what that means? She might die!" the doctor said, shaking his head. "With the amputation, she can still live. But if we delay, if the bacterial infection worsens, what then? How old are you? Can you take responsibility?"

"Henry..." Mr. Miller anxiously whispered. If they didn't proceed with the surgery, would they just let Jessica die? "Let's agree, at least Jessica will be able to live."

"I don't agree, doctor. Let me ask you, can you guarantee my mommy's life within one day?" Henry asked, "I want to hear the truth!"

Night of Destiny

The doctor's face turned red. This child was too despicable, openly questioning his medical skills. In all his years of practice, it was the first time he encountered such a child. His mother's life was hanging by a thread, yet he remained so calm.

"And what about the day after? If she doesn't have the surgery, she will die!" The doctor became angry too.

Implied in his words, two days would be fine. Henry breathed a sigh of relief; he still had time.

"Don't always bring up death so easily. My mommy can still live a vibrant life without undergoing amputation!" Henry said coldly, his tone extremely domineering and arrogant.

A respected doctor being challenged by a child was truly a bizarre event. The doctor became furious but then thought that he was just a child. Perhaps he couldn't accept his mommy becoming disabled, hence his stubbornness.

How could he argue with a child?

"Sir, if you want your daughter to survive, then sign the consent form!" The doctor turned to Mr. Miller and said, "Your grandson is too ignorant. Keeping the patient in this state is extremely dangerous for her."

"Henry..." Mr. Miller was indecisive and looked at Henry.

The doctor trembled with anger. What was wrong with this family? "He's just a child. He protests like this because he can't accept his mommy becoming disabled. Do you have to wait until the patient dies before you regret it?"

Henry narrowed his eyes and snorted, "Grandpa, just wait, I'll make a phone call."

The little boy quickly opened Jessica's bag, took out her cell phone, found Marcus's number, and hesitated for a second. He was too young, and his words might not be enough to convince the doctor. Besides, his grandpa was worried about Mommy's life. If he signed the consent form after Henry left, it would have led to a lifelong regret for Mommy. He would regret it to death.

If the one speaking was his daddy, with his social status, the doctor wouldn't dare pressurize them!

This was the first time Henry felt hatred towards being so young.

He dialed Mr. Marcus's number, and it connected quickly.

"Hey, where are you?"

Chapter 26

Mr. Marcus's Feeling

Mr. Marcus looked at the number displayed on his phone, Jessica's phone?! He frowned. Who is this?

"At home!"

"My Mommy had an accident, and the doctor wants to amputate. I refuse. Can you help me talk to the doctor?" Henry briefly explained the situation.

Mr. Marcus stood up with a swish. His actions were too abrupt, and the files on the table were scattered. Mr. Marcus had a grave face, without any hesitation. He grabbed his car keys and swiftly left, commanding as he walked, "Give the phone to the doctor!"

Henry obediently handed the phone to the doctor. The doctor took it, and upon hearing Mr. Marcus identify himself, his attitude immediately became respectful.

"How is the patient's condition?"

Night of Destiny

The doctor dared not conceal anything and told Mr. Marcus about Jessica's condition in detail. He emphasized, "The patient's condition is very critical. If we don't perform the surgery, there definitely be a risk to her life. It's just that her child is too stubborn and refuses..."

Marcus asked a few more questions to the doctor, and then the phone returned to Henry's hand. Marcus, driving and asking, was calmer compared to Henry, asking questions that the doctor hadn't asked.

"Why refuse the amputation?"

"I have a friend on vacation in City F. He can come here in half a day, and with his presence, he can find a way to restore my mommy to her intact self," Henry said softly, causing the doctor to glare.

Provocation, this was a blatant provocation. This child was not only stubborn but also arrogant. Was he suggesting that the doctor had misdiagnosed and was an incompetent physician?

He was a renowned authority in surgery, both domestically and internationally. And yet he was being repeatedly provoked by a child.

It was infuriating.

"Are you sure?"

"Absolutely!" Henry asserted firmly.

Perhaps the child's voice was too calm, his speech and reasoning too composed and organized. Despite talking over the phone, Marcus felt like he was talking to an adult. He couldn't completely treat him as just a child, but he still had some basic rationality.

That doctor from earlier had a considerable reputation, both domestically and internationally. He said amputation was necessary, indicating that Jessica's condition must be very dangerous. But this child... did he really have a solution?

Regardless, he had to personally go and verify it.

"Boy, you might indeed have a solution, but your mommy's condition is very unstable. No one can guarantee what will happen in the next second. So, you must be mentally prepared and take responsibility for your confidence!" Marcus tried to be more gentle in his words.

However, damn it, he felt extremely panicked inside.

How could that woman suddenly have a car accident and end up in such a severe condition?

Her son vouched for him to come, but what if something really happened, if she had a mishap? What would he do?

Marcus clenched his hands, trembling slightly. Just the thought of a world without Jessica made him feel like all colors would turn black and white.

Even his breathing became weak.

Her son, how old was he? Were his words mere stubbornness, or were they genuine?

Should he agree?

Rushing through countless red lights, ignoring the blaring sirens behind him, Marcus couldn't spare a second to think as various thoughts flashed through his mind.

What should he do?

"My Mommy, I'll take responsibility!" Henry said in a deep voice. "You just need to come and hold the fort for me."

Impressive dominance!

Marcus secretly praised him, feeling a slight relief in his anxious heart. "Alright, I agree. I'll be at the hospital immediately!"

After hanging up the phone, Henry said in a grave voice, "Doctor, I beg you, don't perform the surgery on my mommy. Mr. Marcus will arrive soon, you just need to ensure that my mommy stays alive, can you do that?"

That doctor, already angered by Henry, responded angrily, "Fine! That's your decision. If anything goes wrong, don't blame the hospital!"

With Mr. Marcus to vouch for them, the doctor didn't dare make decisions without consultation.

Night of Destiny

Henry calculated the time and pondered that Marcus would arrive soon.

"Grandpa, don't worry. I will make sure Mommy is intact," Henry persuasively spoke to Mr. Miller, tightly gripping his hand. "I know that Mommy has a chance to stand up completely healthy. It's unfair to Mommy if we agree to the amputation right away. I can't accept it without giving it a try."

"Henry, do you really have a solution?"

"Yes!"

"Grandpa, I'll go home first. You wait here. I'll be back soon!"

Mr. Miller nodded as the little boy gave a few more urging words, quickly rushing downstairs. As soon as he descended, he heard a continuous stream of blaring sirens. He keenly observed Mr. Marcus rushing into the hospital, followed by two police cars.

Daddy, you're really making a scene!

However, he was satisfied with the result. Daddy cared about Mommy, and it was a good sign.

Inside the taxi, Henry clenched his fists.

Mommy, please trust me and hold on! You will get better!

I am your unstoppable son. How is it possible that I can't even protect your health?

Back at home, Henry went to his study, turned on the computer, inserted a CD, and swiftly entered a series of commands in the popping window. Soon, the screen switched to the top floor of the VT building.

In the video, a young man was focused on his work when suddenly the alarm bell rang throughout the entire building. The man looked up in alarm, and his deep eyes were filled with caution as he swiftly stood up.

"Victor, it's me, Henry!" The image on the large screen in the room switched to Henry's face.

Sect Elder Breeze

Victor's eyes widened suddenly. He had seen many storms and experienced countless life-and-death battles, but the calm and wise Victor was now pointing at the face appearing on the screen, his handsome face turning red with anger.

"Henry?" The man exclaimed in a shocked voice, his fingers trembling. "No way!"

The phone rang in the room, and Victor gestured for Henry to wait as he answered the call, saying, "It's fine. Cancel the alarm!"

With a click, he hung up the phone. Victor hadn't recovered from his shock yet. He never expected that Henry was indeed just a little kid. Damn it, he was the mastermind behind global online transactions. For over a year, he, Truman, and Robin had followed his commands. Whenever there were problems, they immediately turned to Henry for a solution.

They had secretly speculated about who this "Love My Mommy The Most" person really was, but they never expected him to be such a little boy. Just thinking about how much they admired him during this past year made them feel overwhelmed.

Victor felt like smashing his head against the wall.

"Damn it, so you really are Mr. Marcus's son?"

Henry nodded, saying, "We'll talk more later. Victor, I need to find Antonio. My mommy is in trouble and it's urgent!"

Seeing the tenseness on Henry's face, Victor didn't say much.

"Wait a moment!"

He took out his phone and dialed Antonio's private number. After a moment, the call was connected. All of them had their own ways of contact, and although Antonio was the most unpredictable among them, it wasn't difficult to find him.

"Henry, are you in Paris?"

"W city!"

Night of Destiny

Victor nodded, "Antonio, where are you now?"

"W city, D airport. Next stop, Egypt!"

"Wait, don't get on the plane yet. Henry has something urgent to tell you!"

"Henry?"

Henry let out a sigh of relief. Excellent! He reported the name and address of the hospital and Victor relayed it to Antonio. He also gave Antonio Henry's mobile number before ending the call.

"Henry, luckily he's in W city. He is rushed to the hospital now, don't worry, there's still time. Antonio's medical skills can bring back the dead!"

Henry nodded. It would only take an hour from the airport to the hospital.

That's great!

"Was it an accident?" Victor was perceptive, and from Henry's expression, he knew it wasn't a simple matter. Although Henry was young, his thoughts were more mature than ten adults combined. If it was an accident, he wouldn't have such a serious expression.

Henry shook his head, "It wasn't an accident. Once my mom gets through the critical period, I'll slowly settle the score!"

The little boy's face turned cold, with a hint of arrogance in his serious expression. Whoever dares to harm his mommy, he will make them pay back a hundredfold!

"Do you need help?"

"Yes! I'm worried about my mom right now. Can you help me check a license plate number?" Henry coldly reported a license plate number. "A limited edition Lamborghini, hmph, not many people in W city can afford it. He's really lawless."

Henry gritted his teeth and spoke with emphasis. Obviously, it was a murder. His mom never offended anyone, so who would want to kill her?

No matter who it was, they are as good as dead!

Victor nodded and snapped his fingers, "Understood, wait for my message!"

Henry nodded, "I'll go to the hospital first!"

He closed the computer and left, heading straight to the hospital.

******

In the hospital, Mr. Miller looked at the arrival of Mr. Marcus in astonishment, dumbfounded...

He was Henry's father? They really looked so alike!

How could he have died when Jessica said so?

Mr. Miller was completely confused. Jessica's life and death were unknown, and now there was another big Henry. The old man's mind was in chaos, unable to understand what was going on, but he wanted to wait for Henry to come before figuring it out.

The doctor showed great respect for Mr. Marcus and naturally assumed they were family. That child was Mr. Marcus's child, no wonder he was so arrogant and domineering.

Waiting was torturous.

Mr. Miller briefly explained the details of the car accident. The culprit fled, and Jessica was seriously injured while trying to protect Henry. He didn't know anything else.

Marcus immediately made a phone call to investigate the car accident. He couldn't hit someone and run away.

It's better to hide tightly. If they're caught, I'll make them regret being born!

"Mr. Marcus, the patient's condition is really critical. Are you really going to listen to the young master's words?" After examining Jessica, the doctor came out and a few drops of cold sweat appeared on his forehead. He mostly knew about Mr. Marcus from the media, as they had never met.

Rumors had it that he was a ruthless and cold-blooded man. Even if the patient lost a leg after an amputation, they would still be alive. If the patient died while being dragged on like this, the hospital would be held responsible.

How could he believe the words of a child?

The doctor was in a difficult situation. In his professional career, he had never encountered such a thorny situation before. It challenged his ability to endure.

"Young Master?" Marcus questioned in confusion. Was he referring to Jessica's son? He didn't think much about it. To be honest, he was also very worried. The woman inside was in a critical condition, and her illness was complicated. If anything went wrong, he would regret it!

"Is it serious?" Marcus asked.

The doctor nodded seriously. It was very serious.

Marcus waved his hand, signaling the doctor to be quiet. He needed a moment of silence.

He walked to the window, a gentle breeze blowing, carrying the summer heat, making him feel restless. Marcus clenched his fist and stiffened, his composure on the brink of collapse.

Jessica, you have to hold on!

Apart from this sentence, he didn't know what else to say to himself.

The memories of the two of them from the first meeting to the present flashed through his mind, scene by scene, like a movie.

The memories he shared with that woman were not many, but Marcus realized that all the memories involving them were vivid and deeply engraved in his mind.

Outside the restaurant, the woman stumbled into his arms. When he looked into her eyes in that instant, it was a fleeting moment of brilliance. He saw a pair of bright eyes that seemed to hold all the colors of the world.

At that moment, Marcus felt his previously still heart quicken its pace.

Sect Elder Breeze

Knowing she was Quincy's girlfriend, Marcus was furious. He didn't understand why he had such strong emotions for a stranger. He wanted to pull her into his embrace and possess her.

During her time as his secretary, she was very competent. She was his rare and capable assistant, and they had a great understanding. It was as if they had known each other for over a decade. With just a glance, she knew what to say and do in any given situation, never making a mistake.

By chance, he noticed that she resembled that woman, and he felt something nearly formed in his heart shattered.

It was like crystal, beautiful, but fragile, and easily shattered by a blow.

Damn it!

She looks so similar to her, is it a coincidence?

During that time, he tormented her in every way, wanting to tear her apart mercilessly, making her suffer for the years of torment he endured.

However, reason told him that their similarity was purely in appearance.

During that period, Mr. Marcus struggled. He wanted to investigate but was afraid of the results. He would start and then tell someone to stop midway. This conflicting feeling was new to him.

He even considered firing her. Out of sight, out of mind, to end everything, preventing him from impulsively strangling her.

But every day at work, when he saw her with a smile on her face, politely saying, "Good morning, Mr. Marcus!" he felt that the sunlight of that day was particularly bright.

The thought of firing her was interrupted again.

Mr. Marcus analyzed his own mentality and felt that he must be going crazy. He knew her smile was fake, intentionally masked, yet he foolishly longed for it.

What else could it be if not madness?

Night of Destiny

At Old Mr. Lee's birthday banquet, Marcus had never considered using Jessica. If it weren't for Quincy making a provocative phone call, warning him not to touch Jessica, he would have never thought of using her.

He was the kind of person with a dark mentality. The more someone provoked him, the more he wanted to retaliate and show them.

But he didn't expect to find out at the banquet that this woman had a son who was already in elementary school.

It was shocking, he had never been so shocked.

What shocked him the most was the day at Noblefull Group when she poured a cup of coffee on Dennis's head, standing up for him. It felt special and warm, making him long for the feeling of being protected by her from the depths of his being.

But before he could make sense of all these feelings, she had an accident and was in critical condition.

She couldn't die!

Marcus had only one prevailing thought: she absolutely could not die.

He hadn't even figured out these feelings yet, how could something happen to her?

That woman, sinister and sharp-tongued, had an angelic face that could often deceive people and conceal her true nature.

That woman, intellectual and composed, had a fake innocent face that could often deceive her opponents and hide her intelligence and wit.

That woman, proud and confident, always disguised herself as humble, often disturbing his mind and issuing the most disrespectful challenges.

Marcus hated intelligent women, especially those who were too smart and rational, lacking the femininity and submissiveness that a woman should have.

But ironically, this excessively clever woman had captured his attention and won his focus.

"Marcus, don't ask me if I love you or not. You will never find an answer. If you want me to love you, it's simple. Trade here!" Her words rang in his ears.

Look how arrogant she was.

She dared to say such provocative words that caught his attention. He knew that in high society, if Mr. Marcus wanted to seduce a woman, he would always succeed.

He knew he had that charm that made women flock to him.

Even without his impressive wealth, he could still win a woman's heart.

In other words, he did not need to put effort into wooing a woman when he could have any type of woman he wanted.

No one had ever dared to say to him, take his heart in exchange for her heart.

Only Jessica, this bold and clever woman.

Her actions were always unexpected.

It was a fair exchange, to give back with a heart for heart, just as she said. She was right, he indeed had no reason to make such a special person love him.

Jessica, if you want my heart, trade it with yours, please, stay alive!

Only if she stayed alive, he would know if this transaction could continue.

Only if she stayed alive, he would know if he, Marcus, was really capable of loving a woman.

As long as you're alive, I'm willing to give it a try!

Marcus had never been so clear in his mind.

Yearning for her smile, enjoying her companionship, infatuated with the very air she breathed, how could he bear a world without Jessica?!

A gust of wind blew across Marcus' forehead, lightly brushing it. Deep within his profound gaze, there was nothing but worry.

His heart was as though it was being seared in hot oil, hot and painful. This waiting agony was particularly unbearable. The person he cared about had an uncertain fate, and he had to wait in silence for news. It felt like a sharp knife piercing his bones.

Chapter 27

Father and Son

Mr. Miller looked at the man's back and felt much calmer.

He might be Henry's father. With him around, Mr. Miller felt a lot of reassurance. Although he didn't know the specifics of the situation, when a family faced a disaster, they always hoped for a pair of strong shoulders to bear all the panic and worries of the family.

Jessica was the backbone of the family, and HE was getting older and didn't understand anything. Henry was too young and couldn't do anything. Now that he was here, standing so upright, seemingly fearless even if the sky were to fall.

Mr. Miller's fondness for Mr. Marcus rose sharply.

"Mr. Marcus..." The doctor, seeing him silent for so long, tried to persuade him to agree to the surgery for Jessica.

Marcus turned around, glanced at Mr. Miller, and firmly said to the doctor, "We won't proceed with the surgery!"

Dominant and unquestionable!

He chose to believe in Jessica's son. Although reason told him that a small child couldn't be trusted, he was willing to take a gamble! He wagered on that child's confidence!

It was not that he disregarded Jessica's life-threatening situation, but rather, the proud Jessica, if she were to lose a leg and spend her whole life in a wheelchair, being inconvenienced in her movements, would be a lifelong pain for her.

He thought about that scene and felt heartache! Therefore, amputation was not an option he accepted. Unless there was no other way!

"Mr. Marcus..."

"We will bear all consequences!" Marcus firmly uttered those words, causing Mr. Miller's eyes to well up with tears.

Great! Mr. Miller was practically treating him like a son-in-law.

The doctor wanted to say something, but Marcus gave him a cold glance, his imposing presence pressuring him as if he would throw him out if he dared to say anything unnecessary.

The doctor turned his head. He was too scared to utter a word. This man's aura was too terrifying. He fell completely silent and could only obey to save Jessica's life.

******

Outside the hospital, Henry was waiting for Antonio.

When a handsome man dressed in casual clothes got out of the car, Henry immediately determined that he was Antonio.

Antonio had an extremely beautiful face, blessed by heaven, with distant eyebrows, emitting an aura of indifference.

He was the Miracle Doctor, Antonio.

At the age of fifteen, he became famous and had been in the field for ten years. His medical skills were excellent, but his temper was peculiar. If you wanted Antonio to save someone, either your status had to be high enough or the person requesting his help had to have a high status.

Otherwise, forget about it!

"Antonio!" Henry went up to greet him. Antonio was slightly taken aback. His mouth opened and closed. Although Victor roughly briefed him on the way, it was still a shock to see Love My Mommy The Most in person. Antonio felt that his mental preparation was insufficient. It was too impactful.

"Hi, Henry. If Captain knew that not only are you underage but also this young, he would jump off a building!" Antonio smiled brilliantly, walking over and lifting Henry. He quite impolitely rubbed his cheek with one hand, turning his tender cheeks red.

So tender!

Henry kicked him with his short legs in protest. He knew that once people discovered his true appearance, it would be like this.

"So adorable!" Antonio laughingly trembled.

"Antonio, save my mommy!" Henry grabbed his hand and forcefully dragged him into the hospital.

"I got it, I got it." Antonio let him lead the way, smiling. "Indeed, you love your mommy the most!"

"By the way, forgot to tell you something, when you see Marcus later, don't mention our relationship..." Henry reminded him as they entered the elevator. They could talk about it after his mommy was safe.

The doctor came out of the operating room for the third time. This time, his face was slightly pale, and his tone was filled with warning. "Mr. Marcus, if we don't proceed with the surgery soon, it will be too late. The range of the bacterial infection has expanded. If we delay any longer, she will..."

Marcus furrowed his eyebrows deeply, and Mr. Miller trembled nervously, unable to produce any sound from his dry throat.

"Just a little longer..." Marcus was burning with anxiety as if there was a fire blazing inside him. Every nerve in his body was tense, and his throat felt as if it was being squeezed. He could hardly bear it. And he almost agreed to the doctor's suggestion!

Damn it, Jessica's condition seemed to have worsened. What should he do?

Marcus was so anxious that he broke out into a cold sweat on his back. His fingers trembled incessantly. Should she proceed with the surgery?

Once he agreed, there would be no turning back...

"Well, this is quite a severe injury, to the point of amputation? Tell me, are you sure you've received a medical license?"

The man broke the tense atmosphere outside the operating room with a gentle yet icy tone.

Although his voice was melodic, it carried an unparalleled arrogance!

The doctor was furious and trembling as he pointed at Antonio, too angry to speak.

It was an absolute humiliation!

"Henry..." Mr. Miller breathed a sigh of relief when he saw Henry return.

Henry held his hand and gave a gentle pat as Antonio confidently walked into the operating room in front of the doctor and nurses.

Marcus felt like thunder had struck, his eyes widened in disbelief at the face that resembled his own. His usually agile and sharp mind went blank.

The doctor and nurses, witnessing Antonio's unabashed entry, hurriedly followed him inside. And in a moment, the doors of the operating room closed.

Night of Destiny

In the corridor, only Marcus, Henry, and Mr. Miller remained.

With just a glance at Marcus, Henry's lips curled into a slight smile. He sat beside Mr. Miller and comforted him gently, "Grandfather, Mommy will be fine. If you're tired, rest for a while. I'll let you know when the surgery is over."

"Henry, who is that man? Can he save Jessica?" Mr. Miller was worried.

Henry nodded, but before he could speak, the operating room doors opened, and a nurse came out to inform Henry that Antonio promised to give him a healthy mommy in five hours.

Henry and Mr. Miller finally breathed a sigh of relief, releasing the tension in their nerves.

"That's great!"

"Grandfather, the surgery will take a long time. You should go home and rest. I'll call you as soon as Mommy wakes up!" Henry said with a smile.

Mr. Miller looked at Mr. Marcus, then at Henry. He knew his grandson had something to say to the man. He nodded and took the key from Henry.

"Let me know immediately when she wakes up, understand, Henry?"

Henry nodded, and only then did Mr. Miller feel at ease and returned home.

"Are you...are you Jessica's son?" Marcus stammered, his exquisitely handsome features filled with shock.

He involuntarily glanced at the operating room, then at Henry, feeling as if he were floating. He felt like there had to be something heavy to hit him hard and wake him up.

If you told him one second was the end of the world, Mr. Marcus would probably agree, indeed it was!

"Hello, I'm Henry!" Henry elegantly introduced himself with his name, like a little gentleman.

The little boy really liked Marcus! Liked him a lot.

Sect Elder Breeze

Maybe it was blood, maybe their personalities were too similar, but ever since Henry had a conversation with Marcus, he fell in love with him.

Seeing how nervous he was for his mommy today, the little boy decisively raised Marcus's score from nine to ten.

It could be said that other than Jessica, Marcus held a very high position in Mr. Miller's and Little Henry's hearts.

"What exactly is going on here?" Marcus muttered to himself.

The usually composed, elegant, and cold-blooded Marcus was stunned.

Shock, confusion, nervousness, complexity... Countless emotions flashed through Marcus's mind one by one. He was at a loss, not even knowing if he was dreaming or not.

The elegant smiling face of the little boy kept flickering in front of him, and Marcus's heart raced like thunder. His hands clenched into fists. Why?

What on earth has happened?

Why does it feel like he just woke up from a nap and suddenly has such a big son?

He felt like he was going insane, shocked to the point of madness.

Anyone with eyes could tell that they were definitely father and son. Such resemblance, one couldn't believe there was no blood relation, it was too much of a coincidence for anyone with a bit of intelligence to believe!

He had had countless women, that was for sure, but he didn't remember ever being involved with Jessica!

If he had ever had a relationship with Jessica, he wouldn't be able to forget it. She was so special, and it was too far-fetched to not have any impression of her after several years apart.

"How old are you?"

"Seven years old!"

Henry answered each question, giving Marcus time to reflect and remember.

Seven years old? Seven and eight years ago, Marcus was still studying in Australia. He was abroad, encountering foreign beauties. It was true that he had returned to W City because he wanted to visit his mother's grave. During that time, his mood was very low, filled with hatred. How could he have possibly been involved with other women?

No matter how hard Marcus thought, he couldn't figure out when he had a relationship with Jessica and got her pregnant.

Was it really just a coincidence?

Damn it! He didn't even believe that reason.

Suddenly, he remembered the first time he met Jessica. When she saw him, she ran like a mouse encountering a cat. Why? Before that, if they were strangers, why would she want to escape?

He vividly remembered that Jessica at the time had panic in her bright eyes.

He believed he was presentable enough, not some freak from the tower. How could he make her panic? Why would she want to escape?

Unless, she had already known him!

No wonder, a few times, her gaze would always get lost when she looked at him. A few times, she would become slightly flustered when she realized he was looking at her, as if afraid he would discover some secret.

Could it be they really were acquainted from before?

Was this child in front of him really his son?

Damn it, what has that woman been hiding from him?

"Who is your father?" Marcus asked.

"It is said that my mommy was unmarried when she became pregnant. I am an illegitimate child. As for my father?" Henry blossomed a smile that could enchant anyone, "Unknown!"

Marcus's breath hitched, feeling like a heavy stone was pressing on his chest, making it hard to breathe.

The child spoke nonchalantly, but he felt a heavy pressure.

Sect Elder Breeze

"You are my son!" It was almost a statement.

Though Marcus's intelligence may not be as mind-blowingly high as Henry's, it was several times higher than the average person. The weirdness revealed by this matter was too much.

That day, when he answered the call, Henry deliberately misled.

When Jessica had a car accident, why did this little boy immediately call him to stabilize the situation? Didn't they have any friends? At best, Jessica was his secretary, not a relative. Why would he call him?

Henry smiled, "Don't you even know if you have a son or not?"

Knowing well that Marcus had been in a car accident and had forgotten some things, Henry deliberately said so. He originally wanted to say, "Daddy, why did you lose your memory, but only forget Mommy?" But he did not say so.

Marcus couldn't say a word, he truly had no memory. But this face was too similar!

"Do you have any free time?" Marcus suddenly asked.

Henry raised an eyebrow, seeming to have plenty of free time, but what did he want to do? His thoughts were difficult to guess.

"Let's do a paternity test!" Marcus said domineeringly. He couldn't accept not knowing the truth, especially when they were in the hospital. Coincidences were rubbish, he didn't believe it.

But if they were father and son, why he had no memory of Jessica?

Well, let's speak in scientific terms. This is the most authoritative evidence.

Henry felt silent: Daddy, you really are a man of action! It's too decisive.

But a paternity test doesn't need to be done twice!

"I refuse!" Henry calmly said, with a smile on his face resembling Marcus. "Why don't you ask my mommy?"

"I bet she'll deny it for sure." Marcus snorted. After knowing that Jessica was safe, he wasn't so worried anymore. His only shock now was the little boy in front of him.

"A paternity test? I'm not interested. When my mommy wakes up, you can go ask her. If she says yes, you can do it, and then no matter what the result is, we'll sever ties with you. If she denies it, it's none of my business, you can play your games on your own." Henry said with a smile. The decision-making power in this matter was in his mommy's hands. He only resorted to Marcus this time because he had no other choice.

If his mommy admits it, Marcus doesn't believe it and still wants to do a paternity test, he will accept it, but he will never admit that Marcus is his father.

A man whom his mommy doesn't trust doesn't deserve to be his father.

Chapter 28

He Was My Son

The child's words were light and his attitude was good, but the implications in his words were extremely cold and decisive, without any hesitation.

Such a young child, yet so methodical in handling things, very determined and efficient.

Take Jessica's situation as an example. If it were another child, they wouldn't be able to withstand the doctor's advice and sign a consent form for Jessica to undergo amputation surgery. But he wouldn't, he knew he was too young to convince anyone.

He found someone who could handle the situation and then went to find someone to treat Jessica.

From the moment he said, "My mommy, I'm responsible," Marcus knew that this son of Jessica was resolute and ruthless, a formidable person.

And in their meeting, in just three or five words, he was even more certain.

This kid is a tough character!

Marcus glared at him, and Henry curled his eyebrows, flashing him a bright smile.

The feeling of being annoyed by Jessica's hypocritical attitude came back to Marcus, his eyes narrowed.

Damn it! Like mother, like son!

Marcus walked over, his deep gaze falling upon Henry's rosy face. He slowly crouched down, his hand gently caressing his face, tracing over his features. Henry felt Mr. Marcus's hand trembling.

Night of Destiny

A smile crept onto Henry's lips. Daddy was not as calm as he appeared to be.

Would Dad love him?

Henry pondered silently, feeling a mix of excitement and unease. No matter how mature he was mentally, and no matter how composed he appeared in times of crisis, Henry was still just a 7-year-old child. He knew his dad was right in front of him, yet he couldn't acknowledge him. There was inevitably a sense of regret in his heart.

Jessica had long been aware of her son's astonishing intelligence, but she had raised him like an ordinary child. She sent him to school when it was time to go to school, and played with him when it was time to play. Henry had enjoyed almost all the childhood happiness that genius children missed out on.

Aside from his remarkable intellect, Henry was just a child.

He also worried if Dad and Mommy would love him, and hoped to win their hearts and receive their love.

The desire for familial love is a primitive longing in everyone's heart, regardless of gender or intelligence.

Moreover, this was the first time he and Marcus had met.

The first time he had been gently touched by his dad, the first time he had been so close to his dad, and the first time he had felt his dad's attention.

For Henry, this was a very special feeling.

Warm and bittersweet.

Excited but also worried.

He really loved his dad, but he didn't know if his dad loved him.

Marcus held his rosy hand. The child's dad had beautiful fingers, long, rounded, and still bearing a hint of childishness. Holding them in his palm felt warm, soft, and comfortable.

Marcus realized that he didn't reject having such a big son at all. He was even ecstatic because he was proud to have such an outstanding child.

Sect Elder Breeze

This little boy was exceptionally intelligent, delicate, and beautiful, a true gentleman like someone from England, making people love and care for him from the depths of their hearts.

Marcus's throat was dry, unable to produce a sound as if a sharp, thin silver needle occasionally pricked his heart.

The more he looked at him, the more distinct his emotions surged from the depths of his heart— love, protection, and fondness. For Marcus, this feeling was also unfamiliar.

A stranger's love.

Is he his own son?!

This feeling of blood being thicker than water was so special. He really wanted to give him all the best things in the world and make him the happiest child in the world.

He was my son! Unconsciously, this thought deeply imprinted in Marcus's heart, never to be erased.

When did he and Jessica have a child?

He couldn't remember anything. He used to find Jessica's figure familiar, but later on, he realized it was similar to Crystal's figure. He had thought it was just an illusion caused by the resemblance. Now, he thought they might know each other.

Eight years ago, he had lost a month's worth of memories. He couldn't remember what happened during that month. Did she enter his life during that time and did he accidentally forget her?

But why, eight years later, when they faced each other every day, did she never mention it, even pretending not to recognize him when they first met?

So many questions clustered in his heart, and Marcus felt angry and impatient. He wished the woman lying there could wake up immediately and tell him that this was his son. And tell him what exactly happened eight years ago.

This hazy feeling was awful.

If they had a complicated relationship and such a big son, then he did miss out so much!

Night of Destiny

The only family affection Marcus had enjoyed in his life was what his mother had given him until he was ten years old. After that, there was only himself in the world, no one to love him, only harm and darkness, without a trace of sunlight.

His longing for family was stronger than anyone else's.

"Henry..." Would this child love him? Marcus felt anxious.

"If I am really your son, what will you do?" Henry let him hold his hand and asked with a smile.

It was said that he had a fiancée he was ready to marry.

"What do you want to do?" Marcus quickly regained his senses from the ecstasy and anxiety. He realized that this child was different from others, extremely intelligent!

"Can I do whatever I want?" Henry blinked. Well, it seemed that his dad wasn't very easy to talk to after all. Maybe it was mom who was biased against him, so her evaluation wasn't fair?

"No!" Marcus categorically rejected it. Even if he was his son, it didn't mean he could do whatever he wanted. Some requests had to be within reason. Marcus never agreed to overly vague conditions from others.

Indeed, not easy to talk to. Mom, you're truly clever!

"Then I'll ask first, and you have to answer first." Henry brought the conversation back.

Father and son really had the same negotiation tactics.

Marcus's face turned serious as he sat in the chair and had Henry sit beside him, his gaze fixed on the operating room. He honestly answered, "I haven't decided yet!"

Henry was satisfied with this answer.

Not deciding yet meant that Marcus would seriously consider what should be done between him and Mom.

"I really want my dad to know that he has such a son like me. But my mom's happiness is more important than my wish!" Henry expressed his choice implicitly.

If one day he had to choose between mom and dad, he would definitely choose mom. After all, he was strong enough, and even Marcus couldn't separate them.

Of course, if there was no need for such a choice, that would be even better!

Marcus gazed deeply at this face that resembled his own, feeling a dull ache in his heart. This topic seemed too serious, and this statement seemed like a deliberate message from this child.

Mr. Marcus was almost certain that Henry knew something but chose not to say it because he was concerned about Jessica lying inside. His heart sank slightly, and he changed the topic, "Who was that man just now? Can he really save your mom?"

Henry nodded and smiled, "Antonio. If he can't save her, then probably no one can."

"Antonio?" Marcus raised his eyebrows in surprise.

There was one particular incident that caused a great stir regarding Antonio, which happened last year and spread throughout the underworld. Marcus had heard a little bit about it.

During the trade between Victor and Robin with an arms dealer in the Port of Paris and Mexico, they were ambushed, and Victor was shot 10 times. It was said that he took as many as 3 bullets in his heart. Many people claimed that he died on the spot.

However, a month later, Victor miraculously woke up.

His attending doctor happened to be Antonio.

Antonio was a man with exceptional and mysterious medical skills.

This incident caused a sensation last year. Almost everyone involved in arms trading and diamond smuggling knew about it.

Marcus found it quite suspenseful and, for a moment, thought that it must have been a body double for Victor. But then, the arms trade remained unaffected and everything was in order. Marcus had to believe that there were indeed people capable of resurrecting the dead.

Night of Destiny

When Marcus mentioned this to Henry, Henry smiled faintly, saying that no one could truly come back from the dead.

Antonio's medical skills were indeed remarkable, but not to the extent of defying the laws of nature.

"How do you know him?" Marcus asked in a serious tone, feeling nervous. It was well-known that Antonio was associated with three major terrorists. How could his son be connected to such a peculiar person?

Henry casually made up an excuse, saying, "When Mommy and I were in Paris, Antonio owed me a favor. Coincidentally, he was in City W, so I asked him to come and repay the favor."

Henry spoke calmly, and his innocent voice was quite convincing. Most people would not suspect a child of lying.

Marcus couldn't find any flaws and stopped pursuing the matter further.

Little did he know that not only did his son know Antonio, but he also had connections with the top three international terrorists and worked behind the scenes to eliminate all obstacles in their trades.

"When it comes to the car accident, what happened exactly?" After asking Mr. Miller, Marcus inquired about it with Henry.

Henry half-lowered his eyes, filled with anger. He said, "I don't know either. Another car suddenly rushed over from behind. Mommy pushed me away, but she got hit herself. The culprit ran away."

If Mommy hadn't pushed him away, both of them could have been injured by that car.

Obviously, it was premeditated murder! However, he didn't want to tell Marcus.

Regardless of who did it, this time, he would make the person pay a painful price. The person who almost cost his mommy her life would pay with their own life.

Sect Elder Breeze

He recognized the brand of the car, Lamborghini, and it was a limited edition. The person who could drive such a top-tier car must have come from a wealthy family.

This person dared to be so arrogant in broad daylight, indicating that they must have some background. Otherwise, they wouldn't dare to drive a Lamborghini to hit someone.

If this matter were to be handed over to the police, even if they caught the person, what would happen? It would just be a formality, and in the end, the person would walk away without any consequences, at most just drinking a cup of coffee at the police station.

How could he let this happen?

Any creature that threatened his mommy's life had to be eradicated!

This matter had to be handled privately with as few people knowing as possible.

He still hoped that in his father's eyes, he would be seen as an excellent, cute, clever, and well-behaved child. It would be best not to ruin his image in Daddy's eyes before they officially acknowledged each other!

"I have assigned someone to investigate this matter. We will definitely get to the bottom of it. Don't worry," Marcus reassured while patting his son's head.

Although they were keeping secrets from each other, the way these two father and son operated was surprisingly similar. Marcus had also arranged for someone to investigate this matter discreetly.

If it was an accident, at the very least, the person responsible should be severely punished before being handed over to the police.

If it was murder, that person would not escape!

Anyone who dared to cause such a ghastly accident should be prepared to face retaliation.

Night of Destiny

However, Marcus thought that this matter was likely an accident. After all, Henry and her mother did not have any conflicts with anyone to the extent of being targeted for murder.

Regardless, he would definitely not let this matter end without a clear resolution.

Henry nodded. Yeah, it seemed like he had to make Victor create some mysteries to divert attention from his father. He wanted to handle this matter himself and didn't want Marcus to get involved, because instinctively, he felt that his Daddy was somehow implicated.

Just in case...

The two cunning father and son had their own schemes in mind and remained silent for a while.

Marcus quietly observed Henry's profile, feeling more and more moved and proud.

On the other hand, Henry pondered on how to make his enemies suffer a more gruesome death.

Time passed silently.

Although Henry was mentally strong, his body was still weak. He had a habit of taking afternoon naps and knowing that Jessica was safe, he relaxed a bit. The drowsiness hit him, and he dozed off while sitting in the chair.

Marcus couldn't bear to see it, so he carefully laid him flat, using his thigh as a pillow. He clumsily protected the little boy in his arms.

Henry was really tired and didn't pay much attention. He found a comfortable position and hugged Mr. Marcus' waist, falling into a deep sleep.

This was his son! A warm smile curved Marcus' lips.

The usually cold features softened, becoming gentle, and charming, as if he had transformed into a different person.

Then his thoughts shifted to Jessica, and a surge of anger engulfed him. That damn woman had hidden this from him for so long. She better give him a perfect explanation.

Marcus now unquestionably accepted that this was his son.

Sect Elder Breeze

Even if Jessica denied it, even if there was no paternity test, Marcus had made up his mind!

Lost in his thoughts, Mr. Marcus couldn't help but admire the creator's marvel when he looked at this small face so similar to his own.

Holding him like this, Mr. Marcus felt an unprecedented softness in his heart, gazing at his face with affection, as if he could never get enough.

Suddenly, his phone rang. Mr. Marcus was about to turn it off and ignore it, but looking at the display, he saw it was Old Mr. Alston. He frowned and answered.

"Return home immediately!" Old Mr. Alston's voice came through the cold machine, and the person on the other end could feel the chill.

Chapter 29

Miraculous Doctor Antonio

Whenever Old Mr. Alston spoke to him, it was always in commanding tones, and Marcus had grown accustomed to it. But he rarely heard him sound so urgent.

If it wasn't an emergency, Old Mr. Alston wouldn't contact him.

"I'm busy right now!" Marcus refused, glancing at the operating room. Even though Antonio was the surgeon and he had reassured him that Jessica would be safe, Marcus still felt uneasy. He had to wait for the surgery to be successful before he could relax.

"Come back immediately!" Old Mr. Alston's voice became sharper, laced with anger.

Marcus was puzzled. What was going on?

After thinking for a moment, he realized that apart from Dennis' incident, there hadn't been anything significant recently.

In a cold tone, Marcus said, "Dad, I'm really busy right now. If there's something, we'll talk about it tonight!"

"I don't care what you're doing right now. Come back immediately!" Old Mr. Alston repeated for the third time.

Marcus coldly curled his lips and hung up the phone. To avoid any distractions, he coolly powered off his phone.

Who cares!

Before he achieved his goal, indeed, he didn't want to have a falling out with Old Mr. Alston. At least he could maintain a false peace. However, this time, Dennis offended Jessica.

He had almost had a falling out with Old Mr. Alston, and this time Jessica's life hung in the balance. Old Mr. Alston couldn't make him leave.

Old Mr. Alston could do whatever he wanted.

He didn't believe it. Even if he brought down the entire Noblefull Group, let's see who could be more ruthless!

Henry was dozing. He had woken up as soon as the phone rang and listened carefully to their conversation. He couldn't help but give a thumbs up.

His dad was indeed formidable, he was full of courage.

In fact, sometimes he thought his dear dad was very adorable.

If he dared to leave the operating room at this moment, the little boy would not be happy.

No matter how big the world was, Mommy was the biggest now!

No matter how big the matter was, mommy was more important.

Hmm, more points!

The operating room, which had been closed for over four hours, opened!

Antonio walked out first, followed by doctors and nurses, all of them looking at him with admiration as if he were a god.

Henry and Marcus immediately went up to them.

"How is it?" Henry anxiously grabbed Antonio's hand.

Antonio smiled and pinched his rosy cheek, "Little boy, why don't you believe me?"

Just as they were speaking, a nurse pushed Jessica out. Jessica had a pale complexion, no trace of color, her eyes tightly shut, and she looked extremely weak, like a withered flower.

Marcus's heart tightened, and there was a slight pang of pain.

The woman who usually smiled and was humble lay pale before him, and it was heart-wrenching.

"Mummy!"

"Don't worry, she'll wake up tomorrow!" Antonio said, and the nurse took Jessica to the VIP ward.

Henry nodded, "Thank you!"

"Say hello to me!" Antonio blinked his eyes. The usually indifferent man had a radiant smile as he teased the little boy. There was no way around it. Everyone in the online community had been deceived by this little boy.

What was even more frustrating was that this little boy had always been telling the truth, but no one believed him.

Henry wrinkled his nose delicately, "You're leaving anyway, so hurry up and go!"

"No way! Using me and then abandoning me, Henry, you're really heartless!" Antonio playfully scolded. "Wait for his message. I'll stay to help you deal with some bloody matters. Don't refuse."

This was what Victor instructed. Everyone in the chatting group liked Henry, and they had been talking for a year. Even if they hadn't met in person, their friendship was close.

Victor asked Antonio to stay because he wanted to protect Henry.

They were all not righteous men and women, and they even killed without batting an eye. They were used to bloodshed and violence, almost always living in danger. But Henry was different. He had always been behind the scenes, never appearing amid bloodshed. They didn't know he was a child. Knowing that he was a child, neither Victor nor Antonio would agree to let him get involved in overly bloody affairs. Even if Victor hadn't given instructions, Antonio would still stay.

Henry nodded. He wasn't trying to be strong. He didn't want to rely on Marcus's dark forces. He could only rely on himself, but he was too young to handle many things personally. It was inevitable that someone had to support him.

Marcus saw that Antonio and Henry's relationship seemed more than just owing a favor, and he couldn't help but worry. After all, Antonio was a dangerous person, and excessive contact was not appropriate.

"Henry, sweetheart, come online when you have time. They're going to explode."

Henry frowned. After he left, Victor would immediately go into the group to announce the news.

Just thinking about that group of terrorists possibly all rushing to W City, Henry deeply mourned for the city's police.

"Don't worry, Victor is the most rational and protective of you. He knows how to measure things." Antonio smiled and waved his hand casually. "I'll contact you later!"

With that, he left.

"That... " The doctor called out to Antonio, trembling and shaky, completely changing his previously angry demeanor. His eyes were full of admiration. He was considered an authority in surgery and had a great reputation internationally. He had always been arrogant, but today he witnessed what true medical skills meant.

Who is that man?

Someone with such a level of medical expertise, he couldn't possibly not have heard of him. And he looks particularly young, it's unbelievable.

"May I ask for your name, sir?"

Antonio turned back, devoid of his usual humor in front of Henry. His eyebrows were cold and indifferent.

"Just a passerby!"

His attitude was extremely arrogant and self-righteous as he left with great pride.

The doctor's face turned red with embarrassment, feeling ashamed of his earlier assertion.

The world is vast, and there are all sorts of wonders.

Night of Destiny

    The patient's bacterial infection had already spread to the point where amputation was necessary. After some time passed, the success rate of the surgery also decreased significantly. But he managed to heal the patient.
    Completely and perfectly!
    It's unimaginable.
    He is far superior in that regard, and what's even more remarkable is that he is so young.
    Marcus watched his figure deeply, feeling like something was off, but couldn't pinpoint it at the moment. What kind of people had this little boy been associating with?
    "I'm going to see Mommy, do you want to come?" Henry asked softly, with a graceful smile.
    Marcus nodded.
    Henry took the initiative to hold his hand, their actions natural and intimate.
    Marcus tightened his grip, holding Henry's hand, and they went together to see Jessica.
    Father and son stayed by Jessica's side until Mr. Miller came to take over. Henry was a child, so it was only natural for Mr. Marcus, Jessica's superior, to stay overnight with her. Despite the presence of nurses, Mr. Miller was still very worried and insisted on staying by Jessica's side until she woke up.
    Marcus had planned to take Henry home, but to his surprise, Antonio was waiting downstairs at the hospital. When he saw Henry coming down, he opened the car door and got out. The man's usually cold face was now smiling softly.
    "Antonio, why are you here?" Henry was surprised. He had been operating for hours and must be tired, how did he recover so quickly?
    Antonio turned his wrist and smiled politely, "I haven't stretched my muscles in a long time, just going out for a walk and to pick you up."

With a year of understanding between them, Henry easily understood what he meant.

"Mr. Marcus, can we have dinner together next time?" Henry asked with a smile.

The two of them had planned to have dinner together. Marcus didn't want to part with Henry so quickly. The little boy also wanted to spend more time with his father. But Victor's efficiency was so high, that it seemed impossible today.

Marcus didn't like Antonio getting too close to Henry. One was an innocent child, the other was a hidden terrorist. Who knew if he would corrupt his son?

But now Jessica was still unconscious, and even if he had accepted Henry as his son in his heart, he still had no say in the matter.

Marcus's icy gaze swept over Antonio, showing curiosity and wariness. A layer of frost covered Marcus's delicate features. Which parents in the world would willingly hand over their child to a terrorist?

Antonio was clever enough to understand what was on Marcus's mind. It was natural for parents to worry about their children, and he could understand that.

But Mr. Marcus, your son doesn't need you to worry about him for a lifetime, I'm afraid. In terms of intelligence, decisiveness, and ruthlessness, few could compare to your son. He only had the role of bullying others, how could anyone bully him?

"Mr. Marcus, don't make such a scary expression. We may engage in arms dealing, diamond smuggling, and money laundering, but human trafficking is off-limits," Antonio said with a light smile, a hint of wisdom gleaming in his distant gaze.

There was a sense of trustworthiness in his indifference.

Marcus was astonished. He didn't expect him to be so direct. His lips curved, a faint and invisible chill passing over them, "Even if you want to engage in human trafficking, you might not be able to get him!"

Antonio smiled, it seemed like Mr. Marcus knew Henry very well.

Marcus then turned to Henry and said, "You go ahead!"

Henry nodded and smiled at him before leaving with Antonio.

******

Inside the car, Henry asked, "Who did it?"

"Dennis, your father's second brother!" Antonio said, handing the computer to Henry. "Take a look for yourself!"

Henry opened the computer and accessed the information Victor had collected. His delicate face tightened, his expression extremely unpleasant. He snorted coldly, "He wanted to run me over, didn't he?"

"Perhaps!" Antonio said cautiously. The affairs of the Smith family's brothers would become even more interesting in the future.

"Bastard!" Dennis didn't hit him, but he caused his mother to suffer. He would never forgive him!

"What should we do? He's at least somewhat related to you by blood. Do you still want to kill him?" Antonio asked, a hint of a smile on his lips. If it was someone else, Henry would issue a death command. But if it was someone from the Smith family, that required careful consideration!

Henry logged into his tracking system, entered a command, and located Dennis.

In just a few seconds, the system had already tracked the location. Henry pulled up the specific map and said in a solemn voice, "2060 Birch st!"

"You're really going to take action?" Antonio was surprised. He thought this was something that Henry would let go of.

"He has to pay for my mommy's two legs at the very least!" Henry said coldly.

There was no discussion about this matter. Did Dennis think anyone could run him over? He didn't even consider his own strength!

Marcus took out his phone, turned it on, and saw that there were dozens of missed calls from his father. Furrowing his brows, he wondered what had happened.

Driving back to the Smith Family, in the hall, Old Mr. Alston and Monica walked together, both of them wearing unpleasant expressions. Especially Old Mr. Alston, his face was livid, leaning on a cane, looking particularly intimidating.

"Dad!" Marcus greeted half-heartedly.

"Where have you been? Only coming back now?" Old Mr. Alston was furious, his gaze dark and menacing, as if a storm was about to come.

Marcus pursed his lips and sneered, "I've been busy."

"Oh, Mr. Marcus, you have quite the attitude. Your father has to ask you three times to see you. But no one has ever dared to make your father wait for so long. Mr. Marcus, are you really busy, or is it intentional?" Monica said maliciously, a gloating expression on her face.

It was no secret that Old Mr. Alston intended to pass on the Noblefull Group to Leonard. But Leonard was still young, and for now, Marcus was in charge. No one dared to underestimate Marcus. Old Mr. Alston was getting older after all, and who knew what changes would occur in the Smith family once Leonard grew up?

Monica, who married Old Mr. Alston at a young age, had her eyes on one thing, the wealth of the Smith family.

Marcus was undoubtedly the biggest obstacle to her exclusive enjoyment of the Smith family's abundant fortune. She had tried to please Marcus, but he had never given her a nice look, often showing disgust and mockery.

This made Monica, who had strong vanity and conceit, hate him to the core.

She was well aware of the strained relationship between Old Mr. Alston and Marcus.

Every time Marcus came back, she would mock him and deliberately provoke a conflict between them, hoping that Old Mr. Alston would angrily kick Marcus out of Noblefull Group.

Marcus's cold gaze swept over Monica, his face expressionless. His delicate features were covered in a layer of ice, and his brows showed his usual elegant indifference. He snorted coldly, ignoring her completely.

Monica was so angry that her face turned red, "Alston, look at him... Is this how he treats his elders?"

"Dad, if you have something to say, say it quickly. I have a tripartite meeting to attend later!" Marcus didn't care about Monica and spoke coldly. He felt sick being in this so-called family for even a second longer!

Old Mr. Alston was filled with anger, his eyes narrowing dangerously. "Marcus, you have some nerve. You dare to hide such a big matter from me?"

"What are you talking about?" Marcus furrowed his brows.

Monica smirked beside him, and Old Mr. Alston's face darkened.

A tinge of suspicion flickered in Marcus's deep eyes. What had happened?

He understood Old Mr. Alston well. After decades of maneuvering in the business world, he was a ruthless character. Although he was impulsive and domineering in his younger years, his experience had taught him to remain calm in many situations. This blatant anger was the first time Marcus had seen it.

Old Mr. Alston became furious, slamming his cane against the ground twice, startling Monica into pale-faced fright. "You still dare to act oblivious. You have a son, why didn't you tell me?"

Marcus's pupils widened in astonishment. How did he know about this?

Marcus was secretly amazed. He had only found out today that Jessica's son had a face that was seventy percent similar to his. It was highly likely that Henry was his son. It had only been a few hours since then, how could his father have received the news already?

Chapter 30

Never Let It Go

"What's the matter? No words left to say?" Old Mr. Alston taunted, a hint of cunning appearing on his elderly face. "See for yourself!"

After Old Mr. Alston finished speaking, he angrily threw the bag of documents on the table towards Marcus. The bag hit Marcus's chest and fell, causing two photos to slide out. Marcus's heart skipped a beat as he bent down to pick them up.

There were two photos of Henry!

One of the photos was of Henry wearing a primary school uniform, with his rosy face adorned by an elegant smile. The photo was taken beautifully, exuding an elegance that resembled a little gentleman, making him very likable.

Night of Destiny

The other photo was a picture of Jessica and Henry together! In the background was the Eiffel Tower. In the photo, Jessica was wearing a red dress, meticulously dressed up, radiating purity and grace, resembling a blooming red rose, captivating and almost enchanting. She half squatted, cradling little Henry in her arms, both mother and son smiling, creating an extremely heartwarming scene that touched Marcus's heart.

His icy gaze softened instantly, almost luring people to lose themselves in it.

He even realized how much he yearned for Jessica to say to him, "Hey, this is your son. We form a family." Instead of rejecting that notion, he felt a surge of excitement.

"How do you explain this?" Old Mr. Alston fumed, "No wonder when I met this child last time, he had a strange look on his face and lied to me that his father was a teacher."

Seeing these photos, Old Mr. Alston naturally recalled his brief encounter with Henry, which only fueled his anger further.

It was evident that the child had been deceiving him at that time.

He wondered why there could be such striking similarities between people, as that child and Marcus looked remarkably alike. He had assumed it was a coincidence, but it turned out to be a deceitful scheme.

"Have you seen him?" Marcus asked sternly, narrowing his dangerously intense gaze.

"I'm asking you how to explain this case!" Old Mr. Alston shouted in a deep voice. This man, who had once been fierce in his youth, had softened somewhat in old age but still exuded an intimidating pressure that left people breathless.

When he was furious, he appeared even more terrifying, like an old lion brimming with strength.

Sect Elder Breeze

Marcus remained composed, his icy gaze displaying elegance and indifference, with a hint of almost invisible mockery. He courteously said, "Dad, are you unhappy? This is the eldest grandson of our Smith family."

Monica opened her eyes wide and coldly said, "Mr. Marcus, this child must be at least six or seven years old. You kept him hidden so tightly. What are you trying to do? If it were all above board, you would have brought him back to the Smith family. We wouldn't have eaten him. What is the meaning of deceiving us for so long?"

This child was so similar to her Leonard, and one Marcus was already enough to give her a headache. Now, another member of the Smith family appeared, and Monica couldn't be pleased.

She would not allow anyone to obstruct Leonard's path.

Marcus glanced coldly at her, mocking, "What right do you have to meddle in my affairs?"

Just take a look at who you are. Even Dennis wouldn't necessarily show her any respect, let alone him. If it weren't for her giving birth to Leonard, she wouldn't have any place in the Smith family.

He had long seen through this woman's pettiness and selfishness. It was all for the sake of the Smith family's wealth. Old Mr. Alston knew that as well, but for the sake of Leonard, he didn't pay much attention to it.

"You..." Monica's face turned red with a mixture of shame and anger. She turned to Old Mr. Alston for support, "Alston, look at him..."

"You shut up!" Old Mr. Alston warned her with a glare, his gaze showing a sense of darkness.

Monica dared not throw a tantrum anymore, and she glared at Marcus resentfully, afraid to say another word.

"Marcus, you have grown up. Have you become defiant?" Old Mr. Alston's voice deepened as his cloudy eyes glistened with sharpness, "What are you planning to do?"

Night of Destiny

In reality, what angered Old Mr. Alston the most was not Marcus's concealment of Henry. He didn't know that Marcus had just found out as well. He thought Marcus had intentionally hidden it from him for years. Over these years, Old Mr. Alston's control over Marcus had been extremely perfect, or at least he believed it to be so.

He knew everything about Noblefull Group's business, both the public and the secret.

He even had people investigating Marcus's private life, monitoring him constantly. He would never allow Marcus to escape his control.

And Marcus had always behaved commendably. Except for his cold demeanor, Marcus had been obedient and played the role of his pawn. That was how they maintained the facade of harmony, despite their twisted father-son relationship.

Furthermore, Old Mr. Alston had placed Crystal by Marcus's side. Even if Marcus had a promiscuous private life, Old Mr. Alston felt assured.

But now, the news broke that Marcus had a secret child, and Old Mr. Alston was furious.

He believed that Marcus was unfathomable and had long escaped his control. Otherwise, with his means, how could he not discover that Marcus had such a large secret?

To Old Mr. Alston, this matter was like a slap in the face. He deeply felt that this son of his was slipping out of his control.

And there was another reason... the woman in the photo...

"Dad, what do you mean? I don't understand. Having a son is a happy thing. Why are you angry?" Marcus asked knowingly, smiling elegantly, though the smile didn't reach his eyes. "What are you worried about?"

Worried that he would swallow Noblefull Group?
Who cares!

Old Mr. Alston erupted in anger, his face becoming extremely ugly. "What am I worried about? Hmph, Marcus, don't you know?"

"How could I guess Dad's thoughts!" Marcus's delicate features seemed to don a thin, cool mask. Despite his smile, it conveyed a sense of chilliness.

"I warn you, Noblefull Group belongs to the Smith family, not you. Just because you're the CEO now, doesn't mean you can do whatever you want. You don't have that capability!" Old Mr. Alston lost his composure due to Marcus's indifferent attitude and spoke bluntly.

Old Mr. Alston would never hand over the Noblefull Group to Marcus. Even if Marcus had a son, so what? That woman...

"Dad, you're just being overly suspicious. You think I don't know? Brother Dennis warns me every time we meet. Noblefull Group is his, not mine. Why are you worried that I can't see the situation clearly?" Marcus smiled gracefully, but his eyes turned cold.

Old Mr. Alston snorted heavily, "It's good if you can see through it. I will never acknowledge that child!"

Marcus's eyes darkened, and a hint of darkness passed over his cheek as he coldly laughed, "Dad, you're joking again. I'll acknowledge my son, that's enough. Whether you acknowledge or not doesn't matter!"

We don't need your acknowledgment either!

Marcus clenched his fists, his face full of coldness. Old Mr. Alston had never acknowledged his own son, so how could he acknowledge his grandson?

If he wasn't talented in management, he would have been kicked out by Old Mr. Alston long ago, just like he did over a decade ago, how could he have survived until today?

Cold-blooded, ruthless, indirectly subjecting him to the darkest and most humiliating years!

Night of Destiny

This hatred had been buried deep in his heart for over a decade. Neither the Lee family nor the Smith family could escape from it.

Old Mr. Alston didn't acknowledge him, and he didn't care about his acknowledgment either. The title of 'Dad' was merely a formality.

Did he think Marcus couldn't survive without the Noblefull Group? Hmph!

Marcus, in his heart, only had his mother, not a father!

"On another note, Dad, how did you find out?" Marcus asked, curious if it was just a coincidence?

Or...

Why did it have to be today? It brought him a dark association. It would be better if it wasn't like this, otherwise...

Marcus half-lowered his eyelids, thinking about the nearly amputated Jessica, thinking about Henry, who was terrified but portrayed himself as calm and composed. His eyes were filled with murderous intent.

This car accident almost destroyed Jessica. It nearly destroyed that family!

But don't let him find any clues, otherwise, he will never let it go!

"If you don't want others to know, don't do it yourself. I saw that child a few weeks ago!" Old Mr. Alston sneered coldly. At that time, he thought it was just a coincidence, but now...

"You changed your secretary, and I suggested Crystal, who is capable of work and can take care of you nearby. But you refused and brought this woman into Noblefull Group... She is the mother of that child," Old Mr. Alston pointed coldly at Jessica in the photo, suppressing the tremor in his voice. "Who is she?"

Marcus was about to speak when suddenly his phone rang, breaking the tense atmosphere between them.

"What did you say?" Marcus's face changed, he glanced at Old Mr. Alston, hung up the phone, and quickly walked out.

"Marcus, stop, where are you going?" Old Mr. Alston was furious.

Marcus turned around, a stern and murderous expression on his face. "You better pray that Dennis was tough enough!"

******

At Birch st, an underground parking lot!

Henry turned on his computer, infiltrating the surveillance system of the building, and disabling the monitors!

Antonio admired his skillful operation. Victor and Robin were also computer geniuses, but their talent was honed through intensive training at the special ops training camp. As for Henry, it was evident that he possessed natural talent. The cold machine seemed to come to life in his hands, allowing him to do whatever he wanted without leaving his seat.

"Hey, when did you develop such a high talent for computers?" Antonio couldn't help but ask curiously.

"At five years old!" Henry said, tilting his head, smiling, and cutely blinking his eyes. "I assembled and configured my first computer by myself. At that time, my mommy had to go to school and take care of me, so we had a tough time. I collected materials from an electronic waste factory and built a computer that was several hundred times better than what was on the market."

"Impressive!" Antonio praised with a smile, and then his eyes suddenly flickered. "They're here!"

Two cars entered the parking lot and as soon as they stopped, Dennis was thrown out. He screamed in pain, holding his head that had been smashed, and shouted angrily, "Who are you people? What do you want?"

Night of Destiny

"Do you know who I am? I am the second young master of Noblefull Group, and I will be the president of Noblefull Group in the future. If you dare to touch me, the Smith family won't let you go!"

Six men got out of the cars, and an oppressive atmosphere immediately filled the parking lot. They wore black suits, exuding strength and coldness. Their every move filled the parking lot with a dark and intimidating aura.

Dennis retreated in fear, trembling and terrified.

The six men remained silent, but their mere presence almost shattered his courage.

This kind of menacing atmosphere couldn't be faked, nor could it be cultivated overnight. It was developed through countless battles and trials, in the realm of life and death. They were far from ordinary underworld figures.

Dennis was a paper tiger. He indulged in pleasure and was lawless, often involved in illegal activities and had been to the black market. He had encountered people from the underworld before.

But this was his first time encountering someone with such intense killing intent.

"Please, spare me, spare me. I'll give you as much money as you want, just don't kill me, don't kill me..." Dennis pleaded while crawling and clinging to one of the men's thighs, crying.

He was originally celebrating in his bar, waiting for good news from Monica. Who would've expected six big men to suddenly rush in and tie him up here? Throughout the journey, he had been scared out of his wits. His previous shouting was just an attempt to intimidate them, but it had no effect whatsoever.

Dennis was scared and trembling.

Sect Elder Breeze

Ordinary people would have their hearts pounding and experience exceptional fear when facing these cold-blooded men in black. And now he had to face six of them at once. The murderous intent emanating from them was too strong to ignore.

"Please, spare me, spare me..."

He had no idea who he had offended. Dennis racked his brain but couldn't figure out who in W City would dare to kidnap him.

He was known for his bad habits and had a somewhat infamous reputation in the underworld. Those involved in the underground world would let him be because of his connection to the Smith family. Dennis felt inflated with self-satisfaction.

He thought that with the Smith family's status in W City, he could do whatever he wanted. A typical spoiled brat, brainless and spineless, only acting tough because of who he knew.

"This guy is such a coward," Antonio sneered, a hint of disgust lingered in his indifferent gaze. Dealing with this kind of person would be an insult to him if he took action.

Wow, such a low level.

He even despised being the target. Shooting him would lower his standards.

Henry tilted his head, a cold smile playing on his lips. He closed his laptop with a snap, and got out of the car, ready to reclaim his father's humiliation and his mother's pain. The show was about to begin. He wouldn't stop playing until they went crazy, and then they wouldn't deserve to be his parents' son!

His father had reservations about Dennis, but he had none!

Antonio smiled and followed him out of the car. Fortunately, this parking lot was rarely frequented, and they had closed it off. They had something to play with!

"Hey, Mr. Dennis, do you know me?" Henry greeted with a smile, slowly approaching Dennis. His smile was elegant and graceful. Coupled with the rosy cheeks unique to children, this scene appeared exceptionally adorable.

Dennis widened his eyes. Was it him? That stubborn brat, was he here for revenge?

"You..." Dennis pointed at Henry, his finger trembling. He rolled on the ground twice, then tried to run away.

Henry slightly turned his head, and instantly two men in black blocked Dennis. Dennis crashed into the solid shoulder of one of the men and rebounded forcefully, falling to the ground in a miserable state, desperately crawling forward. The remaining men in black swiftly moved, encircling him.

"Mr. Dennis, bullets have no eyes. Don't move recklessly!" Henry drew a jewel-encrusted handgun hidden on Antonio's waist. His smile was elegant. "I won't shoot. I've never touched a gun before, and it wouldn't be good if it accidentally went off."

The black muzzle was aimed at Dennis!

Antonio remained silent. This wasn't his original intention, but he couldn't suppress Henry's presence. Fine, this little boy would have to encounter the world sooner or later, so he might as well start training early.

Terrified, Dennis dared not move. Frantically shaking his hands, he pleaded, "Don't kill me, don't kill me...I was wrong, I was wrong, spare me..."

"Trash!" Antonio spit out the word in contempt. If he wasn't Dennis, Henry would have already shot him and left. Why waste time talking to this useless man? Asking for mercy was trash behavior.

This man, crying and howling before a young and delicate child like this, didn't he feel shame?

"Keeping a person like him alive is an embarrassment to all men!" Antonio said coldly as if even a glance at him felt dirty. Crossing his arms, he stood aside and watched the show.

"Agreed, he shouldn't be alive!" Henry said, then swung the gun back and it landed in Antonio's hand. He took a few steps forward, tilting his head to make the men in black step aside.

Dennis was so frightened that his legs weakened, and he retreated repeatedly.

Chapter 31

Henry's Revenge

Dennis wanted to run, but couldn't summon any strength. He looked frantic and sweat poured down like rain. His eyes revealed his fear without any concealment.

That little boy, who was adorable and elegant in every move, exuded an air of elegance. But it struck fear into his heart. How did he find him? How did he know that he had collided with them?

Damn it, if only he had killed the child!

"You're wrong? What mistake have you made? Let me hear it," Henry asked softly.

Dennis froze, then suddenly covered his mouth. Oh no, he let slip the fact that he was the one who hit Jessica and her son. No one was supposed to know about it since there were no surveillance cameras on that street.

Night of Destiny

"I..." Dennis was blocked, unable to say a word. He felt both scared and anxious, his face turning an unattractive shade of red. He looked disheveled and sleazy.

Henry sneered in his heart. It was unfortunate that they were related by blood. What a tragedy for the family!

"You can't say it?" Henry smiled innocently, blinking his eyes. "Driving a limited edition Lamborghini to hit someone in broad daylight, Mr. Dennis, were you trying to announce it to the world?"

"It wasn't me, it wasn't me... I didn't do it..." Dennis waved his hands frantically, his eyes panicked. The group of men in black had almost driven him insane. Henry, maintaining a cute and innocent appearance, spoke in a way that sent chills down one's spine. The stark contrast was too much for the psychologically fragile Mr. Dennis to bear.

"Mr. Dennis!" Henry blinked his eyes, revealing a row of white teeth. "I forgot to tell you, I may not be good at everything, but I'm excellent in computer technology and memory. If I want to find out whose car it was and who hit someone, it won't be difficult. So..."

"Can you stop denying it?" Henry furrowed his brow in distress, his pink lips grazing with a sneer. "Didn't your kindergarten teacher teach you to be honest when dealing with smart people? If you keep denying it, I'll feel like an idiot and start questioning my high IQ, okay?"

Antonio chuckled, finding this scene greatly impactful. He couldn't help but smile, wondering how there could be such a cute yet cunning child in the world.

Look at his flawless skin, still radiating the rosy glow of childhood. One could say he hadn't even grown out of the kindergarten stage, yet he carried such elegance in his smile. Anyone who saw him would think he was such a refined and adorable child.

Sect Elder Breeze

However, from his little mouth came words even colder and more ruthless than those of the terrorists. Though Henry said it with a smile, the underlying mockery and danger seeped through. He silently mourned Mr. Dennis' impending fate.

Raising an eyebrow, Antonio couldn't help but pull out a miniature video recorder, wearing it on his wrist to capture everything and let them witness it.

"I... I was wrong, I was wrong, I was the one who hit you. Spare me, please! I was wrong..." Mr. Dennis wailed, not even understanding why he had become so terrified.

In theory, he shouldn't be scared of a child like this.

Moreover, this little boy had a face that looked very similar to Marcus. Throughout their lives, how many times did he bully Marcus?

When Marcus first joined the Smith family, it was almost like this. The two brothers fought and abused each other, making it quite enjoyable. How did this face become so terrifying now?

Dennis didn't know! He mustered up the courage to suppress him with the identity of the Smith family, but as soon as he made eye contact with those deep, blue eyes, he was too scared to say a word.

Such a terrifying child. An angel disguised as a demon!

"Good boy!" Henry laughed, clapping his hands and wearing an expression of a savior's blessing. "Now, tell me, how do you want to die? I will fulfill your wish!"

Dennis trembled like falling leaves in the autumn, cold sweat flowing. "Please, spare me... I... I am your second uncle, you can't kill me, can't kill me..."

Henry smiled elegantly, with a hint of chilling coercion. If he didn't mention it, perhaps he would kindly spare him from suffering too much. If he did mention it, then he was asking for trouble.

Night of Destiny

"I don't even care about Mr. Marcus' face. How much is your face worth?" Henry coldly said, clapping his hands. "Come, let's simulate a car accident!"

At the moment of the car accident, his mother's fear and unease, he returned it tenfold to this culprit!

"No... Don't..." Dennis screamed.

A man in black came over, grabbed him, and dragged him to stand up straight. Another man in black got in the car, starting it swiftly and deftly.

"No, spare me, have mercy... you demon..."

Henry raised an eyebrow. A demon, huh? That was a good title. He took the gun from Antonio's hand, loaded it, and coldly pointed it at Dennis. "Stand still, don't move! And shut up!"

Dennis was too terrified to move. His mind was in chaos, his expensive suit covered in dust. His eyes were wide open, filled with fear, and his legs were trembling violently.

"Very good, don't move, or..." Henry raised his arm, aiming at his head. "Leave your brain matter behind!"

Antonio clapped, finding that statement harsh, cool, and imposing!

This child was truly talented! If he had the ambition, he would dominate the arms industry in ten years, terrifying them even more!

Antonio thought Truman, the number one terrorist, would have to step aside.

The atmosphere suddenly became tense. The dim underground parking lot with half-lit lights emitted a very eerie ambiance.

Dennis's back shivered, his eyes wide open, trembling there. He dared not move, with that demonic child pointing a gun at him. He didn't think a child could shoot a gun, but he still didn't dare. The sound of the car moving surrounded his ears. He stared fearfully as the car slowly reversed, the fear growing deeper and deeper...

"Spare me, please, I beg you, don't do this, don't do this..." Dennis pleaded, in a pitiful state.

Henry smiled, squinting his eyes, aiming at him, warning him with the simplest movement not to make any sudden moves.

"Move!" After enjoying Dennis's terror enough, Henry shouted with a childish voice, adding a touch of strangeness to the already dark and terrifying atmosphere...

The car surged forward, rushing towards Dennis...

"Oh... Oh...No..." Dennis's scream pierced through the entire parking lot, echoing over and over again... piercing and terrifying.

Antonio shook his head, sneering.

Henry smiled, elegant and compelling. He felt, holding a gun and aiming at someone felt pretty good. Perhaps he should learn to shoot.

The screeching sound of the brakes resounded, leaving a long mark on the ground. The car stopped just an inch away from Dennis...

The engine turned off, and a man stepped out silently, standing aside.

Dennis was almost scared out of his wits, his face pale, and some liquid dripping from his trousers. A puddle spread on the ground.

Antonio chuckled, his voice filled with mockery. "Scared enough to wet yourself?"

Henry nodded seriously, "Seems like it!"

"Mr. Dennis, the car hasn't even hit you yet, what are you afraid of?" Antonio shouted, his laughter mocking. Henry is quite interesting, it's scarier to play with him like this than to run him over at once.

Night of Destiny

In the moment when facing death, it is actually not scary. What is the scariest is knowing death is coming but being powerless to save oneself, only able to wait helplessly for those few seconds of death. That is the most terrifying. That's why they say people who have attempted suicide generally don't try it again. Knowing that one is about to die and experiencing the fear of death at the brink of dying is an unforgettable feeling.

Mr. Dennis cried out, his voice seemed like it wanted to scream, but no sound came out of his throat. Henry's move truly scared him.

"Henry, you're quite ruthless. Standing still and getting hit by a car is more interesting than letting them chase after him and hit him," Antonio laughed with admiration.

Henry put away his gun and smiled, "It's not over yet!"

Antonio narrowed his eyes and raised an eyebrow, asking, "Henry, while he's still not fully conscious, ask him about the bloodshed from eighteen years ago. Maybe there's some hidden truth behind it. Besides, it's your family's matter, it's better to have a backup plan if you find out anything."

"No need!" Henry said. This matter has far-reaching implications, and his father definitely knows the truth. With his father's hatred towards the Smith family and towards him, this matter is not simple.

However, since his father is reluctant to reveal anything, it shows that this matter has caused him significant damage. Why bother involving one more person? It feels invasive to intrude into someone's privacy, and Henry knew it wouldn't be something pleasant.

Henry chose to ignore it!

If his father needs someone to share the burden, he will talk to his mother. If his father doesn't need it, then he doesn't want to know anything!

"Now I only want to seek revenge for them!" Henry's face displayed a chilling smile.

Dennis was already paralyzed on the ground, trembling violently. Henry waved his hand and smiled, "Disable his two legs!"

After breaking his mother's leg, he wanted to compensate with two legs!

Upon hearing this, Dennis's hazy mind suddenly cleared, and he screamed, desperately trying to crawl away.

The agile man swiftly moved towards him and kicked him back with one foot, while the other two held his legs and twisted them forcefully...

Crack...the sound of bones breaking was clearly heard by everyone, followed by Dennis's screams...

"Ouch..." the screams echoed in the empty parking lot, shaking people's hearts and souls...

The black-clothed man let go of Dennis as if throwing away garbage, with a cold and disgusted expression.

Henry approached him, laughing lightly, "How was that? Exciting enough? This is a warning to you. Not everyone can be provoked by you. Why didn't you investigate the other party's background before hitting them?"

With his legs twisted and agonizing pain surging through his body, Dennis almost fainted. He lay on the ground, howling in pain, covered in sweat...

"I will sue you..." Dennis trembled. The hateful child, he was simply a devil, a devil...

Henry chuckled, "Where's the evidence? Do you think a judge will believe that a seven-year-old child crippled you? Mr. Dennis, what kind of joke are you playing?"

"You... you will get what's coming to you!"

"Don't worry, even if you die and reincarnate, karma won't come to haunt me!" Henry laughed happily, finally getting rid of some pent-up frustration.

Suddenly, a sharp warning sound came from the car compartment.

Beep beep beep beep...

Henry quickly turned his head, and Antonio's eyes tightened. It came from his computer, "What's going on?"

Henry looked towards the entrance, and calmly said, "Someone's here!"

He had just installed a warning system around the parking lot. As long as someone crossed the red line, the computer would sound an alarm!

Antonio waved his hand, and six well-trained black-clothed men concealed themselves. Antonio and Henry got back in the car. Henry turned on the computer and started the red line camera, aiming it at the incoming car. A silver Rolls-Royce appeared on the screen.

Chapter 32

Like Father, Like Son

A picture of Marcus suddenly appeared on the screen, and Antonio raised an eyebrow, "Your father!"

Henry's cute and pink face was filled with annoyance and distress. He propped his cheek on his hand and muttered to himself, "I wanted to maintain an elegant and cute image in front of my dad, but it seems... Well, reality and ideals are indeed far apart."

Sect Elder Breeze

Antonio chuckled, "That doesn't sound sincere at all. Come on, you don't need to maintain anything. Your image has always been elegant and cute."

Henry pouted and restarted the warning system.

"Henry, Mr. Marcus is quite capable," Antonio remarked, a hint of admiration flashing in his eyes. "You had Victor distract his people and deliberately mislead them, and made him think this was just an accident. But they were still able to find out the truth and even discovered that Dennis was here. It's quite incredible!"

During their conversation, there was no shortage of praise.

They were both men, standing at the pinnacle of the world. Their every move can have an international impact. They have the ability, power, and courage. They are proud and independent, rarely meeting someone worthy of their admiration.

In male-to-male admiration, it's a strength that speaks! They only admire those who are stronger than themselves and never praise those who are weaker.

Mr. Marcus indeed has some talent. Just breaking through the doubts deliberately set up by Victor and finding Dennis is already enough to impress Antonio.

Henry smiled, "Of course, just look at whose father he is. How can he be lacking in skills!"

The little boy spoke with unparalleled arrogance and pride, appearing exceptionally cute.

When he played the game of tracking and anti-tracking with his father, it took them two consecutive days, the longest time he had played with him so far. Even the four geniuses from the FBI didn't give him the same level of tension and excitement.

Apart from this, Marcus also showed decisive and ruthless business tactics in the market, enough rationality to push Noblefull Group to a new peak. He is a genius in computers as well as in management. With such a father, which son wouldn't feel proud?

Night of Destiny

While they were talking, Marcus's car had already stopped, coincidentally right across from Henry and Antonio's car.

After the headlights turned off, their eyes met, two pairs of strikingly similar eyes, with no time to evade.

Marcus's face darkened, his cold and sharp eyes filled with displeasure, so icy that water could almost drip from them. He gripped the steering wheel tightly, staring at Henry intently, emanating a sinister aura.

This child really dares to make a move! Damn it, doesn't he see how old he is? Yet he plays these tricks.

"Uh-oh, cutie, looks like your father is really angry. Be careful, he might spank your butt!" Antonio teased. He could understand Marcus's thoughts; if he had a son who went behind his back to seek revenge, he would definitely grab him and spank him.

Henry turned his head, gave an elegant smile, and half-jokingly said, "I haven't even been spanked by Dad yet, so getting hit once would be a new experience!"

The three of them almost simultaneously got out of the car, and in the silent parking lot, the only sound was Dennis's wailing.

His wailing echoed again and again, combined with the unique dim lighting here, creating an atmosphere that was indescribably eerie and unsettling.

Marcus coldly glanced at Dennis writhing on the ground, seeing his disheveled appearance, stiff legs, and twisted posture that reeked of strangeness. His eyebrow raised, and a chilling coldness brushed across his lips. He had brought this upon himself, he deserved it!

At the same time, Henry's coldness surprised him. If it were an adult doing such things, Marcus wouldn't be surprised at all. After all, he was accustomed to bloodshed and violence. This level of behavior wouldn't scare him.

But if a seven-year-old child acted this way, the effect was astonishing.

Sect Elder Breeze

What would an ordinary seven-year-old child do when their mommy got into trouble?

Cry, be scared! But he showed none of that. He was calm to the point of being frightening. As soon as Jessica was out of danger, he didn't even eat a meal before immediately seeking revenge. This vengeful nature, who did it resemble?

"Hey, Mr. Marcus, what a coincidence, we meet again!" Henry cutely waved, ignoring his father's furious expression as he smiled brightly and sunnily, as if they had truly bumped into each other.

Antonio admired the child's disguise, it was incredible. He didn't even need to blink his eyes.

"Yeah, quite a coincidence!" Marcus coldly responded, curling his lips. "What are you doing here?"

Henry chuckled and pointed at Dennis, smiling. "This guy needs a lesson, so I'm here to fix him up. Mr. Marcus, do you want to stop me?"

Antonio watched the exchange between the father and son, marveling at their every word and gesture. The genetic inheritance was so mysterious. Not only did they resemble each other, but their aura was also identical.

Marcus scanned Dennis, who was writhing in pain on the ground, and suddenly burst into laughter, with a sinister smile. "How did you manage to torment him like this?"

"Marcus, save me... Marcus, please, save me..." Dennis, in a daze, saw Marcus and screamed in agony. He tried to crawl towards him, but a sharp pain shot through his broken bones, causing him to scream in misery...

The cries echoed in the dim parking lot.

Henry smiled and said, "I want him to experience the pain my mother went through, but ten times worse. Mr. Marcus, you wouldn't beg for mercy for him, would you?"

Marcus crossed his arms, raised an eyebrow, and smirked. His face was gloomy and terrifying, radiating a chilling aura that froze the surrounding air. "Do you think I would beg for mercy for him?"

Night of Destiny

Of course...he wouldn't! Henry secretly thought. How could Marcus beg for mercy for him? He probably wanted to kill Dennis, no, kill everyone from the Smith family, including Old Mr. Alston.

He couldn't fathom the darkness in his father's heart, but one thing he was certain of was that his father would never beg for mercy for the Smith family.

"Marcus, save me..." Dennis pleaded, flailing in mid-air. "Save me, I'm your brother... Save me, I won't compete with you anymore, I won't curse at you again, Marcus, please... take me away from here."

Dennis cried and begged, but Marcus remained cold as ice, sneering at the corners of his lips. "Dennis, compete with me? Are you even worthy?"

Marcus stood there coldly, his well-fitted black suit highlighting his tall and handsome figure. If someone like Dennis could be considered his opponent, wouldn't that be an insult to him?

Over the years, if he hadn't restrained himself, and bided his time, based on Dennis' humiliation, he could have killed him a thousand times over.

Ignoring him wasn't out of fear, but rather out of disdain for laying hands on him.

His true goal was the Smith and Lee families, as well as Noblefull Group. Dennis was just a pawn.

He let Dennis insult him and demand money, just to create an illusion for Old Mr. Alston, fostering the image that Marcus feared him. If it weren't for this, how could Dennis have survived until now?

Marcus now regretted why he hadn't crippled him back then. Instead, he went on to hurt Jessica.

Perhaps, his true intention was Henry.

Unforgivable!

Even if Henry didn't confront him, he wouldn't easily let him go.

Sect Elder Breeze

Marcus approached slowly, step by step, with each step deepening Dennis' fear.

That gaze, wasn't a gaze of salvation, but instead, it looked like a gaze that wanted to send him to hell.

"Don't come closer, don't come closer..." Dennis screamed frantically, waving his hands, his voice piercing, his elbows propped on the ground, ignoring the pain in his legs, desperately crawling forward, trying to escape...

He wanted to escape from this demonic father and son!

Dennis regretted, immensely regretted, if he had known this, he shouldn't have driven to crash into Jessica, oh no, perhaps even earlier, when Marcus was still a child, they should have killed him. Then nothing like this would have happened!

"Help, help..."

Henry's lips curved elegantly, alright, he played two rounds, there were still a few exciting activities waiting for Dennis, since his dad was interested, okay, he would step aside.

Antonio crouched down, and whispered in Henry's ear, "Little cutie, you and your father are quite compatible!"

Henry smiled, blinking his cute eyes, "That's thanks to my mom's excellent parenting!"

Antonio fell silent, if excellent parenting resulted in raising a son like this... then what would bad parenting produce? This question is worth exploring.

"Guess how your dad will play?" Antonio asked in a low voice.

Henry laughed, "Definitely with unique methods, at least ten times more torturous than mine!"

Antonio thumbs up, "Like father, like son. You're strong. I'm sure he'll play dirty."

Henry's recent actions were very devious, and very powerful. At such a young age, every move he made exuded an intimidating dominance, so powerful that even he couldn't ignore it.

Night of Destiny

As for Marcus, this man had a delicate and handsome face, and an elegant and icy aura, he also seemed like a dominating figure.

However, Antonio dared to bet on Henry's high intelligence, that Marcus would definitely play dirty.

"Help? Dennis, scream your throat hoarse, no one will come to save you!" Marcus said coldly, squatting down, gritting his teeth, and spitting out several words, "You deserve to die!"

Indeed, he deserved to die!

Marcus knew Dennis very well. If he left today unscathed, then Jessica and Henry would still be in danger. He wouldn't allow it! He couldn't risk it.

"You can't kill me, I'm your brother..." Dennis yelled, accusing loudly, "You've already killed one brother, do you want to kill another?"

Henry's face turned grim, extremely ugly. Was it true that his father killed Charles? What exactly happened back then?

Antonio's lips turned cold, Dennis was seeking death, bringing up old matters, was he not afraid that Marcus wasn't dark enough in his heart?

"Charles?" Marcus stood up slowly, his face resembling the King of Hell, his cold eyes filled with murderous intent and hatred. Dennis' words had stirred up Marcus' childhood, his darkest experiences. His fists clenched tightly as he swung his fist fiercely towards Dennis' face.

Dennis's cheekbone was almost shattered from the beating, causing him to roll on the ground in pain, clutching his face, his vision blurred with stars, crying out in agony...

"Kill you?" Marcus squeezed out a sentence almost through gritted teeth, "You're not worthy!"

He stood up, a cold smile curling his lips, withdrawing a silenced gun from his waist and fired two shots at the broken bone of Dennis.

It was a silenced pistol, making no sound except for the bullet penetrating flesh, the sound of splattering blood, and Dennis's agonizing scream...

A shattered and despairing howl.

Henry bit his lip lightly, puzzled, wondering what his father was doing. He had already broken Dennis' bones, why shoot him twice more, deepening his pain? It was completely unnecessary. A shot anywhere else would also make him suffer, no need to shoot at the broken bone.

Antonio was also perplexed and asked Henry, "What is he trying to do?"

Henry shook his head, blinked his eyes cutely, and smiled brightly, "My daddy's thinking seems..." He frowned in difficulty, attempting to find the right word to describe this sinister and twisted behavior. "Hmm, very bizarre!"

Chapter 33

Nightmarish Experience

Marcus put away the gun, turned around with a smile, and amid Dennis's horrifying screams, just as elegant and indifferent as ever, he said, "Antonio, could you do me a favor?"

Antonio felt like he had been caught off guard, in this situation, could he refuse?

Night of Destiny

"Okay!" Antonio said, coming over, with Henry following behind.

Marcus swept a look at Dennis and said, "You see, my brother had his bone broken and was shot twice. I've heard you are a Miracle Doctor. Could you kindly teach me how to remove the bullets and mend the broken bone?"

Antonio's eye twitched violently, even the six expressionless black-suited men from start to finish couldn't help but exchange glances.

This situation was truly bizarre!

This father and son duo were torturing Dennis to near death, with the son cutely watching on the side, while the father politely asked the doctor for help in saving Dennis.

This scene was beyond ordinary strangeness.

Henry covered his mouth and laughed. Daddy, your mind is truly twisted. He was starting to worry about his mommy's future.

"Teach you?" Antonio repeated, his eyebrows slightly raised. He said to teach him, not let him do it himself? Hmm, very good, very powerful! Antonio bowed politely, a shallow smile on his face, "I am delighted to serve you, Mr. Marcus!"

"But, we don't have a surgical knife or forceps!" Henry pointed his index finger to his lips cutely and said, looking at Dennis with difficulty, "And there's no anesthetic, so it will be very painful, you know!"

Henry had originally planned to simulate a car accident, scaring Dennis half to death, then breaking his legs, and then playing Russian roulette with him. Of course, it would be empty bullets, but he would make Dennis think they were real bullets and scare him again. Finally, he would make him the target and shoot him twice.

After playing like this, Dennis would probably only have half a life left, and the experience would be unforgettable for a lifetime. He would have to avoid him whenever he saw his face in the future.

Sect Elder Breeze

Unexpectedly, his father proved to be even more ruthless, shooting him twice and then making Antonio teach him how to take out the bullets. Aha, this experience would surely be etched in Dennis' memory! He would probably go crazy even without dying!

This was a method that could drive someone to death.

Father, you're powerful, I will surrender!

He played more domineeringly, while his father played more cunningly.

That was perfect! The pain suffered on Mommy's operating table was returned a hundredfold to Dennis.

"A surgical knife?" Antonio blinked his eyes and pulled out a small surgical knife from his waist. "As an arms dealer, I always carry weapons in case of emergencies. As a doctor, carrying a surgical knife can also prevent sudden incidents."

Henry and Marcus remained silent. Look at which doctor on the street carries a surgical knife?

Antonio laughed and shook the surgical knife in his hand, then put his hand inside his clothes. When he pulled it out again, his hand was already filled with a row of surgical instruments, one by one.

Henry and Marcus remained silent again.

Laughing and shaking the knife, Antonio explained, "During our time at the special agent training camp, we had a simulated mission once. We entered the African jungle to fight a group of assassins. Within four hours, we broke through their encirclement. I and Truman were on the same team, and he accidentally got shot four times. Do you know what I used to perform surgery on him? A military machete... It terrified Robin so much that he would run away whenever he saw me for half a month. Since then, he asked me to carry surgical instruments with me wherever I go. It was because of this that Victor could survive last year!"

Antonio was their exclusive doctor. In the early years when they just started, they were nameless foot soldiers, maneuvering under the eyes of a group of arms dealers and international drug lords. Negotiations sometimes went poorly, and getting shot a few times was normal.

Once something happened, all major hospitals would be locked down and searched. Going to a large hospital was not an option, and private clinics had poor conditions because Antonio would be nearby whenever they negotiated or fought for territory.

He was always ready to save lives. The turmoil and killings in his early years had shaped his habit of always carrying surgical knives.

Now they all stood at the pinnacle of the world, and others could only dream of getting close to them. Naturally, they didn't need Antonio to save lives at any moment, but the habit he had developed over the years could not be changed.

Fortunately, it was because of this habit that Victor could be saved last year.

Dennis was once again scared out of his wits. He really wished he could die immediately. Why wouldn't they let him die?

Henry and Marcus had a good sense of balance, making it painful, but not losing his consciousness. So Dennis could only watch as Antonio taught Marcus how to get out bullets from one's body, which made him shudder with fear.

The sweat and blood mixed and flowed on the ground. Dennis had never been so miserable, so terrified in his whole life...

"Don't... Help!" Dennis cried out.

"So noisy!" Henry squatted in front of him with a smile, speaking gently, "Mr. Dennis, Mr. Marcus wants to save you. Why are you screaming for help? You should be grateful to him!"

"Don't let him save me, take me to the hospital, take me to the hospital..." Dennis reached out to grab Henry, panicked and begging for help.

Henry thought to himself, was he desperate and willing to do anything, or was he just too naive?

Take him to the hospital? That would happen after the surgery! His legs would definitely be useless!

"I'm quite interested in surgery too. Antonio, can you teach me?" Henry smiled and pulled out a small surgical knife, shaking it playfully. It looked very cute.

Marcus coldly refused, "No way!"

"Why not?"

"You're too young!"

"What does that matter?"

"It's too bloody, it's not suitable for you!"

Marcus didn't want him to get involved in these evil things, not realizing that his son's wickedness was inherited from him, and he even surpassed him.

Antonio wanted to say that Henry was much bloodier than his father! However, he found the dialogue between the father and son quite amusing, so he remained silent.

"First, Mr. Marcus, you currently have no authority over me. Second, I choose and like what I want, and you can't stop me. Third, I only listen to my mommy in this world."

Henry coolly stated his position, thinking that he was indeed not as twisted as Mr. Marcus, inflicting surgery on Dennis.

What a loving torment! His father is taking revenge for his mommy with his own hands.

Antonio chuckled as he watched this father-son duo. Marcus squinted at Antonio, then looked at Henry with deep, unreadable eyes.

After a while, a smirk formed at the corner of his lips.

"Come here, let me teach you!" Marcus smiled, oozing the same elegance and arrogance as the little boy, Henry.

Night of Destiny

"You'll teach me?" Henry covered his mouth and laughed, quite cute as he nodded, "Alright!"

Mr. Marcus grinned slightly at Dennis and, amid Dennis's terrified gaze...

Raised his hand, and and the knife fell...

The surgical knife pierced into Dennis's fractured bone, blood splattering out!

"Ouch..." Dennis struggled intensely.

Henry signaled for the man in black to come over and restrain him!

Antonio's eye twitched, "You're too..."

Children who grew up in abnormal environments, this level of twistedness, is truly unimaginable!

Henry nodded seriously, proving that he learned.

Learning from Mr. Marcus, his hand rose, the knife fell.

The surgical knife pierced into Dennis's other leg!

Dennis almost screamed hoarsely, in extreme misery...

"Sorry, I used too much force!" Henry said, without a hint of guilt, smiling at Mr. Marcus, "Mr. Marcus, let's compete and see who can retrieve the bullet first?"

"Good!"

Marcus's surgical knife also pierced into Dennis's fractured bone...

Another scream ensued.

The expressionless men in black exchanged glances, silently mourning for Dennis, who provoked such a twisted father and son.

Henry's force was weaker, and he wasn't very adept at using the knife, inadvertently stirring around, treating Dennis as if he were a piece of meat that he usually cooked, curiously searching for the bullet's whereabouts.

Marcus was much cleaner and more efficient, directly going for the bullet.

The extreme pain made Dennis develop the desire to die for the first time!

Marcus and Henry, on the other hand, wore serious and sacred expressions.

And thus, such a dialogue emerged.

"Mr. Marcus, where's the bullet?"

"A little to the left!"

"I can't see it!"

"Dig deeper!"

"Still can't see it!"

"Then cut off the whole leg!"

"You're too clever, I admire you!"

"Thank you!"

"But the knife is too small, it's a bit difficult to cut!"

"Then poke it!"

"Oh, I see it, it hit the bone!"

"Dig it out!"

...

In the vast parking lot, apart from the eerie flickering lights, there were only Dennis's screams and the dialogue between father and son. One had a deep voice, the other sounded tender.

It seemed like the son was asking the father a highly academic question. And the father was earnestly explaining to his son.

Antonio felt that daughters were better than sons. Yes, he would refuse to have sons in the future. They were too terrifying. On second thought, his own twistedness was not as severe as Mr. Marcus's. Perhaps his son wasn't as fierce and deranged as Henry.

"Oh, you're so ruthless; he seems to have passed out!"

"Then wait, continue when he wakes up!"

...

Henry obediently put down the surgical knife and signaled for one of the black-clad figures to approach. The man took out a bottle and let Dennis smell it. Dennis slowly regained consciousness.

Antonio clapped his hands, "You guys continue!"

Night of Destiny

And so, after Dennis was unable to scream any longer, falling into unconsciousness six times and waking up six times, Marcus and Henry finally extracted the bullet!

Dennis's legs were appalling!

"Next is bone setting!" Antonio pursed his lips, smiling. "We have to go to the hospital for this!" The tools here aren't sufficient!

The twisted father and son duo stood up. Surprisingly, there wasn't a trace of blood on their hands.

Marcus walked around and half-squatted near Dennis's head. With a bloody surgical knife, he tapped it against Dennis's head. "Dennis, I'll give you two choices. A, tonight's events will be forgotten. B, we continue at the hospital!"

Dennis was as limp as mud. The extreme and horrifying pain made his face lose its luster. His eyes were filled with fear, tears flowing uncontrollably. He couldn't endure any longer and hoarsely uttered, "A!"

"Well, if news accidentally leaks..." Marcus coldly sneered, "Surgery won't be as simple anymore..."

The bloody surgical knife left a blood mark on Dennis's face.

Mr. Marcus's face, elegant yet menacing, had cold eyes filled with bloodthirstiness. "Do you understand? Hmm?"

"I understand..." Dennis cried and shouted, nodding frantically, agreeing! If this didn't stop, he would truly lose his sanity.

On one side was the extreme physical pain, on the other was the strange dialogue between father and son. If he didn't leave now, he would go mad. This feeling was excruciatingly painful and desperate.

Unable to live, unable to die. He could only vividly experience the agony of that steel knife striking against his bones. It hurt so much that his nerves were numb, and his soul was weeping.

Sect Elder Breeze

This twisted father and son duo taught him an unforgettable lesson for a lifetime. Perhaps he would wake up from nightmares every night. He would repeatedly experience this pain, fear, and despair throughout his life.

Dennis's lower body was stained red with blood, and his legs were completely crippled. Antonio, proud of his medical skills, swore that even he couldn't save Dennis's legs. They were beyond repair.

Dennis would inevitably spend the rest of his life in a wheelchair.

Antonio silently mourned for the person who had gotten involved with this father-and-son pair. They were too terrifying, too twisted, too horrifying!

"Mr. Marcus, that move of yours is great!" Henry raised his thumb in admiration, smiling happily. Although it was twisted, he loved it, loved it so much! From now on, if anyone offended him, he could deal with them in the same way.

"Not bad, kid!" Marcus grinned, pulling his collar. "Do you do this often?"

Henry blushed as Marcus pulled on his face, giggling. He raised his pinky finger. "First time. It's not like I'm bored and practicing knife skills every day. If he hadn't hit my mommy, who would bother with this trash?"

With that, Henry lifted his leg and kicked Dennis. The already excruciatingly painful Dennis involuntarily moved his already appalling bones, causing him to scream in agony and wet himself...

"He's even worse than trash. Trash can at least be recycled!" Marcus said expressionlessly, disdainful eyes sweeping over the already unconscious Dennis. His thin lips curved in derision.

Antonio and Henry stayed silent. Mr. Marcus not only had brutal and cunning methods but also a poisonous mouth.

Chapter 34

Online Friend

Antonio snapped his fingers, and two black-clad figures approached. He had initially wanted them to just throw Dennis outside a hospital, but upon seeing him covered in blood and urine, Antonio felt sick!

The smell of blood mixed with the stench of urine was exceptionally disgusting and nauseating. Someone like him didn't even deserve to get in their car.

Marcus also realized this and knew they had to take him to the hospital. They had crippled him, but they didn't want to kill him just yet. Leaving him here unattended, he might bleed to death. They had to send him to the hospital.

"Dial 119!" Marcus said.

Antonio agreed and instructed one of the black-clad figures to make the emergency call.

"You ride in my car!" Marcus said, without giving Henry a chance to protest, he picked him up and didn't allow him to go over to Antonio's side.

Henry was taken aback. He usually disliked physical contact with others. But now, he obediently let himself be held by Marcus. He had grown up, and it seemed like besides his mommy, very few people had ever held him.

When Antonio had held him earlier, it had felt strange and uncomfortable. Even though their revolutionary cause was strong, and their relationship was affectionate, he still felt awkward. But being held by Mr. Marcus, he felt a faint sense of reassurance and peace. It was warm and comfortable.

Mr. Marcus and Antonio were about the same age, but the feeling of being held by them was completely different. Perhaps it was because Mr. Marcus was his father. That's why it felt like that.

Okay, he admitted that he was still a child. Despite being mature, he still looked like a baby. It was normal to be held like this by an adult, even more normal. So, there was no need to struggle, right?

Henry thought to himself and smiled at Antonio, "Antonio, I'll ride with Mr. Marcus!"

Antonio nodded and waved dismissively, "Go ahead, contact us if there's anything!"

Henry cutely blinked and waved back, "Let's not contact each other then!"

Antonio burst into laughter. Indeed, what could they contact about? It would be better to not meet when someone's life was in danger and even doctors couldn't save them!

Marcus and Antonio simply nodded and put the little boy into the car, starting the engine and leaving the parking lot.

Antonio whistled and took a small camcorder off his sleeve, smiling gracefully. He would show it to Victor later. Such a lovely scene!

"Let's go!"

"Yes!"

Night of Destiny

Several cars quickly left the parking lot.

In the huge parking lot, Dennis lay all alone, looking particularly miserable from head to toe, as if he had been tortured.

******

After leaving the parking lot, Henry's stomach untimely growled, making gurgling noises. Henry cutely covered his belly skin and grinned, "I'm hungry!"

"Let's eat together!" Marcus said. The plan hadn't changed, just delayed a little for dinner. Besides, they always had a good appetite after tormenting Dennis. He also felt a bit hungry.

Both of them hadn't eaten anything since noon, and Henry was already hungry at the hospital. After all, humans were not made of iron, especially now that it was almost dawn.

Marcus checked his watch and realized the time was almost up. Many restaurants were closing at this time of the night. He hadn't raised a child before, but he knew that children couldn't bear hunger, especially when they were growing.

Fortunately, he knew a few upscale private restaurants that operated 24 hours, so they could fill him up first.

"Mr. Marcus, let's go to KFC!" Henry suddenly said. He knew that with Mr. Marcus' abilities, he could take him to have a meal even at three or four o'clock in the morning, but he now suddenly wanted to go to KFC.

After Jessica gave birth to Henry, she refused the help of her aunt because her aunt's company was facing bankruptcy and their house was being auctioned off. Her aunt's family was also in financial difficulty, so Jessica rented a place to live on her own.

Raising Henry alone was hard, and Henry knew that better than anyone else.

He matured early, as smart children tend to be precocious and sensitive, and Henry was no exception. After all, he wasn't born strong-willed, there was a transitional period.

When he was very young, Henry often saw parents with their children sitting at KFC, enjoying a joyful atmosphere. He envied them greatly. At that time, he was too young to understand what money was all about. He wondered why his mommy had never taken him to KFC.

Once, he saw a child about his age riding on his father's shoulders and felt extremely envious. He fantasized about having a daddy who could laugh and love him like that. They could have together hamburgers and chicken at KFC.

This was his wish when he was three or four years old. Although he is now older and can have whatever he wants, it was still a childhood dream that couldn't be fulfilled, a kind of regret. He wanted to know how it felt for a father and son to eat hamburgers and chicken there.

When he was a child, it wasn't that he really wanted to eat, he just envied and longed for it because he saw many parents taking their children there.

Once, Jessica couldn't bear it and took him there for a big meal.

At that time, their life was very difficult. Jessica was just a student, and there were times when they couldn't afford to eat. Having KFC for them was a luxury.

Jessica survived on only steamed buns dipped in soy sauce for more than ten days. It was only then that sensible Henry realized that his mommy had to go hungry for more than ten days just to have one meal at KFC. After that, he never lingered by the window of KFC again. He began to engage in behind-the-scenes deals, with the simplest wish of making money.

He wanted to make a lot of money, so that his mommy wouldn't have to worry about money anymore, wouldn't have to work hard for money, and wouldn't have to haggle with others in the market for a few dollars.

Night of Destiny

But he never expected to encounter Robin, Truman, Victor, Antonio, and others, things got out of control, and he ended up playing big. After all, he was so confident that no one could catch him. Even if something really went wrong, the Captain was still the highest inspector of the counter-terrorism special operations group.

What was there to be afraid of?

Later, Jessica graduated, got lucky with opportunities, and her aunt and uncle's business gradually improved. They had enough money at home, and his original idea became meaningless, so he kept it a secret.

Because of him, his mommy had experienced the ups and downs of life. Because of him, she lost the most beautiful eight years of her life.

Youth, passion, and happiness were all taken away by life.

Life cannot be rewound to eighteen. Her mother, when she was a young girl, should have blossomed and enjoyed the beautiful and passionate youth reserved for her. But she gave it all to him.

Henry was deeply concerned, so he would do whatever it took to fulfill Jessica's wishes.

When Jessica was hit this time, Henry was extremely resentful. This punishment for Dennis could be considered the lightest. If he wasn't Dennis, Henry would have played with him until he died today!

"KFC, junk food. It's not good for kids to eat too much!" Marcus said, frowning. He still wanted to take his son to eat something delicious.

"You don't know!" Henry smiled, and tilted his head, revealing his longing without disguise. "I want to eat!"

Mr. Marcus initially wanted to veto it, but seeing Henry's deep, hopeful eyes filled with childlike anticipation, his heart softened. Coincidentally, he saw a KFC on the side of the street and parked the car.

Henry smiled with his eyes squinted, making a victorious gesture.

Sect Elder Breeze

They got out of the car. Marcus couldn't help but hold his son's hand and walked into the KFC. It was 1 am and the store was empty with only two female servers dozing off.

Marcus knocked on the table with the key a few times, startling the two sleepy servers. One almost hit her head on the table, suddenly waking up, still looking dazed and confused, staring at them.

One of the servers, who looked like a student, had an especially innocent appearance. She looked at Henry, blinked her eyes, rubbed her eyes, and suddenly had hearts in her eyes. "Kawaii..."

Dream-like screams.

The other server was infatuatedly looking at Marcus.

The father and son duo, in terms of appearance alone, were exceptionally outstanding, standing out among the crowd.

Henry remained silent, Marcus was speechless, and couldn't help but knock the car key again, attempting to wake up the dreamy duo.

Perhaps his aura was too overwhelming, but the two servers quickly regained their senses and warmly greeted the father and son. The smiles on their faces were like blossoming flowers.

After they placed their order, they went to the restroom to wash their hands. When they returned, their food had been prepared. Marcus asked Henry to find a table and sat him down while he carried their late-night snacks over.

They ordered a family bucket and two chicken leg burgers.

They had quite a lot of food, and Marcus was lazy. He didn't want to make two trips, so he insisted on carrying both plates at once. If it weren't for his suit and his refined appearance, he would have been indistinguishable from the restaurant's servers. The posture was so perfect, it was top-notch.

Night of Destiny

    Henry rested his cheek on his hand and watched his dad's performance with a radiant smile. If someone captured this scene, it would be the headline of the entertainment section.

    It felt pretty good to be waited on by Dad!

    Henry opened the burger and took a bite. He was so hungry, he could starve to death. Henry took big bites, his cheeks bulging, and with a hint of rosy pink on his cheeks, he looked extremely adorable.

    Marcus couldn't believe that the cunning and domineering little boy from earlier was the same person. Now, at this moment, he displayed the cuteness expected of someone his age.

    "Slow down!" Marcus cautioned, placing the straw in the cup and placing the cola in front of him. He couldn't understand how his child could like this kind of junk food that had no nutrition at all.

    After taking a bite of the burger, Marcus made a disgusted face. It was really terrible! His picky appetite prevented him from touching such things. However, he was too hungry and had no choice but to eat whatever was available.

    "How did you know it was Dennis?" Marcus asked while eating. Not only did Henry know, but he seemed to have more information than him, it was truly puzzling.

    Henry wiped his mouth, took a sip of cola, and smacked his lips before saying, "I saw his license plate. When Antonio went back, I had it checked. It's not that difficult. By the way, how many Lamborghinis are there in City W? This Mr. Dennis is so arrogant, he's asking for trouble!"

    "You saw the license plate?" Marcus pursed his lips and looked at him. "Since that's the case, why didn't you mention it when we were at the hospital and I said I would send someone to investigate?" He seemed to have guessed something, a slight smile appearing at the corner of his lips. This kid was very clever!

Henry picked at his chicken wing, lifted his gaze to look at Marcus, and then lowered his head. After hesitating for a while, he confessed, "My mother has always smiled at people. How could she have grudges with anyone? I'm just a student, it's even less likely. Most likely, it has something to do with you. So, I didn't want you to get involved at first."

"Not only did you not plan on letting me know, but you also tried to prevent me from finding out, right?" Marcus quickly guessed, "When my people were investigating, someone set up a smokescreen and blurred the focus. Did you have someone do that?"

Henry didn't deny it either. He nodded honestly and turned to look at him. "I don't know the specifics, but... you figured out our tricks and found Dennis. You're so great!"

Henry took a bite of the chicken wing, tender and juicy, really delicious!

Mr. Marcus suddenly stopped, his eyes narrowed slightly, a hint of a smile appearing. Why did this tone sound so familiar?

"Love My Mommy The Most?" Mr. Marcus unconsciously raised his voice, his gaze focused tightly on Henry's young face, not wanting to miss any of his expressions. The way he spoke and the way Love My Mommy The Most spoke were too similar.

No matter how much he denied it, a person's tone and manner of speaking wouldn't change in such a short time.

Marcus couldn't help but recall how he met Love My Mommy The Most. It happened shortly after Jessica returned to America. He was seven years old. And he loved his mommy...

No wonder he felt so familiar with this kid. It turned out he was Love My Mommy The Most on the internet. He was almost certain now!

Chapter 35

I Surpassed You

Henry cutely patted his head, smiling awkwardly, trying to brush it off and smoothly transition past it. Wow, his Daddy's mind was scattered to have made that association so quickly.

He still wanted to delay it a few more days, admit it when his mommy woke up. Maintaining this kind of communication with him on the internet was quite nice.

At the hospital, he had even mentioned that he didn't know if they were father and son. But, on the internet, he was calling him "dad" affectionately.

He dug his own grave. This feeling... well, it sucked!

"Tell me, is it true?" Marcus asked in a grave tone, his face filled with excitement. He took his hand and hit the whole family bucket, causing the cola to spill everywhere. "No answer, no food!"

Henry remained silent.

Dad, you're so talented! No answer, no food? Are you sure this behavior isn't childish? Are you even an adult?

Henry remembered when he was in a kindergarten in France, two kids were fighting, and another one stood on the side waving a popsicle, cheering for them. At that time, he shouted, whoever wins gets to eat, no victory, no food!

His dad's behavior was really... special, just like that kid in kindergarten.

He guessed that perhaps his dad was just too excited, losing control. He should be understanding, right? Hmm, can't laugh!

Marcus seemed to realize that this action was unbecoming of his usual style, so he calmly coughed twice and let go of the bucket he was holding.

Henry raised an eyebrow, huh... Is this giving in and letting him eat?

Henry reached out, grabbed a chicken leg, and looked at Mr. Marcus. He wondered if he would try to snatch his chicken leg and forbid him from eating.

Marcus's face had a slight blush with embarrassment.

"In the end, is it true?" Marcus asked. This time, he was much calmer. He still wanted to preserve a wise and brave image for his son.

"Don't you already know?" Henry pouted, biting into the chicken leg and drinking the cola.

"I want to hear you admit it with your own mouth!" Marcus insisted.

He was really persistent.

"Well, it seems like I have a username called Love My Mommy The Most!"

Although Marcus had mentally prepared himself, he still felt a surge of joy, and he rushed over, immediately hugging Henry tightly to express his exhilaration.

Caught off guard, Henry almost dropped his chicken leg.

Um... Dad, you need to calm down!

Stay calm, stay calm!

Marcus tightly embraced Henry, overwhelmed with excitement and gratitude. A wave of pure joy rushed through him, almost to the point of ecstasy... His typically gloomy and cold face was now filled with unbridled delight...

Night of Destiny

He had already known deep down that Henry was his son, but without confirmation, there was always a sense of unease. What if it was just a coincidence? Marcus was afraid of being disappointed, again and again, his attitude toward family was more cautious than anyone else's.

But this time, since meeting Henry at the hospital, he had developed the conviction that this was his son. Regardless of the circumstances, he would never leave Marcus, forever belonging to him. He yearned for it, this was his son. He prayed that God could give him just one-tenth of the love given to others.

After experiencing so many years of darkness and hatred, he deserved a little warmth. That would be fair, right?

Before receiving confirmation from Jessica, Marcus prayed, even though he didn't believe in God. It was the first time he asked for their blessing.

He knew it was foolish, but there was no other way. When hope faces collapse, divine beings are our only hope. Everyone is like that, whether they are vulnerable or strong.

Receiving Henry's affirmation was equivalent to Jessica's confirmation.

This child was a prodigy, controlling the vast majority of global online transactions behind the scenes. He was cold and decisive, and a child like him would never randomly call someone "dad" online.

They didn't chat much, but true or false, Marcus could tell. He could also feel his son's affection for him. That was just perfect!

Happiness and joy came so suddenly, catching him off guard. The soft spot in his heart was suddenly struck, again and again, with great force, bringing immense happiness.

Happiness is so simple, like a white dove flying past, leaving a trail of fragrance. That fragrance belongs to hope.

Marcus felt that the joy this soft body in his arms brought him surpassed all the honors and luck in his life combined. Involuntarily, he couldn't help but care for and pamper him.

Sect Elder Breeze

"You're choking me!" Henry patted his shoulder, and Mr. Marcus's pounding chest told him of his current state of ecstasy.

But ecstatic joy was one thing, pain was another.

This little body of his couldn't withstand the forceful embrace from his father. He didn't want to be torn into pieces.

"I'm sorry, I'm sorry..." Marcus quickly released him, his eyes slightly red with excitement. "Did I hurt you?"

Henry shook his head, looking deeply at his father, momentarily ignoring the delicious food in front of him. "Are you really so happy?"

"Aren't you happy?" Marcus nervously asked, afraid of even the slightest dissatisfaction from his son.

"I'm happy!" Henry squinted his eyes and nodded emphatically. He was happy, extremely happy!

The tense heart of Marcus suddenly relaxed, and he grinned like a big boy. Henry's heart was moved, feeling a bit tender towards his dad. Although he hadn't investigated his dad's past, he knew from their conversations in the group chat that he must have suffered a lot.

"This is the happiest day of my life!" Marcus's excitement hadn't subsided yet, his chest rising and falling dramatically. He couldn't find the right words to express himself, so he settled for this sentence.

Henry smiled and said, "Well, this life isn't over yet. Maybe one day in the future, you'll be even happier than today!"

Marcus nodded, "Yes, maybe. In that case, let me correct myself. This is the happiest day of my life so far!"

Henry laughed, stuffing a chicken leg into his mouth and gesturing towards the chicken legs and wings on the table, indicating that Marcus should eat. Marcus was too preoccupied with his excitement, his eyes and heart solely focused on his son, forgetting about his own hunger.

Night of Destiny

"Did your mommy tell you?" Marcus asked. How dare Jessica keep it a secret for so long? He had asked her who the child's father was last time.

And how did she respond? Oh, she sadly told him that the child's father had died.

Great! She said it right in front of him, that the father of his son had died. That's just great!

His son is his son, and she is just herself. This account will be settled in due time! But he really couldn't remember when he and her had conceived their son.

Henry shook his head, gulping down some cola. "My mommy said that she and my dad were deeply in love eight years ago. Then, my dad had a car accident and died. The grass on his grave is taller than me. And then, she got pregnant with me and gave birth, raising me with great difficulty!"

Henry, in his tender voice, calmly recited the tragic love story his mom had made up.

A very cliché plot, he bet that his mom either read those online novels or watched those melodramatic primetime dramas to come up with it.

Marcus's face turned completely dark in an instant! That damn woman cursed him! Mr. Marcus smiled twistedly!

Henry fell silent. Dad, your smile is really... so twisted! Mom is in trouble!

"If it wasn't her who told you, how did you know?" Marcus asked curiously.

Henry rolled his eyes, slammed the empty cup on the table, and said, "First, our faces were so similar that when I said we had no connection, you didn't believe me, right? And secondly, you're involved in arms smuggling and diamond smuggling in my territory, and you're skilled with computers. Do you know that? Truman despises your cunningness to the core. He thinks you're too unscrupulous. We could have made a lot of money together, but you insisted on making it alone. So he asked me to sabotage the internal system of Noblefull Group, to teach you a lesson. I got interested in Angel's Tears and discovered your face when I looked through the information."

Marcus's eyes twitched at the corner. "You invaded the internal system of Noblefull Group?"

Henry nodded, showing off, "Frequently!" More than once or twice! Otherwise, how would he know about Marcus's criminal records, and then go and help him destroy them?

"Damn, how come I didn't know?"

Henry pouted and raised an eyebrow, asking, "Don't you think you should be civilized in front of your son?"

Mr. Marcus fell silent. Civilized? Asked him to be civilized? When Henry was using a scalpel to move Dennis's thigh muscles, did he ever think of "civilized"?

"Fine, civilized. But where did you infiltrate from?" He had to fire the technical staff of the security department when he got back. They were all useless!

Mr. Marcus hadn't even thought that this program was written by himself. He always thought it was impenetrable. It had been used for years without any hacker intrusion. If he had to say anything, he could only say that this child... was too skillful.

Henry chuckled cunningly, exuding dominance and arrogance. "I can only say I surpassed you!"

Mr. Marcus couldn't help but feel that his son was too arrogant.

"Okay, let's not talk about this issue. What else?"

Night of Destiny

"And then I investigated your past eight years ago, and suddenly, many things seemed to coincide in time, so I'm 80% sure." Henry smiled even more elegantly. "After my mom went back to America, I was thinking of having her join Noblefull Group and see her reaction to you. It happened to coincide with your father talking about wanting to change secretary for you. I asked Aunt Grace to help and sent Mom to Noblefull Group. I thought, with your decisiveness and iron fist, you wouldn't refuse a top-notch secretary. When she came back one day, her reaction confirmed 99% for me. To prevent any misunderstandings, I went to your apartment building, and asked the cleaning lady to give me your hair. Wow...two strands of hair for 500 dollars, I guess your hair must be the most expensive in the world. Then I did a paternity test..."

Marcus looked at this child, his face so tender, his voice so pleasant, his expression so elegant, but the things he did had nothing to do with his age!

How did Jessica educate their child? Why is he so formidable?

"Don't you want to know the results?"

"No need!" Marcus said. When the conversation had reached this point, how could he still question the paternity test report?

He just felt that his son was so different from other people's.

Marcus drank cola, usually thinking it tasted bad, but now he felt the need to calm himself with these ice cubes.

"So full!" Henry rubbed his belly and cutely yawned. It was already 2 a.m., and the two of them had been at KFC for almost an hour. Fortunately, Henry usually stayed up late, otherwise, he would have fallen asleep long ago. Tired after a day, he felt quite sleepy.

Suddenly, Marcus's phone rang sharply, breaking the silence of the night, sounding terrifying. Marcus took a look at his phone, it was Old Mr. Alston's call, but he hung up and decided to turn off the phone!

Chapter 36

In The Hospital

"Who?" Curious, Henry asked as he noticed Marcus's bad expression.

"Old Mr. Alston!" Marcus replied.

Henry made a sound of understanding, propped his cheek, and pursed his lips. "It's probably about Dennis's matter. Aren't you worried that he'll remove you from the position of President at Noblefull Group?"

"Why?" Marcus asked.

"He might suspect it was you doing it!"

"Evidence?" Marcus raised his eyebrow. He knew that someone had tampered with the surveillance cameras in the underground parking lot, so he wasn't worried.

"Dennis!"

Marcus sneered and shook his head. "No, he won't. I know him better than you. He wouldn't dare!"

Night of Destiny

Dennis was lecherous and brutal but was stupid at the same time. He bullied the weak and feared the strong, and was terrified of death. After this incident, his legs would surely be useless. He could choose death or a lifetime in a wheelchair.

Based on his understanding of Dennis, he definitely wouldn't dare to choose death! He didn't have the courage!

Old Mr. Alston probably just wanted to call him to the hospital to investigate the truth behind his brutalization. Marcus couldn't be bothered.

With Dennis out of the picture and Leonard still young, Old Mr. Alston wouldn't dare to harm him casually.

Noblefull Group was still under his control for the time being. This family business was not important to him. He didn't need to cling to it, but for some people, it was crucial.

It was a rare revenge tool. Not using it would be a waste.

"No wonder!" Henry laughed. No wonder he dared to appear in the parking lot. It turned out he had already planned to teach Dennis a lesson.

Marcus laughed, eating two chicken wings. Then he looked up and said, "Hey, why not call me 'Daddy'?"

Henry pursed his lips and propped his chin on his hand, shaking his head gently. "No, I have to wait until my mommy wakes up. If Mommy tells me to call you that, then I will. But if she doesn't want me to, then I won't."

Marcus almost choked, barely managing to speak. "If she doesn't admit it, then I'm not your daddy?"

"Of course!" Henry said firmly. He dropped his elegant smile and spoke seriously, "My mommy raised me all by herself. Her wishes are my wishes. If she doesn't want a daddy, then I can live without daddy!" Henry spoke earnestly, without a hint of joking. Although he liked Mr. Marcus, if Mommy wasn't happy, he could keep his distance.

This time, seeking out Mr. Marcus was out of necessity, but in other matters, they would have to wait and see.

Sect Elder Breeze

Marcus wasn't angry, just a little disappointed. How much he longed to hear his son call him daddy, but he understood Henry's perspective. After all, Jessica raised him single-handedly. She was only 18 years old when she carried him, still a student. She had to juggle studying and raising a child. He understood just how difficult it was.

He truly didn't have the qualification to consider himself Henry's father without her consent.

"Mommy is always the most important!"

"Absolutely!"

Henry smiled elegantly.

After they had eaten to their hearts' content, Henry grew a little sleepy. Mr. Marcus suggested they return to his villa and visit the hospital in the morning.

******

The next day, at the hospital.

Jessica woke up early in the morning. Her face was pale, almost transparent. Her eyelashes trembled slightly, and her dry lips appeared cracked, resembling withered petals. Her long hair was scattered on her shoulders, the ink-black color accentuating her pale face, giving off a sickly appearance.

Intense pain radiated from her legs, and Jessica couldn't help but groan, "It hurts so much..."

The oxygen mask was making her extremely uncomfortable. Jessica gritted her teeth and forcefully removed it.

Memories of the car accident began to flood back slowly. Jessica's eyes widened, and her whole body trembled. "Henry..."

Where was Henry?

"Jessica, you're awake! Finally, you're awake! Doctor..." Mr. Miller rushed out of the room to call the doctor, and the doctor had already arrived.

Night of Destiny

The doctor immediately began to examine her, he was astonished to find that apart from the external injuries, Jessica was completely fine. It was incredible! That man's medical skills were incredible. He could hardly believe the results of his examination!

He knew the surgery was successful, but he didn't expect the outcome to be this good. The infection was cleared, the broken bones were repaired, and all that was left was for her to recover slowly. Within a month, she would be able to walk freely again.

"Miss Jessica, do you feel any discomfort anywhere else?" The doctor asked. As doctors, having their patients completely restored to health was their greatest wish. Even though he had initially been angered by Henry, seeing that Jessica was okay made him happy for her.

Jessica's face was pale, her bright eyes filled with pain. She tightly bit her colorless lips, enduring wave after wave of pain. A few drops of cold sweat trickled down her forehead. "It's very painful!"

The doctor was impressed by her resilience. Her broken bone was forcefully reconnected and, after the anesthesia wore off, it was indeed very painful. Surprisingly, she managed to grit her teeth and not scream out in pain. Her determination and endurance were commendable, as many people would not be able to withstand such pain.

Just like Dennis who arrived last night. Both of his legs were almost useless after lying in a dark parking lot for a long time, infected by bacteria. He had to undergo amputation. The whole night was extremely busy, and when he was brought in, he was crying in pain. The cries could probably be heard throughout the entire hospital.

"Miss Jessica, this condition is normal..." The doctor briefly explained Jessica's physical condition and gave her some instructions before leaving the ward.

Mr. Miller was overjoyed. He turned his head and wiped away his tears.

Sect Elder Breeze

"Dad, where is Henry?" Jessica's trembling hand clenched the bedsheets, holding her breath, afraid of hearing news that would devastate her. Her eyes were pretending to be calm, full of anticipation.

Mr. Miller held her hand and gently patted her shoulder, comforting her in a soft voice, "It's alright, my daughter. You did a great job. Henry is fine, he will come to see you soon."

"Great..." Jessica let out a sigh of relief. Her strength seemed to have drained away, making her look very weak and sickly. Mr. Miller helped her lie down again, and Jessica stared up at the ceiling with wide eyes, as if lost in thought.

"Jessica, what's wrong with you? Don't scare Dad!" Mr. Miller asked worriedly, unable to resist stroking Jessica's head. She was such a good girl, and seeing her in this condition, broke Mr. Miller's heart.

Jessica grabbed his hand and patted it gently. "Dad, I'm fine, don't worry. I'm just lost in thought for a moment!"

"Good to know you're fine, good to know!"

Mr. Miller went to get water for her. Jessica hid her smile, her face turned serious. Dennis, did he dare to drive and hit them? What exactly did he want to do?

With a glance, she saw it clearly. It was Dennis who drove and hit them, his face full of fierce cruelty. She couldn't have mistaken it!

She had humiliated him in the office, pouring coffee all over him. It couldn't be that he wanted her life, could it? Could it be because he saw Henry...?

Her heart skipped a beat. If he went back to the Smith family and told this to Old Mr. Alston, Henry's identity would be exposed!

The thought made Jessica's heart race, and an unsettling image appeared in her mind. Marcus's delicate face, with a sinister smile, tearing her apart, and then calmly wiping his hands with a handkerchief.

Night of Destiny

Jessica admired her vivid imagination. She felt that given Marcus's dark psychology, it was normal for her to have such thoughts.

The door to the ward opened, and Jessica thought it was Mr. Miller returning. She turned her head and saw Henry's adorable face. Suddenly, her pale face filled with joy and relief. Even though she knew he was fine, she needed to see him with her own eyes to feel at ease.

Jessica forgot about her dry and cracked lips and smiled, causing the wound on her lip to stretch, prompting her to utter a low groan.

"Mummy!" Henry said in surprise, quickly putting down the soup, and anxiously looking at her. "Mummy, don't get excited, you..."

"I'm fine!" Jessica patted her son's face. It had only been a day, but she missed him terribly. Perhaps the scene was too terrifying, as her only thought before losing consciousness was that her baby would be okay. Now seeing him perfectly unharmed, Jessica felt that her injuries were worth it. "Just a split lip, not too painful. It'll be fine soon."

Henry looked at his mom's frail appearance, feeling extreme distress. His cheeks were devoid of any color, and his eyes were filled with utmost restraint. He tried his best to appear calm, but he knew she must be in a lot of pain. He saw the cold sweat on her forehead and the pain in her eyes.

That was how his mom was. She never let him worry, no matter how much pain she was in. Like the time when she worked as a waitress at the restaurant, she concealed from him the fact that she burned her hand with hot water, even though her backhand was bright red.

Now, he regretted not punishing Dennis more severely!

"Sweetie, help mommy sit up a bit!" Jessica propped herself up.

Henry quickly supported her from behind, carefully lifting her and placing two pillows beneath her. He let her lean against them.

"Sweetie, can you stop looking so serious? Come on, give mommy a smile." Jessica pinched her son's rosy cheeks. She loved seeing her son's elegant smile and didn't want to see a grumpy face.

Henry suddenly pounced into Jessica's arms, hugging her tightly around the waist. He said, "I was so worried about Mommy!"

"I'm fine, my sweetheart!" Jessica rubbed her son's head, resting her chin on top. Her eyes showed a hint of tears. My baby, for you, I wouldn't mind losing my life, let alone a leg. He must have been so scared!

It was the first time they had been in such a serious car accident, and to make matters worse, it happened right in front of Henry. She could imagine how terrified he must have been in the operating room, especially since he also had to comfort his grandfather.

"Mommy, you can't do this again. If you scare me like this again, I'll be really angry, very angry." Henry whispered, cherishing the warmth of his mommy. He would rather be the one in the accident than see his mom lying in a hospital bed.

"Alright, I won't do it again!" Jessica gently supported his back, her bright eyes showing a touch of tears. The pain in her leg seemed less severe now. Her baby was truly everything to her. With him, nothing else mattered.

"Hey, sweetheart, now that mommy has agreed to your request, can you please get up?" Jessica teased, her usual dark humor returning. After all, sentimentality wasn't her strong suit. "Although I shouldn't say this, but sweetheart, you do have some weight. Mommy is fragile right now and can't handle your...weight!"

Henry slowly got up, his big eyes glaring at her, perfectly expressing his grievances. "Mommy, there's something I want to tell you."

"Why so serious?" Jessica's face turned pale, a sense of panic creeping in. "Sweetie, you're not going to tell me...about my leg..."

Night of Destiny

Jessica couldn't muster the courage to say it. The doctor had just mentioned that with rest and rehabilitation, she would be able to walk freely in about two months. If that was the case, why did Henry look so grave?

Henry held Jessica's hand and reassured her, "No, Mommy, don't guess randomly. It's because on the day of your surgery, the doctor mentioned the possibility of amputation..."

Jessica's heart skipped a beat. Amputation? Her gaze shifted towards her leg, and for a few seconds, she was stunned. She couldn't imagine what she would become after being confined to a wheelchair for the rest of her life.

Damn it! Dennis, if I end up being amputated, I would gladly hire a hitman to break both your legs!

"What happened next?" Jessica swallowed and asked, wondering why the amputation didn't happen after all.

"Because..."

Before Henry could speak, the door to the hospital room opened, and Marcus walked in as if it were the most natural thing. He was tall, well-built, and had delicate features. His cold, complex eyes glanced at Jessica on the hospital bed.

Jessica's eyes widened to the limit, feeling a sense of confusion. She looked at Marcus, then at Henry, and became puzzled! Someone, please tell her that this wasn't a dream!

Chapter 37

Marcus's Questioning

"I just woke up, so maybe I'm a little dizzy. Sweetie, they say patients often experience hallucinations!" Jessica calmly spoke, her mind was blank.

Henry stayed silent. Dear Mommy, only mental patients often experience hallucinations, right?

"Mommy, please stay calm!" Henry's childish voice contained a hint of amusement.

"Sweetie, can I faint now?" Jessica muttered to herself, looking at Marcus. Her words were directed at Henry. She was considering if fainting now would be a good idea! After all, her body was still fragile, and fainting from a little shock was normal.

Henry pursed his lips, feeling speechless about his mommy's naivety. Marcus's face darkened, and a storm brewed in his blue eyes. He smirked and crossed his arms. "Miss Jessica, you can faint if you want, but I'll be here waiting for you to wake up again!"

Marcus emphasized the phrase "wake up again", almost squeezing it out through his teeth.

"Mommy, I'll go find Grandpa and come back to accompany you later!" Henry kissed Jessica's cheek and looked at her with half-closed eyes, so sweet and radiant. He whispered, "Mommy, you have good taste!"

A faint blush appeared on Jessica's pale face as she glared at him.

Night of Destiny

Henry waved his hand and turned around. "You guys talk!"

As he closed the door, Henry had a sly look on his face. Honestly, he also wanted to know what had happened eight years ago.

He had confidence in his father's cunning and interrogation techniques.

His dear Mommy was no match for his Daddy!

But...

Eavesdropping on the door would tarnish his image, so little Henry put on his headphones and smiled elegantly and charmingly. His cheeks turned rosy, making him even cuter. He openly listened in, aha!

Once little Henry left, the atmosphere in the ward became a bit awkward. Marcus locked his gaze on Jessica's face, his expression complex. This damn woman!

Jessica lowered her eyes, deliberately avoiding Marcus's gaze. Her heart raced, as a secret she had long tried to hide was now exposed. It was certainly not a pleasant situation.

"Miss Jessica, don't you have anything you want to say to me?" Marcus asked coldly, his usual icy demeanor freezing into ice as he saw Jessica's attitude. He wanted to see what else she could say, given the current circumstances.

"Yes!" Jessica quickly raised her head.

Marcus nodded. Good, commendable attitude. He really wanted to know what had happened eight years ago.

"Speak!" Marcus said a few words with a condescending tone.

His attitude made Jessica want to forcefully press him to the ground and step on his face.

She returned to her usual smile, "Mr. Marcus, the doctor said it would take me two months to walk freely again, so... I want to take a two-month leave!"

"Is there anything else?" Marcus bit out the words, his daunting tone accurately expressing his desire to tear her apart. He took steps closer.

Each step felt like stepping on Jessica's heart. When Marcus sat on the hospital bed, less than half a meter away from her, Jessica remained calm on the surface, while cursing Dennis under her breath. If it weren't for him, she wouldn't have ended up like this, unable to escape, and Marcus would never have found Henry.

"Can I take paid leave?" Jessica asked with a smile, driven by her usual love for money. Two months, including bonuses and full attendance, it would be over a hundred thousand. It would be a pity to lose it, especially since she was hit and lying in a hospital bed, and it wasn't even Marcus's fault, yet she didn't even apply for compensation.

Marcus's face had turned so dark. His chest rose and fell dramatically as he took deep breaths. He had to use all his self-control not to impulsively grab her by the neck. Her way acted like an idiot was truly amazing!

Well done, Jessica!

Marcus's anger turned into a smirk as he nodded, "Alright!"

Normally, Jessica would have thought this was an unexpected windfall. But at this moment, she felt that her future was pitch black.

"Thank you, Mr. Marcus!"

Little Henry, who was eavesdropping at the end of the corridor, gave a thumbs up, thinking, "Mommy, you're amazing! Daddy's face must be quite a sight!"

"What else?" Marcus asked with a deep voice. His tone was low, his gaze locked onto her face tightly, not willing to let go of any of her expressions. But he was frustrated to see that Jessica remained calm. A hint of danger glinted in his eyes, and the veins on the back of his hand bulged.

Jessica's heart was beating like thunder. She lowered her eyes, not daring to meet his gaze.

Night of Destiny

"Speak!" Marcus growled when she remained quiet for a long time. He grabbed her delicate chin, forcing her to look at him, gritting his teeth, "I believe Miss Jessica has a lot to say to me!"

"I don't!" Jessica denied it, her scalp feeling tight.

"Very well!" Marcus smirked in anger. He increased the pressure in his hand, causing Jessica to slightly furrow her brows in pain, but she didn't make a sound. Marcus's exquisite features were covered in darkness, "Miss Jessica, you don't have anything to say, but I do. Henry is my son, correct?"

Jessica's pupils shrank. She raised her hand and pushed Marcus's hand away, her expression slightly cold but maintaining her composure. "Mr. Marcus, you are quite funny. Going to an employee's house and claiming my son as your own. If you want a son, there are plenty of women who can help you conceive."

"You know I'm not joking," Marcus said in a cold voice, narrowing his eyes dangerously. "He is clearly my son, why are you denying it?"

"There are many people who look alike. Does there always have to be a blood relationship?" Jessica asked in return. "That woman in the photo you showed me last time also looks very similar to me, but we have no blood relation, it's just a coincidence!"

"And besides, Mr. Marcus, we only met a few months ago. How could we possibly have a seven-year-old son?" Jessica was convinced that he couldn't remember anything.

She didn't want Marcus to recognize Henry. Henry was all hers, and she had worked hard to raise him. Suddenly, someone came along and tried to steal him from her. She was not willing to let that happen.

She knew it wasn't fair to Marcus, but...

There was never any fairness in this situation. She was being selfish! She never had a great sense of morality!

Sect Elder Breeze

"It seems like you want to deny everything?" Marcus wasn't angry, as he had expected this. "Indeed, I don't remember you. Eight years ago, I had a car accident and forgot some things!"

Jessica was surprised. Had he lost his memory? So, he didn't intentionally forget her? This thought flashed through Jessica's mind, and she inexplicably felt a little happy.

Marcus had been observing Jessica's expressions all along. Seeing her surprise, he became even more certain that they knew each other. This woman was pretending. Marcus was a very smart person, skilled in negotiations and debates. It was very simple for him to trick Jessica with a few words.

To use Henry's words, although his Mommy was cunning, she was no match for his Daddy.

"I didn't intentionally forget anyone. If we calculate Henry's birth time backward, it coincides with the time I lost my memory," Marcus said in a deep voice. "Miss Jessica, your reasons are not sufficient. I just want to know if he is my son." He knew that Henry was his son. But only if Jessica admitted it, would he be acknowledged by Henry, so no matter what, he had to get her confirmation!

"I just want to hear him call me Daddy!" Marcus's voice was low, and his Adam's apple moved a few times. There was a hint of anxiety in his deep tone. "Can't you fulfill such a simple wish?"

Jessica felt a pang in her heart. Marcus's tone made her heartache! It was as if she remembered Henry's childhood, when he asked her why he didn't have a daddy while holding onto a bruise on his body. At that moment, just like now, her heart ached.

She struggled fiercely in her heart. She knew Marcus had been lonely for too long and yearned for family affection. It was only natural for him to want to recognize Henry!

But...

Night of Destiny

Mr. Marcus, it's not right to be so ruthless. It's not possible to be tough all the time. Jessica was never one to be swayed by hard or soft tactics, but when Marcus spoke about his wish with such longing and sadness, she wavered!

"Miss Jessica!" Marcus called out, looking at her expectantly. His gaze was full of pure urgency as if he would lose all his radiance if she denied it!

Can you not look at me with that expression, please?

"He is my son!" After a long while, Jessica finally spoke.

"No one can deny that!" Marcus said in a deep voice. "But that doesn't change the fact that he is my son, does it?"

Jessica looked up at him. Mr. Marcus had a deep gaze, and his blue eyes reflected her calm face. Jessica didn't know if she should continue denying it. If Marcus had always been cold and ruthless, she could deny it to the end. Unfortunately, this cunning guy chose the route of sorrow, and it indeed aroused a bit of pity in her heart. She knew he was pretending, but she couldn't help but feel sorry for him.

Jessica, you idiot!

"Well," she muttered to herself, taking a long breath and realizing there was no point in denying it anymore. With technology being so advanced now, all he had to do was get a paternity test and the indisputable evidence would be there. She couldn't possibly deny it.

"Well... he is indeed your son!" Jessica said calmly, then added urgently, "But you are not allowed to take him away from me!"

Marcus pursed his lips and smiled. Finally, she admitted it!

There was something eerie about his smile.

Jessica suddenly realized, infuriated, that he had known all along. Why did he still come to question her?

"You already knew?" Jessica's face darkened.

Marcus smiled, elegantly and smugly. It annoyed Jessica to no end. "Did I ever say I didn't know? I just wanted you to admit it, Miss Jessica!"

Now it was his turn to infuriate her. Mr. Marcus's mood was instantly uplifted, with a smile on his face. The frustration that had nearly taken his breath away when he was angered by her was finally swept away, and even the sunshine felt much brighter.

Finally, he could hear his son call him "dad". Although becoming a father at the age of 28 was early, Marcus didn't care. Not only did he not care, he was grateful to Jessica for giving birth to such a strong-willed son. However, there was no way he would ever express these emotions to Jessica.

The eavesdropping little boy finally understood why his genes were so exceptional! It wasn't just a genetic mutation after all! Because both his daddy and mommy were rather... twisted individuals.

Jessica gritted her teeth. If she had a knife, she would seriously consider throwing it at him as a target. "Why?"

"Our son said that as long as you admit it, he will accept me as his father," Marcus said with a smile, giving her an answer as a reward.

Jessica's eye twitched violently. She couldn't help but think to herself that this man changed his tune so quickly. Son? Ha, besides providing sperm, he hadn't done anything else. He really got off easy as a father. Forget it, admitting it was no big deal.

Suddenly, Marcus leaned forward, his upright figure almost completely covering her, with his hands pressed against the wall on both sides of Jessica's body. His warm breath enveloped her nostrils, leaving her with no way to escape.

"Miss Jessica, what happened eight years ago?" Marcus asked in a deep voice. Now that he knew the child was his, he wanted to know the reason behind why they had a child. Was it the result of a loving union, or...?

It was true that Marcus had countless women, but from his understanding of Jessica, she wasn't the type to casually sleep with men.

Chapter 38

Force Out The Truth

Jessica became nervous as his handsome face suddenly came close. Marcus's scent overwhelmed her. She had nowhere to hide, no matter how much she tried to avoid it, she couldn't escape his scent.

His perfectly exquisite face was just inches away, and she could clearly count his slightly curled eyelashes— one, two... in his profound gaze, she saw her own panic reflected.

Jessica was at a loss. Whenever he deliberately showcased his male charm, every woman couldn't help but be attracted. She cursed herself as a fool, but...

The ambiguous posture was so awkward. In her mind, she couldn't help but recall the intense affair that night, and a faint blush appeared on her face. Pale with a tinge of light red, even her earlobes turned slightly pink.

She had grown up with only Marcus as the only man this close and intimate to her. Marcus was an expert in the dating scene, and Jessica could never be his match.

Her heart was pounding. They were very close, and Marcus could clearly hear the thunderous beating of her heart.

Marcus was satisfied with such a youthful reaction. He was in a great mood, his thin lips curved into a charming smile.

"Miss Jessica, what impure thoughts are you having? Your face is so red!" Marcus teased, his fingers couldn't help but gently brush against her skin. It was fair and delicate, and the touch beneath his fingertips was delightful. He wished he could keep touching it forever. Being so close, he could smell the faint fragrance emanating from her skin. It was captivating. It was a blatant tease!

Jessica wanted to break free, but Marcus quickly restrained her body, warning her, "Miss Jessica, do you want to have another surgery?"

She fell silent!

"Mr. Marcus, didn't you say that you only want to know whether he is your son or not?"

"I changed my mind!" Marcus remained composed, with no change in color on his face and no throbbing of his heart, refreshing his record of being a pervert. He couldn't help but pinch Jessica's cheek.

"Don't pinch my cheek!" Jessica frowned, reaching out to stop him, only to be stopped by Marcus. He looked at Jessica, raised an eyebrow, and pinched her cheek forcefully a couple of times, infuriating Jessica to the point of exploding.

Innocently, he explained, "Your cheek is nice to touch."

"Hahaha..." Henry burst into laughter, clapping at the window with force. He was in awe of his daddy, "Daddy, I worship you so much!"

"What are you doing, Henry?" Mr. Miller, who came back with water for Jessica, was surprised to see Henry laughing at the window. His grandson had always been calm and elegant, it was the first time he was so out of character.

"Oh, grandpa..." Henry quickly adjusted his facial expression and explained, "I'm listening to a French joke!" He was learning French recently, so he made up a lie. Grandpa, forgive me, this is not suitable for you to hear!

"What are you doing outside? Go in, your mommy is awake!"

"Wait, Grandpa, let's go in later..."

Night of Destiny

In the hospital room, Marcus continued to press for answers.

"You are so shameless!" Jessica glared at him. Damn it, Marcus, he kept refreshing his record of shamelessness! How could there be such a despicable person?!

"Thank you for the compliment!" Marcus remained unfazed, smiling as he uttered a word of thanks. He was shameless, so what? He leaned forward again, getting even closer, almost pressing his thin lips against Jessica's. Unable to help herself, Jessica turned her face away, and Marcus's lips landed on her previously pinched cheek.

His lips were warm, unlike the coldness of his usual self. Jessica felt the place he had kissed suddenly heat up, like a pot of boiling water. As time passed, it only grew hotter and hotter, she felt like she was about to be burned.

Her whole body trembled.

Such an interesting reaction, in Mr. Marcus's eyes, created a beautiful scenery. His good mood skyrocketed, his thin lips curling up more and more, and his deep eyes filled with pleasant laughter.

"You better get up!" Jessica said angrily, pushing his shoulder forcefully. Her voice grew a few decibels louder, deliberately disguising her shyness.

Unfortunately, her effort did not effect on Marcus. He couldn't be pushed away at all. Jessica's face turned bright red, unable to distinguish whether it was due to anger or embarrassment. She glared at Marcus and said, "I lost my memory too, I don't remember anything. Can you please move aside?"

"Lost your memory?" Marcus raised his eyebrows and teased as he squeezed her cheek, "When did you lose your memory? Did you panic when you saw me for the first time after losing your memory?"

"I have intermittent amnesia, okay?" Jessica said irritably. Being so close to him, how could she speak properly? He was probably doing it on purpose, intentionally using his male charm to lower her guard and take advantage of the situation. He was going to great lengths to extract a confession.

Continue pretending to be pitiful like you did just now, maybe I'll feel soft-hearted, Jessica thought to herself.

"Intermittent amnesia?" Marcus smiled, showing a lot of patience. "Miss Jessica, is that a new medical term? Coincidentally, we're in a hospital. Should I find a doctor to examine you?"

Jessica waved her hand gratefully, no longer concealing her joy. "Go ahead, go ahead..."

Marcus paused, looking deeply into her eyes. "I think I'll get used to your intermittent amnesia."

Jessica, "..."

"Don't touch my face anymore!" Jessica couldn't take it anymore and slapped his hand, making his knuckles turn red.

Marcus lowered his gaze to look at his hand and commented, "You're quite violent!"

Jessica smiled, "You're a pervert!"

"Violent matches pervert, a perfect match!" Marcus casually accepted her words, leaving Jessica speechless.

She always considered herself quick-witted and sharp-tongued, but compared to Marcus, she was no match at all.

"Mr. Marcus, isn't it enough for you to know that he is your son? Why do you care about how he came about?" Jessica said unkindly. She truly did not dared to tell Marcus how Henry came to be, afraid that one impulsive decision from Marcus would send her to see the King of Hell.

Marcus twitched the corner of his lips, what kind of theory was she spouting?

"I refuse, I want to know the process!"

"Go buy yourself an adult video!"

Marcus almost choked, "..."

Night of Destiny

Henry laughed heartily, realizing that his mommy was truly extraordinary. You're so talented!

Mr. Miller was confused, wondering why this joke was so fascinating.

Marcus silently looked at her. She seemed used to such situations, but as soon as he teased her a little, her whole body turned red and she didn't know how to react. And she appeared so innocent, yet she could casually say something that would leave people dumbfounded.

Marcus's face darkened, with a sharp gleam in his eyes. "You know I'm not talking about that!"

Jessica raised an eyebrow, curling her lips innocently. "Weren't you asking me how the child came? Isn't every child born like this? Unless they come out of a rock?"

"Why are you pretending to be dumb?"

"You can pretend to be shameless, why can't I pretend to be dumb?" Jessica replied coldly.

Marcus stared at her, and Jessica stared back. Were her eyes bigger? She was pretty sure hers were bigger.

"OK..." Mr. Marcus took a deep breath. Dealing with Jessica required a stronger ability to endure. "Let me be clear, was our child conceived out of love or...a one-night stand?"

Jessica's heart tightened, and she fell silent. Of course, it was a one-night stand. Love? That was a joke of cosmic proportions. But she didn't dare say it, because the more she twisted the truth, the closer he got to the truth.

Moreover, no one else knew about this except her. Why add one more person to the circle of knowledge? If she accidentally let it slip someday and her precious child found out, how would she handle it? Even if her son seemed indifferent on the surface, his heart would definitely be hurt. This matter would forever remain buried in her heart. It's best if no one ever mentions it.

Protecting her child was every mother's instinct!

Sect Elder Breeze

"Could it be that you seduced me?" Marcus raised an eyebrow, teasing and deliberately provoking her. He didn't believe he couldn't force out the truth.

Jessica calmly raised her eyes, meeting Marcus's gaze and giving him a dazzling smile. "Seduced you? Mr. Marcus.. My vision is 20/20, with no nearsightedness, and no astigmatism. Even if I wanted to seduce someone, I would choose a more...pure man. I suggest you go look at yourself in the mirror in the bathroom, with your butterfly face. Stay inside and don't come out to seduce women, or you might get haunted by a female ghost in the middle of the night."

Mr. Marcus was so furious that he couldn't catch his breath.

Henry burst into laughter again.

Henry touched his own face, pausing for a moment, as his appearance was also something his mommy despised.

"Jessica!" Marcus gnashed his teeth. This infuriating woman, with a mouth as sharp as poison needles, always hit the nail on the head. Just look at her, clearly her cheeks were red, yet she could calmly come up with this classic insult. What kind of brain did she have? Damn it!

Jessica pushed his head away, raised her chin, and had a look on her face that said, "I'm arrogant, what can you do about it?"

Mr. Marcus, angry but smiling, leaned closer, staring at her with a disdainful expression. "You're not interested, and I'm not interested in you either. I'm quite confident in my judgment. How old were you eight years ago?"

His gaze maliciously moved downward, landing on her chest, and he smirked. "A flat-chested little girl, even if I had no standards, I still wouldn't choose you!"

When it came to poisonous words, Marcus was unrivaled.

Night of Destiny

Jessica gritted her teeth. Perfect, he better regains his memory now. Let him remember how her figure was even better than the golden ratio eight years ago. Even better, let him taste what it feels like to be showered with money. How impressive!

"Mr. Marcus, you have high standards, and I, as a flat-chested little girl, don't meet your criteria. So, can you stop asking?" Jessica smiled, coolly asking, "Since we both hate each other, you can just assume that the heavens dropped a baby for you."

The two exchanged witty remarks, their breaths intermingling, without realizing the provocative nature of their posture. Such a position, such teasing, can set one's imagination running wild.

Marcus's gaze darkened. Unable to get an answer, he was unwilling to give up. He desperately wanted to know if they had been in love eight years ago. Otherwise, how could they have a child? Given his personality, he couldn't have let her have a child if she wasn't the girl he loved. He always took contraceptive measures very well, otherwise he would have illegitimate children running all over the place.

"Miss Jessica, do you have any misunderstandings about me?" Why was she holding onto this memory so tightly, unwilling to reveal anything?

"We're not familiar, so I don't have any misunderstandings about you. If you don't get off me now, I might develop some misunderstandings!" Jessica smiled lightly.

"I want to know what happened eight years ago."

"I'm sorry, I have nothing to disclose!"

Marcus smirked sinisterly, his face dark and menacing. After a long time of interrogation, his patience had worn thin. "Were you involved in some heinous crime that you're afraid I will find out?"

Jessica's breath hitched, and her heart skipped a beat. She had forgotten how sensitive and clever this man was. If he continued to press her, she would explode. "Was it a car accident that caused your memory loss?"

Changing the topic abruptly, Marcus didn't understand but nodded. "Yes!"

Chapter 39

Did We Love Each Other Before

Jessica nodded knowingly, indicating that she understood. She paused, put on her customary smile, and made a reasonable suggestion. "I've seen it on TV and in novels. Usually, when the male lead has a car accident and loses his memory, it's because of a blood clot in the brain. Then, someone hits him, and inexplicably, his memory is restored. Mr. Marcus, how about you go out and find someone to hit you on the head with a steel pipe? It might help disperse the blood clot and restore your memory!"

Marcus's face turned pitch black, his anger raging. He really wanted to smash that smiling face of hers. It was too damn dazzling. Hitting himself with a steel pipe? It was unbelievable that she said such a thing. By doing this, did he even have a chance to survive?

"Before doing that, I'll tear open your head!" Mr. Marcus gnashed his teeth.

"You're so bloody and lack a sense of humor. It's just a joke! Tell me, why are you so insistent on knowing what happened eight years ago?" Jessica was very curious.

Night of Destiny

Marcus's heart tightened, and his eyes flickered, avoiding Jessica's radiant gaze. He was afraid that looking into her eyes would make him blurt out the question, "Did you ever love me?"

This question had been stuck in Marcus's throat since he found out Henry was his son. He desperately wanted to say it out loud but forcibly suppressed it. Especially when Henry mentioned that Jessica had once said they were in love, and she went abroad because he died in a car accident.

So many things were so coincidental.

Marcus couldn't help but make this connection, wondering if they had been a couple eight years ago. He was very persistent in seeking the answer to this question.

But he didn't want Jessica to see through him, so he tried to coax it out indirectly, but none of his methods worked. Marcus was very frustrated! As for why he was so persistent, he had never thought about it.

Seeing him avoid her gaze, Jessica became curious. It wasn't quite appropriate to be so close when talking, as it affected her train of thought. She didn't understand why he suddenly took a more delicate approach.

"Hey, if you have nothing to say, get up!" Jessica pushed his shoulder. "You are pressing a hundred pounds on top of me, do you think you're my baby?"

Marcus wanted to punch her. Wasn't he just supporting himself?

Marcus grabbed her hand, pressed her onto the bed, and burst into anger. This woman could even drive a saint crazy. Since she claimed he was pressing her, he decided to confirm the accusation. Mr. Marcus moved himself and pressed down hard, gritting his teeth, "If I never pressed you. Where did Henry come from? I didn't see any damage!"

Sect Elder Breeze

    A red cloud exploded on Jessica's cheeks, so red that it seemed blood could drop from them. The original posture of the two was already ambiguous, but now it became even more intimate. Their upper bodies were tightly pressed together, no air passing through. His firm chest squeezed against her softness, seemingly unwilling. With one hand around her waist, he tightly enveloped her in his embrace.

    No matter which direction she leaned towards, his breath followed her like a shadow. Especially when erotic words escaped from his mouth, it easily evoked inappropriate imagery.

    "You..." Jessica was utterly defeated. Alright, Mr. Marcus, in terms of shamelessness, I dare not compete with you!

    "Henry said..." Marcus looked at her, prolonging the tone, then suddenly exerted force. Their bodies, which were already tightly connected, became even tighter. He could feel the squeeze of her breasts on his chest, a very... pleasant feeling. He could enjoy it while extracting a confession, a great idea. "You told him that his parents were deeply in love eight years ago. His father had a car accident and died. You were heartbroken and went abroad, and that's how he came into existence, right?"

    Jessica's pupils widened, and she froze for a moment, slightly panicked. What was he saying?

    Her reaction, seen by Marcus, naturally conveyed a sense of guilt. So this was true?

    As soon as Marcus thought of this possibility, his face, which had turned livid with anger, cleared up like dispersing dark clouds, and sunlight shone through.

    Henry, you traitor! After all the love and care she gave him for eight years, he betrayed her for a deranged father he just met that day. Henry, oh, Mommy blames you so much!

    Henry in the hallway elegantly sneezed!

    "Yes, or no?" Marcus pressed, not allowing her to deceive.

    Jessica was at a loss, looking at his just radiant face. You narcissistic madman, if I say no, will you tear me apart?

Night of Destiny

If she had known back then, she would have come up with a less melodramatic story. Why did he have to get into a car accident so conveniently?

Jessica regretted her past lies.

"I forgot!" Neither of the two answers was beneficial to her, so Jessica decisively chose another option, which was safer.

Little did she know, Mr. Marcus raised the corner of his lips. Jessica was horrified, her skin crawling. A man who rarely smiled, who was perpetually icy, suddenly smiling... the effect was incredibly... terrifying.

"What are you going to do?" Jessica trembled, her voice shaking as she watched his increasingly lowered head and approaching lips. She kept stepping back until there was no more room to retreat.

Mr. Marcus allowed her to escape, loosening his grip on her. His gaze shifted evilly towards her chest as he smirked, "Miss Jessica, I take back what I said earlier. Your breasts are not flat, it's quite big..."

Jessica was dumbfounded. Why was he so perverted? Her thoughts suddenly turned to impure matters.

"Miss Jessica, since you've forgotten, let me help you remember!" Marcus smirked, a trace of lust flashing through his eyes. His slender fingers landed on the buttons of her shirt, starting to undo them...

Jessica was frozen in shock. It wasn't until he was about to undo the third button of her hospital gown that she snapped out of her daze. With all her strength, she forcefully pushed his hands away. "You... pervert! What are you doing?"

Because of her intense struggle, she accidentally aggravated the wound on her leg, causing Jessica to break out in a sweat from the pain and shock.

Marcus felt a twinge of pain in his heart. He reached out to wipe the sweat off her forehead but then clenched his fist midway, smirking seductively, "You said you forgot, so let me help you remember, alright?" Such a pity. He was just about to catch a glimpse of her beautiful breasts.

Gasping for breath, Jessica wanted nothing more than to bite him. "Do you have to be this perverted? My leg is still hurting."

Uttering those words, Jessica nearly bit her own tongue. You idiot, what are you saying? Are you implying that he can continue if your leg is not broken? Speaking without thinking was truly foolish!

Marcus chuckled lightly, his gaze becoming even more wicked as he looked at her. "It doesn't matter, even if your leg were amputated, it wouldn't affect our intimacy!"

Once again, Jessica was shocked by his perversion!

Henry finally understood what his father was doing and was also taken aback by his father's perverseness!

"Don't you dare!" Jessica was slightly afraid, but she did not doubt that Marcus would carry out his words. That look in his eyes, was exactly the same as that night eight years ago. Impulsive, and... lustful.

"That depends on whether you cooperate or not!" Marcus smirked, his slender fingers gliding over her face, savoring the smoothness beneath his fingertips. "If you don't cooperate, I'll make love with you on the hospital bed! Even though it's a VIP room with good soundproofing, Henry and your father could enter at any moment. I wouldn't mind giving Henry a younger sibling! What do you think..."

"You can shut up!" Jessica said in a low voice, glaring at him. The time they had spent together had taught her not to doubt Mr. Marcus' words. She understood the situation!

"Okay!" Marcus cooperatively spread his hands. "Can you tell me the truth now?"

Jessica sighed weakly. "Stay away from me."

Mr. Marcus once again cooperatively obeyed, stepping back from her.

After considering for a moment, Jessica chose to go along with his words. "Alright then!"

"What do you mean by 'alright'?"

Pushed by his provocation, Jessica replied with a stern voice, "That's what it means!"

"Is it real?" Marcus anxiously confirmed, wondering if they had truly been in love before. Did she love him? Did he love her? Was it really like that?

Jessica turned her head slightly. Is he ever going to stop? When she saw Marcus' hopeful, somewhat excited, and bewildered gaze, her heart skipped a beat and she suddenly felt guilty! Is it too late for her to take back her words now? She didn't want to deceive him, but... she didn't want this matter to be dug up either! She didn't want Henry to find out.

"Yes!" Jessica said in a deep voice, leaning on him exhaustedly. Talking to him was as tiring as fighting a battle.

"What about now?" Marcus couldn't help asking.

Jessica was taken aback. Now? Her mouth opened and she hesitated for a moment before saying, "Now you are you, and I am me. We can't go back to the past, nor can we go back to the beginning!"

"Why?"

"No reason, just... don't love anymore!" Jessica lowered her gaze, saying these words softly. She didn't know if she said them for Marcus to hear or for herself.

It's not very common for people to still have feelings for each other after being separated for eight years and then reuniting. Especially for them!

"So, who do you love now, Quincy?" Marcus said coldly. He was very dissatisfied with this fact, his tone was cold. The thought that his arch-enemy had been with Jessica all these years, witnessing their son's growth while he knew nothing, made him want to tear Quincy apart.

"Quincy?" Jessica breathed a sigh of relief and shook her head. She knew that in most cases, she should tell Marcus that she loved her Quincy to avoid his further questioning. But Jessica couldn't do it.

Love is love, not loving is not loving. She wouldn't treat emotions as a joke, and she definitely wouldn't use someone as a shield.

"Quincy is just my senior. Right now, I just want to raise Henry. I don't want anything else," Jessica said, looking at Marcus with a serious expression. "Besides, you don't have the right to meddle in my feelings, do you? If I remember correctly, Mr. Marcus, you had... let me recall, 20 women in a month, not including Miss Crystal, your supposedly perfect fiancée."

Marcus deeply regretted it now. Why did he intentionally make things difficult for her, allowing those women to constantly call and harass her?

And Crystal, she wasn't his fiancée. They hadn't officially gotten engaged, it was just a rumor that got blown out of proportion... but why think about these things now?

She was right. Eight years later, indeed, everyone was different!

"Why don't I have any memories at all?" Marcus wondered.

Jessica's lips slightly curled. "Mr. Marcus, if you keep pressing, don't expect to recognize your son!"

Marcus's gaze darkened. "You dare!"

Chapter 40

Hilarious Argument

"Do you think I won't dare?" Jessica challenged. "My son was born and raised by me. He considers everything for my sake. If I don't let him recognize you, do you think he would dare to disobey me?"

Marcus's face turned pale, and he sneered, "Ha, you have a nerve to say that. He considers everything for you? How can you be a mother? Such a young child can cook and do all those household chores so skillfully?"

They slept late last night and planned to wake up later today, but his son woke him up early in the morning and asked Marcus to take him to the market to buy fish because Henry said the fish in the supermarket wasn't fresh. However, the market was not open at that time.

Driving to the market, Marcus was initially feeling sleepy, but then he was shocked to see his son skillfully picking fish, and negotiating prices.

He was the innocent one. Just think about it, he, a well-dressed, exceptionally handsome man, who clearly wouldn't come to a market like this. He followed behind his little boy, and didn't do anything but watch him pick fish and bargain all the way. The women selling vegetables at the marketplace looked at him and pointed fingers, indicating something. They probably thought he was abusing a child or something, making him feel extremely embarrassed early in the morning.

Sect Elder Breeze

Henry said that he learned all this when he was very young, following his mommy. That remark was unintentional, but the listener could infer something. He could imagine what kind of days they had back then.

Things got even more ridiculous when they got home.

In the kitchen, Henry was quick and skillful, with precise movements. Not only did he cook fish soup, but he also made two breakfast plates, leaving Marcus dumbfounded.

Back when Marcus lived with his mother during his childhood, his mother loved him so much that she hesitated to let him do household chores. The most he did was sweep the floor. At that time, their financial situation wasn't good either, and they lived in a low-income neighborhood. Until he was ten and returned to the Smith family, he hadn't learned to cook.

And this little boy not only knew how, but his skills were exceptional!

Henry said he had been doing the household chores for a year. Hearing that, Mr. Marcus couldn't help but feel a pang of heartache and was furious at Jessica.

Anyone could use their toes to figure out who cooked their lunch every day!

It was truly outrageous. The two of them, as parents, not taking care of their child and making their son serve them every day. The mere thought of it made Mr. Marcus feel a mix of emotions.

Jessica felt guilty for a moment, then retorted, "What's wrong with my son being able to cook? Nowadays, which man doesn't know how to cook? Girls are valuable, and men who can't cook can't sell themselves, you know? I'm just training him! If you don't understand, don't make baseless claims, okay?"

Jessica's words left Mr. Marcus speechless. She was the one neglecting their child and yet she dared to talk back, spouting nonsense. Did his son need to sell himself like that?

Night of Destiny

"You, great!" Mr. Marcus squeezed out two words through his clenched teeth.

Pretending not to understand his sarcastic tone, Jessica laughed nervously, "Thank you for the praise."

Mr. Marcus felt hot blood rushing to his head, and he wanted to strangle her, "Why did I fall in love with you in the first place?!"

"I'm also curious as to why I was interested in you. You can't even cook, what else can you do besides having a pretty face? As expected, ignorant people are naive!" Jessica coolly retorted. Let's argue, great, we'll argue first!

"Are you looking for a husband or a nanny?" Marcus sneered and taunted.

Jessica smiled gracefully, "Don't you know? Husbands are meant to be used as nannies!"

Listening eagerly outside the corridor, Henry almost laughed his guts out. He rarely laughed so uncontrollably. His parents were such special individuals, both his dad and mom were adorable.

Who would have thought that the ruthless and cunning CEO of Noblefull Group and the capable Chief Secretary would argue like children? And the content of their argument was so hilarious!

"Off-topic, off-topic..." Henry cutely shook his head. He didn't want to go inside anymore. He was afraid they would start fighting, and his mom would end up at a disadvantage. Otherwise, he wouldn't mind. "Grandpa, let's go see Mommy!"

When Henry knocked on the door, the two were arguing with great enthusiasm. Marcus quickly stood up, and Jessica smoothed out the wrinkles on the bedspread, silently eliminating evidence of their disharmony.

Henry sat obediently beside his mommy, stealthily removed his earphones, and placed them in his pocket, looking innocent and pure, without a trace of mischief.

Sect Elder Breeze

Mr. Miller, upon seeing Mr. Marcus, was filled with gratitude. He busy thanked Mr. Marcus incessantly. Mr. Marcus was polite, elegant, and modestly told Mr. Miller that it was his duty while gently inquiring about Mr. Miller's health.

Jessica and Henry exchanged a glance on the bed, both turning their faces away in silent agreement. One had an expressionless face while the other elegantly smiled, watching Mr. Marcus perform. It was such a pity he didn't become an actor. he made Mr. Miller laugh his heart out.

"Jessica, is he really Henry's father?" Mr. Miller asked, filled with joy. He felt that his son-in-law deserved a perfect ten. He couldn't be more satisfied.

Reluctantly, Jessica nodded, "Yes, Dad. You've been with me all day. Go back and rest now. There are nurses here, I'm fine!"

"Yes, Grandpa. I'll stay with Mommy here. You go back and rest!" Henry added.

Mr. Marcus voluntarily and conscientiously escorted Mr. Miller downstairs. Once he left, Henry immediately jumped one meter away from his mom, his face showing a pitiful expression like a puppy. "Mommy, can you be a little gentler?"

Jessica's lips curved into a sinister smile. She turned her wrist and thumped her fist, then beckoned with her finger. "You traitor, come here!"

Henry pouted cutely, his eyes welling up with tears. "Mommy, you're so fierce. Be careful not to scare away Daddy!"

"Daddy?" Jessica gritted her teeth, clenched her fists tightly, and squeezed out a few words through her teeth, "What a close address! Tell me, when did you start conspiring with him?"

Night of Destiny

Henry protested loudly, his pink cheeks showing utmost innocence. He quickly exaggerated the incident of Jessica and cleverly concealed their early online chats. Then he raised his hand and swore, "Mommy, it really isn't my fault. Don't falsely accuse me of anything. What kind of conspiracy are you talking about? It sounds so harsh."

Jessica sneered at Mr. Marcus; he was taking advantage of the situation. "So, should I thank him, then?"

"In theory, yes!"

"What did you say?"

"No, no, I mean, it was me who saved Mommy, so you don't have to thank Daddy... I mean, Mr. Marcus..." Henry gracefully fake smiled.

Jessica glanced at him, "Why did you tell him everything I told you?"

Henry felt even more wronged. Mommy, it was you who lied, feeling guilty yourself. Such a bossy attitude!

But he dared not resist. They say an angry woman is unreasonable, and a man should have gentlemanly manners.

"How was I supposed to know Mommy was lying to me?" Henry showed his innocent eyes, accusing Jessica of a deceptive upbringing.

After eight years of being together, if Jessica could be fooled by his appearance, then she wouldn't be Jessica anymore.

She beckoned him with her finger, smiling deviously, "Come here, would you like to give yourself two slaps or should I do it for you?"

Henry obediently approached, Jessica pinched his cheeks and rubbed them. Revenge. Just because Mr. Marcus had been rubbing her cheeks earlier, she wanted to retaliate! Indeed, they were so soft and tender, it was hard to let go. Marcus bullied her, so she would bully his son. It all balanced out!

Sect Elder Breeze

Jessica glared at him, pouted her lips, and let go of his cheeks. Henry covered his cheeks with a mournful look, Jessica showed no remorse as she playfully poked his face and asked, "Do you like him?"

"I do, but..." Henry said confidently, then quickly clarified his position, "But Mommy is still my favorite!" No one could replace her. At most, he liked Daddy a little less than Mommy.

Jessica nodded, satisfied. She was about to say something when Marcus walked in, his face dark and gloomy, probably having overheard their conversation at the door.

He felt elated when Henry said he liked him but quickly realized that the little guy was just being mindful of people's feelings. As Marcus pushed the door open and saw their interaction, he confirmed his suspicions.

Jessica saw his face turn ashen, knowing that he had heard everything. She didn't hold back, smiling and saying, "Son, remember your life motto. You were born and raised by me, whereas he hasn't contributed anything so far. So, you're not allowed to like him more than me, understand?"

Marcus's face went through shades of blue, purple, black, and white, finally settling on black. Damn, did anyone have a mother like her?

Henry looked at his mommy's sweet smile and then at his daddy's grim and pale face. He fell silent. Mommy, did you have to be so audacious? You dared to say such things in front of Daddy, you have some serious guts. You should know, you're no match for him. He's strong and you should be weaker. That's the wise choice!

"I think..." Henry barely spoke when Jessica and Marcus simultaneously looked at him, one with a smile still on her face and the other with a grim expression. He seemed to see a gruesome image of them tearing him apart. Oh, his parents are so frightening!

Night of Destiny

Marcus glared at Jessica. Without him, could she have given birth? Why didn't she allow their son to like him more than her? Damn, it's unfair. Who said he didn't contribute anything?

"Who said I've never contributed anything? Who gave you the bonus and salary for the past two months? Last night, I treated him to KFC, and it was on me!" Marcus couldn't stand it anymore and foolishly blurted.

Henry's mouth dropped open, completely shocked by his father's thinking. Daddy, you're so... talented... and childish!

Jessica smiled, "Mr. Marcus, please understand that the bonus and salary I received were the result of my hard work. With your twisted personality and difficult work attitude, I feel that my efforts and my salary are not commensurate. As for KFC... well, just look at your physique, you're the one who eats more!"

Marcus's face darkened, unable to say a word as she cornered him.

Henry saw his father temporarily defeated and silently mourned for him.

"Mommy is right, of course, I love Mommy the most!" This is undoubtedly the truth!

"You're such a good boy!" Jessica smiled gracefully at Mr. Marcus, her face so pure, her smile so formulaic, yet he felt the urge to step on her face.

"Mommy, have some fish soup, I made it for you!" Henry changed the topic as the battle came to an end. He poured fish soup for Jessica, luckily it was still warm.

"Daddy!" Henry suddenly called out, catching Jessica off guard. The fish soup almost sprayed out of her mouth, choking her.

Marcus's face lit up, a big smile spreading across his face. He reached out and held Henry's small hand lightly. "Henry..."

Henry smiled back at him, while Jessica quietly drank her fish soup, her lowered eyes filled with complex emotions. What should she do in the future?

"Daddy, I think we should keep things the way they are, okay?" Henry asked with a smile.

Jessica paused, raised her eyes, and looked deeply at Henry. Did his son understand her thoughts? She smiled in relief because it was her baby, so obedient and understanding in front of her. She had forgotten that her baby was so clever. They had been relying on each other for eight years, how could they not have such understanding?

"Keep things the way they are?" Marcus frowned, instinctively rejecting this idea. He wanted to spend every moment with his son, having missed him for eight years, he didn't want to miss any future days.

Henry nodded and said calmly, "Daddy, you have your own life, and Mommy and I have our own lives too. Let's keep things the way they are. It's a fact that I am your son, but Mommy and I want a peaceful life without any disturbances. If you want to see me, you can come anytime. As for the rest, we can discuss it later."

For now, this was the best they could do. Although he yearned for his mommy and daddy to get married, it couldn't be rushed. Love takes time, and even though he was a genius, there were some things he couldn't control. Maintaining the status quo would be good for everyone. If there are changes in the future, they'll deal with them later.

"No!" Marcus objected. This was not how recognition should be. Having a son meant so much to him, it was such a meaningful thing.

Jessica raised an eyebrow, placed the fish soup down, wiped her mouth, and said, "Mr. Marcus, then what do you want?"

Jessica's calm and indifferent words baffled Marcus.

What did he want? He suddenly fell silent, stood up, walked to the window, and stared coldly at the patients walking downstairs. He remained silent, emitting an icy and gloomy aura.

Jessica and Henry glanced at each other, both looking at Marcus's cold figure, neither of them said a word.

After a while, Henry asked through lip-reading, "What's wrong with Daddy?"

Jessica replied through lip-reading as well, "I don't know!"

"Does this count as abandoning him?" Henry slowly said with a hint of guilt, looking at his father's cold figure with worry.

Jessica looked at her son's lip movements, remaining silent.

"If..." Marcus's low voice drifted over with a touch of seriousness, "Well, forget it!"

Chapter 41

Keep Things The Way They Are

Sect Elder Breeze

Marcus laughed strangely, and both Jessica and Henry perked their ears to listen to his opinion. Hearing this eerie laughter, they both lost their smiles at the same time.

Jessica gritted her teeth and said, "Mr. Marcus, there haven't been any changes, you just have an additional son. You can see him anytime you want, and if you want to take him to live with you for a few days, I have no objections." This was her greatest concession. So, Mr. Marcus, please don't laugh so pitifully as if you've been abandoned.

Marcus remained silent. Jessica and Henry looked at each other, both devoid of smiles. Though Henry was smart, he didn't know what to do in this situation. After all, it was not something that human effort could solve. He really wanted to say, "Why don't you two get married?" But he knew that his mommy would be the first to say no.

Getting married for the sake of the child was not something that either his father or mother could do. Unless they were in love with each other.

But with his father acting like this, it felt as if they had abandoned him. Heaven knows, he really liked his father, and maybe his mother did too, but not to the extent of needing to marry him.

On the pristine window, the man's deep and chilly eyes were reflected. He had thought about getting married. He wanted to ask Jessica if she could fall in love with him, and if so, if could they get married. He didn't reject the idea himself, as long as she agreed. But in the face of Jessica, who was so manipulative and arrogant, he couldn't bring himself to make such a proposal.

"Henry, don't you want to be my son?" Marcus turned around, facing Henry with a serious expression, locking his gaze onto Henry's tender little face. "Daddy really loves Henry!"

Night of Destiny

These were the most sentimental words Marcus had said since he could remember. He yearned for this bond, this blood-related kinship. So far, Henry meant more to him than Jessica did.

Henry smiled lightly, mischievously blinking his eyes, "Thank you for loving me, Daddy. I love you too!"

Marcus's face softened, filled with joy. He couldn't hide the happiness that leaped into his eyes. His usually delicate features relaxed, and he exuded a touch of sunshine, no longer so deep and serious.

Jessica thought to herself, so the twisted and abnormal Mr. Marcus can also transform into a sunny big boy!

"Okay, then let's maintain the status quo as you said!" Marcus said, looking at Jessica. "Miss Jessica, what you said won't stop me from seeing him, and it also allows him to stay with me!"

Jessica cursed inwardly, did he fake that depth just now to elicit her sympathy?

Marcus laughed brazenly, causing Jessica to almost grind her teeth. She vowed to never trust him again, she should have taken her maiden name back!

"Okay, but..." Jessica added.

Jessica glanced at her son, and it was evident that this topic was not suitable for children. She didn't want her women coming to her door one by one causing trouble. Especially now, with her broken leg, if someone came to challenge her, she would be at a disadvantage. While others stood, she sat or lay down. It was quite clear that she was losing in terms of aura!

Marcus's gaze darkened as he also looked at Henry. They had worked together for some time and had a good understanding. He could somewhat guess what Jessica was thinking. He gave her a stern look and nodded, indicating his agreement.

Henry clapped his hands and smiled, "Dear Dad, Mommy, have you reached an agreement?"

Jessica and Marcus glanced at each other and both nodded. For now, it was settled. Who knew what variables the future held? Future matters could be dealt with in the future.

The reason Marcus agreed to maintain the status quo, apart from Henry's wishes, was largely because he didn't want Henry to get involved in the conflicts between the Smith family and the Lee family. Dennis was disabled, and their father had exhausted all his tricks. But there's always a "what if!"

He needed to keep something up his sleeve! It was better for Henry to temporarily stay with Jessica. It would be good for him! He wanted to see what actions his father would take next.

"Dad, sit!" Henry obediently pulled Marcus and made him sit down. He wore a flattering smile, "Dad, since Mommy will be in the hospital for a while, can I stay with you?"

"Of course!" Marcus couldn't contain his joy and pulled his son into his arms, "I was just thinking about that."

Henry, being held by Marcus, smirked, "Mommy, Dad's house is so beautiful. One day, I'll take a picture to show you!"

"Traitor! Ingrate!" Jessica gritted her teeth, feeling resentful seeing her son's flattering face. They were enjoying a blissful family time while she was left alone in a wheelchair, it made her frustrated just thinking about it.

Wait a minute...

"I'll be discharged in two weeks, what will you do if you stay with him, Henry?"

"Huh..." Henry was surprised.

Marcus frowned, "Didn't you say you would stay in the hospital for over two months?"

"Who said that? My leg will be fine in two weeks at most. After that, I'll just come back for regular rehabilitation sessions."

Night of Destiny

Father and son exchanged a glance, clearly both of them thought she would be staying in the hospital for two months. Henry was about to speak, but Marcus arrogantly interrupted, "Let's talk about it when you get discharged!"

Jessica snorted coldly, while Henry smiled, "Mommy, don't worry. I will come to see you every day, don't get jealous!"

Marcus chuckled lightly, and then looked at Jessica's angry face. He enjoyed seeing this side of her much more than the office version of her. He realized that he liked this version of Jessica even more. She was particularly charming when she was full of life and anger. Though it was just a fleeting look, it captured all his thoughts. Perhaps, eight years ago, he truly loved her!

"Hi, Mr. Marcus..." Jessica's lips curled. "You're letting my son stay at your house. I hope he doesn't witness anything inappropriate." Mr. Marcus is charming and devilish, capable of attracting women from all over W City. Who knows whom he brings home? Other women maybe, but his legendary fiancée is surely one who gets brought home. It doesn't seem quite right for her son to witness that.

"Our son!" Marcus emphasized those words.

"What?" Jessica raised an eyebrow, speechless for a moment, then smiled. "Yes, our son!"

"It won't happen!" Marcus was satisfied to see Jessica correcting her words. His villa has never had any women being brought back, not even Crystal.

Henry elegantly smiled as he watched his mommy. Wow, the stench of jealousy was something!

Sect Elder Breeze

"Mr. Marcus, can you find someone to teach your Brother Dennis a lesson?" Jessica suddenly said, her calm eyes bursting with anger, a slightly sinister smile on her lips. "I don't have high demands. Just find someone to beat him up, break his legs, and send him to the hospital!" After all, broken legs can still be mended. He would only suffer some flesh wounds. Daring to hit her baby with his car, he's asking for death!

Henry and Marcus exchanged glances. And then Henry lowered his eyes, playing with the golden button on Marcus' sleeve, as if it was a precious item worthy of study.

Mr. Marcus asked knowingly, "Why?"

"He deliberately crashed into us!" Jessica said angrily. That Dennis deserved to die.

"No need for me to find someone to beat him up, someone has already taught him a lesson. He's lying in this hospital, half-dead," Marcus said nonchalantly as if it was not him who did it.

"Hmm?" Jessica raised her eyebrows in surprise. It was quite a coincidence. Her gaze couldn't help but fall on her darling Henry. "Henry..."

"Mama…" Henry looked at her with an innocent expression, blinking his eyes to prove his innocence. However, deep down, he was secretly distressed by how sharp his mama's mind was.

Jessica's facial expression froze for a moment before she smirked. After a while, she uttered two words, "Well done!"

Henry stayed silent, and Marcus was completely speechless. Now he finally understood why his son was so cunning.

"Thank you for your praise, Mama!" Henry smiled and leaned in to kiss her, looking sweet and adorable.

Marcus looked at the smiles of the mother and son, and his empty heart suddenly filled with some tender emotions. He felt content and uplifted.

Night of Destiny

The father and son stayed with Jessica in the hospital until noon, and then Marcus took Henry to have lunch.

As they walked down the hospital corridor, Henry suddenly asked with a smile, "Daddy, what do you think of my mama?"

Marcus bent down to pick him up and replied with a smile, "What do you want to say?"

Henry wrapped his arms around Marcus' neck and used his fingers to count, saying, "My mama is beautiful, elegant, brave, quick-witted, resolute, resilient, intelligent... Countless virtues. Don't you think she's rare?" Henry said it with great pride.

Marcus chuckled. He didn't want to burst his son's bubble. "You've used all the beautiful adjectives. That's blind love!" She wasn't as perfect as he described. In his opinion, she was petty, cunning, treacherous, twisted, and perverted...

"You really don't know how to appreciate a gem!" Henry pouted. "My mama is the strongest mama in the world."

"That's true, otherwise she wouldn't have raised you!"

"Daddy, you really don't like Mama, do you?" Henry leaned in closer with curiosity, not believing a word.

"Your mama doesn't like me either!" Marcus snorted. The thought of Jessica's smiling face made him furious. With Marcus' good looks, great physique, and exceptional intelligence, any woman would come running like bees to honey. She was the exception, constantly pushing him away.

Henry covered his mouth and laughed. "Daddy, you probably don't even realize how much you sound like a jealous lover."

"Daddy, Mama is desired by many. Like Mr. Quincy. If Mama gets stolen, don't go ruin their wedding, okay?" Henry whispered kindly, reminding Marcus.

"I would never do something so twisted!" Mr. Marcus scoffed. Wedding? An image of Jessica in a wedding dress flashed through his mind, and he couldn't remain calm. "Any man who marries her will have bad luck for eight lifetimes."

Henry, "..."

"Marcus, stop right there!" as they reached the elevator, Old Mr. Alston's voice suddenly came from behind as if carrying a storm that blew the two of them away.

They both sensed the tense atmosphere around them.

Chapter 42

Old Mr. Alston's Rage

Marcus squinted his eyes, a dangerous glint passing through his eyes, chilling his delicate features. He turned around with Henry in his arms, only to see Old Mr. Alston, Monica, Leonard, and the old butler Vincent behind them.

Monica screamed, "Oh my god!"

Leonard's mouth dropped open, his small face filled with shock. His innocent eyes darted back and forth between Mr. Marcus and Henry, filled with confusion.

Even the composed and taciturn Vincent was taken aback.

Old Mr. Alston was first shocked, then his face turned ashen, as he stared straight at Henry. He remembered him, it was indeed the child he met that day.

"Alston..." Monica suddenly became excited, pointing at Henry and Marcus. "Look at them, it's undeniable evidence. Marcus really has a child!"

Night of Destiny

She seemed extremely thrilled. She had been colluding with Dennis all along, planning mischievous plots behind Old Mr. Alston's back for the sake of the Smith family's wealth. Dennis was impulsive and dumb, and she always worried that Old Mr. Alston would discover their schemes and kick her out of the Smith family.

Finally, Dennis had been crippled, with both his legs amputated, barely clinging to life. He was no longer a threat. She was just happy that fate had removed an obstacle for her.

Regarding Marcus having a child, she had initially been skeptical, after all, she couldn't fully trust Dennis' words. But she never expected to run into it face to face.

"Dad!" Marcus coldly called out, his gaze sliding over with faint impatience. Dennis' hospital room and Jessica's hospital room were on different floors, yet they still managed to cross paths. If this wasn't fate, what else could it be?

"Daddy, put me down!" Henry charmingly smiled at Marcus.

Marcus let Henry down and instead held his small hand.

Henry's gaze swept across his dad's and Old Mr. Alston's faces. The corners of his rosy lips lifted, and he still preferred his dad's appearance - delicate and handsome, albeit ice-cold but not malicious. As for Old Mr. Alston, it was evident that he was a handsome man in his youth, but his features gave off a fierce aura.

"So, this is your son?" Old Mr. Alston's gaze locked tightly onto Henry's face. No one could deny their blood relationship—they looked too similar, with a striking resemblance.

Old Mr. Alston looked at Henry but directed his question at Marcus, his gaze like that of a judge. Henry felt uncomfortable under his scrutinizing gaze, but he responded with a bright smile to Old Mr. Alston's livid face, causing him to freeze and grow even darker!

This child was intentionally being provocative!

Sect Elder Breeze

"Yes!" Marcus replied, purely as a formality. His attitude was cold as if the fact that his father saw his son was intolerable, as if he wanted to hide Henry away.

"Grandpa, hello!" Henry greeted elegantly, not caring at all about the disgust in Old Mr. Alston's eyes. Mama said that other people's attitudes didn't matter, but one's own attitude mattered first.

"Shut up! Who do you think you are, calling me Grandpa?" Old Mr. Alston shouted sternly. Although the child was cute, elegant, and had a smart face, looking at him reminded Old Mr. Alston of the young Marcus when he first came to the Smith family – just as innocent and delicate, almost destroying his family. He had always believed that Marcus was the culprit of the Smith family.

"I will never acknowledge you as anything other than Marcus' illegitimate child, a bastard! Don't even dream of earning my approval!" Old Mr. Alston exclaimed angrily.

Marcus' face turned cold, tightly gripping the hand of little Henry in his arms. A raging storm of anger flashed in his blue eyes as he smirked, "Dad, who told you that my son needs your approval?" Nobody cares if you acknowledge it or not!

He forcefully suppressed the anger in his heart and spoke coldly, "Stop calling him an illegitimate child, what's wrong with being an illegitimate child? I am also an illegitimate child, yet I am still astute and invincible, with an iron fist. As for your so-called legitimate son, Dennis? Ha, he's nothing. Apart from my identity, I can still make a name for myself, while your legitimate son, without your protection, is just a piece of shit, worthless even as garbage!"

Marcus twisted his lips into a distorted smile, "Oh, right, if we trace it back, even you, Dad, are an illegitimate child. It seems that the good seed of the Smith family is concentrated in the illegitimate children. It seems that illegitimate children are more popular. What do you say, Dad?"

Night of Destiny

He ruthlessly mocked and ridiculed the ancestors and current generation of the Smith family with these words, exposing their shortcomings and failures, taunting and jeering at himself. He exposed his hidden pain and aired it out in the sunlight.

Monica gasped in shock. Marcus was too arrogant and venomous!

Vincent was also taken aback. How could someone as proud and dominant as Old Mr. Alston bear such clearly insulting words?

Once again, Henry was stunned by his dad's sharp tongue. Indeed, there is no limit to cruelty, only further cruelty.

Old Mr. Alston flew into a rage. He had a naturally fierce temperament. During his youth, iron-blooded, intelligent, and fierce were the three prominent features of Old Mr. Alston, with ferocity being the most famous. He founded Noblefull Group with his own hands, ascending to a position of great influence on the international stage, demonstrating his intelligence and ability.

But in his youth, Old Mr. Alston had a terrible temper and was an undisputed tyrant. With age, he had reined in and suppressed himself out of helplessness, otherwise, with his temperament, how could he tolerate Marcus' ice-cold attitude?

This time, Mr. Marcus struck at the most painful and regretful aspect of his life, igniting Old Mr. Alston's anger to its peak!

"Bastard!" A furious shout could be heard as Old Mr. Alston's anger surged. He lifted his cane and swung it towards Mr. Marcus' head. This old man had a background in the underworld. Fighting and brawling on the streets was a common occurrence in his youth, and later, he often made deals with the underworld in his business, honing his skills.

After more than a decade of inactivity, his movements were slightly rusty, but his strength and speed were just as before.

Sect Elder Breeze

Leonard screamed in fright and immediately threw himself into Monica's arms. Vincent wanted to intervene, but it was too late. He believed that this swing of the cane would undoubtedly strike Marcus' head. If it had hit, it would not only shatter Mr. Marcus' head but also cost him his life.

However, unexpectedly, Old Mr. Alston was fast, and Marcus was even faster. Marcus swiftly embraced Henry, protecting him in his arms. He lowered his head with agility, narrowly avoiding the cane, which dangerously grazed the top of his head and struck the nearby window, causing a loud crash...

A large piece of glass shattered into pieces, cascading down.

This floor was the top-level VIP ward, and there weren't many people who could afford to stay there. Only a few nurses were on duty, and when they heard the commotion, they immediately came out of the duty room, bewildered by the scene, not knowing what to do.

"Sir, please calm down. This is a hospital!" Vincent quickly stepped in to stop him from swinging the cane again.

Old Mr. Alston trembled with anger, his old face filled with furious rage. He was gasping for breath, realizing that he had exerted too much force with that cane. After all, he had gotten older and hadn't engaged in physical altercations for a long time. He desperately tried to catch his breath, his face turning red.

"You bastard!" Old Mr. Alston shouted, gasping for air between his words. If he had known earlier, he would have killed him back then!

Marcus sneered, amused by the idea that he could even touch a single hair on him. It was a joke. He was quite skilled at close combat, few people that could match him in the world.

"Are you scared?" Marcus asked Henry in a soft voice.

Night of Destiny

Henry shook his head, smiling. He was just a momentary surprise. He knew that Old Mr. Alston and Mr. Marcus had a bad relationship, but he didn't expect it to be this much of a conflict. However, the feeling of his dad defending him felt good and warm!

"This old man, you refused to acknowledge me, and I don't believe you were qualified to be my elder." Henry elegantly said with a smile.

"You...!" Just as Marcus had enraged him, he was now infuriated by this little brat. Old Mr. Alston had never suffered such humiliation in his entire life. The most hateful thing was that he couldn't do anything to Marcus now.

"Marcus, you've gone too far. How could you make your father so angry? Dennis just had an accident, and what are you really up to? Is this how you teach your son? You have no manners." Monica scolded.

Henry's lips curled elegantly, politely saying, "Manners vary from person to person. Yes, you're right. I've always kept that kind of thing at home!"

"Kept at home?" Monica still didn't understand what he meant.

Henry explained graciously, "This old lady, you're really dense. Manners are precious, naturally locked in a safe when not in use."

Old lady?

Monica widened her eyes in anger. She was just in her thirties and took good care of herself. With her fair and flawless skin, she looked like she was in her early twenties at most. Yet, a little brat called her an old lady? And he mocked her for being dense?

Monica was furious.

Henry turned his head and smiled, asking, "Dad, is it appropriate to call the old man's spouse 'old lady'?"

"Good son, you're clever!" Mr. Marcus smiled with satisfaction.

Old Mr. Alston took a while to regain his composure and stared at Marcus and his son with a malicious look, as if they were not his family but rather his archenemies of ten generations.

Marcus sneered and looked at him coldly. "Dad, I hope you won't use such offensive words toward my son anymore. Since we've been able to coexist peacefully for over a decade, let's continue to do so. There's no need to tear each other apart."

Old Mr. Alston's heart skipped a beat. He had never dared to underestimate Marcus. In those words, there was a clear warning. Without absolute confidence, he truly didn't want to have a falling out with Marcus. Just now, anger overwhelmed his reason, and he couldn't control himself!

"Vincent, take them downstairs and wait for me!" Old Mr. Alston said sternly.

Monica resisted, about to speak, but Old Mr. Alston gave her a cold glance, making her instantly silent and obediently following Vincent downstairs. What were they going to say that she couldn't hear?

Vincent followed orders and took Monica and her son downstairs.

Once they left, Old Mr. Alston stared sharply at Marcus and asked coldly, "Did you do this to Dennis?"

Marcus smiled, feigning innocence. "Dennis? What happened to Dennis?"

"Don't pretend you don't know!" Old Mr. Alston shouted angrily. "He not only got shot but also had his legs broken and forced to consider amputation. Your secretary called you last night to inform you, didn't she? And you claimed ignorance?"

Chapter 43

Quincy's Visit

Marcus maintained a poker face. Old Mr. Alston called him yesterday, but he hung up. Later, Susan and a few secretaries called him, informing him that Old Mr. Alston had been looking for them to go to the hospital. Marcus chose to ignore it.

"They said Brother Dennis was in the hospital, but they didn't say what happened exactly. Gunshot wounds, broken legs, amputation. It sounds quite tragic," Marcus smiled, his expression chilling, a hint of mockery crossing his lips. "Dad, when I was ten to twelve years old, I had multiple fractures, got shot six times, and almost had to undergo amputation. Why weren't you as caring then? Oh, maybe you didn't know."

Henry looked at him in surprise, tightening his grip on Mr. Marcus's hand. Ten to twelve years old, wasn't that the time he spent in the New York black market boxing arena? They said he escaped from a rehabilitation facility and was sold to the underground market.

Old Mr. Alston was caught off guard, his face darkening. How could he not know about this? Not only did he know, but he also arranged it secretly, deliberately having Marcus fight against those highly skilled boxers.

The underground market was full of life and death contracts. In other words, once you stepped into the boxing arena, you didn't have the freedom to choose life or death, only the fight for survival.

Sect Elder Breeze

"Now, we're talking about Dennis, not your old story. Did you do it or not?" The cane in Old Mr. Alston's hand slammed hard on the ground a few times, hitting the broken glass, and making a crisp sound.

The glass shattered.

Henry smiled and said, "Old Sir, this accusation is slander. To put such a serious charge on my father, it's wrongful. Maybe it was your son who made someone angry and got into trouble, so you blame it on my father?"

"Adults are talking, what's a child doing interfering? Don't you have any upbringing?" Old Mr. Alston snapped at Henry, his anger flaring up whenever he saw their faces.

Henry turned his head, his pink lips curling up. "I've said it before, manners are a valuable thing. I keep them locked up in a safe most of the time, only taking them out when I have the time to bask in the sun."

Old Mr. Alston erupted in anger while Marcus spoke coldly, "Ask Brother Dennis when he wakes up, and you'll know who did it. Why ask me?"

"How coincidental that your woman gets into trouble and then Dennis is targeted. Marcus, do you think I'm a fool?"

My woman? Was he referring to Jessica? Heh, Marcus felt satisfied with this term. It suited him. But...

"Dad, Jessica gets into trouble and then Brother Dennis is targeted. Is there a direct connection between these two incidents?" Marcus smiled, no warmth in his gaze. It seems Old Mr. Alston knew all along.

Indeed, when it comes to him, whether it's his own life or the lives of those he cares about, Old Mr. Alston doesn't care at all. Very well.

Marcus regretted not disabling Dennis's hands earlier, leaving him crippled.

Old Mr. Alston paused and suddenly realized that he had let slip a secret. He felt extremely frustrated and retorted with a cold smile, "Jessica humiliated Dennis in the office. What does it matter if Dennis wants to teach her a lesson?"

Night of Destiny

Henry's eyes turned cold, and he smiled fakely sweet, with a chilling kind of sweetness. "Old Sir, look at what you're saying. It doesn't matter if he teaches my mommy a lesson, why should it matter if someone else teaches him? Whether he is beaten up or killed, it's his own fault. With such behavior, who do you think he resembles? My dad is wise and brave, dignified and elegant. He is not at the same level as him, it's like heaven and earth."

"Suit yourself!" Marcus said indifferently, holding Henry's hand and walking away. But Old Mr. Alston stopped them.

"Tell me the truth!" Old Mr. Alston said sternly, with a cold face. "What did you mean by that last sentence before you left in a hurry last night? Do you know who harmed Dennis?"

"Even if I knew, what's it to you?" Marcus asked with a wicked smirk. "Do you think I would tell you?"

"You..."

Henry tugged at Marcus's sleeve and pouted cutely, rubbing his little belly. "Daddy, I'm hungry!"

Marcus gently stroked his head. This son of his was talented, and his cute face was simply adorable. He couldn't help but think of giving him a pinch. "Alright, let's go eat!"

"Marcus!" Old Mr. Alston shouted harshly, thumping his cane on the ground. The two nurses nearby were scared and prayed that these two terrifying father and son would just leave the scene.

Marcus didn't want to pay attention, but Henry did. He turned around with a smile, his immature voice filled with Marcus's usual elegance and dominance. "Old Sir, as for your son, let me say, if he hit my mommy with a car, it's her own fault. And if he gets played and ruined by someone else, it's still his own fault. In fact, you should be grateful. Considering how trashy he is, people fear that killing him would dirty their record, that's why they let him off lightly, just to have some fun with him."

"Old Sir, your son is too weak, it undermines his dad's worth. Look at how wise and brave my dad is, and I am such a cute, clever child. And then look at your trashy son... It's just that we share the same last name, but how can there be such a disparity? Genes can mutate. Otherwise, how could my dad and I exist?"

"And you, don't be so hot-tempered. Damaging public property is not the behavior of a good citizen," Henry looked around at the shattered glass pieces, his smile elegant, showing no concern for the fact that Old Mr. Alston's face had turned ashen from anger. "I'm really hungry. Stop bothering us. My mommy says that only women will stick to this kind of thing. Daddy, let's go!"

Marcus's lips curled into an admiring smile. This son of his was good, powerful, and talented. His mouth was sharp, and he inherited the best!

"My baby, you are right!" Marcus echoed repeatedly, "Let's go, Daddy will take you somewhere delicious!"

"Okay!" Henry laughed, holding Marcus's hand and not even bothering to say goodbye to Old Mr. Alston. They left haughtily, leaving Old Mr. Alston almost with a brain hemorrhage!

At his age and with all his experiences in life, he had never been mocked by a child like this. The old man stared at the broken shards of glass on the ground and smiled sinisterly.

Marcus, do you want to be happy? I won't let that happen!

******

Henry buckled his seatbelt and smiled at Marcus, saying, "Daddy, I don't like your father!"

"If you liked him, then you wouldn't be my son!" Marcus said, pursing his lips and sneering, "He doesn't need people to like him, he only deserves their hatred!"

Mr. Marcus had never thought about teaching his son about respecting the elderly or showing them reverence.

Night of Destiny

Henry smiled, "I guess when Dennis wakes up and sees my mommy staying in the same hospital as him, he will be terrified."

The image flipped in Mr. Marcus's mind. He smiled, good, it's even better if he's terrified. This time, he feels like he has avenged everything. Who knows, he had wanted to kill Dennis a long time ago. But Dennis himself had willingly walked into this trap, only blaming himself for being too unlucky!

******

Jessica had finished lunch and was taking a short rest. She had just undergone surgery and her appetite wasn't very good. Besides, Henry had spoiled her taste buds, and although she didn't mind the presentation of the dish, she was very picky about the taste. After all, Henry's cooking skills were on par with those of a five-star hotel chef.

Although the food in this top VIP ward was delicious, it didn't satisfy Jessica's palate, so she didn't eat much.

Just as she lay down for a while, her nurse informed her of a visitor, and it turned out to be Quincy, which startled her.

"Hey, Quincy," Jessica was surprised. It had only been a day since her surgery, and even Grace didn't know yet. This news spread really fast.

Jessica got up, feeling quite tortured. She had just been tormented by that psycho, Marcus, and moving around pulled her wound, causing her intense pain and sweating. Now she had to get up again, not a single bone in her body wanted to move.

Nevertheless, she greeted the visitor with a smile, suppressing the discomfort in her body.

"Why didn't you tell me about your accident?" Quincy reproached lightly as he helped her lean against the soft pillow. A tinge of anger flashed through his gentle eyebrows, displeased with her concealment.

Sect Elder Breeze

"Quincy, I just woke up this morning." Jessica smiled, "I'm really sorry for making you worry!"

Quincy shook his head and instinctively stroked her hair. His usual doting for her was evident, but in his heart, he sighed lightly. Jessica, eight years have passed, and you still treat me with such politeness, always keeping us on the friend line. He couldn't cross over. When would she open up to him completely? Was it because he didn't do well enough?

"With a boyfriend like me, it took me a whole day to find out that my girlfriend was lying in the hospital after an accident. You, really..." Quincy pretended to exclaim, staring at Jessica. A faint hint of bitterness mingled within the warmth on his face.

Jessica inwardly sighed. This boyfriend-girlfriend act was just for show, right? Quincy, please don't take it seriously, we'll both be embarrassed.

Pretending to be his girlfriend was his idea, and she hesitated for a moment before agreeing. But she had no intention of actually dating him.

"Okay, okay. It's my fault! Can you just forgive me?" Jessica smiled, lowered her gaze to hide her sharp eyes, and said lightly, "Back in Paris, my son and I caused you a lot of trouble. We were young and didn't have the ability, especially Henry. Now that Henry has grown up, he can handle things on his own. He doesn't like to trouble others, that's just his nature."

With these few casual sentences, she spoke slowly but conveyed her thoughts. Quincy was a friend, not a family member. She didn't mind troubling her family, but even with good friends, there should be limits. How could she expect him to do everything for her?

Quincy looked deeply into her eyes, and a hint of bitterness flashed across his clear eyebrows.

Night of Destiny

This was Jessica's personality, always clear in her love and hate. She never told lies or feared hurting others. She knew he understood her meaning, so she gently told him that they were only friends, but not lovers.

If it were someone else, she would have been more direct.

Could he pretend not to understand? He didn't expect anything. He just hoped that with sincerity, even the hardest hearts could be softened. Occasionally, she would turn back and see him waiting for her, for eight years. Hoping for her to finally look back at him!

"What exactly happened?" Quincy's voice turned cold. Although she considered him a friend, he treated her like a precious pearl in his palm. Seeing her pale lying on the bed, the usually calm and gentle Mr. Quincy couldn't help but feel angry. He wished he could tear the person responsible to pieces.

"What else could have happened?" Jessica smirked, indignant. "The traffic in W city is horrible. Cars are everywhere, it's crowded and chaotic. If the driver makes a small mistake, accidents happen. The traffic police in our city never skip handling a few traffic accidents. This time, it was just my turn to be unlucky."

She playfully wrinkled her eyebrows, complaining about the traffic in W city, using anger and complaints to cover up the reality.

There was no benefit in Quincy knowing about this incident. Firstly, Dennis hitting her was likely because she had humiliated him in the office, and seeing Henry may have caused a misunderstanding. In the end, her son was the one who took action and injured Dennis. The matter was considered closed. It would only cause trouble if more people knew. She didn't want outsiders to know about what her son had done.

Moreover, this was ultimately a matter for the Smith family and Marcus to deal with. If she told Quincy and he got involved, with Marcus's twisted personality, who knows what he would do to her?
    "You, you're always careless when crossing the road. Be more careful in the future!" Quincy lightly scolded, sitting beside her and asking about her injuries.
    "I know, I know, I'm not a child." Jessica chuckled, sensing that Quincy had something on his mind. But if he didn't say it, she wouldn't act like she knew. She carried on chatting as usual.
    She had a feeling that Quincy was in a bad mood and it must have something to do with her. So it was better not to ask, to avoid unnecessary awkwardness. Besides, if he didn't bring it up, it would be impolite for her to ask.

Chapter 44

The Panic Of Losing Her

"Just now I came to the hospital and saw Henry walking with Mr. Marcus. Jessica, have they recognized each other as father and son?" Quincy looked at Jessica and asked, his gaze deep and unreadable, suppressing the panic of losing her.

Jessica's heart trembled. Indeed, she should have anticipated this!

"Quincy...actually..." Jessica didn't know where to start, so she had to recount the whole situation. She sighed bitterly, "I thought I could keep this secret for a lifetime, but I didn't expect it to be exposed so quickly after returning to America, and Henry willingly walked into the trap himself. As a mother, I have no right to deprive Henry and Mr. Marcus of the opportunity to recognize each other. Although I am extremely unwilling, I cannot stop it. Otherwise, it will be unfair to both Henry and Marcus."

Quincy looked deep into her eyes, trying to find a trace of false helplessness in her face, but he realized she was sincere. Plans always lag behind changes, and nobody could have anticipated that a car accident would lead to this. His arch-enemy's luck was so enviable!

Quincy smiled obscurely, his handsome face filled with pain. He had taken care of them for several years, and Henry also respected and was friendly with him. But at a critical moment, the person Henry thought of wasn't him. It was his biological father!

Sect Elder Breeze

    Perhaps, this was what family was like. In life and death-situations, everyone's thoughts would be of their beloved family.

    "This kid is very astute. He has been colluding with Mr. Marcus for a long time. If it weren't for fear of provoking me, he would have long gone to Noblefull Group to recognize his father." Jessica didn't hide anything, talking about her son's thoughts. Besides feeling heartbroken, there was only heartache. "He really likes Marcus. Maybe it's in his nature as a father and son. At the beginning, I was puzzled as to why he agreed to join Noblefull Group without even asking me first, but now looking back, it must have been the plan he made himself. I won't refuse any request from Henry as long as I can fulfill it. How could I hurt his heart when he desires Marcus's love so much?"

    "What if Henry asks you to marry Mr. Marcus?" Quincy suddenly asked, his tone serious, a faint trace of panic in his usually doting gaze.

    Quincy knew how much Jessica loved Henry. For Henry, she could give up everything, and no one held a higher position in her heart than her son. She wouldn't refuse any of his requests.

    Jessica was taken aback, and then burst into laughter. A faint blush rose on her pale charming face due to her emotions. She was quite enchanting. "Quincy, don't joke like that, okay? How could my son, with his personality, let me marry someone?"

    "I mean, if. Jessica, every child wishes to have a healthy family, no matter how mature they are at a young age, they inevitably have such thoughts," Quincy said, his words profound, with a hint of weariness.

    If it were Jessica, as long as he worked hard and was sincere enough, maybe he could win her smile and perhaps her heart one day.

Night of Destiny

But Henry, that child was frighteningly intelligent. Despite being friendly to him in the past few years, his boundaries were even clearer than Jessica's. One could say that he was distant from everyone except Jessica. A graceful distance, even for him.

But just now, he saw Henry and Mr. Marcus holding hands, talking and laughing, and the smile on Henry's rosy face was something he had never seen in the past few years, so pure and devoid of any disguise.

This made him feel afraid. He vaguely felt that he was about to lose Jessica!

"There won't be such an 'if'!" Jessica said solemnly, her bright eyes filled with unwavering trust and no reservation towards Henry. "If he were my son, he wouldn't make such a request."

"Henry likes Mr. Marcus so much, but if I won't agree, no matter how much he likes him, he wouldn't dare to say that he wants to recognize his father. Before my son has a wife, I will always be his favorite person! He won't ignore my happiness and make such a request." A mother knows her child best. She knows her own baby!

"Is that so?" Quincy chuckled lightly, relieved by her tone. Didn't she seem to like Mr. Marcus?

"Quincy, you've spent enough time on me over the years. If you can..." Jessica wanted to try telling him that perhaps they could only be friends, and that he shouldn't be so persistent.

People you fall in love with when young and impulsive may not be the ones you love for a lifetime.

"Jessica, let's not talk about that, alright?" Quincy's voice softened, but there was a firmness that brooked no interference.

Even Jessica silenced herself, but she looked at him fearlessly, very calmly.

Love is love, and not loving is not loving. She wouldn't lie or fake it. Love is a sacred feeling, and she wouldn't desecrate it. That was her principle.

She had made her stance clear, but Quincy had been persistent all along, sinking deeper and deeper. It wasn't a good thing for both of them. If she had known, she shouldn't have saved him when she saw him injured in the rain that year.

If she had ignored him, maybe this entanglement wouldn't have happened. It had brought hardship to Quincy and bound her as well.

"Alright, let's not talk about that. How have things been recently? Is your project going smoothly?" Jessica helplessly changed the subject, discussing work was the safest topic for her at the moment.

Quincy confidently smiled, clear and domineering. "Of course, that case has been followed from the beginning, and we played the biggest trump card in the board of directors. How could it not go smoothly!"

...

The two of them chatted about their respective work for a while. Quincy hesitated for a moment, feeling a bit awkward, and said to Jessica, "After the banquet, my grandfather asked you many things. Did you know each other before?"

"Your grandfather?" Jessica puzzledly raised an eyebrow and teased, "I'm just a nobody, how could I know a legendary figure like Old Mr. Lee!"

She was smiling on her face, but her heart tightened. Did Old Mr. Lee ask her about Diana? Because they looked so alike?

What feud existed between Noblefull Group and Gootal Group? These two internationally renowned companies had been in secret competition for decades.

Night of Destiny

In the business world, there were many rumors about the conflict between Noblefull Group and Gootal Group. Rumor had it that Old Mr. Alston and Old Mr. Lee used to be great friends, but for some unknown reason, they became bitter enemies.

After that, they never had any contact in their lifetimes, and even in public business gatherings, they would only make brief appearances and try to avoid each other.

What kind of reason caused good friends to become enemies? There were many speculations, after all, they were both legendary figures, very topic-worthy. There were numerous versions of their relationship.

Jessica had heard some rumors, most of which were unreliable. She thought that it was probably related to Diana. Otherwise, Marcus wouldn't have brought her in front of Old Mr. Lee just to provoke him, causing him unbearable pain.

But Marcus is much younger than them, so why would he hate Old Mr. Lee? It's really baffling. There must be twists and turns that she doesn't know about.

"What did he ask me?" Jessica asked curiously.

"Many things, such as, where are you from, who are your parents, how do we know each other...he asked a lot," Quincy pursed his lips, with a distant frown.

"My grandfather hasn't been involved in matters for the past few years. He just stays in the backyard, sometimes for a whole day, hardly paying attention to any affair. I report the operations of Gootal Group to him every week, and he only gives a few suggestions for reference. He has never been so curious about anyone before, not even his beloved Gootal Group. It's unusual, I thought you two would know each other."

Jessica smiled and playfully touched her own face, teasing, "Do I have such an intriguing face?"

Quincy was amused by her adorable look, his smile indulgent and caring, like basking in the spring breeze. He was flawless, perfect in every aspect.

Jessica's mind wandered. Old Mr. Lee only had one son and one grandson, both outstanding individuals. On the other hand, Old Mr. Alston had four sons, and the youngest was still a child, so she didn't know much about him. As for the oldest son, just by looking at the second son, she knew he wasn't a good person.

"My grandfather said he wants to meet you. Would you like to meet him?" Quincy suddenly asked, looking at Jessica with calm eyes, an elegant posture, and no hint of coercion.

He gave Jessica the space to think independently.

If he was just curious because she was his girlfriend, he didn't believe it. He really wanted to know why.

Jessica opened her mouth in astonishment, her pale lips moved and then closed again. She lowered her eyes, lost in thought, Old Mr. Lee wanted to see her? What for? What would he say? If Marcus found out, would he still ask her to bring Angel's Tears to see him and intentionally provoke him? With that his dark mentality, there was a high possibility.

"My grandfather has mentioned it several times, he really wants to see you!" Quincy said with a smile. He had always been gentle like this, like a gentle breeze, the most perfect gentleman in high society. It was probably difficult for any woman to refuse his request!

"Just look at me now, how can I visit him? Let's wait until I'm discharged from the hospital!" Jessica said. When it came to seeing Old Mr. Lee, she inexplicably felt a bit scared, afraid of hearing things she didn't want to hear from his mouth.

"Alright, I'll tell him that then!" Quincy didn't insist. "We'll arrange for you to meet when you're fully recovered."

Jessica nodded, and lowered her eyes, feeling exhausted. Why did it seem like she had some feud with the Smith and Lee families, getting involved with them again and again?

Night of Destiny

Quincy stayed for a while before leaving, deliberately avoiding Mr. Marcus and Henry. The father and son returned to the hospital close to dusk, with Henry holding a large model airplane, a military aircraft. He elegantly played with his model, looking cute and tender.

Jessica glared at Mr. Marcus. Mr. Marcus coldly looked at her, the implication being clear: I bought toys for my son, do you have any objections?

She forced a smile without any sincerity, causing the father and son to exchange glances, wondering why she was in such a bad mood.

Mr. Marcus: What's wrong with your mommy?

Henry: Seems like...she's gone crazy!

Jessica smiled mockingly as she watched the eye contact between the father and son, her smile filled with cunning. "I mean, can't you buy normal toys? Buying these things easily makes me think that our son is a big-time arms dealer. I heard that the most popular heavy weaponry in the arms market now includes aircraft carriers and military aircraft, which have good sales and high profits. Isn't that right, my precious son?"

Mr. Marcus arched an eyebrow and looked at Henry. Henry looked back at him stiffly and weakly retorted, "Mommy, actually...biochemical weapons have the highest profits..."

"Shut up!" Mr. Marcus slapped the back of Henry's head, and Henry pouted in distress. He was just refuting his mommy's misconception!

Jessica's expression became terrifying. "Hey, if someone bombs our front door one day, remember to tell them that we're not familiar with each other, got it?"

Damn it! Marcus plays with firearms, and my son plays with firearms too. Life...indeed, the smell of gunpowder is strong.

Henry pouted again. He was scolded by Mommy again!

"Don't worry, Mommy. If someone bombs my front door, I'll bomb their whole family," Henry said calmly.

"Why don't you say you'll bomb their country?" Mr. Marcus replied angrily. He strongly opposed his son doing such things. Completely opposed. It was too bloody, too dangerous.

Henry and Jessica rolled their eyes at each other in perfect harmony.

Henry's immature voice had a clear disdain, "Daddy, you're so dumb. What if he and we are from the same country? Are we going to blow ourselves up too?"

Jessica nodded, making sense!

Mr. Marcus looked at Jessica, then at his son, speechless!

This woman had worn several masks. Earlier, she was supposedly outraged, but now in the blink of an eye, she was proud of her son's intelligence. So, were the words she said earlier just empty talk?

Seeing that his dad was speechless, Henry smiled happily. He had a feeling that with his dad and mommy together, it would be very amusing.

Chapter 45

Someone Wants To Kill Me

The next day, Mr. Marcus escorted Henry to school. For him, this was an incredibly fresh experience.

Watching the parents who brought their children to school, Mr. Marcus felt that he would also step into this line in the future. He was very happy.

"This is your school?" Marcus looked at the elegant school gate, feeling that it was quite good.

"It's beautiful, right? Mommy said she chose it because she liked its appearance," Henry stuck out his tongue, undermining his mommy's choice. He really liked this campus, tranquil and simple.

"Shallow!" Mr. Marcus snorted.

Henry smiled, waving his hand. "Goodbye, Dad. I finish school at 4:30!"

"Got it, go!"

"Henry, is that your dad?" a classmate girl happened to meet them, smiling warmly as she approached.

"Yes, that's my dad!" Henry said. Usually, he would come to class alone, but this time his dad brought him, attracting curiosity from some of the new classmates who noticed the resemblance between Mr. Marcus and Henry.

They all knew that Henry only had a mom and no dad. When he first arrived, a few bullies in the class had even picked on him, but after Henry took care of them, no one dared to say anything about him being a bastard child.

Mr. Marcus felt a surge of pride, standing up straighter. Being acknowledged by his son, Mr. Marcus felt fulfilled.

Sect Elder Breeze

The cute girl exclaimed, "Wow, such a cool car! Henry, let's go together!"

Henry glanced up and down at the girl, his gaze causing a twitch in the corner of Mr. Marcus' eye. It reminded him of some amusing incidents from his own primary school days.

"Sure!" Henry smiled and waved, saying goodbye as he turned around.

Mr. Marcus also waved and watched with a gentle smile as the two little kids happily entered the school. He heard that geniuses were often loners, but his son was an exception. Look, he was so popular among girls.

Good genes! Mr. Marcus walked away with great pride!

As soon as he left, another car arrived at the school gate. Raymond and Florence sneaked out of the car. Raymond was somewhat fearful. "Hey, do you even know which kid is Jessica's son?"

Naturally, they needed to know what the target looked like for the hostage plan.

His voice was shaking a bit.

Florence gave Raymond a disdainful glance. She really wanted to kick him to death. Such a useless man. They weren't asking him to commit murder and arson, what was there to be afraid of? If he was afraid of dying, then didn't agree to this plan!

"His name is Henry Miller. Just find him directly from the outside!" Florence said coldly. "What does a kid know? If an adult asks him to come out, he will come out. If we kidnap her son, she won't dare to defy us!"

"Will this plan really work?"

"I said it will work!"

******

"Hey, baby!"

Henry heard Antonio's voice as soon as they entered the school. He turned his head and saw Antonio sitting casually on a seesaw, waving and calling him over.

Night of Destiny

    This was a small amusement park in Henry's school, filled with colorful toys and slides for children to play on. Antonio, dressed in white, sat there like a jade tree in the wind, looking quite eerie.

    After exchanging greetings with the other little girl, Henry walked over to Antonio.

    "Antonio, what are you doing here?" a terrorist appeared among the group of kids. If news of this got to the government, it would probably mobilize the entire city's police force.

    "Just waiting for you!" Antonio yawned and said, "I was at the harbor yesterday taking care of some business and happened to pass by, so I waited for you here to say farewell before heading to Egypt."

    "What were you doing at the harbor?" Henry frowned. When they mentioned the harbor, people in their line of work were sensitive to it. The fastest and best way for arms smuggling was by air, but a large portion was also done by sea.

    In order to facilitate smuggling, Victor had opened a shipping company early on, specifically responsible for transporting illegal goods for their group. Antonio and Victor primarily handled any issues that arose during transactions and negotiations with buyers. On the other hand, Truman, Robin, and others were responsible for manufacturing and researching arms, including the development of biochemical weapons. Whenever Henry heard about the harbor, he easily associated it with a batch of arms that might be experiencing problems.

    "No worries, just a minor issue. By the way, I have something good for you!" Antonio smiled and pulled out a mini pistol from his waist, cheerfully handing it to Henry. His pure white shirt made him look as pure as an angel. His smile was as bright as the sun, not indicating at all that he was leading an innocent young boy astray.

Sect Elder Breeze

Henry took the pistol, carefully examining it before smiling, "Thank you!"

Antonio laughed and introduced the structure and power of the gun to him.

Henry looked left and right, feeling frustrated. "I don't know how to shoot!"

"Don't be afraid, just aim at the enemy's head and shoot!"

"Wanna give it a try?" Henry raised the gun, and aimed it at Antonio's head with an elegant smile, devoid of any hint of killing intent.

"Hey, baby, I forgot to tell you. You have to enter the correct password to activate this gun. It's just a toy to play with most of the time."

Henry took it reluctantly, shook it a bit, and packed it in his backpack.

"My mommy will scold me if she finds out!" Henry pouted, feeling extremely distressed.

"Here, I'll give you a pack of chewing gum too!" Antonio smiled and handed him a pack of chewing gum, whistling towards Henry. "Did you think I have nothing better to do than to give you guns and explosives?"

Henry furrowed his brow. "Someone wants to kill me? Who?" Why did he keep encountering people who wanted to kill him recently?

He and his father recognized each other, resulting in several murders. Henry began to consider whether or not to disassociate himself from his father. Even though he had such a dangerous and terrifying identity, no one wanted to kill him. But as Mr. Marcus' son, he was informed of a murder attempt for the second time within a few days. It seemed that not everyone who claimed to be Mr. Marcus' son could handle it. It was too challenging!

"Old Mr. Alston wants to take you out. I just overheard a phone call yesterday. The assassin is from Italy, and you're right, Saxon's relationship with him is not as simple as it seems. This time, it's a deliberate trap for Mr. Marcus."

Henry's expression turned cold. Old Mr. Alston wanted to eliminate him? Was it because he posed a threat to his son? Were they afraid of the Noblefull Group falling into their hands?

Damn it! Did they really think he was after their fortune?

Antonio put a watch on him with two small buttons, one red and one green. "The red one is for global emergencies. Once activated, personnel with a rank of F or above will be at your disposal at any time. Generally, you won't need it. The green one is for local emergencies. When you press it, for example, if you're in Paris, people in Paris will come to rescue you. If you're in City W, people from City W will come to rescue you. Understand?"

Henry's mouth fell open in astonishment. This watch?

"You're not going to tell me that I'm the only one who has it, right?"

"No, there are five globally. This one is mine, I'll give it to you for now, and get another one from the technical department later," Antonio laughed, taking advantage of Henry's young age to guide him onto the "right" path.

Henry raised an eyebrow and simply smiled, asking with a pout, "When are they planning to strike?"

Antonio shook his head, furrowing his brow. "Old Mr. Alston is very cunning. We can't find out the exact time, but it's probably within the next few days. Both you and your mother need to be careful."

"If he comes after me, I can let it go. But if he dares to touch my mother, I won't show him any mercy. I'll make him die in a gruesome way!" Henry's adorable little face filled with a murderous aura, his determination firm.

Antonio smiled. This child was good. Despite his astonishing intellect and control over so many terrifying resources, there was no denying that he was a good child.

Victor had said that a child who was so filial to his mother couldn't be all bad.

"Antonio, how many people did you send to protect me?" Henry asked.

Antonio was amazed, his smile elegant. "How did you know I sent people to protect you?" This child was truly perceptive!

"You knew someone was trying to kill me, so how could you just give me a pistol, a tracker, and a few explosives? These are all just in case, right?" How could he not guess Antonio's intentions? How could they really trust a child like him to deal with assassins? He didn't even know how to use a gun.

Antonio chuckled. "There are four people. They will do their best to keep you safe. Carrying these things has its uses too. You are Mr. Marcus' child, and he has had conflicts with people in business. They may trace you and use you as leverage. Once the tracker is activated, Victor will be notified immediately." After all, the child was still young. No matter how strong he was, he was still flesh and blood and couldn't withstand bullet attacks.

Antonio's greatest skill was medicine, not killing. It was much more effective to leave other professionals to protect Henry than to rely on him.

Henry nodded. "And what about my mother?"

"Don't worry, someone has also gone to protect her. Once the alarm is lifted, I will recall the personnel. Be careful when coming and going, understand?" Antonio repeatedly warned, and Henry nodded.

"I understand!"

At that moment, the bell for class rang. Henry waved his hand and ran off to the classroom.

******

Hospital, VIP room.

Jessica calmly watched the sudden arrival of the old man, her whole body tense with nerves, filled with anxiety and fear, pulsing through her organs, her heart racing.

Old Mr. Alston leaned on a cane with one hand and rested the other on his wrist, his sharp eyes coldly fixed on Jessica. He was accompanied by four tall men wearing black clothes and sunglasses, exuding a sense of killing intent.

Jessica saw clearly that they had pistols holstered at their waist. She inwardly panicked, sweating profusely. Could today be the day of her demise? This feeling was too terrifying!

Chapter 46

Assassination

Old Mr. Alston remained expressionless, and in his murky eyes, there was a suppressed complexity of emotions. It seemed like hatred, like infatuation, colliding furiously.

Similar! Too similar!

Looking at the photo, it was about seventy to eighty percent similar. Seeing her in real life, it felt even more like Diana Brown, a seventeen or eighteen-year-old girl, appearing vividly in front of him.

"Mr. Alston, may I ask what brings you here?" The nurse was knocked out and fell in the corner. Jessica could only rely on herself and adapt to the situation. Clearly, the visitor was unfriendly!

Inside the sick ward, she dared not move, fearing that any slight movement would result in bullets being fired at her.

Tension was in the air.

She fumbled under the quilt, and found Mr. Marcus' phone, trembling with fear of being discovered. It took all her composure to dial the number.

"Jessica, Miss Jessica..." Mr. Alston spoke slowly, his sharp eyes fixed on her face, revealing a deep hatred. The old man's finger twitched slightly as he asked, "Who is Diana Brown to you?"

Diana Brown again!

"I don't know her!" Jessica replied, her gaze unusually calm, her pale face radiating a deadly stillness. Stay calm, Jessica. No matter how arrogant and wanting to kill her Mr. Alston was, he wouldn't be foolish enough to attack her in the hospital! Stay calm!

Old Mr. Alston slowly approached, squinting his eyes, carefully examining her face. Suddenly, the wrinkled face burst into laughter, a laughter that seemed like a release. It was also a burst of laughter after extreme pain, heavy and stifled.

Jessica's heart tightened. Another lunatic.

Whether old or young, if they were from the Smith family, they were either crazy or perverted, or simply trash. Couldn't there be a normal person among them?

"Looks so alike," Old Mr. Alston laughed and mumbled to himself, his tone low and chilling. "If it wasn't for the age difference, I would have thought she had come back, come back to die!"

Jessica felt a pang in her heart and forced a smile. "Old Mr. Alston, I am not the Diana Brown you mentioned. My name is Jessica Miller!" She had to make it clear. If he had someone to hate, it shouldn't harm her!

"It's better not to catch you lying, otherwise..." Old Mr. Alston didn't finish his sentence.

From his malicious expression, Jessica could easily guess how ruthless the words he held back were.

"How long have you known Marcus?" Old Mr. Alston suddenly asked. "What is your purpose for joining Noblefull Group?"

"Old Mr. Alston, I... I must clarify that I am not familiar with your son. Furthermore, he has a twisted and perverted personality. If you want to take him home for further education, I have no objection." Self-preservation was always Jessica's style. Without hesitation, she distanced herself from Mr. Marcus, saying, "As for why I joined Noblefull Group, of course, it was for the high salary here!"

"Not familiar?" Mr. Alston sneered, believing that Jessica was lying. The old man was angry at this and slammed his cane on the ground, causing Jessica's heart to race. "You are not familiar, yet you have a child together. Not familiar, yet Marcus keeps defying me for you. Miss Jessica, do you think you can escape punishment?"

Jessica's gaze fell on the black-clad man beside him as she coldly smiled. "Old Mr. Alston, this is getting boring. What exactly do you want? As an elder, isn't it inappropriate for you to threaten me?"

Old Mr. Alston was slightly angered. "You talk back so brazenly! Aren't you afraid that I'll shoot?" She and Diana were different! Perhaps they looked very similar, but his Diana was gentle and sensitive, while the Jessica before him was strong-willed and resilient - two completely different characters.

Jessica hesitated for a moment. "Based on common sense, Old Mr. Alston, you will not shoot. After all, this is a hospital, and you don't want to attract any trouble. But...you Smith family...please allow me this rudeness. I think not a single person in your family is normal, so I can't infer with normal thinking. The conclusion is, shoot if you want, or get lost!"

Sect Elder Breeze

Jessica spoke with extreme arrogance and arrogance, as if she was certain he wouldn't dare to make a move.

If he had acted at the beginning, maybe she would have been frightened. But after all the nonsense she had said, it was clear that her fear had a time limit, and she was not as scared now.

A sinister smile curled at the corner of Old Mr. Alston's lips. He nodded and gestured for one of the men in black to approach. He lifted her blanket, and Jessica could only watch helplessly as he took away her phone.

"Sir, she called the Young Master Marcus!" the man said in a deep voice.

Old Mr. Alston nodded. "Very good!" He instructed everyone to put away their guns and smiled like a benevolent elder. "Miss Jessica, Marcus is on his way here. What do you think I will do?"

Jessica's face darkened as she sneered, "Even beasts know to protect their children. And you, Old Mr. Alston, you constantly trouble your own son, harm your own son, and even viciously want his life. You are worse than an animal!"

"How dare you!" Old Mr. Alston became furious. He raised his cane and swung it fiercely at Jessica. There was a muffled sound and a groan. Old Mr. Alston's cane landed forcefully on her shoulder, heavy and fierce.

Jessica was hit and slumped on the hospital bed, sweating from the pain, but she stubbornly bit her lip and remained silent.

"Young girl, don't get too cocky with your words. Marcus is coming to save you, but I wonder, who will save your son!" Old Mr. Alston taunted.

Jessica suddenly looked up, her pupils widening. "What did you say?"

******

Night of Destiny

Just as the 30-minute morning reading class ended, the beautiful homeroom teacher asked Henry to step outside. Someone was looking for him.

Henry's rosy lips pursed. Antonio had just warned him, and now someone was looking for him? Was it not too soon?

His gaze darkened as he took his books and his small bag, and left the classroom.

Outside the school building, Raymond and Florence were anxiously waiting, discussing what to do. When they saw Henry, they were so startled by his appearance that they almost screamed. One was dumbfounded, and the other was shocked and flustered.

Henry raised an eyebrow as he looked at the two of them. These two people, no matter how he looked at them, didn't seem like assassins, right?

The man could barely be considered handsome, but gave off a creepy vibe. The woman was somewhat attractive, but had a mean look about her. These two were clearly on the same level as Dennis, garbage, and idiots.

"You're looking for me?" Henry flashed an adorable, sweet, and genuine smile, full of innocence.

"You're Jessica's son?" Raymond couldn't help but scream, pointing a trembling finger at Henry.

Florence's eyes turned red with jealousy. She couldn't believe it, was this real?

Jessica's son turned out to be Mr. Marcus's. Wasn't she abroad for eight years? Damn, that hypocritical woman, how could she be so lucky? No wonder Mr. Marcus protected her, they had this kind of relationship.

"Did you not know who I am when you came looking for me?" Henry smiled, raising an eyebrow. He was sure these two weren't assassins. The man looked familiar, like the one he saw upstairs that day. Seems like her mommy's first boyfriend.

This was the first time Henry despised his dear mommy. Her taste was so off?

Sect Elder Breeze

Raymond pulled Florence aside and whispered, "Let's go quickly, we can't mess with Mr. Marcus!"

If this was Jessica's child, they could hold him hostage and threaten Jessica. That woman would probably listen since she doted on her son. She would definitely not call the police. But if this was Mr. Marcus's child, oh my God, they couldn't afford to mess with him! Being bankrupt in Davis Family Group was better than ending up in jail or losing their lives!

Florence looked at him disdainfully, "You're such a disappointment. What does it matter if he's Mr. Marcus's son? Just grab him and threaten Jessica. It doesn't matter whose son he is, as long as Jessica helps us. Think about it, you owe so much loan shark debt. If you can't pay them back, we'll be killed."

Raymond trembled in fear, remembering the towering and fierce men. His face turned pale with fright.

Raymond didn't say anything more, and Florence smiled sweetly at Henry, kindly and amiably, "Little Henry, we are your mommy's friends!"

"So what?" Henry smiled. Their acting skills were blatantly lacking. It was obvious they were being fake. Compared to his dad and mommy, who were masters at this, the two in front of him were too weak.

"Your mommy is in trouble and wants us to take you to see her." Florence looked worried, grabbing Henry's little arm and pulling him towards the exit. They seemed to be in a hurry and genuinely concerned.

Henry's lips curled coldly. These two probably didn't even know that his Mommy was hit by Dennis and was still in the hospital yesterday, right? Henry broke free from her grip and was about to speak when his expression changed slightly.

He saw a red dot moving on Florence's chest, sweeping by quickly. Little Henry's face changed drastically. Oh no... there's a sniper!

"Run!" Henry sprinted towards the school gate.

Night of Destiny

Raymond and Florence thought that they had successfully tricked Henry. They followed closely behind him, walking quickly.

"Don't run so fast, slow down!" Florence, in high heels, exclaimed and shouted.

Henry ignored her, running as fast as he could.

This was a school, full of powerless kids. There should not be a gun battle here. Stray bullets don't discriminate. If they accidentally hurt someone, Henry would regret and feel guilty for the rest of his life.

This was a clean land, absolutely not to be stained with blood. Otherwise, it would become a nightmare for every student.

He didn't know how many assassins there were but he was certain that someone was sniping from a high point.

Fortunately, long-range snipers had a flaw. Once the target moved or there were obstacles, the shots would surely miss. Henry guessed that the person must be in the building opposite his classroom, taking advantage of the time when he was in class.

Damn it! They came so fast, and he was with no preparation at all.

Henry pressed the green button on his watch. Activate the alarm!

Starting today, there would definitely be someone protecting him. Though they probably didn't expect Old Mr. Alston to send assassins so soon.

Henry had just reached the school gate when a bullet struck near his feet, kicking up dust. It was a suppressed gun, so he didn't hear any sounds. Henry was startled and quickly took cover, agilely darting out, narrowly avoiding a row of bullets that swept just below his feet.

Raymond and Florence screamed in shock.

Suddenly, a few gunshots rang out not far away. Henry felt a sense of relief. Good, his people were nearby and it seemed they took care of one.

"Get in the car!" Henry shouted, jumping into the passenger seat.

Raymond and Florence had never experienced a situation like this before and were in a panic. They quickly got into the car upon Henry's loud command. Raymond stepped on the accelerator and they hastily left the school.

After a while, everything went calm. Except for a few distant gunshots, there were no other sounds. As the car drove away, even the gunshots became inaudible.

Henry didn't dare relax, his eyes fixed on the rearview mirror, attentively observing the road behind.

Florence, still in fear, cried out in a desperate voice, "What just happened?"

Henry's phone rang. It was Antonio calling from W City. "Henry, are you okay?"

"I'm fine, I left the school!"

"I saw it!"

Henry took out his handheld computer from his backpack, quickly entered a series of commands, and investigated the situation near the school. He soon found several locations of gunfights on the screen, with casualty numbers displayed: 2 people!

"Henry, brace yourself. Today I only sent four people to protect you. I didn't expect Old Mr. Alston to act so quickly!"

"How many are they?"

"2 people!"

Henry raised an eyebrow, having a foreboding feeling. As expected, Antonio continued, "Old Mr. Alston found out about the failed plan and sent out another team of assassins, a total of twenty people."

"He spares no expense!" Henry sneered coldly.

Antonio was already at the airport, giving orders to his men while investigating Henry's nearby location. He smirked, "Henry, have the person next to you drive the car to DC Avenue, and take the north side to DC Port."

"Alright!"

Night of Destiny

Henry hung up and checked the GPS. He spoke in a deep voice, "Go to DC Avenue!"

"I don't want to, I want to go home. What's wrong with you, you little brat?" Raymond trembled in fear, not listening to Henry's words at all.

Florence had no more thoughts of kidnapping this time. She coldly said, "Raymond, push him down, don't let him drag us down!"

Chapter 47

Unlucky Kidnappers

Raymond nodded, opened the car door, and tried to push Henry out.

At such a fast speed, pushing a child out of the car would give him n chance to survive. Raymond and Florence knew this, but to avoid being implicated, they had to sacrifice Henry.

Unfortunately, they miscalculated!

"Go to DC Avenue, immediately!" Henry pointed his gun at Raymond's forehead, smiling brightly. "Option 1, live. Option 2, die. Which one do you choose?"

"Don't mess around!" Raymond screamed.

"Push him out, he's scary. This is a toy gun!"

Sect Elder Breeze

Henry turned around and shot a bullet next to Florence. There was no gunshot sound, but the seat cushion had a big hole in it.

A smirk appeared on Henry's lip as he elegantly said, "A toy gun, huh? Should I try shooting you in the head?"

"No!" Florence fearfully stared at the hole. "Raymond, listen to him."

Raymond closed the car door again, turned the car around, and drove towards the DC Highway.

It must be said, these two were the most inexperienced and unlucky kidnappers in history!

In the early morning, every road was congested. The traffic in city W had always been terrible, and they were stuck in traffic before they even reached the DC Highway.

Florence was scared and wanted to get out of the car, but they were on the highway and she couldn't get out. Raymond was filled with sweat. Henry checked the bullets in the handgun, there were only nineteen left, as one was just wasted.

Chewing gum was almost useless. It was only effective for close-range destruction and escaping. Henry cursed silently.

Time passed slowly as they remained stuck in traffic. The atmosphere in the car became more and more tense. Raymond trembled with fear. Henry gave him a cold glance and said, "Hey, stop shaking. If you want to stay alive, focus on driving!"

Raymond nodded nervously, and the car started moving slowly. Henry was glad that they were stuck in traffic because the pursuers were far behind. They wouldn't catch up for a while.

Henry checked the GPS and it showed three routes to the north side of DC Port on the DC Highway. He frowned, "Turn right, we're going on the DC Bridge!"

"It will waste a lot of time to go through the bridge."

Night of Destiny

"Nonsense, I told you to turn, so just turn!" Henry sternly commanded. His young voice was filled with authority. The traffic flow was too high, and if there was a shootout, many innocent people would die. The DC Bridge had a lower traffic flow, avoiding unnecessary casualties.

Raymond gritted his teeth and turned the car to the right, onto the DC Bridge, stepping on the gas pedal, and moving forward.

Henry's phone rang, it was a call from Marcus. He answered, but before he could speak, he heard Marcus's anxious voice, "Henry, where are you?"

"Oh dear, Daddy, I've been kidnapped!" Henry said cutely. However, these two kidnappers were unlucky to have been unwittingly involved in this assassination plot, and he couldn't help but feel sorry for their misfortune. Otherwise, he might have died in the classroom today. Considering this, he could ignore their kidnapping this time.

"Henry!" Marcus shouted sternly. "Who? Where are you?"

"Daddy, where are you?"

Marcus went silent for a moment. "The hospital!"

"That's good, protect my mommy!" Henry said, still calm and composed. "I believe in Daddy!"

"Mom and Dad are worried about you!" Marcus said a few times.

Jessica couldn't help but grab the phone and say, "Darling, where are you? Don't scare Mom!"

"Mom, how can you not trust me? It would make me sad," Henry said lightly.

"When are you coming to see Mom? "

"At noon, for sure!"

"Don't get hurt!"

"No worries, who am I? How could I get hurt!" Henry proudly laughed.

Marcus took the phone and asked, "Is someone protecting you?"

385

"Yes!" Henry relaxedly replied to avoid worrying Marcus and Jessica.

Raymond, who was beside him, almost screamed. Who was protecting them? No one!

"That's good!" Marcus's worried heart finally relaxed. The people with Henry were probably much more skilled than those on his side. With someone protecting him, Marcus felt relieved. "Your mom will be fine, I promise!"

Henry looked at the rear-view mirror and saw four cars chasing after them. His eyes narrowed dangerously. "Daddy, I have visitors. I'll hang up!"

As soon as he hung up, gunshots rang out!

Florence screamed in fright, and Henry furrowed his brows, shouting, "You, shut up, or I'll kill you right now!"

Florence covered her mouth in fear and cowered in the back, afraid to make a sound.

A barrage of bullets hit the car, making a clanging sound. The sound of death was near, almost within earshot.

Raymond immediately stepped on the gas, and the car sped up, running as fast as possible.

Henry narrowed his eyes. These two cowards, how could they dare to come out to kidnap him?

"Don't panic, if you don't want to die, listen to my commands and drive!"

On the DC Bridge, five cars were chasing each other. Luckily, this car was a Lexus limited edition sports model. It had excellent performance and enough horsepower to easily leave the other four cars behind if driven at full speed.

However, the little Henry knew better. There must be an ambush on the north side of DC Port, enough to eliminate them. He trusted Antonio's deployment, and reinforcements were coming from the DC Highway. They just needed to hold on for a while longer.

But Henry wanted to personally take them all out.

Night of Destiny

With his identity, he would encounter many assassination attempts in the future. If he always relied on support, he would have no means to escape or counterattack. There would come a time when his luck would run out. So, these people were his first batch of training targets!

Clang clang clang... Bullets hit the car's body continuously, making a clanging sound. Florence leaned against the car window, head lowered, covering her ears, afraid to even breathe, fearing the bullets would hit her.

Henry opened the car door and shot at the car behind him. The bullet didn't affect the glass of that car. He quickly turned back. Damn it, it was bulletproof glass. Suddenly, a car rushed towards their side, the window opened, and several handguns were fired desperately.

"Go!" Henry shouted, and Raymond stepped on the gas.

Bullets hit the car's body, and one bullet hit the glass, causing it to shatter and scatter throughout the car. The rear glass was also shattered, leaving it wide open!

"Oh...no..." Florence screamed.

Henry impatiently grabbed her collar. "If you don't want to die, do as I say!"

Henry tore open the packaging of the chewing gum, revealing a red and black alternating sticky explosive. He placed it in Florence's hand and said in a deep voice, "In a moment, two cars will be driving on either side of us. You need to knead the chewing gum and stick it on their car bodies, understand?"

Florence shook her head frantically, "I can't, I can't... I can't do it..." She cried, tears streaming down her face.

"Listen, if you don't want to be buried here with me, then do as I say. You only have one chance!" Henry said in a low voice while tearing open another piece of the chewing gum. He finally figured out the use of the explosives!

******

Sect Elder Breeze

In the VIP waiting hall at the airport, Antonio looked at his computer screen and smirked, "Well done, kid! You didn't disappoint!"

A cold female voice came from another computer, "Shall we take action now?"

"Wait, don't move yet. Keep your distance and observe the child's performance!" Antonio chuckled. He gave Henry the opportunity to prove himself!

"If anything happens to him, be prepared to be hunted down by Mr. Marcus to the ends of the earth!" Another female voice rang out, different from the previous cold voice, carrying a clear sense of elegance.

Antonio chuckled, "I trust Henry!"

******

Suddenly, a car rammed into them from behind, sparking a shower of sparks. The tremendous force almost threw Henry towards the front.

Florence screamed again as bullets hit the car, creating a clattering sound. The sound of shattered glass continued as almost all the windows of their car, except the front one, shattered.

The car moved, aiming at the target, but hitting accurately was uncertain.

Henry knew without thinking that there must be a row of bullet holes on the outside of the car.

"Do you want to die?" Henry looked at Florence calmly. His young face looked solemn.

Florence swallowed nervously and took the explosive from him, saying, "I'll do it!"

"When the red and black are kneaded together, it will explode in three seconds. You have to be fast!"

Florence's face turned pale with shock, but she nodded quickly. Her hands trembled violently.

Night of Destiny

"Good!" Henry said resolutely. "You bring those two cars over and align their speeds with ours. We'll detonate it immediately."

"...Okay!"

Raymond purposely slowed down the car, and the other three cars behind quickly formed a triangle formation. One car rammed heavily into the rear, while the other two attacked from the sides, resulting in a shower of sparks. Without the protection of the shattered windows, the sparks fell into the car, crackling.

At the moment they were about to break through the encirclement, Henry shouted, "Go!"

Both of them opened the car doors simultaneously and quickly stuck the explosive on the other cars. Florence was slightly faster than Henry, after all, she was an adult with longer arms. So Florence came back first, and Raymond immediately accelerated, almost throwing Henry out of the car door. He pulled back forcefully, but the car was too fast. He rolled inside the car and hit Florence, and both of them almost fell out of the car door together.

It was incredibly thrilling.

At that moment, two loud bangs were heard, and the two cars instantly exploded, flames reaching up to the sky...

Antonio whistled at the computer, amazed by what he saw. "This kid is really good at making use of waste. Look at how well he's commanding those unlucky kidnappers. Not everyone can do that." So impressive!

Florence cheered excitedly, raising her hands in celebration. Henry rubbed his arm and realized that he had been scratched by the broken glass. Oh no, Mommy is going crazy!

"Don't get too excited, there are three more!" Henry said in a low voice.

And Florence became even more excited. "Let's do it again!"

Sect Elder Breeze

Henry glanced at her, wondering if killing people could really make someone excited. He had doubts about her excitement.

"Old tricks won't work!" Henry said flatly.

The other three cars quickly caught up, shooting desperately from behind. Ding ding ding, the sound of bullets hitting the car increased, and they seemed determined, firing wildly. Florence screamed again in fear.

One car hit them from the side again. Henry gritted his teeth. Who does this guy think he is, showing off with his horsepower?

He squeezed next to Raymond, snatched the steering wheel from him, and said, "Step on the gas!"

Henry quickly turned the steering wheel and aimed at the other car, colliding with it. The cars collided, and both were fast, creating a particularly dangerous sound of friction. Sparks flew everywhere. Henry didn't let go; instead, he kept turning the steering wheel, continuing the collision!

Raymond, who usually liked to play with cars, had good driving skills and coordinated perfectly with Henry.

But on the other side, they couldn't hold on. Henry managed to squeeze their car into a hopeless situation, crashing into a complete barricade. With a loud bang, the entire front of the car sank in!

"Beautiful!" Antonio clapped. Kid, you're too cool!

"Antonio, you're really mean!" that elegant female voice spoke again.

Henry loaded his gun and handed the steering wheel to the stunned Raymond. Seeing that he was clueless, Henry slapped him to wake him up. "Drive!"

"Step on it!" Henry shouted sternly.

Raymond nodded and stepped on the gas pedal to the maximum. Antonio raised an eyebrow. This kid, is he going to lead them into a trap instead of doing it himself?

If he thought that, then he was wrong!

"Antonio, what about the other two cars? What should we do?" Henry asked anxiously while loading his gun.

Antonio smiled. "Let me make a practical suggestion. Aim for the tires!"

"Shoot the tires until they burst?"

"No, shoot the tires off!"

To save resources, Henry connected to the internet and quickly looked up the structure of the vehicles. He smirked. "Got it!" Indeed, it was a wise choice not to shoot randomly earlier.

Chapter 48

Reveal His Weaknesses

"Drive to the intersection up ahead and immediately make a U-turn, understood?" Henry said.

Raymond's pupils shrank in fear. "A U-turn? That's facing them head-on?" This was suicidal behavior, and Raymond shook his head fearfully.

But Henry said in a solemn voice, "Trust me!"

Raymond looked deeply at Henry, feeling like he wanted to cry. He thought today was the unluckiest day of his life. If he ever saw this kid again, he would keep his distance.

Florence, who had gone from excitement to pale in the face, and Raymond gritted their teeth. Raymond was brave enough to admit that he was timid, but along the way, this kid had taken down three cars and over a dozen assassins. He believed in him. If they were lucky, they could escape this nightmare of a day.

Henry took a deep breath. He wasn't fearless, holding a gun for the first time, shooting for the first time. He had no idea if he could aim accurately.

It was a gamble! His luck had always been good!

The car suddenly turned around, and Henry struggled to steady himself. Because of the sudden turn, the two cars couldn't brake in time and continued to rush forward. A gunman in black raised his weapon and aimed at Henry. Little Henry quickly drew back and avoided the shot.

The bullet hit the mangled car door, leaving a few more bullet holes.

Henry agilely crouched down. Squinting, the handgun in his hand had already been switched to fully automatic, with over double the power...

He shot at the top of the tires, firing seven or eight rounds. He only saw the tires detach. Due to the car's momentum, the detached tire flew three to four meters high. The car flipped a meter high due to the impact and crashed fiercely into another car. With a loud bang, both cars shattered. Henry hit the fuel tank, and gasoline gushed out.

Henry revealed a cute smile, sweet and elegant. "Goodbye!"

He fired another shot, and with a booming sound, the remaining two cars also exploded...

Bang!

Debris from the cars flew everywhere!

"Wow!" Raymond exclaimed in astonishment, dumbfounded. It was too powerful, too impressive, too shocking. He didn't know what words to use to describe it. He felt that he was the unluckiest and most ridiculous person to have kidnapped this kid.

In 40 minutes, 20 people were skillfully killed. Little Henry emerged victorious!

Antonio clapped his hands and cheered. The force displayed by this promising talent was excellent. It was amazing!

Henry let out a long sigh of relief, turned around, and grabbed his handheld computer to start destroying the surveillance footage from this period on the road, erasing all incriminating evidence.

The process took less than 15 minutes.

"My enemies have been killed. Now, let's deal with our problem!" Henry playfully blinked his eyes.

Florence had already been scared into a puddle of goo, and Raymond's hands and feet were shaking.

They looked at the little boy's pursing and opening mouth in fear, afraid that in one impulsive moment, he would shoot them in the head.

"Misunderstanding, it's a misunderstanding. We're not kidnapping you!" Raymond quickly clarified. From now on, he would keep his distance from Jessica and her son. They were too terrifying!

"Did I say you were going to kidnap me?" Henry asked curiously, raising an eyebrow and smiling innocently.

Raymond almost choked on his breath.

"What do you want from us?" Henry asked. He had always made a clear distinction between friends and enemies. If it weren't for them, he wouldn't have been able to take down this group of assassins so easily. They were his assistants in training, after all.

They deserved to be rewarded!

As for kidnapping, it didn't exist!

"Can we ask for money?"

"You asking me for money?" Henry smiled.

Raymond thought he would reject, but unexpectedly, Henry said, "If you ask me for money, you're asking the right person!"

******

Hospital, ward.

The three of them formed a deadlock. Jessica lay on the bed, with the Smith family - father and son - one at the door, the other at the window. It created a tense atmosphere but also presented a strange picture.

Everyone was silently waiting for news.

Old Mr. Alston was very confident. This time, he would get rid of Henry. The assassins he sent out were all highly skilled, some even having received intense training at special operations camps. He was very confident and would not fail. After all, Henry was just a child, and there were more than twenty killers.

If it weren't for Raymond and Florence going to his school to stage an unlucky kidnapping, perhaps Henry wouldn't have escaped the sniper's shot today.

These two not only disrupted his assassination but also helped Henry take down the group of assassins!

Old Mr. Alston had miscalculated in his elaborate plan.

Mr. Marcus and Jessica received the message from Antonio, informing them that Raymond and Florence had intervened, successfully taken Henry away from school, and were currently engaged in a clash with them on the road, escaping a disaster.

Mr. Marcus and Jessica exchanged glances, both wearing perplexed expressions. It was too comical, too dramatic. Raymond and Florence had actually helped Henry, playing the role of bad guys to do him a favor.

Night of Destiny

Antonio remained calm and courageously told them that his people had been monitoring from behind the scenes the whole time, watching how the little boy skillfully eliminated the enemies.

Mr. Marcus's face immediately changed from gloomy to thunderous, dark, and menacing. Antonio could pay with his life for his sadistic sense of humor if anything happened to his son.

Old Mr. Alston saw his gloomy face and thought that Henry had already been secretly killed by his people. His aged face burst with a gleam of joy, making Jessica want to grab an apple from the table and throw it at him.

"Old Mr. Alston, I'm curious. My son is cute and beautiful, obviously intelligent. Any parent would love their child to the bone. What has he done to upset you?" Jessica asked coldly, her face pale, devoid of color.

Although she knew her son was not an ordinary child and had people protecting him, as a mother, how could she be at ease with her child navigating through bullets?

"Miss Jessica, if you want to blame someone, blame Marcus. It's him who has caused the death of your son!" Old Mr. Alston said coldly and cruelly, his muddy eyes filled with mockery and sowing discord. He intended to make Marcus lose everything he cared about.

Marcus coldly stared at Old Mr. Alston, with a touch of despair and extreme disgust that he struggled to suppress from bursting out. Standing tall, facing Jessica's gaze, he had no regrets. He had acknowledged this son. Although he had brought him into danger, he had no regrets. They were father and son, separated for eight years. What reason could prevent them from recognizing each other?

"Indeed, my son acknowledged Mr. Marcus as his father, which is not a wonderful thing," Jessica looked at Mr. Marcus and said each word sharply. Old Mr. Alston smiled arrogantly. Jessica's gaze fell back on his face, cold and mocking, "But the reason you blame Mr. Marcus for harming my son ultimately comes down to you being a complete failure!"

Old Mr. Alston's face transformed drastically, brewing a terrifying storm in his murky eyes.

The atmosphere in the hospital room reached its breaking point due to this statement.

Old Mr. Alston's face became incredibly ugly, filled with fury, humiliation, and shock.

Decades turned back in time, when there was once a young girl, standing under a streetlight, her usually gentle face twisted with mockery, "Alston, you're a complete failure!"

Memories from his youth rushed in like a snowstorm, sweet, painful, despairing, and hateful... flooding his mind one by one. Old Mr. Lee grew furious, trembling as he raised his cane, once again swinging it fiercely towards Jessica!

"Shut up!"

He had just struck Jessica with a hint of rationality, hitting her shoulder, this time his sanity shattered. The cane mercilessly struck toward Jessica's head. The faces in his mind and Jessica's face morphed and overlapped, his anger and shame grew, and he only wanted to shatter that face to pieces.

Jessica was startled, forgetting about her injured leg. She tried to dodge the cane but ended up aggravating her wound, causing her to frown in pain. The cane was about to strike her head when, in the blink of an eye, a dark figure rushed towards her, using his back to shield her from the blow.

She was enveloped by a warm and solid chest, protected from the imminent pain.

Night of Destiny

With a dull thud, the cane hit the figure's back, its weight resonating heavily in Jessica's heart. She heard a muffled grunt followed by Mr. Marcus's heavy, restrained breaths, quivering in pain.

Jessica's face turned pale; she had witnessed the force of Old Mr. Alston's blows before, but this time, fueled by fury, his strength was astonishing. She almost doubted whether Old Mr. Alston would break Mr. Marcus's back.

Jessica erupted into anger. She despised her current situation, unable to do anything but be beaten. If she had a gun in her hand, she would not hesitate to shoot Old Mr. Alston. Jessica grabbed an apple from the table and forcefully hurled it at Old Mr. Alston, "Get out of here!"

Old Mr. Alston dodged to the side, narrowly avoiding the apple's attack. The apple slammed against the hospital room door, then bounced back, rolling on the ground several times.

The bodyguard who had been sent out wondered what had happened, quickly opening the door. Old Mr. Alston turned and shouted, "Get out!"

"I'm telling you to get out!" Jessica scolded.

At that moment when Old Mr. Alston turned his head, Jessica threw another large red apple, which smacked Old Mr. Alston on the back of his head with a loud thud. In pain, Old Mr. Alston let out a cry, leaving the bodyguards stunned, completely confused about what happened!

Old Mr. Alston grew furious, turning around, and with a loud thud, the third apple hit him on the forehead, causing him to stagger back, stumbling several steps before falling backward. One of the bodyguards quickly stepped forward to support him.

The fourth and fifth apples missed their mark, and the basket was emptied. Jessica's anger subsided when she saw the swelling on Old Mr. Alston's forehead. She felt satisfied! Hitting him twice and causing him to swell up made her feel much happier!

Sect Elder Breeze

As for Old Mr. Alston, gnashing his teeth, his aging face turned red. He, the once illustrious figure who had braved life and death in his youth, victorious in every battle, was now left with a swollen head after being struck by two large red apples.

For Old Mr. Alston, who was proud and conceited, this was incredibly shameful and left him in a state of extreme rage!

"Marcus, how are you?" Jessica helped him sit on the hospital bed. Mr. Marcus maintained the position in which he had pounced for a long time, motionless. A drop of sweat fell onto Jessica's hand, shattering and splattering.

It must hurt a lot!

Jessica's heart tightened, fearing that he had suffered a broken bone from Old Mr. Alston's blows.

"Jessica, you've gone too far. Do you believe that I'll shoot you dead?" Old Mr. Alston erupted in anger, never expecting Marcus to rush to her rescue. It seemed that the girl meant a lot to Marcus. He had been keeping an eye on his son for more than a decade but had never seen him go to such great lengths for anyone. This was an exception. He had to seize this opportunity and make good use of it. Marcus, revealing your weaknesses to the enemy is so foolish!

Chapter 49

You Care About Me?

"If you dare, go ahead and shoot!" Jessica raised her eyes and said coldly. Jessica had always been a strong and assertive presence since she was young. She refused to believe that Old Mr. Alston would shoot in the hospital. "What's the use of just talking? Do you think I'm someone who can be scared? Old Mr. Alston, you are brutal. You are cruel. You're not qualified to be a father, and even less qualified to be Marcus's father. If I were him, I would have gone to court a long time ago to request severing the father-son relationship with you."

"You..." Old Mr. Alston's face turned red as Jessica's provocations choked him with anger. He wanted nothing more than to dismember this audacious girl. "Alright, alright, alright! You're good with words. I want to see how long you can keep from crying!" He was convinced that their son had probably been killed by now!

Narrowing her eyes, Jessica coldly chuckled, "You mentioned my son, didn't you? Do you think anyone can harm even a single hair on him? You don't even know who will die in the end. I advise you to behave yourself and stop your underhanded schemes. Otherwise, I can't guarantee that your son Leonard will remain unharmed!"

"Are you daring me?"

Jessica coldly snorted, "Why not? You dare to touch my son, but I can't touch yours? What a joke."

Sect Elder Breeze

Old Mr. Alston didn't expect that this delicate-looking woman would be so strong-willed. Being intimidated by her and thinking of Dennis's tragic state, he shivered at the thought that Leonard could end up the same way. So far, Leonard was his only hope, and he couldn't risk using him.

Marcus slowly straightened up, and a bead of sweat dripped down his forehead. There was no visible pain or anger, just a serene stillness, concealing his emotions. However, his tense body and heavy breathing revealed the heaviness of the blow from the cane.

"You called me by my name for the second time!" Marcus softly spoke, staring deeply at Jessica. From the time they met until now, it was the first time he heard her call him Marcus. It was when she adamantly told him that if he wanted her heart, he should exchange it with his heart. The second time she called him Marcus was accompanied by a strong sense of concern. This feeling was warm and special.

This woman always politely and distantly referred to him as Mr. Marcus. Even when she mocked him, she would call him Mr. Marcus.

Jessica was taken aback. Really? There had been many times when she had called him that, but it was always in her mind while angrily scolding him.

"Your name is so unpleasant!" Jessica pouted, "How's the injury on your back? Does it hurt?"

"You care about me?" Marcus asked.

Jessica was puzzled. At a time like this, when did he have the mood to care about this? Wasn't that insignificant?

Marcus's gaze remained cold and calm, as deep as ever. The two of them were very close, and Jessica could see her own face reflecting in his blue eyes. They silently locked eyes, as if nothing else existed in the world but each other.

Jessica's heart quickened its pace. Suddenly, she felt a bit flustered and confused. Her sharp mind became muddled and blurry, unaware of the fact that they were still in a hospital room, their crisis unresolved.

Night of Destiny

He was the kind of person who would only say and do what he wanted, no matter the situation. Arrogant, proud, and dismissive of everything. But she wasn't...

Jessica felt like she was going crazy.

"Mr. Marcus, isn't it normal for me to care about you?" Jessica smiled, deeply concealing her agitation and chaos. She shrugged her shoulders and said, "If something happens to you while protecting me, how can I live with myself?" She was the one who should bear the pain from the cane. He came to bear it, even though it wasn't what she desired or expected. But ultimately, it was because of her that he was injured. So, caring about him, wasn't it normal? She wasn't a heartless person.

Marcus's eyes deepened, his thin lips lightly curled, and he murmured with a smirk, "Jessica, you really enjoy being contradictory!"

This sentence, filled with tenderness, didn't fit Mr. Marcus's strong demeanor at all. The way he said Jessica sounded three times softer, enough to numb a person's heart. Jessica's heart, once again, beat uncontrollably several times.

"Oh, well, this is a virtue!" Jessica smiled.

Marcus smiled as he hooked her chin and commented on her recent actions, "Your move was quite bold!"

"Thank you for the compliment!"

Mr. Marcus's eyes deepened, his blue gaze veiled as if to prevent anyone from peeking into his emotions. It was a tempting taboo that made people even more curious.

What was he thinking at this moment?

Jessica didn't think it was a wonderful idea for the two of them to be tangled up in these inexplicable emotional issues on the hospital bed.

"Mr. Marcus, I think you should deal with your father first!" Jessica said indifferently, driving away the annoying old man and making the air much fresher.

Sect Elder Breeze

Suddenly, Marcus held Jessica's head with one hand, leaned down, and planted a kiss on her forehead. His Adam's apple moved a few times as he softly said, "Thank you!"

His usually deep voice now carried three parts of charm, three parts of ambiguity, and four parts of emotion. It sounded magnetic and... sentimental.

Jessica was bewildered by his actions. Thank her? For what? And why did he kiss her?

Seeing her confused expression, Marcus simply chuckled. This woman could be clever at times, but she could also be more clueless than anyone else. He was grateful for her protection, this was the second time! He had been protected by a woman, not just once but twice! Once against Dennis and now against Old Mr. Alston, each time she had shown her ruthlessness, delivering a heavy blow to them, leaving them in a miserable state. How could he not be thankful?

Old Mr. Alston coldly chuckled and sarcastically said, "Marcus, you have a son and a lover. How are you going to explain it to Crystal?"

Jessica furrowed her brows and looked deeply at Marcus and saw absolute calmness in his eyes, without panic, without difficulty, not even a trace of guilt.

Marcus slowly stood up, and straightened his spine, his exquisite face briefly displaying a coldness before he smiled arrogantly and icily, "Why should I explain to her?"

The air froze as these words were spoken.

A cold atmosphere pervaded the entire hospital room. Marcus didn't appreciate people meddling in his life, whoever tried to control him was foolishly wishful thinking.

Crystal understood this, which was why she had been so compliant all these years.

Night of Destiny

Old Mr. Alston waved his hand, signaling the bodyguard to step back. His sharp gaze swept across Jessica, and he pointed his cane at her, "Old Mr. Walker and I will have a meeting the day after tomorrow to discuss your marriage with Crystal. Marcus, this is the first condition for you to take over Noblefull Group!"

Jessica was momentarily stunned, silent for a moment. He was going to marry Crystal? That was fast. He just recognized his son, and now he's getting married – double happiness, isn't it? Although she wasn't the bride, it was still a joyful occasion, and she should congratulate him.

After all, these few years, it was only Crystal who had been faithfully by his side. It was only Crystal who had been allowed to be by his side without leaving or abandoning him. Marcus treated her differently from other women.

A jealous feeling welled up in her heart. Jessica suddenly detested Old Mr. Alston's sharp face. This person was a tyrant, an emperor if the Smith family was an empire. Others were just subjects, controlled by him, not allowed to resist. Marriage was a common way for elders to control younger generations. If Marcus married Crystal, this union would have a very elegant name – a business alliance.

Great! Perfect!

"Marriage?" Marcus raised an eyebrow, with a smile that seemed both mocking and teasing. His wishful thinking was echoing loud and clear. Without thinking, he glanced at Jessica, and his anger suddenly surged out of nowhere.

Jessica's face remained calm, even carrying a sense of, "He's getting married. That's great."

Marcus glared fiercely at her, but Jessica wore an expressionless face, turning away and not looking at his charming face.

Sect Elder Breeze

"Dad, you have planned it well, but I don't want to get married for now." Marcus vetoed it outright. He had considered it before, that one day he would marry Crystal and use each other. If one day he did get married, Crystal would definitely be the bride. This idea had been entrenched in his mind for several years.

But ever since he found out about Henry and Jessica's existence, within a short day, this deeply rooted idea had begun to waver. Marcus now had the whole world with his son. Anyone threatening his son's rights would be mercilessly dealt with.

"You don't want to get married for now? What an excuse!" Old Mr. Alston angrily pointed at Jessica and said, "Do you want to marry her, a woman from a common family? Do you want people to mock you? This woman absolutely cannot enter the doors of my Smith family. If you dare to entertain that thought, you can resign and leave Noblefull Group. Don't think that we can't do without you!"

Old Mr. Alston was furious and made it clear that it was either Noblefull Group or Jessica.

Marcus wasn't surprised at all. His icy gaze remained icy, devoid of any emotions. It was Jessica who retorted with a cold disdain, "Old Mr. Alston, I suggest you don't overestimate yourself. Is the entrance to your Smith family adorned with gold or jade? Do you really think any woman would throw themselves at it just because?!"

Old Mr. Alston's face changed, his expression darkening as he dangerously looked at the seemingly innocent and beautiful girl in front of him. Why did she speak with such a sharp tongue? Bold and unyielding? She didn't care about the Smith family. He didn't believe it! Every woman was driven by vanity. In his eyes, Jessica was just a shameless woman who coveted the Smith family's wealth.

Night of Destiny

A fleeting smile grazed Marcus's lips, and his initially gloomy expression brightened a little. This woman was not someone who could be bullied without fighting back. And if she couldn't handle it, a powerful son was standing behind her.

"Well, with your temperament, I doubt anyone would want to be your daughter-in-law. When you're old, you should learn to control your temper. If you keep getting angry like this, watch out for a brain hemorrhage. It would be such a pity if you die early and miss out on so many good things, don't you think?" Jessica spoke with a smile. Don't blame her for not respecting the elderly. Some people simply didn't deserve it.

Old Mr. Alston's face turned purple with anger at her words, and if Marcus hadn't stopped him, he might have hit her with his cane!

Marcus raised an eyebrow. Jessica's mouth was becoming equally venomous as his.

"You..."

"Sir, there's a phone call!" a bodyguard entered the room, pushing the door open.

The expressions of the three people in the hospital room changed simultaneously.

Old Mr. Alston's face turned fierce as he swept his gaze over Marcus and Jessica. "Your son is as good as dead! Prepare for his funeral!"

Jessica wished she could crush his face, feeling nervous inside. She couldn't help but look at Marcus, his gaze becoming even colder and his fists tightening involuntarily as Old Mr. Alston answered the phone. Suddenly, Marcus's phone rang too.

Chapter 50

Nothing Is Impossible

Marcus swiftly answered, his eyebrows raising higher in surprise. Antonio was reporting his son's achievements, describing them as if he were there himself. If Marcus knew that Antonio had been monitoring the whole scene, he would surely be furious.

"How is this possible?" Old Mr. Alston's voice suddenly escalated. "This can't be!" He simply couldn't believe that a child, a seven-year-old child, had single-handedly eliminated the twenty assassins he had sent, leaving not a single survivor. What kind of scene was that? He could hardly imagine it.

Old Mr. Alston had dominated his entire life and had never heard of such a miraculous event.

In a situation like this, most seven-year-old children would just cry. How could anyone escape the pursuit of twenty professional killers?

This was impossible!

Jessica saw the starkly different reactions of the father and son and knew that her son was safe. The tightness in her heart was finally released.

Marcus hung up the phone and smiled at Jessica. "He is fine, and will be at the hospital soon!"

Night of Destiny

Jessica nodded. Marcus's expression became strangely complex. He increasingly suspected that Antonio had intentionally given Henry firearms and explosives, and that he was pretending not to know that Old Mr. Alston would attack today. He was sure that Antonio wanted to see how Henry would escape from this chase.

Henry's future seemed to be predetermined. He would inevitably enter the arms industry with the help of Truman, Robin, Victor, and others. He would comfortably sit in the seat of the top arms dealer, without any problems. However, this matter carried too much risk, and Marcus was strongly opposed to Henry continuing down this path.

But, his son seemed very interested this path, and Marcus understood that the child's future had long been planned by himself. Having Old Mr. Alston as an example, Marcus would never try to control Henry's future. The path his son chooses, he must bear the consequences, but...

"Is he injured?" Jessica asked. She couldn't be bothered to appreciate the scene of Old Mr. Alston raging. The most important thing to her was that Henry wasn't hurt.

Marcus shook his head, his delicate features clouded with complexity. Jessica, if you know that your son can take care of twenty adults in half an hour, even trained killers. what would you think about it? In any case, he was about to be stunned by his son. He unexpectedly turned out to be so brave. Perhaps this child had mutated genes.

Jessica didn't think much about it when she thought of her son being safe. She was eternally grateful to his unfriendly group of friends who protected him from harm.

If she found out that these seemingly friendly guys had dragged her son into a terrorist organization. It seemed that she would have to change her face again!

"Who is he, really?" Old Mr. Alston put down the phone and asked in shock.

"What did you say?" Marcus jeered coldly. Just thinking about the unpleasant face Old Mr. Alston had earlier, his mood improved a lot. Didn't he think that anyone could touch his son? He was overestimating himself.

"Who was your son in the end?"

"My son is my son, what kind of stupid question are you asking?" Marcus disdainfully mocked. "Dad, I hope this is the only time. Henry is fine this time, I can overlook your attempt to assassinate him. But if you have such thoughts again, listen carefully... If Henry has injured one arm, I'll take two arms from Leonard; if Henry gets shot once, I'll shoot Leonard ten times. If my son is harmed, your son will pay the price. You better remember that and stop having any evil thoughts. You also know that I'm not as pure as I appear on the surface." Did Old Mr. Alston think that my huge Ghost Gang was a pushover?

Old Mr. Alston was too shocked to say a word. "This can't be, it's absolutely impossible!"

A youthful and elegant laughter drifted in as Henry pushed open the door to the hospital room. His exquisitely handsome face appeared in front of everyone, accompanied by his unique melodious voice, full of dominance and arrogance. "With me around, nothing is impossible!" He was the one who turned impossibility into possibility!

"Baby!" Jessica exclaimed in surprise, reaching out her hand for Henry to come over and embracing him tightly. "Scared mommy to death! Are you hurt? Let me see..."

"Mommy, I'm fine!" Henry affectionately kissed his mom.

"Why is there blood here?" Henry pressed on the broken glass, causing a few minor cuts and leaving some blood stains on his school uniform.

Marcus thoughtfully rolled up his sleeve, only finding a superficial scrape with no serious injuries. Both of them breathed a sigh of relief as Jessica held Henry tightly, her voice choked with emotion. "You little rascal!"

"You..." Old Mr. Alston tremblingly pointed at Henry, unable to comprehend how he managed to kill those assassins!

Henry turned around, gracefully smiling with a youthful voice laced with undeniable coldness. "Old Sir, I wouldn't mind finding a few people to keep your little son company, if you'd like."

Demon...

This was Old Mr. Alston's second impression of the little boy!

He had initially thought that this child had inherited some of Marcus's sharp tongue, but a seven-year-old child saying such chilling words with calmness was truly shocking. Apart from demon, he couldn't find another word to describe him.

Old Mr. Alston recalled Marcus at the age of ten, standing next to the lifeless body of his mother, silent and tearsless. Marcus at ten and Henry now were roughly the same age. Marcus had a difficult life, living with his mother in harsh conditions, suffering from malnutrition, and growing at a slower pace. His complexion was also very poor, not as fair and lovely as Henry's, but equally delicate and beautiful.

Everyone thought little Marcus was frightened, as no servant approached to comfort him due to Old Mr. Alston's anger. Thus, he was left alone to face the tragedy of his mother's death. They all thought that this child was scared and didn't say a word.

But when the crowd dispersed, little Marcus suddenly lifted his head, revealing a refined smile, and calmly uttered a sentence, "Twenty years later, I will destroy your pride!"

That sentence, like a curse, lingered in Old Mr. Alston's heart. It was even the reason why he pretended Marcus had a mental illness and sent him to a rehabilitation facility in Australia, where he received the harshest and cruelest treatments.

Now, more than a decade has passed, and everything seems peaceful.

Sect Elder Breeze

But Old Mr. Alston never forgot the tone and coldness in little Marcus' words when he said that, just like the current Henry, they were exactly the same. The absolute killing intent behind the elegant smile! The unwavering determination to not stop until the goal is achieved! That's why he was afraid, afraid that once Marcus gained power, he would truly destroy his pride.

What is Old Mr. Alston's pride?

Noblefull Group!

That's why Old Mr. Alston needed to rely on Marcus' abilities and tactics while also controlling him. He wouldn't allow things to go beyond his control, and if they did, he would definitely suppress it. Just like with Henry! Having another successor would introduce too many variables, and Old Mr. Alston couldn't afford such uncertainty.

He never thought about resolving the hatred between him and Marcus. He only thought about how to deal with Marcus' hatred towards him and how to better control him.

Marcus had indeed been obedient for over a decade, but recently, he has changed. This obedient child was just pretending, and Old Mr. Alston couldn't tolerate it, nor could he accept Marcus's rebellion. He had planned to use this opportunity to tell Marcus that he would always be under his control, never able to escape. But he never expected that Marcus's son would eliminate all the assassins, overturning all his plans.

"Dad, if you have nothing else to say, please leave!" Marcus said coldly. He didn't like Old Mr. Alston's gaze towards Henry, judgmental, mocking, and complex. It reminded him of the unbearable years when he first returned to the Smith family. It felt like a venomous snake crawling across his cheeks, extremely disgusting.

"Daddy, no need to rush!" Henry elegantly smiled, standing by his father's side. He smiled and said, "Old Sir, I always do what I say. You shouldn't test my patience. The only one who can change my decision is my mommy. If that day comes, I'll make you beg my mommy on your knees, and it won't be a pretty sight!"

"You..." Old Mr. Alston became enraged, his icy gaze sweeping over the three of them. He let out a heavy snort and left, filled with anger.

"Wow, he has such a bad temper!" Henry cutely frowned and turned back to his hospital bed. "Mommy, did he do anything to you?"

Jessica shook her head, looking deeply into his eyes.

Henry's face lit up with a big, sparkling smile. He playfully rubbed his hands and asked, "Mommy, what's wrong? What's wrong? Tell me!"

Marcus was taken aback by his son's pitiable appearance. He stared at him fiercely, wondering why his son turned into a cute boy whenever he was in front of Jessica.

"Did you send someone to hurt Leonard?" Jessica frowned, her innocent face showing disapproval. It was a terrible idea, but... she had to admit that their way of thinking as a family was surprisingly similar. Her, Marcus, and Henry, all using Leonard as a threat against Old Mr. Alston. His weakness was too easy to find, or were they all focused on Leonard?

"No, no, absolutely not. I just wanted to scare him, that's all," Henry chuckled. "I'm your sweetie, I'm always a kind boy. How could you think I would do something so bloody?"

Kind boy?

Marcus and Jessica both twitched their eyes in unison. Jessica rolled up Henry's sleeve, revealing a few superficial scratches on his little arm. It was just some minor cuts, and only then did she fully relax.

Sect Elder Breeze

"By the way, that old man failed to hurt me, but he did hit him with a cane," Jessica suddenly pointed at Marcus. Her tone was cool and sincere. She added, "He beat him so hard he couldn't stand up straight."

Marcus was infuriated by this. What did she mean by saying that he beat him so hard he couldn't stand up straight? She was spreading rumors!

"Wasn't it because I was trying to protect you that I got beaten?" Marcus couldn't help but retort. "If it weren't for me, your brains would have been splattered all over the place. Heartless woman!"

"Dad, well done!" Henry praised him, giving him a thumbs up. A man who could protect his mommy was a great man!

Marcus suddenly realized he had fallen into a trap. He glared at Jessica fiercely, completely speechless. Was this how she was trying to help him to gain his son's favor? She had such a twisted personality.

"Henry, does your arm hurt? Let Dad take you to bandage it up," Jessica softly asked. This child had grown up without a single scar thanks to her care.

Henry shook his head. "It's fine, just a small thing!" Though it stung a bit, it wasn't particularly painful, just some minor cuts. It would be fine in a couple of days.

"Henry, do you have classes this afternoon?"

Henry nodded and then went on to tell them about the unfortunate incidents where Raymond and Florence had kidnapped him. Marcus and Jessica were both speechless. It was true that they had done a good deed by saving their son's life.

"This time, I'll take care of the favor for the Davis Family Group. I owe them that," Marcus hesitated for a moment before decisively making the decision.

Jessica didn't say anything. Although she didn't have any positive feelings towards Raymond and Florence, even disliking them, she didn't say anything considering they had saved Henry's life. Marcus wanted to help, so be it! After all, it wasn't her money on the line!

"Mr. Marcus, what if your father attacks Henry again?" Jessica's eyebrows turned cold as she asked in a deep voice. She looked displeased, as it was a serious problem. She truly regretted Henry's decision to recognize Marcus as his father, and within a day, her little sweetheart was being chased and killed. The issue with Old Mr. Alston had to be resolved!

Chapter 51

Being With My Son Is The Most Important.

"Don't worry, there won't be a next time!" Marcus confidently stated, a hint of hostility flickering across his icy gaze. If there was a next time, he wouldn't have to be polite and considerate. Dennis was an example of what would happen!

Knowing Old Mr. Alston, Marcus knew that the next move would be to control his marriage!

It was ridiculous!

Sect Elder Breeze

Well, it was for the best. At least Henry's crisis was resolved. It wasn't fortunate like this every time. Although he won through this fierce battle!

"Henry, I think you should move back home. You only moved in with him for a day and look what happened. If you stayed a few more days, would you even still be alive?" Jessica teased, patting her son's tender face. "Shouldn't you consider my suggestion?"

Marcus pursed his lips. Was this what he wanted? Even if he didn't move back, he would still be chased and killed. These two things weren't necessarily connected, were they?

Henry shook his head and leaned in, affectionately hugging Marcus. With a sweet smile towards Jessica, he said, "I want Dad!"

His words made Marcus very happy. He provocatively looked up at Jessica, as if to say, "See, our son loves me so much!"

Childish!

Jessica curled her lips. Mr. Marcus, you should take a good look at yourself. You're exceptionally childish.

Marcus stayed at the hospital for a while before returning to his company.

Henry curiously picked up the apple from the ground and waved it. "Mommy, why is Grandpa's apple being treated like this? Are you venting your frustrations?"

"Throw it in the trash bin!" Jessica calmly said. "I just used it to hit Old Mr. Alston. Didn't you see the big lump on his forehead?"

Henry said, "...Mommy, you're really strong!"

Extraordinarily powerful!

So amazing!

"What did he say? Did you get angry and hit him with apples?" Henry asked curiously. It was a lovely weapon, and she was clever to think of using it.

Night of Destiny

Jessica blushed slightly. "Marcus defended me against that cane. He was in pain, and I got angry in the heat of the moment, so I hit him."

"You hit him for Dad?" Wow, this was a good sign, very good!

Upon hearing her son's teasing tone, Jessica's cheeks turned red, and she coughed lightly. "Who said that?"

"No need to explain, explaining is just covering up!" Henry blinked.

Jessica's face turned red with anger. She gritted her teeth and glared at him. "You, go buy me a few more apples!" She had thrown them at Old Mr. Alston and hadn't eaten any.

"No money!" Henry replied bluntly. Besides the money for groceries, he never carried any cash on him. Now that he didn't need to buy groceries anymore, he naturally didn't need money.

"Why didn't you ask your dad just now?"

"You didn't say anything. How about I use this apple to cut it for you? It's not spoiled and can still be eaten."

"Just go away! I just used it to hit Old Mr. Alston, and now you want me to eat it? Get lost!"

Henry stuck out his tongue. Jessica found herself bored, and it was the perfect timing. She turned on the TV and watched financial news. To her surprise, a news report came on, showing the brutal game of killing and being killed between Henry and the twenty assassins.

Eyewitnesses claimed to have seen five cars chasing a Lexus, and some even said they saw a child shooting at them. The police found sixteen bodies at the scene, along with severed limbs and arms scattered about due to explosions.

Because the surveillance footage was damaged and couldn't be retrieved, the police had formed an investigation team dedicated to solving the case.

Jessica watched the news anchor report in astonishment and turned her head. Henry had a strange smile on his face...

She trembled. She had always thought that someone had saved Henry, but never thought... "Baby, you... single-handedly took them down?"

As the lights flickered on, night adorned the city with a magnificent color.

The darkness in the city always carried a touch of fervent beauty, even at night, it couldn't shake off the scorching heat in the air from the daytime, and it exuded a profound sense of mystery, tempting people to peek into it.

In an elegantly decorated French restaurant, Crystal sat near the window, gazing out through the glass at the bustling streets below, her delicate face tinged with a hint of sadness.

She was wearing a light blue dress that was both delicate and pure, with finely arching eyebrows that seemed as if the most famous painter in the world had meticulously drawn them, appearing so perfect under the illumination of the lights, a perfect reflection of her sorrow.

Such a woman aroused the protective instincts in men the most - tender, melancholic, and slightly sorrowful - making one yearn to offer the best treasures of the world just to see her smile.

Marcus approached the restaurant and quickly spotted her, coincidentally tilting her head, revealing a perfect half-face, lost in thought, with a faint hint of desolation on her face.

Mr. Marcus furrowed his brows and walked over, "Crystal, how long have you been waiting?" He pulled out a chair and sat down.

A glimmer of joy flashed through Crystal's eyes, and the sadness dissipated, replaced by a shimmering radiance. She brightened up completely, as if Marcus was her entire life, and she lived solely for him. Indeed, it had been these few years!

"Not long!" Crystal softly replied. Even if she had been waiting for an hour, she wouldn't have considered it a long time, as long as Marcus arrived, she was willing to wait no matter how long.

Night of Destiny

"What would you like to eat? Let me order for you!" Crystal considerately offered, her gentle face filled with tenderness.

Marcus shook his head, a faint smile of affection passing through his refined and cold features. He calmly said, "No need, I'll have dinner at home later!"

Before recognizing his son, Marcus used to snatch Jessica's lunchbox for his lunch. Later, she spontaneously brought two portions, although they were home-cooked dishes, they were delicious, no worse than those prepared by the chefs at five-star restaurants.

Recently, he had been living with his son, and every day, he would come home to have dinner with Henry without fail. If he had no urgent matters at work, he would postpone them to the next day, preferring to free up time to accompany Henry to the market, buy groceries together, and return home to cook and eat together. He didn't know how to cook, but he was learning recently.

Henry said that a good man must have the ability to cook. He patted his chest with a childish air, saying that he was the perfect example of a good man, which amused Marcus. His little sweetheart said that he would train his dad to become a master chef in the shortest time possible to take care of his mommy.

Look, what a biased little cutie.

But...

For Marcus, this rare experience of enjoying a warm family was something he cherished deeply.

"Have dinner at home?" Crystal was taken aback, feeling inexplicably nervous, and tentatively asked, "Did you hire a housekeeper?"

"No!" Marcus looked deeply into Crystal's eyes, realizing that his father hadn't told her yet. Indeed, Old Mr. Alston still hoped that he would marry Crystal and receive assistance from the Walker Family Group. Naturally, he wouldn't tell Crystal the truth.

Sect Elder Breeze

"Crystal... Well, never mind. Do you need something from me?"

A trace of bitterness flashed across Crystal's lips. When did their relationship become one where she could only approach him when something was wrong? Marcus, I am your girlfriend, your fiancé. You said that if you got married, I would be your bride. Have you forgotten?

"Have you been busy recently?" Crystal disguised her pain and asked softly. Lately, every time she tried to contact him, either his phone was off or he claimed to be busy. When she called Noblefull Group, Susan said her boss had been absent from the office frequently and arrived late.

Marcus, he had never been like this before! Even if he was busy, could he really be too busy to spare time to have dinner with her?

"Quite busy!" Marcus smiled. He wanted to spend every waking moment with his son. Just the thought of adorable and cunning Henry made his cold demeanor warm up naturally, revealing a doting attitude.

"Is that so?" Crystal forced a bitter smile. The sorrow in her melancholic gaze added a touch of sadness to this romantically infused restaurant. Did he have another woman? During this period, he hadn't attended any social events, nor had he been rumored to be with any woman. He went straight home after work. For a girlfriend, such a change from her boyfriend would be a good thing. But if it was Marcus who changed like this...

Crystal would only feel restless and anxious, a cascade of negative reactions flooded her mind - lies, conjecture, jealousy, and wild suspicions. She felt that if she didn't see Marcus soon and get things clear, she would go crazy!

In the past, even if Marcus had other women, he never forgot about her. Yet, how long had it been since he last called her?

Once a woman starts feeling insecure, she becomes restless.

She wanted to ask who it was, but as she saw the tenderness and affection on Marcus's face, something he had never shown before, Crystal lost all the courage to question him. She was afraid she couldn't handle the consequences.

"Oh, by the way, where is your chief secretary? Susan has been answering your calls lately." Could it be her? His chief secretary? That woman who caught Marcus's gaze. How coincidental, she hasn't been around the company during this time either.

Marcus's gaze sank as he looked at Crystal, his expression turning slightly cold. Was she testing him? Hmph!

"She had an accident and is lying in the hospital," Marcus said indifferently, checking his watch. It was already 7:00, and his son would be expecting him. "Do you still need something? If not, I'll leave."

"Marcus..." Crystal called out to him in a panic, her tone revealing her pain. "Can you spend the night with me? It's been so long since you've been with me!"

With her delicate and tender appearance, anyone with a heart of stone wouldn't be able to bear rejecting her invitation.

Marcus had an expressionless face, completely cold, and firmly refused, "No!"

Marcus took two steps and turned around, giving Crystal a cold glance. He said lightly, "Crystal, don't have any expectations of me!"

Cruel, heartless, without any emotional fluctuations, as if he was simply stating a fact. With that, he turned and walked away.

Crystal watched his departing figure, gritting her teeth in frustration, feeling it deep in her bones. Her delicate white hand involuntarily clenched. How could he be so heartless? Although Marcus had never treated anyone with tenderness in the past few years, he had never used such a heartless tone with her. She had always believed that she was different from other women.

But Marcus, why did his attitude change so quickly?

She wouldn't give up, she would never give up!

Her grandfather had said that he and Old Mr. Alston were already planning their wedding. She was about to become his wife, the president's wife of Noblefull Group. At a time like this, where was his heart? She would not allow anyone to ruin their relationship.

seven years, a long seven years. She had been with him, walking this long road, using up her youth. How could she be willing to give up on Marcus at this moment?

She had always known that Marcus didn't love her. He didn't love anyone. If it didn't matter who he married, why couldn't it be her?

Crystal stood up, her soft face showing a hint of melancholy.

She wanted to see who was waiting for him at his villa, something that made him rush back without even sparing her a minute.

Chapter 52

The Provocation From His Girlfriend

Hospital, early morning.

Jessica had the nurse take her downstairs to get some fresh air early in the morning. Lying in bed all day was boring. The past few years had been too busy. She had gotten used to a fast-paced life. Suddenly having free time felt uncomfortable, as if a part of her life had been forcibly taken away.

The greens in the garden outside the hospital were well-maintained. Many patients were walking or sunbathing downstairs, old and young. From their faces, she saw signs of suffering, as well as serene calmness.

The most eye-catching was a pair of twin boys playing with a small soccer ball in the garden. They were around seven or eight years old, similar in age to Henry. They looked adorable, like little dolls, slightly clumsy in their movements, displaying the characteristic slowness of children. Their faces were rosy from running around, looking pink and tender, incredibly cute.

Their mother smiled as she watched the two children frolic, occasionally reminding them to be careful and not fall. The entire garden was filled with the laughter of angels, dispelling the heaviness of the hospital.

Several elderly people were also practicing under the trees, observing the children's play with interest.

She took another walk in the courtyard, and then the nurse pushed her back.

It's been such a pleasant day today!

Just as she returned to the ward, the joy disappeared. A visitor arrived in the ward uninvited.

And she was the kind of guest that Jessica didn't want to face.

Crystal! Marcus's girlfriend!

"Miss Jessica, I'll leave first!" the nurse exited the ward.

Jessica pushed her wheelchair, giving a faint smile, "Miss Crystal, what a surprise!"

Crystal's face looked extremely pale and bloodless. She was still wearing the light blue dress from last night.

Jessica didn't need to think much, Crystal definitely knew! Did Marcus get caught being too conspicuous, or did she happen to find out?

Jessica guessed it was the latter. Generally speaking, a cat that steals fish will wipe its mouth. Why would they be foolish enough to leave such solid evidence and go bragging about it?

"Jessica, what exactly is the relationship between you and Marcus?" Crystal asked through gritted teeth. She had cried, her eyes had bloodshot veins, losing their usual charm and showing a touch of melancholy.

"The relationship between a boss and an employee!" Jessica answered with a smile. She wanted to challenge her, but it seemed like she chose the wrong target!

"You're talking nonsense!" Crystal got a bit agitated, trembling hands pointed at her. "Which boss and employee would have a child together? It's you... What's your purpose for getting close to Marcus?"

Jessica continued smiling, as she said, she should have torn Dennis into pieces and fractured her legs. Now, Marcus's woman came to challenge her. Crystal stood, and she sat. In terms of momentum, she had lost!

Why does everyone ask this question? What is her purpose?

Night of Destiny

Old Mr. Alston did, and so did Crystal. They all came to ask her after they had figured out her purpose, waiting for her to speak, so they could refute her and then humiliate and mock her. Is it interesting?

In the usual drama, when a third party interferes in someone else's relationship and the official wife shows up. What should the third party do?

Option A, simulate a pitiful appearance, gain sympathy, and without saying much, immediately promise to leave him. This belongs to the delicate and beautiful type.

Option B, be very arrogant, speak rashly, and say, "Yes, I am the third party, so what? Get out. This man is mine." This is the fierce and bold type.

Option C, as his wife chatters a bunch, she remains silent, selectively deaf until the other side finishes venting, and slams the door with a bang. This is the upgraded version of being fierce and bold.

So what should she do? If she could choose, she would choose Option C. She really didn't want to listen to Crystal's hysterics.

However, looking at her pitiful broken leg, it would take a lot of effort to get her to leave at this time.

"My purpose?" She paused and then said, "Mr. Marcus, after all, is the number one person on the W City's Golden Singles List. He's handsome and comes from a good family. I'm greedy and flirtatious. And Mr. Marcus fits the criteria."

Crystal couldn't believe her eyes. How could she be so shameless and arrogant?

"You're shameless!" She trembled for a while before cursing her as shameless. She was furious, shaking all over. Someone took away her precious treasure, which she had held tightly in her hand. It felt as if she had swallowed a fly. She was extremely uncomfortable.

Sect Elder Breeze

If it was just Jessica, Crystal was confident that she could defeat her, and ultimately Marcus would be hers. But now, she found out that Jessica and Marcus already had a 7-year-old son. Just with this, she had lost! She had lost miserably.

Last night, she drove to his house near the mansion before Marcus did, and was shocked to see the lights on. Marcus's house had always been dark unless he was home.

He valued his privacy and didn't allow anyone to step onto his territory, except for the designated cleaning staff every week!

At that moment, she speculated who had moved into his house.

But she never expected to see a child coming out, carrying two garbage bags to throw away. Crystal was stunned and thought she was dreaming. Otherwise, how could she see a child who resembled Marcus so much?

Coincidentally, Marcus came back at that time. The sound of "daddy" almost drove Crystal to the brink of collapse. Father and son were talking and laughing, their relationship was excellent. It was the first time Crystal had seen Marcus smile so pure and sunny, his eyes filled with endless affection.

Crystal drove back to her house and smashed everything she could out of anger.

She cried for most of the night, scaring her family. In the middle of the night, she had someone investigate the child. The news was delivered to her early in the morning. The child was Jessica's, and it was also discovered that Marcus had been coming home late lately, picking up and dropping off the child, taking him to the hospital, and going to see Jessica together.

These pieces of information were like a loud slap to Crystal's face, igniting a series of negative emotions within her – humiliation, jealousy, hatred, and resentment – engulfing her.

Night of Destiny

She was just a hair's breadth away from losing her sanity and taking a gun to shoot Jessica and Henry.

After a night of madness, her emotions settled.

Crystal was a very smart girl. She knew that at that moment, she had to pretend to know nothing. Her father and Old Mr. Alston were meeting, already discussing their marriage. Marcus hadn't mentioned anything, neither denying nor admitting. She thought he would accept this marriage.

After all, he had said that if he got married, he would marry her.

She was the most suitable woman for him, a perfect match in terms of status and talent.

However, things suddenly became complicated and unfavorable for this marriage. She shouldn't have been so irrational. Once they were married, her position would be secure, and she would be in a more advantageous position to deal with Jessica and her son. It should have been simple.

But she just couldn't swallow her pride. She wanted to understand what exactly was going on. So, early in the morning, she went to find Jessica.

"Shameless, right?" Jessica smiled, not getting angry. Compared to Crystal's impatient anger, she appeared calm and composed. "Miss Crystal, you have already accused me of this crime. No matter what I say, you won't believe it. So, why not directly tell me what you want to do? Isn't that better? We're all adults. There's no need for beating around the bush in our conversation."

Last time Susan said they looked somewhat alike, and Jessica didn't mind at all. But now, somehow, she suddenly thought of her words. Upon closer inspection, there was indeed a trace of similarity in their aura.

Jessica's heart skipped a beat. She disliked this confusing and unresolved situation. Yet, her expression remained calm and composed.

Sect Elder Breeze

Crystal's breath caught, and she arrogantly lifted her noble head, saying coldly, "Miss Jessica, you can't compete with me!"

"Compete?" Jessica smiled, tilted her head, pretending to contemplate, and after a while, she said, "What do you mean by 'compete'? Competing is when opponents of equal strength meet. If the difference in strength is too great, competing becomes meaningless."

Crystal believed that Jessica would give up, after all, as she said, the difference in their strengths was too great. No matter from which aspect, Crystal could easily crush her. The Walker Family Group was not something that they, common folks, could provoke.

"Now that you know the difference in our strengths, why don't you leave W City with your son!" Crystal acted magnanimously, assuming a high and mighty pose. Arrogantly, she said, "As long as you leave, I can forgive you!"

Jessica covered her mouth and laughed. Bright eyes revealed a cold sneer. "Crystal, it seems like your ego is inflated. 'Forgive me'? Miss Crystal, may I ask what authority you have to forgive me? You are not Marcus' wife, even though rumors say you are his fiancée, you two have never officially gotten engaged. In this day and age, divorce rates are skyrocketing. Even after getting married, people can still get divorced and mistresses can take advantage. You're just one of his many girlfriends and absurdly think of yourself as his wife. It's ridiculous."

"You..." Crystal trembled with anger, her beautiful face completely distorted, looking at Jessica with hatred. "You're just after Marcus' wealth. What right do you have to talk to me here?"

"So, we both have no right to judge each other, right?" Jessica smiled lightly. Who could win an argument against her? She had quite reputation for her debating skills during her schooling years. "Besides, haven't you figured out the situation yet? It's you who came to talk to me, not the other way around. Speaking of reasons, I have more than enough. Marcus' child's mother is me, not you. What do you say?"

"You..." Jessica's words almost made Crystal faint. She pointed at her tremblingly, unable to speak for a while, gasping for breath continuously. Her face turned red with anger. Her opponent was so difficult to deal with, like never before.

Over the years, Marcus never stayed with a woman for long. It wasn't that he hadn't found one that suited his taste. The so-called "suitability" referred to a woman who could handle his temper and keep his interest for a longer period. Or perhaps, someone who resembled the girl in his subconscious memory a little too much, causing Marcus to be captivated.

Once he lost interest in a woman after two weeks, Crystal would make her move. Two girls had been forced into miserable situations by her – one was disfigured and quietly sent out of W City, while the other was scared and fell down the stairs, becoming partially disabled.

While Crystal presented herself as gentle by Marcus' side, she closely monitored every woman who was with Marcus. Once a highly threatening individual appeared, she would eliminate them without hesitation. Her methods were ruthless, after all, she was an only child in her family, who had been trained to be the successor since childhood. She was far from being as innocent and clean as she appeared.

This behavior could be called jealousy or envy.

But, the more primal explanation was that beasts have absolute aggression towards creatures that pry into their mates, with destructive tendencies!

This time, meeting Jessica was encountering the most formidable opponent she had ever encountered!

Chapter 53

He Loves Me, Not You

Jessica wasn't afraid of her cunning or the power behind her. And she could casually spout a series of infuriating words. Crystal was used to being in control her whole life and couldn't bear this kind of frustration.

"Miss Crystal!" Just when she was about to explode with anger, Jessica said calmly, "Instead of talking to me here, why don't you confront Marcus about this? After all, he is the key to this matter, isn't he?"

The root of this matter was Marcus himself, and Crystal was too confused about the situation!

"I will find Marcus. Don't be arrogant. Even if you give birth to his son, you still won't be able to enter the Smith family." Crystal calmed her anger, saying arrogantly. With the support of her father and Marcus's father, she would not lose.

Marcus must know that Old Mr. Alston has already talked to her father about their marriage, he did not deny it, didn't he implicitly acknowledge this marriage? She won't lose!

Night of Destiny

"Who cares!" Jessica sneered coldly. Mr. Marcus has a twisted and dark personality, Old Mr. Alston is like a ruthless dictator, Dennis is a walking garbage, and Leonard is just a naive little kid. This family is too bad. Getting into the Smith family is like entering a prison. Only an idiot with a squeezed brain would marry into the Smith family.

Jessica finally understood why Marcus had Crystal but still sought other women. If her guess was correct, it had something to do with the Smith family that Crystal often mentioned.

Marcus hated the Smith family, and he wanted to destroy the Noblefull Group. However, Crystal felt proud of being associated with the Smith family, which violated one of Marcus's taboos.

Crystal had been with Marcus for seven years, she must know Marcus's taboos, but perhaps due to her upbringing in the entrenched upper-class society, she unintentionally mentioned it.

Wow, how blind!

Miss Crystal, you don't love Marcus enough. If you love him enough, what have you done in these seven years?

Loving someone is not just silently accompanying them.

Anyone can provide companionship, why does it have to be you?

"Miss Jessica, you're so hypocritical!" Crystal said coldly. "You also said that our strengths are too disparate, and you cannot compete with me. Now you say you don't care, contradictory!"

Jessica smiled, "Don't be delusional. Did I say my strength is inferior to yours? I'm afraid a hundred Walker Family Group couldn't match my son."

Her son, a person who can make ten Walker Family Group collapse within an hour. Who can be more powerful than him?

"Besides, Crystal, are you sure Marcus really cares about the power behind your family?"

Sect Elder Breeze

The Marcus she knows is not the kind of person who would sacrifice his marriage for power. Even if he wants to marry Crystal, it's not because he values her wealth and influence. By saying that, it's just an insult to Mr. Marcus!

Crystal smiled confidently, "Miss Jessica, do you think you can demand sky-high prices just because of your son? You're too naive. Anyone can have a child, why should it be you?"

Jessica's expression turned slightly displeased. It's her business when she mentions her son, she is very resentful when others mention it. Especially in this situation.

"Your words don't match your thoughts. I don't believe you don't care, otherwise, why did you give birth to his son?" Crystal sneered coldly.

Jessica's brows furrowed, "It's none of your business whether I give birth to a son or not. Stick to the topic, don't bring up my son. At least I can give birth to one, unlike you who couldn't in seven years!"

Crystal's face turned completely black!

Jessica's words were harsh and ruthless, piercing straight into the heart.

Why do women make it difficult for other women? Jessica was not really ruthless, just targeting others' weaknesses. If Crystal spoke kindly, she would naturally calmly tell her everything. But she was really annoyed by those women who relied on their wealthy background, acting superior from the beginning, with a face of benevolence!

Her politeness varied depending on the person.

Her son had just experienced an assassination attempt, so she was sensitive when hearing about her son from Marcus's girlfriend. Yes, Henry was strong, taking down twenty people in an instant, but luck also played a part.

Not every time would be so fortunate. Jessica worried that someone would once again harm her precious child.

"You're going too far!" Crystal was so angry that she could hardly speak. She cursed at Jessica ten times, but couldn't match the impact of Jessica's words. All the flavors of sweetness, bitterness, and anguish from the past seven years surged up all at once. Jealousy and anger intertwined. So miserable and bitter.

The graceful woman seemed to have lost all her strength. She was like a fallen flower, pitifully beautiful and worthy of pity. It made people want to bring the whole world to her, just to see her smile.

However, her vulnerability, and her pitiful state, meant nothing to Jessica. Therefore, it is said that a woman's charm is not suitable for use against other women. It not only has no effect but also elicits aversion.

Especially for independent and resilient women like Jessica, she hated women who easily put on a show of crying, making a fuss, and threatening to commit suicide. It was so boring.

"Miss Crystal, the thief accusing the thief, don't you find it ridiculous?" Jessica smiled lightly, elegantly leaning back in her wheelchair. A cold arc curved at the corner of her lips. "You have no position at all to accuse me. You're not qualified!"

"I'm not qualified? Are you qualified then?" Crystal stared at Jessica with intense resentment. Her entire face twisted in a terrifyingly. Just a moment ago, she had a pitiful and charming aura, but now she displayed a monstrous and horrifying expression.

Never underestimate a woman's jealousy. It's the most unpredictable and destructive weapon in the world.

"Say whatever you want!" Jessica was too lazy to argue with her. Envious women were the most irrational; once they started going crazy, there would be no end. She had already said so much, and if Crystal continued to say anything offensive, she shouldn't blame Jessica for being ruthless!

Sect Elder Breeze

Crystal laughed out loud, a laughter with a touch of misery. Jessica was reminded of the laughter of those female ghosts in horror movies. It seemed to have a similar effect, conveying a sense of resentment, despair, and a hint of resistance and hatred. It sent shivers down one's spine.

"If you're qualified, why hasn't Marcus married you even after you've given birth to his son for eight years?" Crystal cynically taunted. "You're delusional to try to control Marcus with your son. You won't succeed, he won't marry you. Who do you think you are, and why do you think you can monopolize him? You're simply not worthy of him. See, even when there's such big news like having a son, there hasn't been a peep from the media, it's all to save face!"

Crystal thought that by saying this, Jessica would be humiliated. After all, no woman could remain composed after such an insult. Not only did she humiliate Jessica, but she indirectly denied Henry as well.

However, to her surprise, Jessica smiled slightly.

"Miss Crystal, I feel like there's something wrong with your brain," Jessica's index finger tapped her forehead, a hint of coldness gleaming in her bright eyes. "People like you, with fixed thinking patterns, no wonder you lack creativity. You're too afraid to reveal your true nature to Marcus, and instead, you only dare to imitate the image he likes. How pathetic! How do you know it's Marcus who doesn't want to marry me, and not the other way around? You're too self-righteous."

"You..." Crystal retorted with a mocking smile, "I imitate the image he likes? Hmph, what do you know? Isn't it all women who imitate my image?"

Jessica chuckled, thinking this Miss Crystal was quite foolish and naive.

"Mr. Marcus is truly exceptional. He had a girlfriend whom he deeply loved, yet he was fooling around with other women. Since he already had a woman he loved, why was he still seeking so many women who resembled his beloved? Why look for substitutes when he already has the genuine one? That just shows how poor the quality of the genuine one must be."

"You..." Crystal seemed to have realized something, her face suddenly turning pale...

Eight years, seven years...

Marcus met Jessica before anyone else, including Crystal!

Seeing Crystal's pale face, Jessica's mood immediately improved. She had absolutely no sympathy. "Miss Crystal, you finally figured it out. Who is the substitute after all?"

This matter still needed further confirmation! Didn't it?

"No, it's impossible..." Crystal's large eyes welled up with tears, she gritted her teeth and held back the urge to cry out in despair, "This can't be possible..."

She had always known that there was another woman in Marcus's heart, someone who could never be replaced by anyone else, except her. She had asked Marcus if he had ever loved anyone before, and Marcus had said no! He said it so convincingly, with a determined expression.

She thought it was just her imagination. Women are often perceptive when it comes to their partner's feelings, and after being together for a long time, she could sense it when his heart was not fully with her.

He often looked at her absentmindedly, as if seeing someone else through her. Crystal always pretended not to notice, for only by pretending could she maintain a semblance of peace and suppress her jealousy deep inside.

She often wondered if that woman had already died! It wasn't worth holding onto such grudges. But who knew that not only was she not dead, but she had also given birth to Marcus's son and become his secretary.

This woman's temperament was somewhat similar to hers, gentle and pure. From behind, their figures were almost indistinguishable from each other.

She had no choice but to believe that the person Marcus truly loved was, in fact, Jessica!

"It's impossible!" She couldn't accept this answer. "You're talking nonsense!"

"I didn't say anything!" Jessica innocently shrugged her shoulders, wearing a face that appeared to be as sincere and honest as possible. Yes, she deliberately led Crystal to think that way. Actually, Jessica was just making things up.

It was mainly because Susan had mentioned to her before that Marcus's women all had a certain characteristic, which happened to be similar to her, while Crystal, unfortunately, also bore some resemblance to that characteristic.

It happened that she had known Marcus eight years ago, while Crystal knew Marcus seven years ago.

It happened that she and Marcus had a seven-year-old child.

With so many coincidences linked together, it was easy for people to have twisted thoughts, especially for someone as sensitive as Crystal. Even Jessica herself, if she were to put herself in Crystal's shoes, would believe that Marcus truly loved her and had been constantly searching for a substitute.

It was indeed a tantalizing idea, and Jessica felt a momentary surge of excitement.

But she knew...

This was an impossible situation!

Their encounter was extremely dramatic. With Marcus's twisted, cunning, and sinister personality, she had treated him as a money boy. Her arrogance had trampled on his pride, and in that situation, Mr. Marcus would only wish to tear her apart. How could he love her?

Night of Destiny

She still remembered the brutality and ferocity of that night; she was probably one of the most miserable girls to experience her first time. That heartless man toyed with her all night long, every bone in her body protesting.

Later, she had cunningly tossed $100 at him, which had probably twisted him even more. He probably wished he could find her and beat her up, but fortunately, she had escaped quickly back then.

In this situation, how could there be a melodramatic plot of Mr. Marcus falling in love with her?

Even she thought it was impossible!

As a renowned sexologist said, that love was born from sexual intercourse.

However...

This theory did not apply to them at all. It was simply nonsense, and even she found it too fantastical!

But Crystal, it serves her right to provoke her with such malice. She gave her a way out, but she refused, so she deserved her ill fate!

"Did Marcus ever love you?" Crystal's lips trembled, her face turned extremely pale, and all the strength seemed to have been drained from her body. She almost collapsed on the ground. Because he loved Jessica, so...

It was impossible!

Jessica didn't directly answer but instead smiled lightly, "Marcus is such a playboy, and having so many women for so many years, how come he hasn't fathered any children?" As she said this, she felt a hint of guilt. That night, Marcus was obviously in a bad mood, and it wasn't like he had any intentions of seeking other women. It was just her being young and naive, willingly walking into his arms.

Women who willingly offered themselves in that kind of place usually knew how to take contraceptive measures, but she was too innocent.

The next morning, she ran away too quickly, and Marcus didn't have the chance to remind her. As a result, she ended up with Henry in a confused and fortunate manner.

"But if that's the case, why did he hide you for eight years?"

"Miss Crystal, you really are persistent. Who told you that he was hiding from me for eight years? Eight years ago, I thought he had a car accident and died, so I went abroad. I only recently returned. Did you know?"

The meaning is, if she hadn't left, could you get close to Marcus?

Crystal completely collapsed!

"No..." Crystal collapsed to the ground, holding her head, letting out a mournful scream... Overwhelmed with anger, she fainted!

Jessica frowned, feeling a bit sorry for her, and was about to call the doctor when the door of the ward was forcefully pushed open...

Marcus?

Jessica was startled and inwardly cursed...

It's over!

I've gone too far!

Chapter 54

Sudden Kiss

When things go wrong, even drinking water can choke you. Jessica felt that she was now extremely unlucky!

Crystal was taken away by the doctor for examination, while Mr. Marcus stood coldly, his eyes chillingly fixed on her, not saying a word. Jessica lifted her gaze and saw his deep and icy eyes.

The ward itself was already all white, and she thought it was creepy enough, but she didn't expect Mr. Marcus to be emitting such a cold aura here. She felt a chilly autumn wind blowing, a hundred miles of killing intent, truly... a desolate scene!

During the summer in W City, it was very hot, making it unbearable. Jessica thought that the woman who could marry Mr. Marcus must be very happy in the summer. Look, they wouldn't even need an air conditioner, just stand within a meter of him.

Saving energy, money, and trouble.

Okay, she admitted that she had provoked his sweetheart to the point of fainting. She was guilty, having a sharp tongue sometimes wasn't a good thing. But Mr. Marcus, if you want to explode, do it quickly! What's the meaning of standing there motionless?

She anxiously wanted to know which of the two demons would come out victorious in their struggle.

After a long silence, two sets of gaze clashed in mid-air, one cold and one tranquil, neither winning nor losing.

Sect Elder Breeze

Miss Jessica suddenly felt that this was indeed a waste of time. She smiled lightly and asked, "Mr. Marcus, may I ask what you have to say?"

Marcus gave her a cold look, and suddenly his phone rang. He pressed his lips together, turned around, and walked out. With a bang, he forcefully closed the door, the sound striking her eardrums with a dull pain. Jessica thought to herself, did he get angry? With such force, was he trying to break the door?

She shrugged her shoulders and waited for Mr. Marcus for a while, but he didn't come back. Jessica assumed he had urgent matters to attend to.

She leisurely opened her computer, connected to the internet, and started watching the latest episode.

When Marcus came in again, Jessica had already finished drinking the soup and was enjoying watching the anime.

"Mr. Marcus, what exactly do you want to say? Can you please get to the point?" The anime was paused halfway, and her heart felt uncomfortable, scratching like a little cat.

"Just now, I heard everything at the door!" Marcus said coldly, a smirk playing at the corner of his lips, his voice chilling. "Once again, I get to experience Miss Jessica's sharp tongue!"

"You should say 'quick reflexes'!" Jessica retorted!

"Quick reflexes, huh!" Mr. Marcus sneered, walking closer, step by step, emanating a daunting pressure that left people breathless. Some men were accustomed to sitting on the throne, their every move imbued with an intimidating power.

He sat next to her, causing the bed to slightly dent. Jessica's heart skipped a beat, and a warning alarm rang in her mind.

Danger!

"I love you..." Marcus's voice was low, soft, and magnetic.

Night of Destiny

Suddenly, he burst out with these words, throwing Jessica's mind into chaos. Her heart raced, and her cheeks burned even hotter, as a deep blush took over.

Oh, Jessica, stay calm, stay calm, don't act like a foolish girl. There's more to this!

Compose yourself, and stay composed!

Damn it, this perverted Mr. Marcus, why did he pause after one sentence? He's not going to die if he completes his sentence, right?

If he wanted to gauge her reaction, well, congratulations to him, because she remained calm beneath her mask. Despite her inner restlessness and rapid heartbeat, she smiled serenely, making the effect even more perfect if it weren't for the uncontrollable flush on her cheeks.

"So, all these years, the women I've been with were just substitutes for you?" Marcus finally finished his sentence, looking at the blush on her face with a smirk. Wow, he thought she wouldn't know what shyness was.

Jessica smiled lightly and said slowly, "I carefully recalled what was said just now, and I assure you, I never said those words. Mr. Marcus. Have you fantasized too much?"

Mr. Marcus nodded. Very good, she didn't say it. "But you mislead Crystal into thinking that, didn't you?"

Jessica smiled faintly. "Mr. Marcus, you're overthinking things. It absolutely did not happen!" Miss Jessica denied it categorically!

"No?" Marcus glanced at her, suddenly moving closer and pulling her towards him, narrowing his eyes dangerously. "Do you really believe that I went around looking for substitutes because I love you?" He ignored her denial!

The danger in Jessica's heart reached a critical level.

He was so close, and Marcus's breath brushed against her face, his clean and refreshing scent surrounding her, forming a cage that trapped her. She wanted to break free, but her strength was too weak compared to Marcus's.

"Hmm?" Marcus dangerously dragged out his voice, his thin lips nearly touching hers. Just an inch closer, and he could have kissed her. Jessica felt helpless and frustrated. Why did it always have to be this forced position? Couldn't he try something new?

Perhaps Jessica had never imagined that Marcus would only use this perverted method of interrogation on her.

"Illusion..." Jessica chuckled weakly. "Mr. Marcus, maybe you should choose selective memory loss!"

"I already have selective memory loss, and I choose to forget you, Miss Jessica," Marcus said coldly, his profound gaze locking onto her eyes. In those radiant eyes, he could see the hidden amusement in her own.

This woman was always saying one thing and meaning another. But as she said, her reflexes were quick! However, her words just now gave him an epiphany.

Over these years, he had indeed only been attracted to one type of woman — pure, graceful, and possessing a certain quality that could captivate him. He paid attention to every detail.

But it always felt insufficient.

Far from enough!

Searching and seeking, never staying. He had never stopped to think about why he was like this!

Why was he so greedy, never satisfied?

It turned out that because none of them were her?

"So..." Jessica, now being held by him, found it difficult to ignore his burning breath and deep gaze. It felt like a blue vortex that wanted to engulf her soul.

This feeling made her heart race and left her utterly confused! Even her smart brain had become a little slow.

"What did I used to call you?" Marcus suddenly asked. Miss Jessica, Miss Jessica, he had been calling her that for so long. Maybe it was time to change the way he addressed her?

Night of Destiny

"What?" Jessica was confused, momentarily stunned. This man's ever-changing nature was driving her crazy. Just now, he was acting like a stranger to avoid, and in the blink of an eye, he switched to an affectionate approach.

Mr. Marcus, you didn't even know my name eight years ago!

Tears welled up in Miss Jessica's eyes. One lie led to countless others, and the lies grew bigger and bigger. If he remembered everything, she wouldn't be able to escape his pursuit. So, she remained silent!

"Answer me!"

"I forgot!" Jessica decisively replied.

Marcus chuckled lightly, and within his refined features, a charming smile emerged. His eyes focused on her luscious red lips as he asked, "Did I ever kiss you before?"

Jessica's heart skipped a beat, and under his gaze, she unconsciously nodded. Marcus's smile grew wider. Perfect. He leaned in and kissed her lips forcefully.

Startled, her eyes widened to the maximum, and she tried to escape, but he firmly controlled her. Marcus took it a step further, pinning her down on the bed, carefully avoiding her legs. He locked her between his chest and the mattress as he kissed and dominated her mercilessly.

Jessica was taken aback by his sudden kiss, leaving her mind in disarray. She dumbly allowed him to take advantage of her, until her lips stung, and she instinctively parted her teeth, clumsily welcoming his warm and slippery tongue into her mouth.

Marcus's fervent kiss frightened Jessica. She was unfamiliar with matters of love between men and women, like a pure white paper that couldn't withstand Marcus's passionate kiss. Her entire body felt weak, as if small electric currents ran through her. Trembling all over, she forgot to react, tightly gripping the bedsheets beneath her, knuckles raised, her heart throbbing.

Sect Elder Breeze

Marcus kissed with force, unstoppable. He pulled her tongue into his mouth, sucking and teasing, savoring the warmth and tenderness brought on by her struggles!

The temperature in the entire room rose, and the romantic atmosphere in the air soared exponentially. This scene made one's face blush and heart race.

Marcus was no longer satisfied with just kissing. His hands reached under her hospital gown, cupping her soft breasts, manipulating it through her bra. Jessica felt like lightning had struck her as she struggled, forgetting about her injured leg. She desperately tried kicking him.

But with just one movement, the pain made her groan and break out in a cold sweat. Miss Jessica couldn't help but feel frustrated!

Marcus released his hold on her slightly, with the young girl's head in disarray, cheeks flushed red. Bright eyes took on a hint of dark red, a captivating allure. Marcus's breathing became rapid, taking a while to calm down before he uttered in a low voice, "Maybe what you said is right!"

Jessica was left a bit dumbfounded by the kiss, momentarily unable to grasp what he was saying! Was what she said right? What did he mean?

Marcus helped Jessica up, leaning in and lightly pecking her lips. His exquisitely enchanting face was full of a triumphant smile. He spoke in a casual tone, "Miss Jessica, in my memory, you are the only woman I have ever kissed!" Only her!

Jessica was stunned. Marcus's expression was serious, lacking any sign of guilt. Jessica understood that he was telling the truth!

Damn, should she kneel and thank him for his grace?

Jessica's anger flared up. How many times had Marcus kissed her already? "Why did you kiss me?"

Night of Destiny

Miss Jessica wasn't the type to act coy. Just because he kissed her didn't mean she would shyly retreat into her world and revel in self-indulgence. On the contrary, she was braver than most in asking why.

It was precisely this kind of innocent impulsiveness that made her radiate a bit more sunshine and vitality.

"Just remembering your taste, maybe it will trigger some memories!" Marcus responded. There was a strong hint of a smile in his eyes as he observed the cracks in her perfect facade. In that smile, there was a hidden sense of pride and awkwardness.

He just wanted to kiss her, that's all. There was no need for a reason.

However, he would never let Jessica know about this mood. Two proud individuals, neither willing to be the first to back down!

"Very well!" Jessica gritted her teeth. She should have bitten Marcus hard just now. It would have been delicious. Jessica thought spitefully, and in that moment of absent-mindedness, something crossed her mind, causing her expression to change slightly.

Maybe what you said is right!

Jessica finally understood why Mr. Marcus said what he did. He believed that he loved her, so he went to find a substitute?

No, Mr. Marcus, you're always so wise and powerful. How did you become so foolish this time?

In Jessica's mind, the image of Mr. Marcus tearing her apart and calmly wiping his hands with a handkerchief flashed again. Her shoulders slumped, feeling like crying without tears.

Disdain!

Severe disdain!

She greatly despised men who enjoyed listening to two women argue!

Sect Elder Breeze

It would be best if he didn't regain his memory! Jessica prayed to God.

"Miss Jessica, has your personality changed a lot between eight years ago and now?" Mr. Marcus suddenly asked, slightly confused, inexplicably rubbing his chin.

Jessica sneered inwardly. What change are you talking about? Eight years ago, you had no idea about my character. If she knew that Mr. Marcus was so twisted, she would have run far away and never met him.

Thinking this, Jessica still nodded honestly.

"No wonder!" Mr. Marcus raised an eyebrow, giving a very wise assessment of his own speculation. "With this type of personality, you were never to my taste! If it was the same eight years ago, how could I possibly love you!"

He didn't love overly intelligent women, and this Miss Jessica was not only intelligent but also quite fierce!

He explained it as being a result of living with Henry for these past few years, compelled by the environment, which had turned an innocent and tender girl into a fierce woman.

Jessica's delicate face turned various shades of green, purple, black, and white, finally settling on black. She really wanted to bang her head against a wall. Come on, Mr. Marcus, you never really loved me, did you?

Indeed, one cannot lie!

Self-inflicted!

"Hey, shouldn't you go see your fiancée?" Jessica forced out a smile, coldly saying, unable to continue any further, she was going crazy!

Marcus's gaze fell directly onto Jessica's face, narrowing his eyes slightly. The corners of his lips formed a straight line, with a hint of coldness. "She's not my fiancée!" Subconsciously, he explained. Before, he didn't explain because he was lazy. But now?

He suddenly felt like explaining, but as for the reason, Mr. Marcus disregarded it as usual.

Chapter 55

Pitiful Substitute.

"You really have a talent for pissing people off!" Mr. Marcus sarcastically remarked.

Jessica accepted the praise sheepishly, "Thank you for the compliment!"

Mr. Marcus's eye twitched. This woman, really...

"Mr. Marcus, I think we should, um, have a good... communication about something. If you want your son, to at least sort out your history of love affairs, settle your playboy debts once and for all. If you can't, then be straightforward and give someone an answer. Whether you don't want her anymore or want to marry her, make it clear. Don't let her hang on and cause trouble for me and my son. I don't care, but I don't want anyone approaching my son. If you want to ruin the image you have in your son's eyes, that's fine, but I don't want my son facing the consequences of your playboy debts."

Mr. Marcus regretted for the nth time why he chose her as his secretary in the first place. But then again, if she wasn't his secretary, he wouldn't have had his adorable son.

Sect Elder Breeze

He suddenly remembered a sentence Henry once said online, "Mr. Marcus, you better be careful. Don't create a surprise younger brother or sister for me, I'll deduct points from you."

Although it was said jokingly, his son's words already indicated his attitude!

Mr. Marcus frowned, "You don't have to worry about that, I will handle it!"

"Very well!" Jessica said calmly, not asking how he would handle it. It wasn't her question to ask. There was a line in Jessica's heart, and for now, she didn't want to cross it.

Marcus looked at Jessica, with a dark expression, and suddenly asked, "You don't mind at all?"

Mr. Marcus smirked coldly, "You just said you're greedy and lustful, so you were attracted to me?" Knowing that she was speaking out of anger, he couldn't help but taunt her.

Jessica smiled elegantly, "Mr. Marcus, let's play a question-and-answer game, shall we? First question, who is more handsome, you or our son?"

"Of course, our son is more handsome!" Mr. Marcus didn't hesitate at all, answering resolutely. There was no doubt about it.

"Second question, who is wealthier, you or our son?"

"Of course, our son is wealthier!" Mr. Marcus didn't think much about it, answering readily. His son's money came the easiest. He hacked into a bank's system alone, and he could do whatever he wanted with it. Besides, his money would be his son's in the future. In conclusion, our son is wealthier!

"Very good!" Jessica smiled lightly and slowly said, "Since our son is more handsome than you and wealthier than you, why should I be interested in you? Is it necessary? I should be with my son. At least my son is loyal and won't abandon me!"

Mr. Marcus's face turned dark! His hand was itching to move, and he really had the impulse to strangle her.

In her words, he was disloyal and had abandoned her?

Not only was Mr. Marcus's face dark, but it was also distorted. He gritted his teeth. Couldn't she say a few nice words occasionally?

He then thought about his promiscuous behavior, constantly changing women like he changed clothes. He began to seriously consider whether he had done something wrong to her eight years ago, otherwise, why would she avoid him and keep pushing him away?

Jessica found it quite fascinating to see his changing facial expressions. It was like watching a silent movie from years past, and it felt quite amusing. Finally, when she saw Mr. Marcus's gaze become deep and calm, no longer distorted, but rather focused on her, Miss Jessica's heart skipped a beat. What was happening?

To avoid any further complications, Jessica smiled faintly, "Mr. Marcus, shouldn't you go see Miss Crystal?"

Marcus furrowed his brow, lips curling in a half-smile that held no warmth. His focused gaze instantly turned icy cold. "Miss Jessica, you are truly competent!" Even though she was severely injured, she didn't forget her true nature as a secretary. Very well, very well indeed!

"Alright!" Jessica knew he was angry but remained calm, still smiling, elegantly leaning against the bedside, her gaze filled with fondness drifting towards her notebook.

A surge of anger rushed from the soles of his feet to his scalp. With the simplest action, she made it clear to him that Marcus's charm was nothing compared to an animated series.

Marcus stood up abruptly, gave a cold snort, and left in a huff!

Miss Jessica remained unfazed as if it had nothing to do with her. It was only after the door to the hospital room closed that she let out a long sigh, her face slightly sullen.

For a long time, she sat in silence, deep in thought, not knowing what she was thinking.

******

Sect Elder Breeze

Crystal had already woken up. She had fainted due to anger, lying on the hospital bed, her face pale and bloodless, tears filling her eyes. Her pale lips trembled like wilting flowers.

Jessica's words kept echoing in her mind, each word stabbing into her heart, causing a pain that made it hard to breathe. She didn't want to believe that what she said was true!

Marcus pushed the door open and entered. When Crystal saw him, her eyes brightened, and she suddenly stood up. Tears flowed down her face, her pale complexion turning red due to extreme suppression. Only her trembling lips remained pale.

The brightness in Crystal's eyes gradually faded away, disappearing bit by bit. In just a few seconds, they became dull and lifeless, empty and vacant, as if she didn't recognize Marcus. Slowly, a bitter smile appeared on her face.

Tears, like pearls falling off a broken string, streamed down, revealing all the grievances and bitterness of the past seven years in front of the man she loved.

Attempting to gain even the slightest bit of his love! To obtain even a few words of commitment from him. Otherwise, she would collapse!

Marcus approached her, a hint of reluctance in his cold gaze. After a long silence, he placed a hand lightly on her head and patted it gently. "Crystal..."

"Don't say it, please, don't say it!" Crystal grabbed Marcus's hand, crying heartbreakingly. She was terrified to hear Marcus's choice, afraid for him to admit that he truly loved Jessica, and that she, for the past seven years, was nothing but a pitiful substitute.

Marcus faintly furrowed his brow, her tears falling onto the back of his hand, warm and making him feel somewhat guilty.

Night of Destiny

"I'm sorry!" Apologizing was not Mr. Marcus's style, but he still apologized. He had once said he would marry her during these seven years of companionship, but it seemed that none of that could become a reality now. He owed her an apology.

But he couldn't afford to give her anything more!

"Why are you apologizing? Out of pity? Or guilt?" Crystal became somewhat hysterical, her eyes filled with scorn and self-mockery. Could it be true that she was just like any other woman?

Marcus pursed his lips, there were certain things he didn't want to say explicitly. After all, Crystal had been with him for seven years, that was a fact!

"How do you know about this?" Marcus didn't answer but instead asked a question in a cold tone. He had kept this matter hidden so well, recently Old Mr. Walker and his father were discussing their marriage plans, and Old Mr. Walker would definitely not tell Crystal. He had planned to reveal his refusal at the very last moment, thereby embarrassing his father and breaking the trust of Old Mr. Walker to sabotage their collaboration. Unexpectedly, she discovered his intentions before them.

Crystal laughed with an unclear meaning, seemingly mocking, "You hid such a big secret child in your home, could you really keep it hidden? Marcus, you are truly despicable. I have been with you for seven years, without any complaints or regrets. I even accepted your dalliances with other women. But you never let me get close to you. But they... they only spend a few days with you!"

She felt extremely unwilling! She had given everything, even going against his father, Old Mr. Alston's wishes, but in the end, she was defeated by them, who were just with him for several days.

"He is my son!" Marcus lowered his voice, slightly displeased. At the same time, his gaze became as cold as a knife. "He is the closest person to me in this world!"

Sect Elder Breeze

"He is your son, then what about me? Am I just an outsider?" Crystal asked while crying. Over these few years, she never even got to see what his home looked like.

"Yes!" Marcus said ruthlessly. Indeed, she was an outsider!

"You..." Crystal felt a great pain, she froze, and closed her eyes, letting the tears flow. "You are truly cruel!"

The corner of Marcus' lips curled slightly. Cruel? Indeed, regardless of how the business world perceived Mr. Marcus, he was as an iron-blooded and ruthless person, with methods akin to a judge of hell. Even if more people called him cruel, what difference would it make? Marcus didn't care at all!

"What about Jessica?" Crystal opened her eyes and asked. "What is your relationship with her?"

"Crystal, you shouldn't have come to the hospital to find her!" Marcus said calmly, a hint of warmth passing through his cold gaze. If his son knew that someone had bullied his mommy, he wouldn't be able to stop his son's retaliation.

However, Crystal misunderstood his words, believing that he meant that she didn't have the right to come find Jessica.

"You promised to marry me, Marcus!" It was his own words, why had he forgotten so quickly?

Marcus furrowed his brows, somewhat helpless. "Crystal, when you initially approached me, didn't you have an ulterior motive?"

Crystal was stunned, her crying stopped abruptly. She looked at him with a surprised expression and frantically explained, "I didn't do anything, I really..."

"No need to explain!" Marcus said coldly, his gaze particularly icy. "He sent you to me just to control my every move. As for what you have done or not done, you know it in your own heart. This time, the intelligence I traded with Saxon, was leaked to him by you, wasn't it?"

"That's because..."

"As expected!" Marcus' face was cold as ice. Seeing the icy gaze in her eyes, he guessed that it was Crystal who had done it, but he didn't expect it to be true.

Night of Destiny

"Did you trap me with your words?" It was already too late for her to understand. She had accidentally seen the document which fell out of his briefcase.

"Why did you tell him? Well, I don't care. What he promised you, that's your business. My relationship with Saxon, I'm not afraid of it being exposed, as long as he can catch the evidence." Marcus coldly curled his lips. "So, Crystal, don't cry in front of me, as if you're so wronged, can you?"

Crystal felt as if struck by lightning, fiercely biting her lower lip. "When did you find out?"

"From the very beginning!" Marcus said calmly. The struggle between him and his father had never stopped. His father thought he had done it unnoticed, but little did he know that Marcus had known all along.

Crystal smiled bitterly. "Then why did you keep me around?"

"Because..." Marcus frowned, why indeed? It was a bit distant now, he could hardly remember. He recalled that at that time, he had no intention of keeping her around as a ticking time bomb.

Perhaps it was because she had an overly familiar charm! Well, who knows?!

Crystal seemed to have also figured it out, her smile becoming even more bitter. It turned out she was able to stay by his side for seven years, thanks to Jessica... heh, what irony!

"Marcus, I truly love you!" Crystal said sorrowfully. "Apart from leaking that document, I haven't done anything to harm you these past few years!" Not a single thing!

Except for monitoring him and reporting his every move, she hadn't done anything to harm him.

"I know!" It was precisely because of this that he didn't treat her too cruelly.

Sect Elder Breeze

Everyone had their purposes and positions, and he was tired of it. These people who came and went by his side, each one of them approached him with despicable motives. He was truly tired of it.

Crystal cried softly, feeling extremely sad. Marcus just looked at her coldly, remaining calm for a moment before saying, "Crystal, we..."

Marcus had just wanted to talk to Crystal about their marriage, it was bound to happen sooner or later. This marriage proposal wouldn't work out, although it was a bit cruel to say it at this moment, it was a good opportunity, wasn't it?

But unexpectedly, the door to the hospital room opened, and a middle-aged female doctor in a white coat walked in. Seeing Crystal crying miserably, the doctor's expression changed. "Crystal, why are you crying?"

"Aunt!" Crystal threw herself into the arms of Betty Walker, seeking comfort from her elder, crying even more bitterly in her embrace.

"Don't cry, my good child, don't cry..." Betty patted her shoulder, gently comforting her. She looked up and glared fiercely at Marcus, with a hint of anger in her eyes.

Marcus remained expressionless, cold, and unaffected.

Betty comforted Crystal for a while before calming her emotions slightly. She looked at Marcus coldly. "Come out with me!"

Marcus glanced at Crystal once, then followed Betty out. He asked in a deep voice, "What's the matter?"

"What happened between you and Crystal?" Betty asked.

Marcus jeered, "I don't have an obligation to report my affairs to you."

"You..." Betty was slightly angry, and she slapped Crystal's medical record onto Marcus' body, saying in a low voice, "Take a look for yourself!"

One of Marcus' eyebrows raised, a sense of foreboding emerging. He glanced at it and his face changed slightly...

Night of Destiny

How could this be?

Marcus widened his eyes in disbelief.

"That's right, as you can see, Crystal is pregnant!"

---Book 1 completed, Book 2 to be continued---

Printed in Great Britain
by Amazon